BEHOLD THE MAN

By

Toyohiko Kagawa

HARPER & BROTHERS
NEW YORK AND LONDON

BEHOLD THE MAN

By

Toyohiko Kagawa

Edited by
MAXINE SHORE *and*
M. M. OBLINGER

HARPER & BROTHERS
NEW YORK AND LONDON

BOOK ONE

WHAT SEEK YE?

CHAPTER I

EVEN before they had entered Machaerus' palace, the two disciples felt the first light breath of premonition. Yet neither Akkub nor Baasha knew why. They were aware of it as an inner stirring, come suddenly from nowhere and without reason. For the morning was flawless. The peach-glow of sunrise tipped the hills. The valleys still slept in their shadow-filled deeps. The gateman had been courteous and opened at their asking the huge West Gate that had neither creaked nor shuddered as they went through, shoulder to shoulder. They had been glad that now, at last, they could petition King Herod for the body of their teacher, John, that they might go forth and give it decent burial.

But no sooner were they within the gates than foreboding came. It could not be because they had left the other thirteen disciples outside the fortress walls. Nor was it because the palace grounds, rising in lordly terraces to the main entrance, looked unfriendly. The flagged courts and large fountain, guarded by its Libyan lion, were orderly and beautiful. The paths were swept clean. The grass was incredibly green. Somewhere, probably in the branches of a feathered palm near-by, a bird sang. Sang with a throat swelling with happiness. Yet both Akkub and Baasha moved along conscious of a mounting conviction that all was not well.

The sharp grief at hearing the news of their master's death had been dulled by three days of forced marching here to Machaerus. The message had been sent to them by a certain centurion named Joshua. There had been no details. The messenger himself, an ignorant fellow, knew nothing. He could tell them nothing beyond what had already been said in Joshua's meager note, that Herod had had him executed.

That was all—John had been executed. He who had been imprisoned so long, their beloved leader. He was gone. A beacon once flaming across the world. A spirit crying out through the far reaches of the wilderness.

Holding their heads high, Akkub and Baasha walked up the marble steps and were ushered into the royal audience chamber, eyes dark with an unnamed, unreasoning fear.

There followed six hours of negotiations that no man, Akkub thought, however strong his will or steadfast his purpose, could easily endure. Six hours of pleading and praying for the body of their master. Six hours of broken conferences with various prelates and commissioners of King Herod. Pompous men rolling speech like pebbles over their rough tongues. Dignitaries without dignity. In those long hours the two men had been speared with questions until their minds bled. The real purpose of their business was often obscured. Akkub had been oppressed by the feeling that they, themselves, were on trial for their lives. Though they had come for but one thing, permission to take John the Baptist's body away for proper burial, it was not this that was discussed.

One of the last to see them had said: "All of you are guilty of blasphemy and outright treason. Your words are a sacrilege and your faith is a devil."

"We want only the body of our master," Baasha sighed. The man stared him down. "Master! Whose master is he?" he pushed his thick neck forward at them and shouted: "The king is wroth. We may throw you into prison. You, too, should be executed along with your mad wilderness prophet."

Akkub shivered. "We have done no wrong. We have no plans for conspiracy. We pay the taxes and obey the laws."

The official made a gesture of contempt. He rose from his chair and smoothed out the front of his gown. He walked to the end of the room, scowling.

"You do not worship in the tabernacles," he said accusingly. "You have baptisms of running water and make wild vows. You speak of a mystical prophet whom you call the Son of Man."

This Akkub was obliged to admit by his silence. But it was not guilt he felt. His eyes sought those of Baasha, but his companion, uneasy under the dark stare of the king's representative, dared not look back.

"You are fortunate the king is lenient," the man said finally. "For my part, I'd order your arrest at once. Let me warn you. Never return here for another favor."

"No, your excellency."

The title seemed to please the man, for he stood straight and pulled in his belly. "I have no more time for you," he declared, "and I regret that your wish is granted."

"Thank you, your excellency."

Their wish was granted! Akkub began to shake. There were tears in his eyes, and his chest rumbled like a cask of newly fermented wine. He could not see the king's man clearly for there were prisms of colored light diffused through the room. Near him Baasha moaned: "God has not forsaken us." Then he coughed and rubbed his coarse, weather-stained hands.

"I'll send a man in to give you your instructions," the king's representative said, and left the room.

They were alone in the council chamber except for one of the palace guards. Akkub looked at him. He was immobile as the furniture. He had as much expression as the table. His iron helmet was no harder than his jaw. Somehow he seemed to Akkub to personify the court, its cold and inhuman atmosphere, its bleak stones, its straight pillars, its strong facades. The spear he held upright before him was more than a spear. It was an iron rod of authority, symbol of all the reigning houses. Here in the office and trappings of the guard had the spirit of the times found expression, thought Akkub.

"We wait a long while," he said, growing impatient. "Soon all the sand will have run out of the glass."

Baasha smiled. He could smile without moving his lips or wrinkling his face. Only his very dark eyes beamed. Satisfaction with the outcome of the negotiations made his voice mellow.

"You must have patience."

"Yea," said Akkub, "forgive me. I was thinking of them —the thirteen who wait for us outside the gate."

"No follower of John would find that hard, considering our task."

"That is true."

Akkub stroked fingers through his black beard, and returned to his contemplation of the guard. In a manner of speaking, the guard was himself a king. In his right hand was the king's power. In his presence was the king's authority. The Emperor Caesar was this man and so had been Nebuchadnezzar. Babylon had seen him behind strutting horses, riding a gold chariot and dragging the bound victims of his wars.

Baasha said: "I hear someone coming."

The great door swung open. Another guard stepped in. He, too, wore an iron helmet, but it was plain that he was no ordinary guard. For a moment Akkub thought it was the same messenger who had originally come from Joshua with the news that John's unburied body was lying in the dungeon in Machaerus' palace. The messenger, so like this man, had been the cause of their expedition thither.

"Not a difficult undertaking," Joshua's note had read. "Even in his own palace the king's reputation is very bad. If you should steal the body and are caught, Herod's enemies will keep you out of prison."

But by none of the disciples had the plan of stealing John's body even been considered. Least of all by Akkub and Baasha. They had gone openly to the palace to ask for what they wanted.

As the soldier drew nearer, Akkub saw that he was no lowly palace guard as he had first supposed, but a centurion. All at once he realized that this was Joshua himself. His interest quickened. Here was the man responsible for their present mission, a person whom even the king dared not oppose, it was said. He had the presence of one who had borne arms and seen much military service. He was tall, without appearing to be; strong, yet not too muscular; swarthy of face and lean of jaw. His measured gait, grown on him from long habit, was not walking. It was marching. He marched into the room, made a military turn. Marched to the table opposite Akkub and Baasha, then halted. Like a true soldier, he wasted no words in greeting.

He said: "Everything is arranged. You can take the body through the Dung Gate."

"The Dung Gate!"

"The king's orders," said the centurion swiftly.

Akkub felt a curious prickling at the back of his neck. All the refuse and litter from the palace and stables was removed by way of the Dung Gate. It was an insult both to them and to the memory of their beloved master. He heard Baasha exclaim angrily. There was a weighted pause during which Akkub could have sworn that the rock face of the palace guard cracked into a sly grin.

"You'll be wise not to protest," Joshua said. "I can do no more for you. I'm sorry."

"Why do you bother at all?" demanded Baasha.

Joshua's lean jaw twitched. He glanced almost imperceptibly back toward the palace guard. Akkub understood. There could be no explanations. Spies were everywhere. No man could trust anyone within hearing.

"I'll help you attend to this matter," the centurion said, "and see you and the other disciples on your way. But first, there is one thing you must know that grieves me to tell you."

"What is it?"

Joshua had ceased to look directly at them. Rather, he looked between them, narrowed eyes on the cold smoothness of the floor.

"There are only the torso and limbs for you to take away."

Akkub stared, his mouth suddenly dry. "You mean ——?"

"John the Baptist was—beheaded."

Baasha sat down as though a sack of sand had dropped upon his head, and threw his hands to his face, moaning.

"Two days ago," went on the centurion, "a man named Salathiel came and demanded John's head, which I let him have."

Akkub could not move. His beloved master, John—beheaded! Up until now he had not thought to ask the manner of his death, nor had any of the pompous prelates they had interviewed today, spoken of it. The details of his murder had seemed unimportant. It was enough that John the Baptist, shouting his vigorous denunciations of this generation, was gone—silenced forever. A great choking rose in Akkub's throat. Now, after the first blunt shock of it, he could not think nor feel. His seeing sense was all that was left to him. But form had no meaning and objects no perspective. He stared through the dimensions of the room into dimensionless space.

Outside the West Gate, the other disciples of John, thirteen in all, resting upon their staffs, or sitting or lying upon the ground, awaited them. From here, the road wriggled to the walled town, making its numerous turnings among bleak and bold rocks. Always on one side or the other were gorges or narrow canyons that ran into the deep-split valley to Lake Asphaltitis. Around on the other side of the fortress there was no approach, nor any opening in that great wall that Herod the Great had caused to be built atop this gigantic mountain. There, in a series of ghastly descents, step upon step, the scarred terrain rushed down three thousand eight hundred feet to the Dead Sea.

Surely, thought Akkub, Herod and his new wife and all their line for generations to come would be safe here. And safe they had need to be. Strife, conspiracy and discord surrounded them within the kingdom. Enemies pressed them from without. Aretas, king of Arabia, father of the former queen wronged by Herod, was even now, it was said, preparing for war upon him. Everywhere, even here in this apparently impregnable place, man lived in dread. There was no trust among them though they broke common bread. Few had heeded John's eloquent warnings to leave their wicked ways before the vengeance of God came upon them. Now, thought Akkub heavily, vengeance of a different sort had come upon John. He was dead, murdered, his noble head served to the queen upon a platter, that a sworn oath might be fulfilled.

Akkub suddenly hated both the king's consort and her daughter. In his throbbing head, Joshua's low-voiced telling of Salome's abandoned dance and its ghastly culmination was still being repeated, word upon word. "Proceed to the dungeon," the king had ordered, "and bring back the trophy the daughter of my queen, Herodias, has demanded. It shall not be said that Herod's word is not kept nor his debts paid."

Remembering, Akkub sweated in agony. A quick glance showed him Baasha's drooping shoulders and set face. Their sandaled feet, nearing the thirteen waiting men, lagged.

Now, at eventide, the sun sat upon a mountain and the far-flung plain of Arabia was sparkling sand and glimmering dust. Camel trains went striding down the trade routes inland. Donkeys were climbing the road of rocks, up and up by tortuous gradients to the town. Because of spring rains, the lower hills were emerald-studded knobs.

Akkub lifted his head. The air was fresher here than in the palace. They could breathe again. They could feel the stir of the earth once more. They could mark the swallows' flight through the slowly winging-up dusk. They could pray.

"Pray—pray!" Akkub commanded himself. "I must put off my bitterness and pray."

But he could not. Nor, he saw, could Baasha. Mockery to move one's lips forming mere words, saying what meant nothing. Repeating over and over without understanding, "I beseech You, O Father. I call upon You. I beg of You—my God—my God ——"

Nay, he could not.

There were swift heavy steps behind. Turning, he saw that the centurion, Joshua, was overtaking them. Akkub sighed. Why was it not possible to walk straight and proud into the midst of the disciples, like this soldier? This soldier, Joshua, who would lead them to what was left of John, direct them along the cold deep passageway into the earth and back—back with the headless body—back to the fresh air, to the cool night, to the clean fresh world of reason.

And suddenly, though he knew he was acting like a child, Akkub wept. But the release of tears could make the telling no easier. How to explain to these faithful followers of the beloved master, these other disciples now running forward to crowd about him? The shaking of Akkub's body smothered the upwelling of his voice. The thirteen were asking questions, no two questions the same. They were looking at Joshua, making signs and demanding to know who this man was.

"Who is he?"

"Why is he here?"

"Are we under arrest?"

Akkub managed to shake his head. Baasha stroked his beard tremblingly.

"I have come to deliver to you," Joshua said, and then hesitated, "—the body of your master."

Their relief was so great that they shouted aloud. They danced around, Akkub thought wearily, in a senseless manner. One man kissed Joshua's hand. Another spread his mantle upon the ground that the centurion might walk upon it.

"After the funeral," Baasha said, his sober voice quieting

the others, "we will go, as we have planned, to Galilee. For Jesus, called the Nazarene, must hear of this."

Akkub wondered if Jesus did not already know of it.

"Through the Dung Gate," he heard Joshua say, "we will take the mutilated body of your teacher, John."

He had told them. They knew—knew that John the Baptist's head had been severed from his body for a woman's whim. They weren't shouting now. They weren't singing their songs of gratitude to the king's centurion. The pitiless fact was now like a pair of glazed eyes staring them down. Whatever they thought they kept under a cold slab in the vaults of their minds. Akkub saw that the man who had flung down his mantle for Herod's officer to walk upon had caught it up and was burying his face in it. Here and there sounded a dry cough in a straining throat.

The sun threw its last rays upon the hills. Soon dusk would be here. Akkub knew they had to hurry. He called them together and they went around in dull silence to the Dung Gate. He could never relive again in his thoughts that next hour—nor the next. The deep, swallowing dark, the infernal clopping of their bare feet over the smooth dungeon stones. The stench, the dank, the torchlight flapping its flame like a one-winged bat. The digging of the grave and the placing of the slab upon it reverently—but not prayerfully. All prayer had gone out of them. Only the stars John loved could offer up a prayer now. His desolate disciples had ceased even to think. It was enough to keep their bodies in motion, dragging their feet and raising and lowering their hands. It was enough—and more.

Akkub could barely remember when it was all over, for he was asleep standing up. He was standing up among the other disciples, feeling the cold from the Samaritan mountain and caring not at all what happened to him.

Presently there was a voice that was quite warm, inexplicably, and very near him. It was not Baasha's nor any of the other disciples'; it was Joshua's. Odd. The centurion was still here. For some reason, he had decided not to return to Herod's fortress. Wonder pricked through Akkub's fatigue. Curious thing—Joshua was *one* of them.

"Gather up your packs," the soldier said, "find your staffs. We will proceed at once on our way to this strange man you call Jesus."

CHAPTER II

WHEN the dawn wind stirred the embers of the fire, Akkub awoke. In the dimness he could see the huddled forms of his brother disciples, crouched together to ward off the mountain cold. Like sheep, thought Akkub. Anger rose in him. What of their shepherd? In the bitter dark he lay and remembered—until at last the crowding pictures could not longer be endured. He moved abruptly and Baasha, whose body pressed his, awoke grumbling.

Akkub rose stiffly. "Come. Let's be on our way."

"But the sun is not risen," protested Baasha thickly, "and we have rested not more than a few hours."

"No matter. These are not hours to dream away."

Groaning, Baasha got to his feet. "What of the others?"

"Let them sleep. We can travel faster without them."

Traversing the heavily wooded coal mountains of Samaria, they reached the slope of Dothan shortly after sunrise. Gay little flowers sprang from the black soil, quickened by the touch of the spring sun.

Baasha's mouth twisted. "Why has the Lord of all made these things beautiful when human beings are the ugly things they are?" He shook his staff contemptuously.

The same thought had been grating in Akkub's mind. He had hoped to find peace in motion. He had hoped to still his heart's rebellion by travel. But the flame in him burned on. Just so, he thought, must his patriot father

14

Hazael have felt. Akkub had been but a child when his father had joined a group of Galileans in the revolt against the tax gatherers, but he could still remember the look in Hazael's eyes the night before he had been slain by Roman soldiers. Perhaps, thought Akkub, his own eyes bore that look now. What wonder, when the very ground his sandals marked was a place of ancient hatred? Here on the slope of Dothan, Joseph's brothers had sold him into Egyptian slavery. So men dealt with one another. Then—and now.

The road wound down to the plain of Jezreel and before them, like an aged picture, lay Shunem where the prophet Elisha had raised the widow's son. Would that the great Elisha might stretch his hand from eternity and restore John the Baptist to his despairing disciples!

"Nazareth draweth nigh." Baasha spat out the words. "Here it was that Jehu dropped the queen Jezebel from a second story window to be devoured by dogs. Hear my prayer—may Herod's adulterous queen meet a like fate!"

His eyes on snow-covered Mt. Hermon towering behind the dingy village, Akkub echoed the prayer—or was it a curse? Well, call it what one wished, he would not repent of it. "I will lift up mine eyes unto the hills from whence cometh my help." There had been a time when, his eyes on the sky-pushing Mt. Tabor or on little Hermon's shining blue to the south, he had been able to repeat David's words and believe that help did come. Today not so. There was a hardness in him—an incredulity.

Almost unnoticed, the travelers on the Jezreel road increased. Groups of five became ten, and ten became twenty—and all were hurrying northward. Their footsteps stirred up the dry lime dust which rose in thick clouds. Akkub began to realize that these were no ordinary wayfarers. No one was in holiday attire. Rather, it was as if they had all come directly from the fields. Sickles were thrust through belts. About one in ten, Akkub saw, had an old-fashioned sword hanging from his waist.

Baasha rubbed his beard. "Queer—it is not festival time."

"Nay, it is not." Curiosity kindled in Akkub and he could see it glow in his companion's face. "It looks—it looks as if something might be going to happen."

Akkub began to run, clutching his coat which was only half on his right shoulder. Baasha followed. After they had gone about half a furlong, they hailed the nearest farmer who was coming from the direction of little Hermon.

"Where is everyone going—and why? Can you tell us?"

Dirt etched lines in the youth's perspiring face. He darted a suspicious glance at the two disciples and, without answering, quickened his steps. Baasha looked after him in perplexity, then fell to coughing from the billowing dust.

Akkub shouted for attention. "Which is the quickest way to Capernaum—by way of Nazareth?"

One of the elder men in a group ahead answered, hardly turning his head. "If you don't go by the mountain road, then of course to go from Nazareth to Cana is quicker, but since the road is the Megiddo highway, it is probably better to go by way of Tiberius."

"Thank you for your kindness," said Akkub.

He and Baasha increased their pace until they drew nearer those ahead.

"Would you object to our joining your company?" asked Akkub.

One or two halted, looking back at them kindly. "Do you also go to see Jesus of Capernaum?"

Baasha coughed croakingly. "Yea, brothers."

"And you?" asked Akkub.

The answer came as one voice from several. "Yea—yea!"

When they came abreast, the man who had first answered them inquired whence they came.

Akkub's face shadowed. "From Machaerus."

"Machaerus?" Eyes grew veiled, suspicious.

"We have just come from burying our master on a Samaritan hilltop," said Akkub.

"We are disciples of John the Baptist." Baasha wiped his veined eyes.

Expressions changed. Sympathy softened narrowed eyes. Shock parted lips. Briefly, Akkub told the details of John's tragic death.

"Beheaded!" The older man wagged his head sadly. "What a terrible thing." The nine in the group crowded about the two, asking questions, listening indignantly to the heavy answers, calling down curses upon Herod and his family.

"We cannot—we shall not—endure such things longer!" A burly man smote his hand hard upon his sword hilt. "I, Onesimas, pledge myself to the cause of justice."

Akkub asked curiously: "But who are you in this group, and for what purpose do you seek the Nazarene? For healing, perhaps, or ——"

"We seek freedom!" Onesimas' voice boomed over the plain. Then he lowered it more cautiously. "We are the remnant of the defeated Galileans who, under Juda, revolted against the Roman rule."

Emotion, hot and searing, filled Akkub. "I am the son of Hazael who was killed in that revolution." He looked at these men, his interest come alive. His father's compatriots!

The older man reached a hand to Akkub's shoulder. "I, Nadab, knew your father Hazael well." His face was grim.

"He died gallantly, and for a righteous cause." His eyes searched Akkub's keenly. "Perhaps this meeting was pre-destined."

Akkub had the queer feeling that his own father, and not Nadab, had his hand upon his shoulder and was speaking thus to him.

He jerked restlessly. "Perhaps!" The words themselves were unimportant, surely. Then why should Nadab smile in that peculiar manner before he dropped his fingers from Akkub's sleeve? And why that feeling of continued pressure on his flesh when the cause of it was gone?

Onesimas was asking a question of Baasha. "Then, since you are John the Baptist's disciples, no doubt you know Simon the Zealot, now one of Jesus' followers?"

"Yea. We were once together in the same tent over by the Jordan river."

Onesimas threw a great arm across Baasha's shoulders and drew him along, talking earnestly. Akkub followed with Nadab. All about them were travelers hurrying northward, some talking loudly, some secretively—now and again bursting into some patriotic song.

When they had walked for some time, Nadab said un-expectedly: "Now is the time!"

Akkub licked his lips. His heart was a loud live thing in his breast. Though he did not speak, his mind flung questions out violently.

Nadab studied the younger man with his deep eyes. "We must raise our flag," he said softly. "We must push the fox from his stronghold and fell the Roman eagle. Now is the time!"

Still Akkub did not speak. Was this it—the outlet for all his new-born hatred of men in high places, men who wielded purchased influence like a bludgeon, who forced tribute from the harassed, who had power to cripple or to slay at a whim? Would he—could he—help to throw off the scarring yoke of oppression?

Beside him Nadab's voice throbbed. "There will never be another chance like this."

"Are all—are all this throng in agreement?" Akkub's voice was no more than a whisper.

Nadab hesitated. Then: "No, not all—but a strong leader could bring about complete union."

Saying no more, they approached Nazareth. It was a mean town, Akkub thought. It squatted among the southern ridges of Lebanon, and there was, Onesimas remarked scornfully, only one spring in the entire village.

"But here the Teacher Jesus was reared," said Nadab.

They passed through the town swiftly, and took the road to Cana, instead of the way which led past Herod's palace in Tiberius. Onesimas pointed out a big helmet shaped rock on the far side of the valley. " 'Twas from that cliff yonder that the people of Nazareth sought to drop Jesus. No one can explain how he could escape. The mob was rioting, shrieking, pressing him ——"

"But he did escape," said Nadab. "He has great powers. Some declare he could escape death itself." He stared at the huge precipice. "They've no miracles in Nazareth—why? Because they had no faith." He turned abruptly to Baasha. "Do you believe?"

Baasha's eyes clouded. "I—I do not know."

Akkub said: "We've heard many strange tales of Jesus. It is hard to tell the true from the untrue."

A man of middle age, slight of stature and serious of expression, came forward. "I am from Nain. See—it is there on the south side of little Hermon. Jesus did a marvelous thing in our village. The son of a widow died and as they were going to bury him, Jesus came and put his hand upon the coffin, commanding the young man to rise—and he did!"

Baasha inhaled sharply. "He did? Were you there?"

"I was standing behind the casket, for the young man is a distant relative of mine."

"He's still alive?"

"More vigorous than ever. As a matter of fact, he desired very much to come with us to Capernaum, but his mother wept and persuaded him to stay."

Akkub walked beside Nadab pondering the strange story. Could such a thing actually be? It was not easy to believe, yet the spokesman was oddly convincing. He had made no effort to dramatize the occurrence, but had simply set forth what he had witnessed.

Onesimas was telling of another incident. At a wedding in Cana, the host had run out of wine. It was very embarrassing, so Onesimas said. "But this Jesus, who had come to the wedding with his family, simply ordered the water in the jugs to become wine!" Onesimas moistened his heavy cracked lips. "One who was there told me it was the best he'd ever tasted."

"Would we had some now," sighed a young man from Bethsaida. "My throat is like dry leaves."

The short spring day came to an end at Cana. They made camp, along with several other groups, in a pasture near a spring. In the background, Mount Hattin was dusky purple and snow-capped Hermon, touched by the sun's last rays, glowed pink.

Long after his fellow travelers slept, Akkub stared into the fire and, when at length it had fallen to coals, at the star-pierced heavens. Tomorrow—tomorrow they would reach Capernaum and meet at last the man some called Messiah. Messiah—King of the Jews! Was he indeed such? Was this the one heralded by John? There had come out of the land of the Jordan strange accounts of Jesus and his works. It was said that he possessed a mystic sixth sense. He knew without hearing or seeing. He had performed miracles and wonders of such great magnitude that even the Pharisees were impressed. The only criticism of Jesus was that he spoke in parables, little understood, whereas John's words had been simple and his meaning so clear that Akkub thought no one could misunderstand.

Jesus was often misinterpreted and misquoted. His gentleness sometimes amused the crowds who were used to the provocative and belligerent attitude of John. "Turn you to God, sinners, before it is too late." On the other hand, it was said of Jesus that he spoke little of sin. He did not look for it. Instead he looked for love and seemed to find it everywhere, even in sinners. Strange, Akkub thought. For his own part, he doubted if the Nazarene were the true Messiah because these were days when one could not temporize. Only rock could withhold the flood. One had to be a wall. One had to hold rigidly against the beating of the great waves of dishonesty, drunkenness, cruelty and war. That had been John's view and Akkub subscribed to it. Of course, there might be a place for gentleness, too, but personally he preferred to think of it by another name. Yet it was true that this Jesus was gathering followers at a great rate. So, because he was the only teacher they could go to in their time of trouble, they must now go to him. But would he indeed be the strong leader Nadab and his fellow revolutionists sought?

The next day when Nadab's band, swelled to thrice its original size, entered Capernaum, the evening lamps were lit. Stars twinkled in the clear heavens, and the sea of Galilee was fluid silver. Six hundred and eighty feet below sea level, the city was already as hot as the first days of summer. Usually ten or twenty fishing craft were out on the lake, but tonight not one could be seen.

As they passed through the town, Akkub tensed at the tumult of excitement. Everywhere, at the crossroads, huddled in byways, upon the rooftops, men were grouped—talking, shouting—making gestures. To Akkub's amazement, he heard them speak mainly of the death of his master John.

"You see?" Nadab nodded. "The time is ripe." After a hurried consultation with his original band, he began to go in and out among the crowds with Onesimas. As he went, the older man dropped a word here, planted a rumor there, spoke of certain plans. Sometimes his voice was low and confidential. At other times, it rose to an emotional pitch. Onesimas' voice shouldered its way from group to group. Soon there surged a wave of activity around the two Galileans wherever they went, and a rumble of eager commotion.

Akkub and Baasha soon lost all track of the others. Standing confused in a doorway, they hailed a passing youth carrying a torch.

"How is it everyone knows of the death of John the Baptist? Hardly has there been time ——"

"A fast horseman brought the news, they say." Someone shouted at the young man, and he was off at a run, his torch waving and flickering.

Inquiring of the next comer where they might find Jesus, they were told he was at the house of Simon Bar-Jona near the seaside. Phrases lifted out of the confusion as they hastened along. "Beheaded John has risen from the dead and was seen walking in Tiberius!" "At last Jesus is going to call down fire from heaven and burn Tiberius." Hundreds of men and women rushed by the two disciples intent on reaching Tiberius in time for the heavenly spectacle.

Simon Peter's house was a small place about one block from the sea on a side street next to a little meeting place which, in its turn, was a poor building of gray plaster with a rounded roof.

Blocking the way to the house was a great throng. Women spoke uneasily to one another. "When do you think fire will descend from heaven?" A thin, white-faced child tugged at his mother's robe. "When will Herod be killed by divine judgment?" he whined over and over. Akkub and Baasha, forcing a passage through the wall of people by sheer persistence, entered the house by a low kitchen door facing the sea.

A loud voice challenged them. "No admittance! Who enters?"

"That voice is familiar," muttered Baasha.

"We are two disciples of John the Baptist!" called Akkub, as they paused uncertainly on the threshold. "We have come to see the Teacher Jesus."

"Two disciples of—!" A short exclamation. "Enter!" A stocky little man came forward to meet them. "Akkub and Baasha—friends!"

"Nicolas!" Akkub looked at him in astonishment. Only ten days before, this man, Nicolas son of Asaph, had been with them in Machaerus when, for the last time, they had brought food and gifts to the imprisoned John. He it was who had acted as emissary between the prison and the world without.

"How did you get here so quickly?" stammered Baasha. "We ourselves have scarcely stopped to sleep."

"I came from Machaerus in the chariot of Chuza, the steward, via Perea. Madame Chuza is a follower of the Teacher here."

Nicolas turned as a young woman of twenty-four or five came into the room.

"Ah, Mary Magdalene, here are two more disciples of John."

She wore a rather elaborate robe which looked a bit out of place in this poor home, Akkub considered, but her smile was friendly and genuine and her manner was sweet and gracious.

"You have come far?" Her great eyes were sympathetic. Akkub realized suddenly how road-worn they must look, he and Baasha. Eyes dust-reddened and watery, lids darkened by fatigue, sandals frayed, garments crumpled and soiled. Weariness swept over him, and a great aching thirst.

"Yea," he said, "we have come all the way from Samaria."

"To see the Master?" Her voice was gentle.

Baasha nodded. "But—such a crowd—I suppose we must wait a long time."

"I will see," said Mary Magdalene quickly, and went into another room.

"Is he in there?" asked Baasha thickly. Then, apparently losing interest in the answer, he slumped upon the floor and tugged at the cords of his sandals. Akkub stood, leaning against the wall. He had a feeling that if he were to sit or relax, he would forget his manners and fall into immediate slumber.

Two men came in the back door. He of the sunken eyes, Nicolas whispered, was Philip. The one with the broad forehead and large eyes was Nathanael. Each carried a small bag and staff. Akkub, watching them, was somehow impressed, and felt his fatigue lessen.

Mary Magdalene returned. Almost at the same moment, from the kitchen of the opposite house where, Nicolas said, she had been baking bread, Peter's wife entered. She had apple red, sunburned cheeks and a clear direct expression.

"Is your husband home yet?" asked Philip.

She said briefly: "He returned two days ago." She walked to the big stone jar in the corner, and with short jerky motions dipped water into a small crock.

"Sit down, Philip. I'm drawing water for your feet."

"Nay, don't trouble."

She smiled firmly.

Mary Magdalene, wringing a towel in water, took it to Akkub and Baasha.

CHAPTER III

A̲KKUB said to Mary Magdalene: "Where is Jesus
now?"

Baasha repeated: "Where is he?"

Both were growing impatient. Outside they could hear
steps and voices. The earth was giving out low, restless
vibrations as it sometimes did under the rhythmic march
of Roman legions. But tonight there was no rhythm, for
the army was civilians in broken step, a mob, a multitude,
preceded by dust and followed by dust. Through the thin
walls of Simon Peter's house penetrated the sounds in all
their variance. Men, women and children talking, muttering, weeping. Sometimes there was singing, too, but
usually weary and suppressed; and again, voices were
raised high in disagreement or in protest.

Akkub, tired from tramping so long, felt that he should
have been in sympathy with them, all of them, no matter
in what mood they were or where they came from or of
what nationality. Wasn't it enough that they were here to
see and hear the man they believed might be the Messiah?
Yet, as he waited for Mary Magdalene to answer, Akkub
knew that he resented them. Each petitioned for some
personal thing—peace of mind, bodily health, freedom
from oppression. Whereas he and Baasha had no thought
of self. They were messengers from John and because their
motives were nobler, they should, of course, have prece-
dence over these self-seekers.

"Where is your teacher?" he asked again.

Mary Magdalene had been hesitating. Suddenly, then, in a burst of confidence, she told them that no one ever could be quite sure where Jesus was at any time of the day or night. He was, she said, unaccountable. He was inexplicable. He seemed to be guided by curious inner promptings. He was at the mercy of every moment and whatever it might dictate. He might start for a certain place and fail to arrive because he found work on the way that took him in a new direction.

Having explained all this very carefully, she concluded: "I expect now, though, that he is outside administering to the throng which ever presses him for more attention."

"Then," said Baasha a trifle gruffly, "let us seek him."

Once through the back door, they were pressed by crowds on every side. Akkub soon learned that crowds will jostle you with their composite strength, but will tolerate no individual jostling. He and Mary Magdalene and Baasha were unanimously rebuked as they made a path through them. One irate man jerked Baasha's beard. Another pushed a hard flat hand into Akkub's face.

"Stand back in your own place!"

"Important," Akkub insisted, "that we see the Master. We carry a message. We must get through!"

A Syrian ground his heel in Akkub's aching foot. "Let the messenger through!" he shouted sarcastically. "Let him through!"

The way opened for a few paces, then closed before a mob within a mob. Here was a mass of fitted-together forms, writhing and twisting, trying to see over each other, pushing toward a central vortex. In this space, only partly cleared, were a woman and several of Jesus' disciples. The woman had just come out of Peter's house walking erect and tall. She seemed unaware of herself or of those around her. It was clear that she was conscious only of a condition—a perfection beyond her faculty to believe. Akkub thought she looked dazed, then he saw that it was no ordinary bewilderment. Her face was almost luminous. A set expression of her eyes made him think that she might be blind, then somehow he knew that to her ordinary sight had been added a more expansive vision. Not only did she see within the scale of ordinary mortals, but infinitely beyond it.

A man shouted: "The cripple's back is straight! She walks! She walks!"

A few minutes before, a girl told Akkub, relatives had borne this woman into Peter's house at the Master's request. And now—now she walked out alone!

Akkub smiled. How credulous they were! The crowd was making its own miracles. Unquestionably the cripple had not yet appeared.

"I wonder," he said to Mary Magdalene, "if Jesus is not soon coming out again?"

"Possibly," answered Mary.

She had turned her head and her gaze followed two torches being carried through an inner garden to the outer gate. Near the gate, a man stood addressing not more than a half score of persons sitting or standing around in small groups of three or four. Beyond the gate pressed the multitude, part of that vast assembly through which Akkub and Baasha and Mary Magdalene had just come.

"There he is!" Mary, suddenly, was trembling—for no reason at all that Akkub could see. "I will lead you to him now."

"But—when did he come out?"

A shrug of her shoulder was his only answer. They walked to where Jesus stood and for the first time, Akkub looked at the man who had been hailed as a Messiah. He looked, almost stared, then his fingers curled deeply into his palms and he pressed them hard in disappointment.

His master, John, had had lines of character worked like a scroll over rugged cheeks; he had had eyes that were fierce and fearless; he had had a mouth that might easily have been carved out of rock. Always, the sight of John gave one the assurance of strength, of deep straight thinking, of a massive unassailable intelligence.

But this man! He had no one outstanding quality, either of mortality or spirituality. He was smiling, young, and extraordinarily good looking. Tall, lean and muscular. He appeared to be in a vastly cheerful frame of mind and occasionally would laugh. John the Baptist seldom, if ever, laughed. Jesus laughed freely and easily. It was not unpleasant to hear, such laughter, but Akkub could not understand how any man, knowing all the weight of sin upon the world, could have the heart to laugh.

Akkub took a few steps nearer, and stopped. The tenseness and strain went out of his body and flowed into the ground. He was in a place of calm, a place of rest. There were singing sounds in his head, not heard at all, but felt as one feels the continued vibrations of a stringed instrument after it has ceased sounding. Around him it seemed as if the earth exuded wholesomeness, and even the dust smelt sweet as thyme at harvest. The horrible fact of John's death no longer oppressed him. The message he bore now seemed unimportant, strangely. Whatever was happening to him at this moment was unaccountable and as sudden as the silence following a stroke of lightning. The realization of a sense of attainment was his, but he did not know what he had attained. He did not care. He could hear a cricket chirping. Baasha was at his side and Mary Magdalene was leaning against his arm. He could hear their breathing in a unity and continuity of effect as though they inhaled and exhaled together to and from one pair of lungs to make one heart beat more strongly.

Jesus spoke to him. "You have come from John?"

"Yea, Lord."

There was no need to say more. The inflection of Jesus' voice when he said "John" conveyed a great deal beyond the ordinary significance of a name.

Then Jesus said: "You have come far. You must rest."

Akkub said: "Yes, we must rest. We are poor and had to walk from Machaerus. For four days we journeyed. That is why we were delayed."

Jesus made no answer. There was rustling and movement behind them. A number of invalids and sick persons and a few cripples approached. In their lead walked two men who were strong and straight and well clothed. Their manner was jubilant. Akkub recognized Philip and Nathanael.

Philip lifted his hand in salute, and almost shouted: "Teacher, we are late. But I must tell you—we have had wonderful results. Wonderful! Didn't we, Nathanael?"

"Yea, truly," said Nathanael.

Philip frowned slightly, then went on enthusiastically: "At this rate, we can drive even the devil out of the world!"

A slow smile came to Jesus' eyes. It was tolerant, and yet it was sad. What meanings could be read upon such a countenance were not always clear, Akkub decided. The man had him completely mystified. He was unlike anyone he had ever known. A very righteous person, undoubtedly —but not the Messiah. He seemed symbolic of all the virtues and graces, apparently. He looked like an aristocrat or a well-bred royalist, or possibly even a scholar. Why he should smile and then look sad was not comprehensible.

John, his own master, had always gazed sternly and defiantly at the world around him and at the people in it. There were no disguises he could not penetrate. Baasha had often said of him, "He sees right into your mind."

"But Jesus sees into your heart," thought Akkub, and was astonished.

The son of the Galilean carpenter drew Philip and Nathanael close to him. "You have done well," he said, "but what of these?"

He turned, looking directly at the motley, shambling, limping cavalcade the two disciples had preceded. There they were in dust and rags, in filth and sorrow. Philip, who would soon drive even the devil out of the world, could not now drive the consternation and humiliation from his own countenance, nor could Nathanael speak a word.

Jesus repeated gravely: "What of these?"

"Before God," wailed Philip, "they were too many for us. These we could not help. The others we did."

"There are no others," said Jesus, "except these." He took a step forward while Akkub's heart thundered. He said to the shuffling throng of halt and maimed, the ill and the needy: "Go, and you will find food and drink and beds to lie upon, according to your need. There will be hands to comfort you. There will be arms to gather you close—the arms of my Father which is in Heaven."

As Akkub stared, the cavalcade turned as one man and walked away silently, moving through the light that came from Peter's house and then into the darkling shadows. No one was limping now, nor moaning, nor offering up a prayer for relief. They had, Akkub perceived—and the shock of this realization was like dagger-points pricking into his skin—all been healed! Every one of them. And now Jesus was smiling once more and he asked informally of Philip: "Where did you hear of John's death?"

Philip took a deep breath of relief. "At the foot of Mt. Carmel. A week ago. Since that time, Master, at every village and farm and wayside inn, the talk is of rebellion."

"Rebellion?" said Jesus slowly. "Rebellion?"

"Yea, my Lord. They say that because you are the Messiah, you will lead them in a revolution."

Jesus looked at Philip. There was a slight lift of his eyelids, and again that strange grave smile. But he did not speak.

"I did not go to ten of the villages as you commanded," Philip said, "but hurried back. They all wanted you to lead the revolution and suddenly I knew why you told us when we left, 'Before you have visited all the towns of Israel, the Son of Man will have appeared.' Those were your words, Master."

"That is so," said Jesus gently.

"They sank deep into my mind," Philip went on, "so when I heard what had happened to John I could not but think that perhaps the time for your leadership has come."

"Verily," said Jesus, "my time is come."

"A great crowd of people is ripe for revolution," Philip was growing enthusiastic and had raised his voice. "Everywhere—everyone is ready. We hurried back to tell you this."

Other disciples of Jesus had come out of Peter's house and now drew near. Akkub knew a few of them by sight. Peter, James, and John. And the man Matthew. Following a short distance behind was Simon the Zealot in a fresh clean robe.

"Greetings!" said Matthew to Akkub and Baasha. "We welcome you most cordially."

The other disciples also greeted them kindly and Akkub was deeply touched. He decided that he would like to be one of them. Now that his own leader was gone, could he

do better? Yea, he would join them in a revolution, help
to put down the power of Herod and avenge John.

Simon Peter took Jesus by the arm. "You must go in
now," he said insistently. "We will all go in and talk for
a while."

On the way to the front of the house, Matthew fell in
step beside Akkub. "I remember you well. You were the
leader of a group in Galilee some years ago who refused
to pay me the taxes due to the crown."

Akkub flushed. He had almost forgotten. "On that occasion," he stammered, "you were tax collector for Caesar."

Matthew smiled reassuringly. "But I'm not reminding
you of this to make you uncomfortable. Your reason, no
doubt, seemed good to you. I am no longer a publican—I
suppose you know that."

Akkub said stiffly: "I inferred as much, seeing you here
with—with him."

"But he pays taxes," said Matthew slyly. They walked
in silence for a few moments, then he went on: "Henceforth, I will follow him wherever he goes. He needs
friends—close, true friends." Matthew raised his arms and
let them fall. It was an odd gesture, but Akkub understood it perfectly. It said more emphatically than he could
have managed with speech, that come what might, the
friendship between him and Jesus could not be severed,
that it was the Alpha and Omega, the ultimate and the
eternal of all friendship. Nor could Akkub doubt that it
was, for he, too, was beginning to want to be Jesus' friend.
He was so absorbed in this thought that he but half heard
what Matthew was saying. Something more about taxes—
and when they had entered the dwelling and were proceeding directly along the hall to the room reserved for
the Master, taxes was still the subject of Matthew's talk.

"Simon, who was called the Zealot, also refused to pay taxes," he said.

They entered Jesus' room and sat down. Mary Magdalene had entered in the company of Nicolas and smiled as she passed Akkub. Baasha was with Philip on a low bench not far from the Master. Someone touched Akkub from behind to draw his attention. He turned to look into a thin, wasted face that had only one mark of strong vitality, a pair of eager burning eyes.

"I am Simon, late of the Zealots," he said. "We met as followers of John, I believe."

Akkub nodded. "I remember."

"I've heard of the horrible experience you've been through. I sincerely sympathize. I mourn with you. I think as you do that something ought to be done. Those responsible should not go unpunished. We're all with you in any plan you may suggest to avenge his death."

Akkub's eyes filled with tears. "Thank you."

"You must rise," urged Simon, "and tell Jesus and those assembled here just what you know and just what you intend to do. Be firm. I doubt not that you are hewn of the same hard rock as John the Baptist."

This was true. Akkub had always known that he was strong and purposeful, else he would not have become his master's favorite. He would do as Simon suggested, make a speech and tell them plainly just what ought to be done. He could feel the words welling up in him, fiery and accusing, words of condemnation, yet words of courage and high purpose, he felt. Personally, he did not believe that Jesus would do anything to punish Herod and his evil consort, Herodias, unless he were pressed. The man was far too gentle. Far too lovable and kind. What he needed was flint and fire in him and blazing wrath that had consumed John when the wilderness prophet was crossed by the exponents of the devil.

Yea, he would tell them. Simon was right. He would tell them. He would make them sting with resentment; he would make them see the bloody, decapitated head of his venerable master. He would show them the funeral procession of broken, weeping disciples, moving through the litter and stench of the Dung Gate.

Abruptly he was out of his seat, standing high above the faces raised to his. As though they were no part of him, he heard the words he spoke, clear and strong in the room. He was inspired, he knew. Perhaps it was the voice of John speaking through him.

"If you have consciences, hearts—if you would hurl down deceit and treachery and low, subtle schemings—if you would be true to the guiding spirit of your God—act!" He heard himself shouting. "Act! Now is the time to prove the strength of all of you, and especially of your teacher, Jesus. You must act! Our leader, John, died believing that he was one sent by divine decree to serve and save you. Because of this we must take our stand with him. Raise the banner that has been stained in his own blood! Is it God's will that we should be forever bound by the fetters of the Roman empire? By the miracles that your new teacher, Jesus of Nazareth, performs, let us feed this puppet of an Antipas and the adulteress, Herodias, to the dogs!"

Akkub sat down amid a roar of applause. Several of the disciples rushed forward to clasp his hand. Mary Magdalene was openly weeping. Nearly everyone had arisen except—except the one he had hoped most to impress and stir, the son of the carpenter.

As the others crowded about him, he could see past them to the small table near which, in profile, a head was bowed. Candlelight fell over it and made a crown of beauty upon the yellow, clustered hair.

CHAPTER IV

THE commotion following Akkub's speech had not yet died when Peter's wife appeared in the doorway.

"Master," she said, "Joanna, the wife of Herod's steward, Chuza, and her young son are here."

Jesus rose. "I will go to them."

"Nay, Lord," protested Peter, "let them come to you."

Jesus seemed not to have heard. "Where are they?" he asked Peter's wife.

"In the garden, Master, but ——"

Jesus was already gone from the crowded room. Akkub looked after him, astounded. "How swiftly he moved! Why, only a moment ago he sat by that table yonder and now ——"

"Now," shrugged Simon the Zealot, "he is in the garden. He is always that way—as hard to hold as a sunbeam."

Akkub followed the others out of the house. He was baffled and disappointed. Jesus had ignored his eloquence. Yet Akkub knew that he had spoken with all the feeling and fury necessary to rouse and influence the human mind. In his words had been all the elements to sway. The reactions of the others proved that. But Jesus of Nazareth was not, it grew increasingly clear, as others.

A woman knelt before Jesus and beside her, a lad of fourteen.

"Teacher," she said in a voice strained as if by tears, "see how the boy you saved last year has grown!"

36

Jesus lifted them both and said pleasantly: "I rejoice with you."

Joanna, Chuza's wife, began to sob. "Oh, Teacher, I was on the king's left when the soldier brought in John's head on a silver tray and gave it to Salome. I——"

"The Master has heard all about it," broke in Peter, putting a restraining hand on her shaking shoulder.

"Let her speak," said Jesus.

Peter dropped his hand.

"Salome took that bleeding head without a single quiver and gave it to her mother. I hid my face."

"And Herod?" Jesus' voice was quiet.

"He bowed his head. Oh, believe me—believe me, Teacher, he was truly sorrowful!" Her wet eyes sought the Nazarene's countenance earnestly.

Baasha said angrily: "It was late for sorrow, then!" Nicolas and Simon the Zealot muttered together, shaking their heads.

Joanna went on, her voice torn: "Chuza left his place and came and whispered to me, 'There'll be punishment from heaven.' I thought so, too." She fell to her knees again, her hands catching at the folds of his robe. "Teacher, will there be punishment from heaven? Can nothing be done to save that family?"

"Why should anything be done?" asked Baasha violently. Torchlight fell upon his face and made it a thing of sharp shadows and burning eyes.

Joanna's gaze flashed to Baasha, then scurried in fright back to the Master. "Teacher, Chuza said to me, 'There is likely to be an uprising in Galilee. You go to the Teacher and ask his help.' My husband was almost in tears. That is why I hurried here, to plead for the king's life."

Jesus reached down and raised her to her feet again. Akkub saw the shimmer of a gold bracelet on her arm, and noted the long flowing robes she wore. Those of a

Roman woman! Her very dress, he thought bitterly, de-
noted her allegiance, her fealty to the oppressive eagle.
Why did Jesus suffer her presence? Why did he waste his
time with her, when he had had no attention to give to
John's disciple, Akkub?

"Teacher," wailed Joanna, "my heart is a weight in my
breast. I admit the wickedness of Herod's deed, but he is
the master who has favored my husband through many
long years. Can't you save Herod's family as you saved
ours?"

Jesus was silent.

Akkub shouted: "God ought to punish a wicked man!
To ask for anything else is a sin in itself."

Joanna burst into loud uncontrollable weeping, covering her face with the purple embroidered neck piece of
her dress. Peter's wife came to her and said comfortingly:
"Do not weep, madame. I shall add my pleas to yours to
save your master."

Simon the Zealot strode forward and stopped before
Jesus, his head thrown back. "Teacher, if you listen to this
woman's request, the Kingdom of God will become but a
nest of sinners!"

Jesus' deep clear eyes met the hot gaze of his disciple
composedly. When he spoke, his words were so low that
Akkub had to move nearer to catch them.

"Simon, Simon . . . you speak of God's Kingdom without understanding. I must repeat again what I have told
you many times. The Son of Man came not to condemn,
but to save."

Little by little, Simon's head lowered. He backed away
from his Master's kindly but firm scrutiny, and was soon
lost in the shadows of the garden. Akkub found, to his
amazement, that his own head was bowed, as if he, too,
had partaken of the rebuke. Confusedly, he jerked his

head up and looked furtively around. No one had noticed, apparently. Jesus was deep in meditation, his eyes raised to the stars of Leo, twinkling above the rooftops. His disciples, too, were silent.

Uneasily, Akkub moved out of the group and made his way toward the end of the garden, drawn by the light of torch flares, rapidly increasing with a gathering crowd.

Someone called his name. "Akkub—is it you?" Onesimas strode forward and clapped him upon the shoulder lustily. Behind him came Nadab and a great Samson-like man who dwarfed them both, tall as they were. From a bushy beard which covered his face, a strong aquiline nose peeked out like a cedar tree from a thicket. This, Onesimas announced pridefully, was Barabbas, the leader of the anti-tax payers.

Spreading his legs, Barabbas grunted a greeting. His close-set eyes stabbed into Akkub's. When he moved, Akkub could see, even in this light, the roll and bulge of muscle. It was like coming face to face with a boulder which had somehow contrived to take human form. Here, obviously, was a man of force and action.

"Will you introduce us to Jesus?" asked Nadab.

But Barabbas scorned such formality. Pushing past them, he called in a voice like the rumble of chariot wheels: "Teacher! Teacher!"

In front of Jesus, he stopped and dug his great feet into the earth, his manner daring anyone to move him from the spot.

"Teacher! We represent the villages of Israel. These men here are the twenty-four elders representing the twelve tribes of Israel!" He waved his hand commandingly to the fifty or sixty men who had followed him. They dropped to their knees. "We've come because we want you to become our king."

Nadab, rising from his obeisance, came to stand beside Barabbas. "Teacher," he said in that inflexible, yet compelling voice which Akkub well remembered, "the time has come. There, in yonder synagogue, we have just taken the oath of allegiance. We pledge you our fealty."

"We will protect you as long as we live!" roared Onesimas.

Baasha broke into loud cheers.

"We beg of you to hear our petition," said Nadab persuasively, "and straightway to take the oath of king."

"Then," promised Barabbas, "we shall immediately set fire to Tiberius, attack Machaerus and avenge John's death!"

The garden rang with shouts. The disciples looked excitedly at their Master. But the carpenter's son stared up at the constellation of Leo unblinkingly. Joanna, tears still tracking her cheeks, knelt at his feet.

"Teacher!" rumbled Barabbas somewhat impatiently, "you are the true King of Israel and Herod should be punished by you."

"But you are also the Saviour," pleaded Joanna huskily. "Please—I implore you, save at least the life of Antipas."

Baasha sprang forward angrily and pushed her away. "No need to ask to save such a life! If such as he is not punished, the Kingdom of God will never come on earth. Stop bothering the Master."

Joanna remained where she had fallen and continued to weep. Peter's wife, her eyes flashing indignation, raised her in her arms.

"There is no need for violence here," she flung at Baasha.

"Who is this woman who pleads for Herod's life?" demanded Barabbas of Baasha. When he heard, his face darkened. "So! One of the group of foxes who slew John!"

"Let's stone her! Let's stone her!" cried Onesimas.

Barabbas drew his sword. Joanna, cowering in the embrace of Peter's wife, held trembling hands out to Jesus. "Master! Master!"

"Put up thy sword, Barabbas!" Jesus' voice was quiet, but imperative.

Barabbas hesitated, his narrow eyes rebellious. Then, resentfully, he sheathed the weapon. The men with him shifted restlessly on their feet, and grumbled. Onesimas glowered at Joanna.

Jesus spoke again. "You have come from the synagogue, Barabbas. Return thither again—and this time pledge allegiance not to me, but to my Father. Pray—pray!"

Without looking back, Jesus walked toward the outer gate, the movement of his robes like flowing light among the shadows. Barabbas, gaping after him rigidly for a long moment, came abruptly to life and pounded in pursuit.

"Teacher!" he bellowed. "Teacher, where are you going? To the synagogue, too?"

At the outer gate, Akkub and Onesimas caught up with Barabbas. "Where did he go?"

"To the seashore, I think." Barabbas flung the words over his shoulder. For a heavy man, he ran with surprising swiftness, and it was with difficulty that Akkub and Onesimas overtook him.

When they reached the Galilean shore, it was dark and such a great crowd had gathered that they could not guess which way Jesus had gone. Everyone asked the same question of everyone else. Where was the Nazarene? Which way had he gone?

Barabbas cursed. "It's black as death here!"

"In this murk, how could you find anyone?" despaired Onesimas.

Akkub went from one person to another, asking: "Where did he go? Did Jesus pass this way?"

Barabbas' followers, guided by the sound of his exasperated profanity, soon rallied about him. Nicolas ran up with the news that he had just seen Jesus and his disciples boarding Peter's fishing boat.

"After them!" ordered Barabbas.

But the boat was already out on the water when they arrived. By the light of the moon rising over the mountains of Gilead and now shining over the eastern lake, the vessel's direction was easily seen.

Barabbas unsheathed his sword. "Let's surround the lake—surround it!"

Those in Jesus' boat stopped rowing, however, and drifted on the waves. Thwarted, Barabbas put up his sword disgustedly, as did his followers. They were about one mile from Capernaum by this time and gasping for breath after their run. Throngs from the town and nearby villages, attracted by the excitement and shouting, had come out to see until the numbers on the shore increased to thousands. There were so many that few knew why they had come, actually, or what they were expecting. One man, guessing that Jesus was going to cure all the sick in the crowd, told his surmise to others. The rumor spread and the sick who had been waiting in Peter's garden and outside the gate were brought by anxious friends and relatives.

Becoming aware of the multitude, Jesus' disciples rowed him out deeper. Akkub, wedged between Onesimas and Nicolas, strained his ears to catch the words of the Nazarene which carried clearly across the water. "Let us sleep here, tonight." The reply of the disciples was indistinguishable. Odd, thought Akkub, how clearly the soft voice of Jesus carried in comparison.

Barabbas blustered: "Then we'll sleep here on the shore."

A watch was posted and the crowd settled down on the beach to wait for morning.

Baasha pushed through to Akkub's side and settled down upon the pebbles, grumbling. "It's an outrage! This Jesus doesn't even thank us for asking him to be our king, but simply walks off as if we didn't exist. And now, in order to keep an eye on the man, we must sleep the night through on stones!"

Akkub did not answer. He was far too weary for complaint. Above them shone a silver crescent, touching the varying purple of the lake and the rough rocks of the eastern slope to majestic beauty. To the right glowed gentle hills and the great Damascus road which framed in white the deep lake waters.

CHAPTER V

Akkub stood among the crowd watching the boat draw near to the mouth of the Jordan. At this place the Galilean coastline made curving indentures into the land. Over the water came the rhythmic stroke of oars and the helmsman's droning voice. Jesus sat in the bow, smiling. Sometimes he would let his arm fall overside and raise his eyes to the gulls wheeling and gliding overhead. Sometimes his figure was erect, detached, giving the impression of one among men, but not with them. It was as if he were alone and sufficient in himself, like a mountain overreaching hills.

All along the hills where the throng awaited the Teacher were moss-covered stones and green banks of rushes. And beyond were sloping fields, disturbed and restless in the strong urge of spring. Oleanders were budding here and new green sprouted from the twigs of the locust trees.

Slowly the boat came closer and Akkub perceived, with an inner start, that Jesus was trailing one hand in the water. Idly and pleasantly trailing his hand so that it made ripples and a grooved line alongside the boat. He was doing this while the multitude waited, baffled and tired from waiting, while it stood wondering why their new leader, who had all the qualities of leadership, did not act. They knew, Akkub suspected, that if he did act he could have whatever he wanted. All he need do was to reach out and it would be his. Then would come the crashing of an empire and the liberation of a people.

No sooner had the boat begun to grate through the shallows than the disciple called Judas Iscariot clambered out of it, holding his robe high. In the strong morning sun his hair and his beard glinted red.

He waded a few paces—and stopped. "Teacher!" he cried. "Teacher, they come—the crowd. It presses toward us."

Akkub saw Peter rise and throw out the anchor. "Nuisance!" he said. Akkub remembered that Mary Magdalene had said that Peter disliked crowds; it would have pleased him to go away alone somewhere with Jesus, and return in triumph to Jerusalem, riding a golden cloud and dispensing justice and largesse to the accompaniment of strokes of lightning and peals of thunder. He was the most impetuous man Akkub had ever met. But he believed thoroughly in his Master's power. To Andrew, his brother, he had just spoken of the possibility of Jesus ascending to a great height and actually riding upon such a cloud. Andrew said, in some wonderment: "Well, I can think of no better way than that."

Peter answered: "It can be done. It is remarkable—it is marvelous, I tell you, what he can do!"

A youth of eighteen or nineteen, standing near Akkub, opened his mouth very wide and stared at Jesus as he and the disciples disembarked. When Peter passed, he ran panting to overtake him.

"Please, sir, can you tell me when your Teacher is going to ascend? I want to be there to watch him."

Peter shrugged him off. "You must wait and see. You must believe as we believe."

Akkub smiled at the faith of Peter and the credulity

of the boy. The next moment the smile left him. Judas, Jesus' youngest disciple, also believed and so, too, James the less, his brother, for they fell to discussing the subject while Jesus made his way forward in no special hurry but evidently with some new intent.

James the less said, finally: "I'm hungry. If we could but find a fig tree. . . ."

But there were no fig trees bearing. It was not, Akkub could have reminded him, the season of fruition but, rather, the season of preparation. The time of the Passover was near. The hills wore thick skirts of grass, garlands of young leaves and flowers; there came upon the wind the heady smell of a refreshened soil, disquieting yet satisfying. Akkub remembered that the country hereabouts belonged not to Herod, but to his brother Philip, whose beautiful wife the king had stolen.

Such thoughts always led back to his beloved master and the manner of his death. Indeed, when Herod came to mind, or Herodias, but chiefly that woman, there followed in his sight a staring grave on a bleak hillside, a procession of men of which he was one moving toward it in a silence so thick it smothered.

He would never forget that. Nor did he want to until John was avenged and the whole unreasonable and infamous regime destroyed by the battalions of Jesus.

Then he heard the youth speaking to James of the very thing that had suddenly occurred to him. "Your Master was clever in coming here where Antipas could not follow. Probably it is as good a place as any to mobilize his forces."

Looking around, Akkub saw that Jesus was proceeding toward the highest of the hills nearby and there was Peter with him, and John.

Andrew said: "They will return presently," and

stretched out on the ground to rest in the sun. He was, apparently, very tired. He and Nathanael were exhausted, he told Akkub, because of their trip yesterday.

Just then Barabbas' party galloped up. The horses were steaming and spotted with mud.

Barabbas, in a violent and heavy voice, demanded to know where the Master was. "We're ready to form ranks. Before another sun, we'll move against the castle whose walls protect the black, cowardly hearts of those in authority." He paused, glaring. "Come—where is Jesus? Where is this wonder-worker of yours? What do we wait for?"

With the branch of a willow he had used to whip up his horse, he pointed along the shore.

"There they come like the uncounted sands. Scores— thousands of them! My army."

"Your army!" gasped Akkub.

"I have been spreading a fury among them. I have taken them by the nose of their intelligence and led them around. I—Barabbas! I did it—I!"

He beat upon his great chest with a doubled hand. Akkub moved closer. Barabbas had girth and strength and fire. Not too smart a man, probably, but one who could match wisdom with cunning. He would make a popular champion for the mob. As a second-in-command taking orders from a leader like Jesus of Nazareth, he would be invaluable.

"You have accomplished much," Akkub complimented him. "We should all be working. I think Jesus is ready— now. He went to that hill yonder and, I have good reason to believe, to make his plans."

"In a few weeks that carpenter's son will be a king," Barabbas boasted, "and I his chosen commander."

"I doubt not."

Barabbas put down his whip and jerked on the halter

line. A quick fleshy smile made carvings on his face and tiny wells in his cheeks. "You speak well. Leap up behind me and we'll go at once to your Master."

"You mistake," said Akkub. "John the Baptist was always and will ever be my master."

"But he's dead now."

"That makes no difference."

Barabbas looked puzzled. "How can you follow a man who is no longer here to lead you?"

"It is not the master; it is the principle."

"Enough of such nonsense! To horse, man, before the phantom son of a carpenter deserts yon mountain for another and is lost to our cause forever."

Akkub laughed as he scrambled up. Barabbas was oddly refreshing. Like a wind strong out of the north; like thundering waves upon a rocky shore. One felt sure of him. At least Akkub, for the present, felt sure of him. If Barabbas changed his mind before tomorrow, he would tell you why. Any man might be privy to his thoughts and welcome. There were those who claimed Barabbas was not to be trusted, of course, that he would lie and cheat and steal and be untrue to his friends. Akkub could believe this of the man, but in what respect did he differ from mankind in general? It was common in this day and generation to do all these things. It was said no one could survive else. A change in government, the destruction of its evil-spawning rule alone could save the country and men like Barabbas.

Up the mountain along a broken and confusing trail the horses carried them. Barabbas whipped his own mount and urged it on. Between times, he told Akkub that he would henceforth be more firm in his dealings with Jesus.

"He dreams," Barabbas said, "and flits from candle to

candle like a moth. Though he is undoubtedly a great prophet, he is as yet unawakened. He must be roused to practicality. Is that not your own estimation of him?"

Akkub could not have put forth truer words himself and to Barabbas' broad back he slowly made the admission.

"Well, then," said Barabbas, "listen to me when we overtake him. Pest! How that fellow must walk!" He raised his whip. "Get on there, you miserable bone-bag, you unschooled foal of a worthless dam. Hurry!"

"I think on the ledge just above we shall find them."

"May God be your adviser," Barabbas snorted. "Ah-h, what was I saying? Now I have it—firmness. That was it. My speech shall burn his ears. He needs strong talk—he needs handling." He slapped his horse. "I'll put life into this cause."

Even as Barabbas spoke, they dipped down through a stony ravine, skirted a few stunted trees and there, most unexpectedly, Jesus was.

Barabbas reined up and Akkub leaned over so that he could see better. The carpenter's son sat on a flat rock, two of his disciples beside him sleeping.

"He is praying," whispered Akkub.

"Nay," said Barabbas. "His eyes are open."

The sun concentrated and focused upon Jesus' bared head. There was sun in his hair and face. His eyes were shining with it, refining and further illuminating it. The white cloth of his simple robe had the brightness of a shield, but none of its glare.

"By the prophet's beard," Barabbas spoke, "the man is burning up!"

Akkub got down from the horse in a sort of numb stupor and began, to his utter amazement, to count the fingers of his right hand. There could be no doubt, there

were five fingers; he had always known—five fingers
on each hand. A little finger, a thumb, and three more
between them. He was a child counting his fingers with
the interest and urgency of a child. And yet he could hear
Barabbas repeating over and over, with a like stupidity:
"The man is burning up. By the prophet's beard, he
burns!"

But, for some reason, Akkub could no longer look at
Jesus. Jesus was there—he was aware of him—but so was
he aware of the mountain and the two slumbering disciples. His state of awareness included the sky and the
sea of Galilee, and all the land and the alive, freshening
spring and the glory of the sun. Yet he counted his fingers. Better that, than to be sheared of one's senses in the
blaze of that breathless white purity.

Then he remembered what Barabbas had said. Barabbas
would be firm. In strong speech he would make this
dreamer understand him.

"Speak to him, Barabbas," Akkub urged. "You told
me——"

The voice of Jesus came to them from the sanctuary
of the rock. "Come, if ye have need of me."

How Barabbas went to him Akkub never knew. But
presently he could hear his companion's voice, dimmed
and shorn of its harshness, not commanding, but pleading. "We have searched everywhere, O Master, for him
whom John said would lead us. Now we know for a
surety that you are he, the Saviour of Judea. We beg of
you to show forth your purpose. Save us, Master!"

Barabbas made low obeisance before the Nazarene.

And then Akkub turned his head at the sound of voices.
The advance guard of the great multitude had just crossed
the ravine. Down the mountains came hundreds of others,
thousands of them, many carrying their bed-rolls. Chil-

dren were among them and old men and women, so weak they had to be helped along.

They were shouting and singing: "Save us, Teacher! Down with oppression. Establish a new kingdom on earth."

Akkub heard Jesus approaching Barabbas. "The kingdom of God is not here, Barabbas, not where we can see it, but in our hearts," he was saying. "The kingdom of God is like a pearl taken from the sea. The kingdom of God is like treasure hidden in the field. Think not of the things of the world seen with the eye, but of the things of the Spirit which are not seen."

With what dignity he could, Barabbas arose, his face dark with disappointment. "I can find no sense in what you say." His tone held rebuke.

Jesus smiled, and lifted his hand in a friendly gesture.

"Go and study by the side of the road," he suggested. "Listen for the wind at nightfall and the sound of children's steps. Make a holiday in the field with the grass to whisper to you. Take a flower from the mountain and breathe its fragrance."

Barabbas turned on his heel, muttering: "The man is mad."

The multitude was pressing closer. Some of them called out eagerly: "Jesus! Jesus! Master!"

Baasha joined Akkub and with him was Simon the Zealot.

"With this many, I'm sure we can succeed!" Simon said exultantly. "If we revolt now, not only the people of Judah but all the people about the Mediterranean and the Jews scattered everywhere will join us. Positively I say that this is the right time."

"Then why does your Teacher shilly-shally?" demanded Baasha.

Barabbas snorted as he walked over and picked up the reins of his horse.

"I'll tell you," he said, "and you'll find me right. Your master is no leader at all—merely a magician. A person of recipes and incantation. Presently he will walk upon coals of fire and find birds hidden in children's garments. Did you hear what he said to me?"

"Yea," nodded Akkub.

"Did you understand him? Be frank, man. I'll have the truth out of someone or run him through!"

"Nay," said Akkub, backing away from that angry flushed face, "I did not."

Baasha wrinkled his nose. "Nor I."

Someone in the fore ranks of the throng called out in a scratchy, excited voice: "Master, how then can the kingdom of God come?"

"It will come on the day when you all repent and love one another," Jesus answered.

Barabbas swung about angrily. "What do you say? Is it, then, as easy as that?"

Jesus rose. His manner was incredibly pacific. "Only if you have understanding." He was quiet a moment, then went on in a strong sure voice. "You think God's kingdom is raised by jealousy and the sword? How wrong you are. From ancient times, we have been taught to love our neighbors and hate our enemies, but I say to you that that is not sufficient. I say, 'Love your enemies, do good to those that curse you, consider those that persecute you. Pray for your enemies.' "

The group of Zealots near Akkub burst into roars of laughter. Onesimas, stout and flushed of face from his climb up the mountain, bristled and began to sputter. When he could speak, his voice rose high.

"Think you that we are fools? Love Herod's followers!

Bless the Romans! Pray for those who killed the teacher, John! What nonsense! How think you we could do that? Should we follow that advice, we Jews would be slaves forever."

Jesus upturned his face to look at the sun, an April sun, warm and radiant over the earth, a cheerful sun, smiling into the fields and laughing upon the sea. Again, Akkub felt that strange uplift in which the mundane and the material were without legs to walk upon, or any reason to walk. Instead was fullness within and calm without.

Whatever he was, this Teacher, Jesus, had a most engaging way with him, a spirit of friendliness and good will difficult to resist. Unconsciously, one was pleased with him, even though one knew him to be wrong.

"Does not our Father in Heaven cause His sun to shine upon the good and the bad, and His rain to fall on the just and the unjust? Think well on these things. If you love only those who love you, where is the virtue therein? Do not the publicans do as much? Even those without God love their own brothers. You must be perfect as your Father in Heaven is perfect."

Barabbas' followers were silent. Akkub leaned toward Nicholas and whispered: "He says, 'Be ye perfect,' as though it were possible of men."

"Hard words," said Nicholas, shaking his head, but not looking at Akkub. "I ——"

"Yea," interrupted Simon the Zealot, "hard words, indeed! But look here—he has some special power, hasn't he? That's certain. We don't know when it may be manifested in its entirety. It's my belief that he speaks as he does so that Rome and Herod will tolerate him—so that they will be unprepared when he is ready to strike the blow!"

"Let us pray that is true," said Akkub.

Then he followed behind Jesus, who was moving down the mountainside to minister to the sick and deformed. For an hour, wide-eyed, Akkub watched the Nazarene; watched him cleanse a leper, give sight to the blind, strength to the weak, wholeness to the maimed. There was no doubt of the things he did. Whatever else one might think of him, of his strange creed, of his curious beliefs, of his tendency to avoid important issues—he was a man who had a healing voice and hands which could restore and comfort. He was, Akkub decided, a physician of remarkable attainments and magnetic presence.

But as a leader of a strong cause, as a soldier who could set up a kingdom in which injustice, murder and persecution were not tolerated, was he fit and qualified?

For a long space, Akkub dwelt on that question while rumors were flying about him—rumors of an impending attack by a Roman army marching hither from Damascus, by Herod's army marching from Tiberius.

Then, with a shrug of his shoulders, Akkub walked alone and sorrowfully down the long slope of the mountain.

CHAPTER VI

Before evening, Akkub returned. Most of the crowd would be gone, or going soon. All the stir and talk, the restlessness and dust would have abated. In a few more hours cooking-fires would light the Galilean shore and the banks of the Jordan. Weary families would press into the courtyards of the inns and crowd about the farm cots to buy, with their few coins, a fish-loaf or jug of milk.

The need of food would drive them from the mountain. Hunger would call them down into the highways to beg or buy; or, if that failed, to steal; for hunger has a set of jaws, Akkub reflected, that will bite anyone. In his wanderings with John the Baptist from one mission camp to another, he had known hunger himself. There had been days of fasting, not always because there was need to try the flesh, but because, often, there was no food to be had. And when food could not be had the body was rebellious and made overtures to the mind, "Proceed hence," it would say. "The stone in this field may be a turnip in the next. This forlorn bush may yield berries beyond the bend in the river." It seemed to Akkub that they went seeking bread more often than they went seeking converts.

And so it would be here at the mountain. But when Akkub looked up he was amazed. Hunger had not driven them out. They were here, all of them, the same crowds

55

of the morning, making shadows upon the ridge, darkening the slope, moving or lying around among the rocks like contented sheep. Coats were spread out. Fires were lighted. The sun was setting behind Hattin mountain, a golden disk that made flame of the sky and obeisance to the coming dusk.

Akkub climbed the path, one of many, until he reached the upper elevation where, he supposed, the Master would be. Voices came to him first, then a slight movement, which he heard rather than saw because of the in-lying dark. Presently, quite clearly, to the front of him, Philip spoke: "Master, are you not hungry? We have not eaten this day, nor has the crowd. Shall we send them away for their supper?"

"Is there bread for them?" Jesus asked.

Philip threw back his cloak and laughed. "Why, Master, even if we had brought two hundred denari worth, it could not possibly feed all."

Before Jesus could answer, Andrew stepped beside them, leading a child who, he explained, had been dumb. Its parents, he said, lived in Bethsaida, not far from his own home and he could vouch for both of them. "Gentle, honest folk," he said, "frugal and generous, and now joyous in the gift of healing you have bestowed upon this child."

Jesus shook his head. "My Father, not I."

Andrew looked confused. "Your father!"

"Our Father," Jesus said.

Akkub pressed closer. After all, what did it matter whose father? Jesus so often dwelt within himself that he could not make ordinary use of his senses. His speech wandered and was irrelevant. It amused Akkub to hear a grown man talk as a child might.

Andrew said: "What I came to tell you was that this

child's brother brought his lunch. In gratitude, he offers you part or all of it: two fish and five small loaves."

Jesus placed a hand upon the child's head and smiled. "It is kind of your brother." Then he turned to Andrew. "Fetch it all," he said, "and I will bless it."

But when Andrew returned, Jesus was playing with the child, raising him up and lifting him down. Akkub was further amused. Jesus had apparently forgotten entirely why he had sent Andrew, and now that Andrew was here, why he carried a basket.

Andrew had the expression of one whose good offices have been disdained.

"Here is the food, Lord," he said a little crossly. "You requested it."

"Up!" said Jesus to the child, raising his arms. "Down!" he cried, lowering them. "Now," he laughed, swinging the child around, "we go in a circle. It is the way of the good moon and the little stars, and of the great glowing sun. Do you like them?"

"I like them!" crowed the child.

"Will you go in a circle like this always?"

"If I may come back to you."

"You were never away from me," Jesus said.

Then he kissed the child and called Andrew to him and Peter. "Arrange the multitude in groups of fourscore and ten."

"But, Master ——"

"Ask them to sit down."

Andrew and Peter stared at each other but Akkub suddenly felt his hands tingle with excitement. Didn't they understand? At last and at length, as he had secretly hoped and prayed, Jesus was about to reveal his intentions, throw down his challenge to the world, organize his following, this great multitude, into integral parts of

a great army and send them forth—praise be to God!—
send them forth against Herod and the Roman oppressors.

The revolution was on. Fool, that he had ever doubted,
ever misjudged this man. Could the time have been more
propitious? With foresight the Master had waited until
now, selecting neither too soon nor too late, the psycho-
logical moment. The realization whirled within the orbit
of conscious thought in Akkub and left no space unused.
Small wonder that he had been drawn back here; forced
back here, almost, by something that he could not name.

He became aware that his eyes were flowing tears. He
had clutched the folds of his gown, straining at the cloth
until it was taut at the waist. He breathed brokenly. He
was trying to feel his way toward Jesus when an arm
touched his and the voice of Baasha, raised in exaltation,
cried: "Barabbas must hear this great news. Come, we
must go to his encampment, a furlong away, and fetch
him."

"Yea, we must fetch him," Akkub said.

"Quickly! Quickly!"

They ran. In the dusk, they stumbled, for the descent
was steep. Persons were in the way and they collided with
them. Fingers of the brush tore their clothing; brambles
scratched their ankles. They buffed their knees upon rocks.
They plunged their feet upon sharp stones. The snares of
the dark were as a hundred devils.

Baasha made a snarling sound in his throat and pulled
his beard in vexation.

"Pest!" he cried. "This mountain is sliding down ahead
of us. The distance increases as we go hence."

But presently they reached the more level land and
now it was full dark, with a dew falling. Pausing to rest,
Akkub heard through the grasses the stirring of a timid
breeze. About them, strong upon their nostrils, were the

smells of fertile earth and opening buds. The first fire-flies were flashing like tiny sparks from stars; and he could almost believe that the lines of trees following the course of the Jordan were soldiers on guard.

That way lay Barabbas' camp.

"Hurry!" urged Baasha, pointing. "It is there where the fires are lit."

From here the way seemed shorter, as indeed it was. A space of fresh plowing black under their feet; a field already planted and then, within a strip of untouched land, near the river, the cluttered tents of him who would be second in command.

Barabbas himself met them near the first enclosure. "Hail!" he said. "What brings you here?"

They told him. The mighty shoulders of Barabbas shrugged. His jutting jaw lifted in unbelieving disdain. He smelled of strong wine.

"I do not believe," he said.

"Come and see."

Leaving two of his men on picket duty, Barabbas returned in force, himself on horseback, his men scattered out behind him, Akkub and Baasha each seated upon an ass. From the first elevation, they could see the disciples dividing the assemblage into groups. Not until then did Barabbas cease sniffing.

"It is true," he admitted.

Akkub soon perceived that it was not easy to divide the crowd. From a short distance off he watched a group disperse and join another group, another and another. Leaders went about looking for each other. Children had become restless and would not stay anywhere. Women cried out that they were separated from their men. Husbands proclaimed the right to have their families in the

particular group to which they had been assigned and
went in search of various straying members.

It was all very confusing until a Zealot, who had once
served in the army of Rome, took charge and summoned
Barabbas to help him. They rode into the crowds with
drawn swords and stern commands. They shouted and
struck many with the flat of their weapons. A small child
fell, screaming, under the hoofs of one of the horses. The
disciples themselves were herded around in whatever
manner it pleased Barabbas, who had no thought for
anyone's feelings or the least respect for their positions.
As matters continued to go wrong, Baasha, Nicolas,
Nadab and Akkub were pressed into service. Then all of
the disciples were called out of the forming ranks.

"Each of you," Barabbas instructed, "will be centurion
under me, taking orders from me and doing exactly what
I tell you to do."

Judas Iscariot stepped forward and said haughtily:
"Not I!"

Simon Peter, quite red with indignation, took his place
by Judas' side.

"Nor I!"

Barabbas scowled darkly, wheeled his horse and, with
an oath, rode away. As soon as the groups were formed,
he called Akkub and Baasha to him, and together they
ascended the slope.

"Master," puffed Barabbas, "the groups are ready! Shall
we attack Jerusalem?"

Jesus smiled at him. Then he looked past him toward
his own disciples who were now clambering and stum-
bling up to the narrow plateau. The wind blew gently.

Awaiting Jesus' answer, Barabbas dismounted and advanced a few paces with confidence and soldierly pre-
cision.

"Master—" he began again.

Jesus stopped and uncovered the basket at his feet—the basket with the loaves and the fish—and he blessed both the loaves and the fish, his eyes raised toward heaven.

It was the most incredible proceeding Akkub had ever witnessed. A man blessing his own food in the sight of thousands of hungry people, preparing to eat, when others could not.

"He is selfish," Akkub thought, and a great despair turned his stomach sour.

He would not look at the Nazarene. He would not believe any more. He was tired and ready to return to some friendly inn and admit his defeat. Search some warming fire for the face of the only man who had had courage in these times and the will to assert his high convictions.

Suddenly he heard the breaking of bread and an exclamation from Baasha.

"Take these," Jesus was saying, "and feed them." A few favored disciples, no doubt.

There was more breaking of bread. Except for that the silence was profound.

"Take these also and feed them."

Jesus went on breaking bread and apportioning the fish. Akkub heard the sound he made. It was the only sound. He looked up. Jesus was ringed round with staring faces.

Akkub thought: "There is much breaking of five small loaves."

The disciples took the bread he broke and returned again and again, and they took the fish he apportioned and returned for more. Always, incredibly, Jesus was waiting with quantities of bread and baskets of fish and still there was no end to it. Akkub, watching him very closely to discover the source or substance from which the food was taken could not find it. There were always five loaves and three fish in the original basket, no matter how many Jesus took out. And these did not appear there—they *were* there, exactly five loaves and three fish.

The multitude, every man, woman and child on the mountain, was being fed by the Master from the puny supply in the basket. Of those who were the most amazed was Barabbas. He stood clucking and drawing in his cheeks. He would rub his eyes, shut thick lids over them in the belief that his sense was at fault and, that by resting a while, he could correct it. So, with new determination, between times, he would jerk up his head and stare fiercely into the basket.

Always he counted, as a child silently counts, forming each number with his lips, "One—two—three—" Five for the loaves and three for the fish. But Jesus still went on, serenely breaking them into many pieces.

"It is a magic basket," Barabbas finally whispered to Akkub. "See—it is replenished from the air. I have heard of ancient magi who could do that trick."

"In the name of the Father," Jesus was saying, "give them this food to eat that they may be sustained and cheered."

Barabbas stared down at the bread and fish given him by James the disciple. He felt it with thick hands. Cautiously, he bit into the broken loaf, swallowed it carefully.

"It tastes real," he said and gulped down the rest of it. He slapped his belly. "It *is* real, by heaven!"

Onesimas pushed through the crowd, his face glistening with borrowed triumph. In his waving fists he clutched portions of bread and fish.

"We've as good as won the battle!" he cried to Barabbas. "Heaven even sends us our food!"

From various groups came surprised voices and the sound of hymns. Voices lifted in chants of hallelujahs.

As night fell, a sudden wind sprang up. The trees down along the shore that had been still, bent and swayed.

"Master," said Barabbas urgently, "it is almost dark. What shall we do with these companies now?"

"Dismiss them."

Barabbas choked. "Are we to dismiss these? We've only now formed them into companies!"

"Dismiss them."

Jesus turned and went along a little path that twisted up higher into the mountains. His white robe presently became but a pale glimmer on a height and, at length, Akkub could see it no longer.

Barabbas, mouth open, also was looking after that far ascending figure. Then, in a thunder of resentment, he began to storm and swear.

CHAPTER VII

G ALILEE seethes like a boiling cauldron!" Onesimas tamed his voice to a harsh whisper, but there was satisfaction in every line of his face.

A great crowd was gathered in front of the little corner bake shop near the synagogue and here, on their way to buy bread, Akkub and Baasha had met Onesimas.

Baasha's eyes gleamed. "Tell us more, friend."

Onesimas drew them into the doorway. Galloping horses, he said, had sped to Herod's castle and, from the tax office where Matthew formerly worked, the same report of political unrest had soon spread to Caesarea where the Roman governor, Pontius Pilate, dwelt. The Capernaum Road, built Roman style and not more than six feet wide, was filled with jostling throngs. Some were coming to the city to buy food, some to attend to matters of property, some to satisfy their curiosity, but some, grinned Onesimas, "to buy swords!"

"Ah-h-h!" breathed Baasha. His dark eyes thirsted for more information from this human fount.

"But Herod's spies and those of the Roman government are mingling with the crowds to learn what they can—and Caiaphas, the high priest, has sent investigators from Jerusalem, as well." Onesimas slanted his eyes from one to the other warningly. "So—until the time ripens—caution is the rule."

Akkub waved his hand toward the crowd around the bake shop.

"Why this large gathering?"

"They are buying loaves enough for a week's lunches," said Onesimas, winking knowingly. "But I have heard complaints that the proprietor's bread is much inferior to the stuff the Nazarene fed them yesterday."

"How does the baker like that?" asked Baasha.

"He likes it little, you may be sure. He is displeased with Jesus who, unmindful of him or of his business, so thoughtlessly makes bread!"

With a brief farewell, Onesimas went off to meet Barabbas about whose ability and leadership he was enthusiastic. Akkub and Baasha made their way into the bake shop.

"If we are going to be subjected to that sort of thing," the short, oily-skinned baker was complaining to a customer, "we won't be able to keep business going at all!"

"He's nothing but a poverty-stricken carpenter from Nazareth, isn't he?" said the Pharisee scornfully. "There's something wrong with the people in this town. Imagine believing that five thousand can be fed with five loaves and two fish! It can't be done!"

"You think not?" The baker looked more hopeful.

"They are simply being fooled by an extraordinarily clever magician. Certainly the man has no religion. Why, he didn't even wash his hands before distributing the food to the multitude!"

"Is that so?" The baker shook his head piously and clucked with his tongue.

"Some say he's possessed by Beelzebub, the chief of the evil spirits." The Pharisee rolled his eyes upward and clasped long hands together. "Heaven defend us! If that carpenter stirs the city up any more, there'll be another uprising."

"I fear it!" nodded the baker. "Verily, I fear it!"

A group of Zealots pushed forward for attention. "Here —sell us all this bread, will you? How much for it all?"

Baasha nudged Akkub. "That fellow is Jehu, one of Barabbas' friends."

Jehu was a large angular man with a flattened nose and deep, searching eyes. A long scar reaching from ear to mouth caught up his upper lip slightly, giving him a threatening expression.

"There's about ten shekels' worth here," said the baker quickly. "If you need more, I'll bake it at once."

One of the Zealots, yawning noisily, sank down on the bench by the bake board. On a nearby chair, a young man began to speak of Jesus.

"The fellow's no good, I tell you. When we tell him our plans and suggest this, he says do that, or if we say that, he says this. Or else doesn't pay any attention at all. I'm completely disgusted."

The man on the bench replied in a whisper without opening his eyes. "It's the truth. He's making fools of the lot of us, that carpenter's son."

About to depart, the Pharisee paused in the doorway and called back. "Jesus is an imposter. He's certainly not the Messiah. He doesn't even wash his hands before meals."

"We aren't concerned about hand-washing," retorted the young man on the chair. "We don't bother with that, either. But we think he's a coward. Here we had five thousand people gathered together and everything ready for a revolution, and what happens?" He clutched exasperatedly in his touseled hair. "He runs away to the mountains!"

"That's natural," said the Pharisee scornfully.

"He's the son of a carpenter and so would have no taste for war," put in the baker.

The man on the bench opened one eye. "Jehu, what did Jesus mean when he spoke in the synagogue a little while ago? He said that the manna that fell in the wilderness was of no value, but that if we ate of his own body we'd never die."

"Blasphemy!" shrilled the Pharisee.

"What on earth did he mean?" persisted the man thickly. "It doesn't make any sense to me."

The baker blew his nose between his fingers. "What about the business of feeding five thousand people? Is it true?"

"Oh, it's true enough," said the young man on the chair. "I ate the stuff, but I certainly don't know where it came from."

"So did I," said Baasha. He was about to say more but Akkub warned him with a glance.

"Remember what Onesimas said about caution. Let the others talk. We'll hold our peace."

The fat little baker looked unconvinced. "You're sure you're not all possessed?"

The man on the bench sat up, blinking angrily. "That's just about what we are!" He sank back, his voice growing tired. "Say what you will, though, the fellow is amazing."

Before Akkub and Baasha could give their orders, a gentleman wearing a Roman toga went by the door, followed by two servants. In a flash, the baker ran out, calling: "Oh, Master Manaen! I haven't seen you for some time."

The gentleman stopped courteously.

"Ah, master, what business brings you again to Capernaum?" asked the baker obsequiously.

"Who is that man?" asked Baasha of Jehu.

"That man, Manaen, is Herod Antipas's foster brother," replied Jehu. "You remember the Essene prophet, Manahem, don't you?"

Baasha shook his head.

Jehu looked condescending. "He was the father of that man there. While Antipas' father was still a bandit, it was prophesied that he would some day become the king of Israel—and the prophet was none other than Manahem."

"Indeed?" said Baasha.

"So when Herod became king, all of Manahem's children were taken to be reared in the palace. That man there grew up with Antipas. He knows everything that goes on, I tell you!"

Akkub looked at Manaen with greater interest. He had heard his name, but never before had seen him. Herod's foster brother! Another of the pack of dogs responsible for Israel's suffering and John's death. He looked with loathing upon the man's fine raiment, and heard with hatred his soft, cultured speech.

The baker babbled on. "I'll never forget your kindness in showing me your beautiful mansion, Master Manaen!"

"I'm afraid I may have been a bit short with you," replied the gentleman kindly, "but I was very busy that day with some official work for Antipas."

"Oh, I understand! Perfectly! Perfectly! You were most kind—most kind. But where are you going today?"

"I am just coming from the synagogue."

"From the synagogue?" The baker looked dubious. "From that prophet?"

Manaen nodded smilingly, then turned as someone touched his arm.

"Ah, Jairus—greetings!"

"I did not recognize you at the synagogue," said Jairus breathlessly. "But when I heard you had been there, I hurried after you."

Jairus' eyes were beaming and he fingered his silky black beard. His glance was keen and kindly.

Lines deepened in Manaen's brow. "They've started quite a disturbance, haven't they?"

Jairus, too, looked troubled. "You heard the talk in the synagogue this morning?"

"I heard it." Manaen's eyes were thoughtful. "Jesus of Nazareth speaks like a Greek philosopher, I think. A marvelous knowledge for a carpenter's son." He nodded briefly to the little baker who stood by smiling nervously and clasping and unclasping his fat hands, and walked away down the street with Jairus.

Pompously the bake shop proprietor returned to his waiting customers. A Zealot, rushing through the door, nearly upset him.

"Bread! Bread!" shouted the newcomer. "Give me something substantial. All this talk of Jesus' about bread from heaven and eating his body nauseates me. My thoughts are like chaff in a whirling wind." He snatched up a newly baked bun and began to eat gulpingly.

Jehu addressed him. "Is Barabbas still in the synagogue?"

The Zealot waved his bun. "Not a soul is left," he mumbled. "They were all offended at Jesus and went off and left him there. Barabbas, Onesimas and the rest were furious, I tell you, and threw over the desks in the building."

Akkub and Baasha looked at one another. Anger darkened the latter's eyes. "I don't blame them. Why doesn't Jesus stop theorizing—and give them control?"

Akkub didn't answer. Deep, up-welling disappointment drowned his hopes. Somehow, being near Jesus and watching him, he had begun to believe that the answer to Israel's problem was this strange carpenter from Nazareth. Undoubtedly his was the power which could command the allegiance of the multitudes; his was the strength to lead to victory; his the wisdom to rule wisely and with kindness a liberated nation. Why then did the man halt and hesitate? Was it cowardice—fear that the rebellion might fail and his own life be forfeit? Or was it simply a womanly weakness in the man, a lack of proper ambition?

Baasha, throwing down a coin, took up two loaves of bread. The Zealots, too, were crowding forward after him, some taking five, others ten loaves and tying them in kerchiefs. Akkub saw that no payment was being made the baker who stood by, uneasily but with growing indignation.

As Jehu, the last, strode unconcernedly out the door, the little proprietor puffed after him and gripped his sleeve with a perspiring hand.

"The money? You forgot to pay!"

Jehu widened his eyes, then smiled crookedly. "What's that? Money? Oh, I forgot my money. I'm on my way now to my friend's to borrow some." He tried to pull away from the baker.

"Don't joke about it, sir. You promised ten shekels for the bread, you know. I'm a poor, hard-working man. I must have the payment."

Jehu sobered. "All right—all right. Here—I'll give you your pay."

In an instant his long sword was pointing at the baker's pug nose. The little man jumped back into the store, his mouth dropped open in alarm.

Jehu laughed loudly, slowly sheathed his sword and walked away. Akkub and Baasha, without looking back, went off in the opposite direction.

As they neared the market place, crowds grew more

dense. Rumors flew everywhere. Herod's army, some said, was approaching Capernaum to destroy it. Pilate was sending reinforcements at once. Soldiers were on the march.

Confusion everywhere, thought Akkub—within and without. His own mind's turmoil repeated a thousand times. Questions, doubts, fears.

"There's Nicolas!" cried Baasha, and hailed him. Nicolas swung about and pushed through the crowd to greet them.

"Were you seeking the Teacher?"

"Nay, not I!" said Baasha decisively.

Akkub said, and was astonished at himself: "I was." Yea, it was true. His steps had quickened with that hope; his eyes had arrowed through the tangled streets searching for one form. His ears, alert and straining for the sound of one voice, had rejected all others as meaningless murmur.

Nicolas looked from one face to another, a half-smile on his lips. "You've missed him then, I'm afraid. Until about five minutes ago he was here in the market place healing the sick, but now he's gone elsewhere."

"It was nothing of importance," said Akkub. "Some other time will do—tomorrow perhaps."

Nicolas said: "Haven't you heard? Jairus, alarmed at all the reports, has urged Jesus to go away for a time."

"Where?" asked Baasha.

"To Syrophoenicia."

"But surely he's not going?" said Akkub, unbelieving.

"He starts on the morrow," replied Nicolas. He lifted his eyebrows, jerking his head at the shrilling, jostling crowds. "It's the part of wisdom."

"Coward's wisdom!" Baasha's face was scarlet with fury. He stamped away from them both without looking back.

Nicolas looked after him ruefully. "Barabbas and Onesimas will react in a similar fashion when they hear the news, I expect. Not all of Jesus' disciples, even, are in accord with his decision. Only six are going with him. Judas Iscariot has refused point-blank and is going to Jerusalem, instead."

Akkub swallowed. "And you—what do you think of it all?"

"I don't know," said Nicolas heavily. "I—don't know."

Akkub knew how he felt. He felt sick and betrayed. He felt a sorrow deep and bitter. He felt as if justice were flattened, and the world gone dark again for him as it had after John's death.

Blindly, he turned from Nicolas and shoved his way through moving, protesting bodies which shoved in their turn. He heard, dully, the shouting of his own name. Again. More than one voice calling: "Akkub! Akkub!"

They ringed him in. Men calling to him, thumping him on the back for attention, gripping his arms. Their faces grew clear to Akkub then, and well-remembered. John's disciples—those he and Baasha had seen last huddled on a Samaritan hilltop in cold pre-daylight. And with them— Joshua the centurion. The soldier was clasping his hand and smiling warmly. They were going to Jerusalem, they told him, for after his journey to Syrophoenicia, it was believed that the Nazarene would return there for the Feast of the Passover.

"Will you also journey with us?" they asked him.

Their familiar faces blurred before Akkub. Yea, they were his loyalty now, these lost groping disciples of John. He was one of them. They were bound by each earthen clod that had thudded into the Baptist's grave, by each ringing word of the wilderness prophet, by each stab of hate for the oppressors of Israel.

"I will go!" said Akkub.

BOOK TWO

HAVE I NOT CHOSEN YOU TWELVE . . .

CHAPTER VIII

SUNLIGHT struck down upon the man's red hair and
beard, glimmered on the dark breadth of his countenance,
highlighted the thin aquiline nose with its flaring nostrils.
He walked slowly through the gate called Beautiful, then
turned right to make his way along the line of stalls and
booths within the walled enclosure.

Looking sharply around, he began to quicken his pace.
Jehoiada should be here. Martha had said so, as she braided
her long hair this morning, her shoulders wrapped in a
towel.

"Jehoiada," she had said, "will be at the stalls selling
sacrificial lambs. He is the only priest I know in Jerusalem. I will give you a letter to him."

"Ask him to make me a bargain," he had said, "and as
surely as my name is Judas, I will reward you."

"It is not money I want," Martha said quickly.

Judas watched the color find her face and stay there
through the few moments it took her to place a clasp
slightly above her left temple. And because of her embarrassment, he had suspected what she wanted. It was
what most women wanted, Judas had found, of whatever
age or condition or understanding. What all of them
placed first in their lives, as if it were some sort of healing
stone; indeed, as if it were the primal and final antidote
for all the negative and upsetting ills of the world. Love.

Martha wanted that, too. Judas was amused. Middle-aged and beginning to grow fine lines in her face; beginning to have puffy lids and not very pleasing limbs, she wanted love!

But to humor her, he asked: "What is it you want, then?"

Her answer startled him. "Happiness. That's all."

He was cynical. "By what right? Who has it? Is there such a thing? Can you prove it? Has it ever been yours or anyone else's you ever knew?"

"Yea," she answered quietly, "I know someone."

"Who?"

"The Nazarene."

Judas Iscariot had it in his mind to disagree with her and so prolong the argument until he had worn down her spirit. But the new plan was too much in his thoughts. If he bought sacrificial lambs from the temple priests, he would gain a diplomatic victory for the revolutionary cause. It would make the Pharisees and Sadducees more lenient in their attitude toward Jesus. It might help to dam the flood of condemnation the priests were pouring out upon the Master and, what was worse, their inciting of Herod and the Romans against him.

He said: "That isn't altogether true. I've seen him in anger and in anguish. I've seen him in tears. I've watched him nervously walking alone in the night. I've heard him pray on bended knees, silently, with the wet on his forehead glistening like sorrowful pearls."

Martha's expression did not change.

"I could tell you more," he insisted, "but the sand drains out of the glass and I must buy those lambs from the priests—damn them—while the urge is still like a green spray in my girdle. Once it withers, I'm lost. I can ill afford the money."

"You are always worrying about money, Judas," Martha rebuked him gently. "Just the same, it's wonderful of you to want to do this."

Judas laughed. "I don't want to do it. I must. I'm compelled to it. Our cause is shaking."

Martha went into the next room without replying. He looked after her dubiously. In a few minutes she was back with a letter for the priest which she gave him.

But now, nearing the middle gate at the southeast corner where the sacrificial lambs were cared for, Judas looked vainly for the priest, Jehoiada. Only a few shepherds and cowherds were in sight.

Turning on his heel, he moved off impatiently in the direction of the priests' quarters. Then, near the pillared temple, his footsteps slowed to match the solemn dignity of the building.

Judas sighed. Such splendor made him feel inferior. Here, he always felt, was not so much a monument to the Lord God as to Herod whose power had built it. Yea, this was Herod's temple—a constant reminder of the king's wealth and might. Throwing his head back, Judas squinted upward. The morning sun shining over the Gate Beautiful fell directly on the gold leaf painting the upper walls and on the glistening marble brought at much cost from the territory of the Mediterranean.

"Like a rainbow studded with jewels," muttered Judas, and his sun-dazzled eyes narrowed to slits. To think of a man like Herod—a man who still had not spent all his substance after the erection of such magnificence! The thought grated in his mind. He would look no longer. Lowering his head, he blinked irritably at three scribes passing the pillars in front of the Holy of Holies, then set off again to find Jehoiada.

The priest was not in his room. One of the twenty-four

priests in attendance during the festival season told him that Jehoiada was living at the home of Caiaphas, the high priest.

What a convenient circumstance! Here was an opportunity, perhaps, to meet the great Caiaphas and persuade him to join Jesus. That would be an aid to the cause indeed. Judas could even now envision the scene when he told of his accomplishment. He could see the Master's gaze bent upon him approvingly, that deep, deep smile in his eyes that seemed ordinarily to be reserved for unassuming John or impulsive Peter, as if they shared with him or were to share some unique experience. Often that special look, which he himself had ever failed to wheedle from the Master, enraged Judas. Oddly, the emotion was akin to that he felt when viewing the temple. Violent. Unexplainable. And, following after, a weakness and despair which drained from life its flavor.

Well, thought Judas, pushing through the streets, if he could bring the high priest into camp, Jesus would be obliged to accord him high commendation and—yea—unusual authority. More money, too, and with enough of it, Judas was confident, the revolutionary cause would prosper, Herod and the Romans would be put down—and all who had followed Jesus would move with him into a prosperous kingdom.

Judas was soon jostled from his reverie. Jerusalem was filled with festival gaiety. The city was solid with pilgrims from north, south, east and west. Day after day they came, thousands of them; men wearing turbans and coats with large patterns, carrying long staves; women veiled, and their long triangular sleeved gowns tied with bright sashes; children darting in and out, like small restless fish in a strange varicolored sea. Above everything was the pipe and drone of merchants calling their wares and, occasionally, snatches of festival songs.

Suddenly, ahead of Judas, there was a change in the tempo of crowd noise and movement. A lane was opening for a carriage. Crushed back with the rest to make way for it, Judas saw that it was Herod's carriage and riding in it with him were Queen Herodias, her profile haughty and remote and—yea—Joanna, the wife of Chuza, the royal steward. They were going, he guessed, to call upon the Roman governor, Pontius Pilate, who had moved from Caesarea into Jerusalem, ready to quell any disturbance which might arise during the feast of the Passover. Pilate had taken up his residence in the governor's mansion which was connected with the Tower of Antonia. Herod Antipas, although slightly troubled about the Moab boundary question, had come to Jerusalem also because of Pilate's presence there.

The throngs closed the passage behind the carriage. Judas was aware of an ominous rumbling and angry shouts. A group of men with staves and stones pressed after the royal vehicle. In the lead was Barabbas, a heavy menacing figure drawing each moment a larger following of rabble. Here and there, Judas recognized men familiar to him. Onesimas, a thick club in one great fist. Nadab, lean and vital. Baasha, plowing through the crowd with his head lowered, bull-like. Akkub, a fierce light in his eyes, the skin of his face tight and shining.

There was likely to be trouble, Judas thought, and was tempted to follow along after to watch the ever-fascinating boil and bubble of a rioting mob. But no—he had other work to do.

Coming at last to the high priest's house in southwestern Jerusalem, he knocked at the gate. When Jehoiada appeared, he presented Martha's note saying he wanted to buy sheep for the feast of the Passover.

"Since I want to purchase four yearling lambs, I thought you might give me a good price on them."

Jehoiada bent his head at an angle. "Well, well!"

The priest was about fifty and it was evident that not only had he had but little education, but also that he possessed no native intelligence.

Judas pressed a shekel into his moist plump hand.

Jehoiada smiled broadly. "Truly, you are a man of faith. There are not many people these days who offer four or five lambs to God. This way, please." He talked on in a flat voice as he led the way to the high priest's office. "By all means, we must accept your devout offer. If you would buy five head, now, we could let you have them for twenty shekels each."

This was exceedingly cheap, but Judas said nothing.

"Who is offering these lambs?" asked Jehoiada.

Now for the first time, Judas gave his name as Judas Iscariot, disciple of Jesus of Nazareth.

Jehoiada grunted. "When did you come from Galilee?"

"But five days ago."

"Is your Master here, too?"

"Nay," said Judas quickly, "he is in the north with six of the disciples."

The priest scratched his chin. "I'll never forget what happened when the Nazarene was here two years ago. It was while John Baptist was in prison, I remember. Do you know what your Teacher did?"

Judas nodded hastily. "But about the lambs——"

"He upset the tables along the corridors in the temple and chased out the money-changers and merchants, and all the doves and sheep and the rest of the animals for sale made a terrible hub-bub in the streets."

"The lambs ——"

"I was right in the midst of it," sighed Jehoiada and wagged his head loosely. "The high priest doesn't like him I can tell you!"

Judas remained outwardly unperturbed. Inwardly, he shook. There it was again. Things of this sort were always cropping up when one mentioned his connection with Jesus. True, it had been a magnificent thing to see, one man with a scourge of cords and an invincible will cleansing the temple single-handed. Like sustained lightning, his eyes had been, and his voice like thunder on Mount Hermon. Still, it had hardly been the politic thing to do, Judas felt, and certainly the result had been but temporary. Only this morning he had passed them all. Money-changers, merchants, sellers of sheep and doves. Now if Jesus had only used that fire and force of his for some more lasting and significant purpose—if, even now, he would kindle it on behalf of trampled Israel—if he would only placate the authorities instead of alienate them. . . .

Jehoiada was looking at him from beneath his brows. "And how about what Jesus said about destroying the temple. Is it true?"

It was in Judas' mind to say that Jesus had not actually threatened to destroy the temple. He had said: "Destroy this temple and in three days I will raise it up." But he could hardly tell Jehoiada that and expect him to believe that it was anything but an exaggerated boast. The temple had taken forty-six years to build, as everyone well knew.

Judas laughed deprecatingly. "There's a little misunderstanding about that. He is a man of faith and trust, I assure you. He comes to worship at Jerusalem at almost every festival."

Jehoiada grunted.

Judas said sharply: "Jesus is really a great prophet. It is nothing for him to raise the dead."

Jehoiada started. "The dead . . . ?" his eyes rounded.

"If the prophet and the priests would only work together they could do great things such as were done by Moses and Aaron," said Judas intensely. "Yea—they could do at least the combined works of Ezra and Nehemiah!" He glared at the gaping priest and for a moment his hand tingled with the desire to smite that stupid jowled face.

Judas looked toward the inner court. "Is the high priest at home?" He would go in to Caiaphas. He would tell his Holiness that the life and hope of Israel depended upon his awakening to the greatness of Jesus. He would tell him that with the combined forces of the Pharisees, Sadducees, Zealots. . . .

"Yea, he is here," said Jehoiada after a stupid wait. "Shall I call him?"

The flaring zeal went out of Judas. He swallowed. After all, perhaps it was better to let things take their course. It might be even more difficult to answer Caiaphas' questions than Jehoiada's. Besides, he might fasten upon himself the high priest's disapproval of his Master.

"Don't trouble him," Judas said. "Perhaps another time. I came today to purchase the lambs. There'll be another time when I hope to hear the words of his Holiness."

Hastily, he stepped from the office. Jehoiada followed, rubbing his hands. "That will be one hundred shekels."

Judas counted out the coins and handed them to Jehoiada.

"The five lambs will be delivered to you this afternoon before the altar," beamed the priest.

Judas had passed the tower of David near the Joppa gate before he sank down on the stone fence adjoining and began to count the money left in his wallet. The lightness of it had filled him with misgivings all the way from the high priest's house.

Only fifty-two shekels left! Less than he had expected, even. He felt suddenly bereft, as if a part of himself were missing and now he were less of a man, somehow. He had been a fool, he decided bitterly. One hundred shekels spent for five sacrificial lambs—and for what purpose? No doubt Jesus would have naught to do with it, anyhow, for he was always saying that burnt offerings were unnecessary. Besides, Jesus disliked the Pharisees and scribes and thoroughly disapproved of the ways of the high priest. Oh, there was likely to be unpleasantness when Jesus discovered what he had done, and sternness in those deep eyes instead of smiling approval.

But inside another voice, at first but a whisper, grew stronger. "But if you want to make Jesus great, you'll have to bring about a compromise between him and the high priest. Only in that way can there be a great national movement."

The first voice broke in rebukingly. "Don't you understand that the religion of Jesus is a religion of conscience? Would you want to bring about a compromise between the high priest who is willing to sell his people to Rome and the one who is using all he has to permit the people to hear the voice of God?"

Judas put long hands against his temples, tightly so that he could feel the pulse beat. He rocked his aching head. Two voices. Always—always two voices. Shouting, teasing, rebuking, arguing within him. Making confusion of his thoughts, dissipating his purpose, weakening his resolve. And because often now he listened and did not deny, that second voice was gathering fearful strength. . . .

Judas Iscariot sat with bowed head looking at the ground.

CHAPTER IX

MORE and more of late, when Judas was troubled or had a problem to solve, he looked down. The habit had grown strong in him. When within walls, he stared at the floor; when outside, at the earth; in a fishing boat, at the water. It helped him to concentrate. Jesus, he had noticed, had a somewhat similar habit. He looked up. When throngs pressed him, when the voices of the needy were a persistent, many-toned discord in his ears, when the diseased, the maimed and the lame struggled toward him, Jesus often paused, lifting his eyes toward heaven. Then, after a bit, he was apparently refreshed and strengthened, ready to give himself up again to his compassionate laboring. Men differed, Judas thought, in their ways. He had tried looking up, but the vastness of heaven with its rolling sun and changeful cloud patterns in daytime, or frosted at night with remote stars, distracted him. Yea, it was easier to think if one's eyelids shut out all but a small portion of a confusing universe.

Judas remembered well his first meeting with Jesus of Nazareth. In Jerusalem, where he had come from Kerioth, his native town, he had heard of the work of John the Baptist. Curiosity and disappointment that he could gain no business foothold in the great city, had combined to send him to Bethabara, east of the Jordan, where John the Baptist was baptizing.

Judas was impressed with John, with his ringing de-

nunciations, his uncompromising manner, the deep-carved
lines in his face that made him seem ten years older than
his thirty years. He listened intently when the wilderness
prophet spake of "one greater to come." He was minded
to seek John privately to learn more of the matter. He
followed the teacher to the cave in the cliff where he
dwelt, subsisting, it was said, upon wild honey and locusts.

One of the disciples guarding the cavern's entrance took
word to the prophet.

When John appeared, standing lean and straight as a
soldier in his simple coat of camel's hair, his loins girded
with a leather girdle, Judas said bluntly: "Who is this one
of whom you speak? The Messiah?"

John's keen eyes burned into his. "Why do you ask?"

Judas dropped his gaze and said humbly: "That I may
follow after and worship."

"Have you then repented?"

"Yea, master."

Judas lifted his eyes to find the prophet's stern glance
going past him—nay, through him—like a shining blade.
He was, for a moment, discomfited, then found his voice
again.

"Tell me of whom you speak."

But John the Baptist turned and was swallowed in the
cave's dusk. Judas put forth his hand, took a step forward.

"Master ——"

"Go now," said one of the disciples at the entrance.
"Our master will not speak with you further."

The next day Judas determined to be baptized. Thus
proving his repentance, he might gain a more satisfactory
audience with John. After his immersion, he again sought
out the prophet, but with no better results.

John repeated vehemently just what he had said before.

"I indeed baptize you with water unto repentance: but

he who comes after me is mightier than I, whose shoes I am not worthy to bear: he shall baptize you with the Holy Ghost and fire."

Judas' curiosity increased, and with it a driving impatience. For three more days he dogged John's footsteps. He drew aside his most loyal disciples and questioned them. Always, he pushed to the front of the throng which gathered about the teacher. He was resolved not to miss any significant word or deed.

The fourth day there came to John's baptism, Jesus of Nazareth.

Baasha, a disciple of the Baptist, whispered to Judas that the young man was the son of a Galilean carpenter and claimed relationship with John.

"He is a cousin, they say, but has never before met our master who has been so long in the wilderness." Baasha's fingers stroked through his beard. "Except that they are both strongly built, I see little resemblance."

Judas watched the young man as he patiently awaited his turn to come before the teacher. He asked no favors because of kinship, and Baasha murmured that he doubted that John knew of it.

When the two men stood face to face, Jesus said humbly: "I also would be baptized."

There came a change upon the wilderness prophet. All who had felt the lash of his tingling rebukes and had trembled under that dominant gaze, were astonished. Judas saw the lined countenance soften and the eyes glow.

"Nay," said John gently, "rather let me be baptized of you."

His heart wild within him, Judas pressed closer.

The young man from Nazareth smiled, but his eyes were deep and grave. "Suffer it to be so now," he said. "So we must fulfill all righteousness."

Judas did not take his eyes from Jesus. As he came up out of the Jordan, a dove circled his bright head, then alighted fearlessly upon his shoulder. It was then, for the first time, that Judas beheld the Nazarene looking up. As if he might be listening to a heavenly Voice and, truly, Judas had seen on no human face a more divine expression.

Yet, when Jesus was again upon the bank, he seemed, after all, but an ordinary youth, and Judas found his conviction wavering. When he sought to make his acquaintance, he found him pleasant, even stimulating, to be with and extraordinarily learned, but could not see that he bore any sure proof of Messiahship.

The following day Jesus still tarried at Bethabara. Now and again, he spoke with John, alone or as one of a group, but oftener he walked by himself along the riverbank. The prophet's eyes, Judas noted, were always seeking out the carpenter's son, always following, following that lone figure.

Finally, Judas' watchfulness was rewarded. Deeply reverent, John spoke.

"Behold the Lamb of God!"

There was an indrawn breath from Andrew, Simon Peter's brother, and then a follower of the Baptist.

"The Messiah!"

Thus had Judas become a follower of Jesus, although, at times, doubts harassed him still. There were so many things he could not understand. In particular, it was difficult for the practical Judas to see why, if the Master's power were so great and good, he did not use it to obtain wealth for himself and his followers. Certainly, he could have vastly aided the poor. Or, at least, he could have rewarded the faithful twelve, who, for his sake, had left all. Money could pave a glittering pathway to the very gate of the Kingdom, Judas was persuaded. He had approached the Master once upon that very subject. He himself, he told Jesus, would assume the responsibility for the proper distribution of the heavenly bounty.

But Jesus had smiled, shaking his head in amused reproof.

"Judas, Judas! Look up! Look around you! Behold the wealth our Father freely bestows. Would you exchange it for small disks of metal?"

Judas remembered now, acutely, his humiliation. He had no answer. Though one might misunderstand or even disagree with what Jesus said, yet there was an assurance in his manner not to be withstood.

Judas' eyes traced the light print of a sandal in the earth. He sighed. If the Nazarene had only cared to, he could have made his disciples prosperous. He could have relieved Judas, for one, of untold mental anguish. Throughout his life, each badly managed business venture had left him with debts, and bills sniffed him out like persistent hounds wherever he went. Often, to stave off creditors, he had to borrow a bit from the funds entrusted to him by Jesus, in order to pay the interest on some loan or other. But, he assured himself again and again, he meant to pay everything back when he received his share of the kingdom established by Jesus.

"It isn't that I'm actually bad or dishonest," he soothed himself. "It's the system which demands such interest that is wrong. If Jesus would only hurry and set up the new order where no interest is demanded as we are taught in Deuteronomy, my troubles would cease. It's really up to him."

But about this present problem of the lambs. He must find some solution. How he grudged the money he had just handed over to Jehoiada!

Judas stared at the dusty footprint. He frowned and gnawed at his full under lip. He raked long nervous fingers through his hair.

He had it, suddenly. Very simple. Chuckling, he rose, passed through the temple grounds, and out through the Gate Beautiful. All the way to Bethany he did pleasant sums in his head.

Turning into the street which led to Martha's house, he met Susanna, one of the older women who followed Jesus. She had come, she said, from visiting Martha.

"We have been speaking of Jesus," she said, and her voice was gentle over the name. "Do you know, Judas, when he will be returning from the north?"

He shook his head. "Not until after the Passover, I'm sure." He looked at her persuasively. "We who are here must make our offerings in his behalf."

She inclined her graying head. "That is so, Judas."

"Of course you'll be wanting a lamb for sacrifice, won't you?"

"Well——"

"I have some. They were thirty-five shekels apiece. You can have one at that price and it will save you going in to purchase one yourself."

"Well——"

"Just thirty-five shekels. For the Master." Judas bent his head piously.

Susanna counted out the money. "That is little enough for a thank offering to God for sending us such a Teacher as Jesus." Turning to go, she stopped and spoke over her shoulder as an afterthought. "Mary Magdalene arrived today."

Judas dropped one of the coins he was slipping into his pouch. He stooped to pick it up before answering.

"Indeed," he said casually. "Will she be staying at Martha's home?"

"Nay, she will be with me at the house of Simon the leper. He welcomes all those who follow Jesus."

"Then I'll walk along with you," said Judas quickly. "I should like to greet her.'"

As they went, Susana spoke at length of Jesus and his works, but except for an absent word or two in response, Judas was quiet. Mary Magdalene. It was a name the unexpected mention of which could strike him like a blow, palsying his fingers, voiding his speech. It was a name which could send his mind back along the blackened path of eight years to a certain street in Jerusalem and a long low tenement. . . .

She had been sixteen, Mary of Magdala, but the world was not new to her nor bright with any sort of promise. It was a tarnished thing, made so by the feet of those who walked thereon, beating away its gilt. Her own feet beat upon it with a sort of frantic abandon, faster, faster, with a hardened unconcern for where they went as long as there was movement and the sound of it. She knew what men wanted and what women, with no other means of livelihood, must give them. And the whole business, because it was a practical transaction with bread for its object, had ceased to be of much interest or importance.

Until that day when Judas, his heart wrung by a new failure, sought surcease with her. A friend had suggested her name with one-sided smile and had told him where she lived. It was odd, but Judas could not afterward remember what friend, but only the smile's crookedness, as if it were a disembodied thing.

But the house he remembered, the middle dwelling in the five apartment tenement back from the alley. The room, too, small with one narrow window, wooden bed and one dingy lamp.

The youth of the girl had startled him. The wisdom in the pale oval face, the large eyes narrowed as she studied him, and the slight limp as she walked—all intrigued him. Seeing that he had noticed, she told him, quite dispassionately, about the lameness.

"I was a dancer in Caesarea and Alexandria. There was an accident with a chariot and I was crippled. My husband, a Roman centurion, deserted me."

There was a studied grace in her every gesture, and Judas saw that her talent for the stage must have been a great and compelling one.

As the months went by, there grew to be a kind of understanding between them, nurtured by a similar viewpoint of life and the living. Judas came to depend upon her and flew into rages to see her with other men.

"But I must get money to return to my mother's house in Magdala," she said. "I can't return to be a burden to her."

"Why return at all?"

Silence grew in the room. He repeated the question testily.

When she turned her head to look at him, there were tears in her dark eyes. He was startled and uncomfortable. He had never seen her thus. He disliked weeping.

"Because," said Mary Magdalene, "I am afraid to die alone."

Looking at her, then, he found for the first time the difference in her. She had always been slender. Now she was noticeably thin. Her cheeks were hollowed; her eyes, shadowed. There was in her gaze an unnatural brightness. Her skin was tautly transparent. She had moods of frenzied gaiety of late, and, after them, spells of coughing.

Dust in her throat, she had always laughed, and had blamed the dingy room and shabby, dirty streets. Like a fool he had accepted the explanation.

Now he looked at her. "Die," he repeated. Then with a rising inflection. "Die! Nonsense!"

She said, stoically now: "Not nonsense, Judas. I really died two or three years ago, when I was about fourteen, I think. My body has simply been a little stubborn, that is all."

Rage swept through him, unreasoning, violent. Sickness was detestable to him. Beholding her, he was revolted. The mad notion possessed him that this illness was to spite him, to spoil his pleasure in her. He stamped about the room, cursed.

Her tears stopped.

She stood, and her towering rage matched his.

"Go now, Judas Iscariot! Go—and never return!"

He had gone. He had been glad to escape that tortured room, to leave that torn remnant of his pleasure, to flee from whirlwind thoughts of past and future.

On the street he paused, and looked back. The darkness which had come at the call of the spring evening joined together the roofs of the houses. In the window of Mary of Magdala no lamp glowed. Always before, she had burned oil so that he might see it from below. He waited. No light appeared. She was there in the dark—alone.

Immeasurably exasperated, Judas strode away.

Two days later when he returned, Mary was gone. No one knew where. Back to her home in Magdala, probably. The neighbors were indifferent.

Judas found other friends—and other worries. Plenty of both, for a time, until business troubles increased. Then the friends dropped away, and only the worries remained to him for company. Finally, a combination of circumstances led him to John—and to Jesus.

He was with Jesus at Bethsaida when Mary came with her mother from the neighboring village of Magdala. He had turned, suddenly shaken, from the wreck of her beautiful body and the pain-marked face. He had seen much of suffering since following the Nazarene and had believed himself inured to it. But this—this was unendurable. Surely, even Jesus must fail here.

Someone shuddered. "She has seven devils!"

But when he had been able to turn back, behold a miracle! She was healed, and in the great dark eyes lifted reverently to the Master was a look all-transforming. An expression of purity and, more astounding than that— hope! Her mouth was sweet with it and her chin steady with new resolve. Judas stared. This was a Mary Magdalene he had never seen before and far more beautiful.

When he dared, he tried to renew their relationship. She was older, yea, but the glow of health lay upon her like the bloom of fruit ripening in Lebanon orchards. There was, too, an inner shining about her which tantalized Judas. He longed to trace the elusive quality to its source and, having captured it, to investigate it with critical thoroughness.

But Mary Magdalene had no eyes for Judas now, nor for any man save the Nazarene. And him she looked upon, Judas was at last reluctantly convinced, not as a man but as an ideal.

But now—Jesus was in the north. That being so, Mary Magdalene might not look so indifferently upon normal companionship. He, Judas, could be both charming and entertaining. Indeed, he might even propose marriage to her. She would make a proper vigorous helpmeet for him now and such a union might even better his position with

Jesus for, oddly enough, he seemed to have a high regard for Mary Magdalene.

However, arriving at Simon's large house, he remembered that the business of the lambs had best be settled first. He sold one to Simon the leper and one to Mary. The money safely in his pouch, he said:

"Was your journey from Capernaum, where we last met, a pleasant one?"

Mary smiled. "Very. I stopped a few days with my mother in Magdala, and then traveled hither with Mary and Lazarus who came to Bethany to be with their older sister, Martha." Her manner was friendly, but reserved.

"I hope I shall see you frequently. I'm staying with Martha, too, you know. Just down the hill a bit."

She smiled politely.

When he left, he felt confused. Meeting Mary Magdalene always baffled him. It was as if she were two women, somehow, and he never knew to which one he was speaking. Yet, in a way, the situation was diverting, and Judas preferred anything to boredom. Sometime, doubtless, there would be a challenging glimpse of the sixteen-year-old dancer of eight years ago, and when there was, Judas would know what to do.

He found Martha in the kitchen preparing lunch.

"You're late," she frowned, then smiled forgivingly. "Did you get the lambs?"

He nodded. "Martha, won't you be making a special thank offering? Jehoiada is charging thirty-five shekels a head, but because I bought five heads, he gave me a slight reduction. I am charging the others thirty-five shekels, but I'll give you one for thirty."

Martha bought the lamb. Judas was elated. He still had one animal for his own use, and had made a profit of thirty-five shekels besides.

"Where are Lazarus and Mary?" he asked.

Martha moved her shoulder slightly. "In the garden, I suppose, talking about the Master. They never tire of recounting his works and pondering his parables."

After lunch, Mary announced that she would not go with the others to Jerusalem.

"But—aren't you grateful to God for all His blessings?" asked Judas.

Mary was small and delicately built. Her eyes were a dark, vivid blue. She didn't believe in burnt offerings any more, she told Judas, and pushed her wavy hair back from her forehead with an independent gesture.

"I shall find another way to express what is in my heart." She looked at Judas levelly. "Jesus knows better ways."

He left her, annoyed. That night, instead of returning to Bethany, he decided to go on to Hebron to pay fifty shekels on the back interest of his most pressing debt.

Three nights later, he walked up the hill to the house of Simon the leper.

He greeted Mary Magdalene abruptly. "Will you walk with me in the garden?"

When they were outside, he turned to her. "Mary—there's something I've been wanting to tell you—to ask you."

She laughed. "I've been wanting to talk to you, too, Judas."

His heart beat loudly. "Have you? Have you?"

"Judas, you haven't changed a bit!"

"Wh-what do you mean?"

"Didn't you buy those five lambs for one hundred shekels?"

Judas cleared his throat, coughed. "Why, Mary, I ——"

"When Martha went to worship yesterday she heard of

your purchase from Jehoiada." She put a hand on his arm. "I'm surprised at your unscrupulousness. I thought perhaps, now that you're a disciple of Jesus, that——"

He said defiantly: "Well, could you buy a lamb for twenty shekels?"

She took her hand away. There was a pause before she replied.

"No, I don't suppose I could. A lamb bearing the seal of the high priest sells for thirty or thirty-five shekels, I know, if you buy only one. Oh, Judas!" Her voice was half-amused, half-despairing. "I'm not saying your price was too high, but I do think it's rather awful for you to make fifteen shekels on a beast that only cost you twenty —and to make it from your friends."

Judas walked beside her in silence, staring at the ground. Then he said: "But you think one ought to pay debts, don't you?"

She laughed. "So that's it! Still in debt, Judas."

He felt tragic. "I'm always in debt. I doubt if I shall ever get out, Mary. This particular one I incurred even before I came to Jerusalem and I'm greatly troubled about the interest. It was to meet this that I bargained for the lambs and made a small profit."

She said nothing.

"You'll forgive me, won't you?" He looked at her pleadingly.

Mary shivered slightly and turned back toward the house.

"Let's go in, shall we?"

CHAPTER X

JUDAS stood upon the western shore of the sea of Galilee. One hand shaded his eyes from the slanting sunlight. Far out, boats were but dark specks upon the water's glare.

Beside him, Simon the Zealot spoke. "Can you tell which one ——?"

"Nay," said Judas, "from this distance it is impossible to distinguish one from another."

Behind him, Thomas murmured impatiently, and James the Less, Nathanael and Thaddaeus crowded closer. They were all here, thought Judas wryly, the obedient six not chosen by Jesus to journey with him to Tyre and Sidon.

"You're sure it was here at Bethsaida we were to wait for him?" asked Nathanael. His eyes were deep and eager.

"So said the message," replied Judas shortly. His eyeballs ached. Sweat beaded his forehead, and his red hair was damp against his dark temples. It was June, a hot dry month in Galilee. Grain ripened upon the hillsides, and the only task of languid shepherds was to take the sheep and goats to the watering. When the wind blew strongly from the east, dust from the Arabian desert swept across the dry slopes of Gilead and settled an inch or more deep upon roof tops and window sills.

Despite the stifling heat, however, great throngs had gathered, waiting for Jesus. News traveled fast in Galilee. Judas had cause to wish it did not. He resented the multitude which clamored after the Master wherever he went. Ignorant folk, for the most part. The time Jesus gave them so generously really belonged, Judas believed, to the faithful twelve and those few others whose minds could grasp the meaning of the Nazarene's parables and teachings.

He closed his eyes against the sun's brightness. With sight blotted to a confused orange glow upon his eyelids, he could hear rather than see what was going on. The rumble of the crowd as it shifted, moved, increased in number. The shouts of little children splashing in the shallows along the beach. The low voices of the other five disciples around him. The slow slap of waves on rocks and their liquid whisper in the rushes.

Simon gripped his arm. "I see them!"

Judas' eyes snapped open. One of the specks had become a boat and it was peopled with men, seven of them. In the prow sat Jesus, the shining head and poise of posture unmistakable even from this distance.

James the Less gave a great shout and ran down the beach into the water among the wading children. Nathanael and Thaddaeus followed. Simon thumped Judas on the back, his thin face glowing.

"The Master—the Master comes!"

They were acting like children, Judas thought. His own demeanor, as he walked down to greet Jesus, was reserved. Let the others give him a carefree welcome. More serious matters concerned Judas of Kerioth. He had news for his Master.

The tidings waited until the importunate lame were made to walk, the maimed were made whole, the sick became well, the crazed were calmed and freed of evil spirits. They waited while Jesus spoke to the sorrowing, and taught those who begged for word of the kingdom of Heaven.

Judas, despairing of gaining the Master's attention for some time, drew the six returned disciples to him instead.

"Conditions in Galilee are worse," he whispered. "A number of Zealots were killed in riots at Jerusalem, during the festival."

Matthew looked gloomy. "That is bad."

"Not only that, but it is said that Barabbas and his followers have taken to robbery to raise revenue for their soldiers." Judas rubbed his hands together, his eyes narrow with remembered excitement. "Great things have been happening."

"Tell us more," urged Philip.

From the tail of his eye, Judas saw that Jesus was within hearing distance. He lifted his voice. "The water works problem came to a climax. The several thousands who protested against it were killed by hidden soldiers during the festival."

John's keen but gentle face was puzzled. "What do you mean by the water works problem? I hadn't heard of it."

Judas threw him a lofty glance. "You mean you don't know? Why, that business of the aqueduct has been going on for almost a year."

John smiled apologetically. "I didn't know. I've been more interested in the kingdom of which Jesus speaks than that of Rome."

"Explain!" demanded Peter, his eyes flashing with interest.

"There's a great brick aqueduct over two hundred furlongs in length already finished," said Judas. "Only the Jerusalem section remains unfinished."

"But it sounds like a good undertaking," puzzled John.

"Oh, it is. If only Pilate had used some other money it might have been all right, but instead, in direct opposition to the people's will, he took the temple money and it isn't completed yet. Otherwise, it would have been done long ago, but the Pharisees have now become obstinate and are doing everything possible to oppose it."

Judas turned to see what Jesus would do. He could not have failed to hear. But the Master was talking to a group of men whom Judas saw were Pharisees and Sadducees. He gave no indication of having heard Judas at all.

The sun was dipping into the west, and the stratus floating gently from north to south was a long shining veil. Lake wavelets reflecting the sky shone like gold lacquer in relief. Round basalt pebbles on the beach glistened as though they were varnished.

The voices of the men around the Master rose challengingly.

"We want some proof of your authority!"

Jesus' voice was low but carrying. "Have you not seen the sick healed, the maimed made whole this very hour?"

"It's proof we demand," came the reply sharply. "You speak in familiar tones of the Kingdom of God. Give us then proof from heaven."

The disciples forgot about Pilate and his aqueduct. With one accord they gathered around their Master. Peter, thrusting himself a little in front of Jesus, scowled threateningly at the Nazarene's questioners.

Jesus put out a gentle hand and placed it upon his shoulder. His glance was an affectionate reproof. Peter stood aside, reddening.

A cripple was making a ragged, tortuous progress toward Jesus, looking up now and again with anguished, tear-filled eyes.

The Master lifted his eyes toward the sunset clouds, riding high above the Gennesaret shores. The muted light fell softly upon his features. His eyes were illumined.

"You behold the red sky at eventide and say that tomorrow will be fair, do you not, people of Israel?"

One of the Pharisees cleared his throat. "That is so, Master."

For a moment, Jesus said nothing. Quiet was a cloak upon the group around him, and the sun's last rays were a glory upon his countenance.

He spoke then, and his voice was unexpectedly strong and firm.

"Yea, you understand the signs of the sky—but the signs of the times you cannot interpret. If you ask for a sign, none shall be given you but the sign of Jonah."

Turning, he laid his hand upon the shoulder of the cripple. The limbs of the man straightened and grew strong. He leaped for joy, crying out that he was healed, and praising the Master. The crowd shouted enthusiastically.

The Pharisees and Sadducees, grumbling, walked away into the settling dusk.

Jesus said gently: "Praise me not. It is God Which doeth all good."

Above the golden clouds, a delicate purple floated, and yet higher the sky was painted deep blue. The shadows bronzed, then slid together into one pattern of dark.

It was Jairus who came again with a money offering to Jesus. He feared for the safety of the Master, he said, and begged him to leave the territory of Antipas and go once more into that of Philip.

Jesus appeared undisturbed, Judas saw.

"Fear not, Jairus," said the Nazarene. "My time is not yet come."

The ruler of the synagogue looked but little heartened.

Jesus said: "Nevertheless, I will go to Capernaum. There is work to be done there, too."

That night Jesus and the twelve left Bethsaida secretly.

Judas traveled with reluctant feet. There was insufficient

money for the expenses of the journey, and the trip was a hard one by foot. The first night, they slept in an olive grove not far from the sea of Galilee, with no protection from mosquitoes. Three equally uncomfortable nights followed, and discontent grew in Judas.

The third night, he caught John by the arm.

" 'Foxes have holes, and the birds of the air have nests, but the Son of Man has not where to lay his head' is what the Master is always saying—but I like it not!"

Jesus had gone to bathe in the waters of the river which wound through the valley. He seemed unwearied by the hot day's journey, and undisturbed by the discomforts of night. He slept, in fact, very little, but spent the majority of the night upon the mountain alone, praying.

Now John looked off along the path the Nazarene had taken.

"At least," he said mildly, "there is no rain."

Judas snorted. "Must we all kneel in thanks for that?" He thrust out his forearm. "Behold how my flesh has been made manna for the mosquitoes!"

John looked at the ugly red welts. "Indeed," he said, "you have been severely bitten. I am bothered but little, and I have yet to see a spot upon the Master, though they swarm all around him."

Judas had noticed that, too, and the knowledge was exasperating. He scratched viciously at his itching legs.

John said: "Sometimes, Judas, I am weary, too, but then I remember Moses' forty years in the wilderness and I know that our hardships are slight in comparison."

Thomas, coming up behind with an armful of fagots for the fire, laughed.

"Forty years!" he said. "And we've been sleeping outdoors but three nights. Consider, Judas. Your suffering lacks thirty-nine years and three hundred and sixty-two days!"

CHAPTER XI

J UDAS turned from the path into the woods. Soon darkness would come striding down along the ridge and there was need of fuel for the cooking-fires and need of warmth and light in the hour or two before bedtime. For some reason, no one else ever had the forethought to make a bundle of fagots ready for the night or raise a shelter against the wind. If it were done, he must do it himself. It had become his duty. More and more, he was left to take charge of the menial work of the camp. The disciples had grown lax and somewhat shiftless under the leadership of a man who took no thought for the morrow, what he should eat or wear or drink; who trusted in God completely and eschewed responsibility for everything that had to do with one's material comfort.

As a piece of ideological doctrine, it was all right, Judas considered; but for practical purposes it was all wrong. At least, it was wrong for him. Peter, of another mind, caught the Master's jeweled words and strung them on literal thread. Yet the chill got into Peter's bones of a cold night, and he suffered material hunger as well as any of them. And what was true of Peter was true of John. They believed, but they suffered. They were not clothed like the lilies, nor did they eat like the birds, nor did they find that the spirit could raise the flesh above the sensory level.

Fools, didn't they realize that what the Master said was only true in its broadest sense? Either that, or Jesus had himself become an impractical dreamer, which Judas doubted. Certainly, he accepted with gratitude whatever material things were done for him, and must have known that each one had been planned long before it had come into being. Yet, strangely, Jesus seldom sought food or thought of rest. He did not ask about the washing of his clothes, or appear to grow weary on a journey.

That might be all right for the Master, who had servants to attend him, whether he bade them or not; but as for Judas—he of experience in the world, he of knowledge of man's struggle to survive, he of the memory of past hungers and bitter nights and wretched surroundings, had learned his lesson. Indeed he had learned a little more than that: a fundamental truth, ungarnished with ideology, and it was—make every reservation for the coming hour and the approaching day; look to yourself and your opportunities, lest you fail from thirst and hunger and thus fall by the way.

What is bitterly learned is remembered, Judas thought, as he went among the brambles picking up sticks for their evening fire. Earlier in the day he had purchased some dried fish for tonight's dinner and, later, vegetables, though on both occasions he had had to haggle over the price so that he might save a few copper pieces for his commission. From the inadequate general funds which he disbursed, he usually managed to save a little. In time, with careful management, he could pay all his debts. But, unfortunately, the whole amount left unpaid would come due in three months. Eliab, a money lender in Jerusalem, fat, unyielding and greasy of skin, the paunch of him lying down in great folds upon his lower belly, would insist upon the full amount being paid forthwith. He would not extend the time. He would take no further surety or bond from another. He would listen neither to pleadings nor to tears. He was rock against subterfuges and excuses. He had, Judas knew, no compassion in him, no love for his fellows, no faith in a man's word. Judas remembered how once he had hated him—hated him so hotly that the inner consciousness he had of the man was red flame in his burning brain. No longer did he have such emotions because of his gnawing perception that one's first duty was to look after oneself. Therefore, Eliab was but fulfilling this requirement. Judas still feared him, but he did not hate him. In a way, he admired him. Often he wished he might be like him.

The fear of Eliab was with him constantly night and day. When the debt matured, then would come the reckoning—prison and disgrace. He could not, unless a miracle occurred, pay that money. What could he do?

Darkness had fallen and the tips of the branches of the trees shone like bright stones in the starlight. The pot of broiling fish over the fire sent forth pleasant odors. Presently, sniffing and glancing about, Peter roused himself to go into the woods to call Jesus. In some secluded spot, the Master meditated or prayed, as was his custom at this hour. Seeing him go, Judas thought: "If our Teacher can be prevailed upon to set up his earthly kingdom within three months I am safe. I will have power even over Eliab. I can outlaw the debt."

Yea, he would outlaw the debt. But there was need to hurry. It was imperative that Jesus act at once. So when the two returned, advancing within the circle of disciples around the fire, he looked up and said quickly:

"Teacher, when will you declare your colors?"

There was silence. The pot boiled, and steam rose and filtered away into the still air. Instead of sitting down, Jesus walked to the fire's side where he stood watching the flames burning along a stick, tiny flames which reminded Judas of cats' red tongues lapping. He was not sure whether the Master sighed or whether it was the broiling in the pot; but he could see what an effect his words had had upon the others. They were waiting, breathless, for the answer.

Judas repeated the question. "Teacher, when will you declare your colors?"

To Judas' dismay, Jesus asked a question in turn.

"Whom do men say that I am?"

Peter coughed and stared into the fire. John turned to look away into the darkness as though expecting to find the answer there. Andrew, who had recently rejoined them, spoke immediately.

"Some say that you are Elijah come again."

"Yea, and there are some who say that you are Moses returned to us," said Simon the Zealot.

Nathanael picked up a stick glowing red with embers and absent-mindedly turned it round and round. Then, as the disciples looked at him, he moistened the end of one finger with spittle. As he touched the glowing end, there was a hiss and the smell of steam.

When the stick no longer glowed, he said: "It is said that you are the reincarnation of Jeremiah."

Jesus smiled and his eyes rested upon each in turn.

"But what say you?"

With decision, Peter spoke. "Teacher, you are the Son of the living God."

There flashed into Jesus' eyes that expression of sublimity and tenderness, of gentle approval, which they had all come to know so well.

"Simon Bar-Jona," he said, "you are a fortunate man. You are well-named Rock. Upon this rock of understanding I will build the habitation of men to the glorification of our heavenly Father."

In vexation, Judas pulled a bundle of fagots toward him and hurled it into the fire. Pest! Another chance gone. In the swirling of sparks and swaying of the kettle upon its crane, he saw his own hopes scattering and dying, leaving behind only dead smoke. And he saw, too, suddenly the Master's gaze upon him, where a moment before it had caressed Peter. In the agony of his heart he was aware of the same tenderness, yet—not the same. There were in the unfathomable deeps of Jesus' eyes two pearls, two holy immaculate tears that somehow Judas realized were not alone for him, but for all men. And, further, as he read the look, he found himself reflected in it during the eternal span of a single moment, the lifetime of the world. There he beheld himself, stripped to his inner core: neither a cloak for his thoughts nor cover for his desires. But it was he, not Jesus, who could see that reflection so mirrored. Jesus would find his own perfect image in the staring orbs directed toward him.

"Forgive me," said Judas.

"You are forgiven."

Judas' hands trembled as he took the kettle from the blaze. "Teacher," he said, "we know who you are—but *where* are you?"

Jesus answered at once, but, again, not as Judas had expected. "I am here and in the hearts of men. I journey in the wind and sleep in the cradle of the land. In the spring plowing and the fresh-turned earth there am I. In a child's laughter seek and find me."

Wood burned to coals made a small noise heaping together. No man in that circled glow moved. The breathing night ringed them, but here was only light and a man speaking.

But when Jesus went on, Judas was suddenly aware of

the world's great darkness all about, a darkness drawing nearer as the fire burned low.

"But, presently—and this you must remember, for soon it will come to pass—I am in Jerusalem, seized by the high priest and the Sanhedrin and made to suffer by them. I am crucified upon the top of a high hill in the sight of multitudes."

Peter and John openly wept. Andrew took a turn about the fire and then paused before the Master, his face drawn and white.

"That, then, is to be the end."

Jesus smiled at him. "Can you find the end of that which has no beginning? I said to you once, before Abraham was, I am. Now I say to you that when the last stone has crumbled and the earth is no more, the Son of Man still lives. Within three days after my death, I will rise again and come among you."

In a deep silence, Nathanael dropped his head on his knees. Thomas looked questioningly at the Master, as did some of the others.

Judas, a curious feeling come upon him, sat listening to crickets chirping in the woods and an owl hooting in the distance.

"It is well it ends well," he said, keeping his eyes downcast.

James, son of Alphaeus, who sat next to Philip, said in a whisper loud enough for Jesus to hear: "What shall we do? What shall we do if Jesus, our Master, is killed?"

Philip shivered. "I know not."

"Nor I." Thaddaeus huddled over the blaze, warming his shaking hands.

"It will be the end," said Thomas with tragic certainty.

Once more Judas thought about his debt to Eliab, and fear shuddered in his bones. If death came to Jesus in

Jerusalem, truly for him that would be the end. His hands trembled as he took the pot from the fire again. In abstraction, he apportioned the fish. In terror he looked upon the man who, by some miraculous means, had read his own doom. Near him, he could hear Nathanael sniffling as if he were a child.

Matthew rose, leaving his food untouched, and groped his way into the woods.

Yet Jesus sat there unaffected. Upon his features were neither lines nor shadows. The fire, springing up, illumined his face and touched his hair, and made his temples glow with brightness. A kind of calmness hovered about his head and quiet smoothed his brow. He ate, but seemed not aware of the food, nor what was going on about him, so great was his in-dwelling consciousness.

Unable to sit there longer and watch him, Judas himself arose and followed some of the other disciples into the shadowing trees. He had gone no farther than a few paces, blindly and bitter-of-mind, when he stopped, hearing a voice. Peter's voice, the precious Peter so lauded by the Master.

"We must stop him. God in heaven, isn't there some way to keep him here? Must he go to Jerusalem? Must he leave us and the world desolate?"

"Nay, let us dissuade him!" It was James, brother of John, who answered. There was the sound of his turning about, and a quick breath of hope from Peter. Back to the fire they went.

Judas followed slowly.

"Teacher," he heard Peter say, "if what you say is true, it must not happen! Tarry with us, Lord, and enter not that iniquitous city."

From his deep abstractions and ponderings Jesus, Judas saw, came back to a clear awareness of them and of Peter's words.

With a swiftness that was startling, he stood up. His eyes, upon Peter, flashed sternly.

"Satan, get thee behind me! You think not of the things of God, but are concerned only with human events. Go!"

His voice carried through the woods.

Quietly, then, he returned to his place by the fire. A moment later, Peter timidly followed. Judas dropped to his knees, swaying there while the black of his mood beat out his thoughts and any hope he might have had, any peace he might have known—all black spaces in a crushing void of despair.

Presently he lay, stricken and tense, staring at red coals and red flame and charred wood and the enclosing circle of grass withered by the fire.

All at once, he realized that the Master was speaking again.

"If you would follow me, you must expect to be crucified. If you do not follow with that purpose, you are false. He who would save his life will lose it. He who would lose it for my sake will save it. The Son of Man came not hither without purpose."

Judas listened. His agonized mind groped toward an understanding, but could not reach the height of it.

"In time," Jesus was saying, "the Son will come again with the angels for the glory of God. When that time comes, each will be rewarded according to his deeds." He looked around about at them all, at each upturned asking face. His eyes rested gently upon John. "Truly there are some of you standing here who will not see death before the Son comes again to rule his kingdom."

Nathanael raised swollen eyes and got slowly to his feet.

Then Judas, realizing that he was the only one not on his feet, hurriedly stood up.

CHAPTER XII

JUDAS, lifting his eyes from the roadway and the dragging sandal prints of his companions, stared resentfully. While his disciples plodded, Jesus' quick effortless stride had taken him far ahead along the winding valley of the Jordan. Only now and then was the light-robed figure even visible in the patterned shade of the oak thickets along the river's edge. The storm within Judas beat the more fiercely. Questions. Questions. Questions. Never any satisfactory answer for any of them. Certainly there was nothing in himself which could quiet their clamoring. Nor, he believed, in those who walked with him. Only one man could make reply but, if he could, he would not. When one wished to query him, either he was, as now, advanced beyond hail or the words of response were, to Judas' groping and exasperated mind, irrelevant.

Today there were so many questions in Judas' mind that sometimes one was uppermost, sometimes another. There was a merging and shifting of his thoughts, a tumbling and struggling of reason so that it seemed as if an Arabian sandstorm raged within him. Ere he clutched at one idea to hold and wrest from it a sharpened meaning, it was swept away and another whirled before him. One after another. A mocking and confused parade. What of Jesus' kingdom? What meant those startling phrases of the Nazarene, those prophecies which etched doubt and foreboding in the mind? Was the Kingdom of Heaven not, after all, to be set up on this earth with Jesus king and all the twelve as lofty lords? What, then, of Judas' debts? What of his future? Would this toilsome discipleship lead to naught but another failure?

Failure! Judas stopped, burned by a recent memory. He shifted his leather bag from one shoulder to the other. That child in Caesarea Philippi with the dumb spirit.

The father had come to Judas bringing the lad who promptly demonstrated his affliction by falling into a fit, his countenance convulsed, his limbs contracted.

"Can you not cure him?" begged the father desperately, and he had clung to Judas' robe in supplication.

Judas' distaste had turned to condescension. Thus, many times, he had watched the needy plead for help from Jesus. Yea, and did not the Master graciously perform the miracle? The act of it was simple. A mere raising of the eyes to heaven for prayer, sometimes silent, often not. A clear commanding glance at the sufferer. Possibly a touch of the hand. That was all. Judas knew well the way it was done. Many of the disciples, too, had had encouraging success. He himself, until now, had not felt inclined to minister unto the unfortunate. But now . . . there was that in the man's manner of near-worship, the groveling at his feet, that made Judas feel benign. It was, in a way, a foretaste of the importance he would attain to when the Master established his kingdom.

"Can you not cure him?" wailed the child's father again.

The child wallowed like a beast upon the ground before Judas.

Judas said: "Yea, I will cure him." He lifted his eyes. He fixed upon the lad a stern glance. "Evil spirit, depart!"

The boy screamed, writhing upon the earth.

Judas, annoyed, repeated. "Depart, I say, O evil one!"

He watched intently. No change, except for the worse. He strode to the child, laid hold upon it violently. "Be healed!" he shouted. The small body wrenched itself from his grasp, and fell to the earth, but not before the sharp hand nails had gouged his flesh so that blood flowed from Judas' face and arms.

Hearing the noise, a crowd gathered, and among them some scribes and Pharisees. Questions were arrowed at Judas. What had happened? Why could he not heal the child? His Master often cured such. Had he not been given power to do so?

Judas said angrily: "I did not expect to cure the child. I but sought to calm him before he was taken before the Master." He rubbed at his stinging cheeks and when he brought his hand down, the fingers were crimson.

The throng laughed derisively. Thomas, Philip and Thaddaeus, hearing the disturbance, pushed through the multitude. One of the scribes put the question to Thomas.

"Can you cure this man's child? Your brother disciple has had but small success. In fact"—the scribe grimaced and waved his hand—"none."

Thomas looked dubious. "I might be able to, but ——"

"Could you?" asked the scribe of Philip.

"The Master could easily," said Thaddaeus defensively.

"But why could not this disciple cast out the demon?" demanded the scribe. "Is he not one of your Master's chosen twelve?"

"Yea," admitted Thomas.

The scribes demanded explanation. Their queries were subtly put and difficult to make reply to. The disciples faltered over their wording.

They were uncomfortable and perspiring when Jesus made a lane through the curious crowd.

"What is this argument about?" he asked quietly.

The dumb child's father flung himself forward. "Master, my son has a dumb spirit. Yea, he is sore torn by the malady. Behold him!"

Jesus' eyes dwelt for only a moment upon the convulsed child who clawed at the soil and screamed.

"Master, I asked your disciples for help, but they could not relieve him."

The scribes murmured together, suspicious eyes going from Judas to the master. Judas rubbed angrily at his scratches and would not meet the Nazarene's probing gaze.

"Oh, faithless generation!" said Jesus. "How long shall I be with you? How long shall I suffer you?"

Judas, bitterness growing in him, would not look up. Was that rebuke either necessary or kind? Was not his humiliation complete enough?

"Bring the child to me," commanded Jesus.

Two men lifted the struggling lad while Jesus spoke in low tones with the parent.

"If you can do anything," cried the farmer, "will you not, out of pity, do so, Master?" His eyes filled with discouraged tears.

Jesus' voice, to Judas' chagrin, was calm and assured. He put a quieting hand upon the man's drooping shoulder.

"Believe. All things are possible to one who believes."

The man fell to his knees, in his face an anguished eagerness. "Lord, I believe!" He caught up a fold of the Master's robe. "Help my unbelief, Lord."

As always, Jesus had healed the child, although for a moment when the child lay unconscious apparently, Judas had believed him dead. So had the knowing scribes and Pharisees. They had said: "He is dead!" and looked accusingly at Jesus, who had stooped then, and lifted the child to his feet. Life came into the small form, a serene normal vitality, and the father had wept for joy.

Alone with the Master, the disciples had asked: "Why could we not cast him out?"

Jesus had given one of his cryptic answers. "This kind must be driven forth by prayer and fasting."

Fasting? The statement was contradictory. Jesus never fasted, as far as Judas knew. He was, in fact, condemned by the pious Pharisees because he often accepted invitations to feasts and ate well when food was placed before him. Prayer, yea, he spent much time in prayer. But fasting—that was another matter.

Judas became aware that Peter was speaking about that very matter, teasing him a bit for his inability to cure the child. He turned on Peter testily.

"Have you forgotten last spring when you tried to walk on the waters of Galilee as the Master did, Peter?"

Peter reddened, coughed, then smiled sheepishly. "Nay," he said ruefully, "I have not forgotten." He clapped Judas good-naturedly upon the back. "We'll speak no more about the unfortunate occurrence at Caesarea."

Thomas trudged abreast of them. "Judas, I've been wanting to ask you something."

"Ask, then."

"What did you do in Jerusalem with our money? You didn't leave a shekel for those of us who remained in Capernaum." Thomas' rather prominent eyes fixed Judas insistently and not without suspicion. Judas was seized with an almost uncontrollable desire to shake his stocky body.

Instead he said stiffly: "It went for a good purpose. To represent us all, I went to Jerusalem and bought a lamb to offer as a sacrifice to God." He glared at Thomas. "Have you any more accusations?"

Matthew, ordinarily quiet and reticent, stepped between

them. "Even if you did go up to the Passover, was there any need to offer sacrifice for us? Were you asked to do so?"

Judas smiled humorlessly. "As it happened, I was buying one each for Mary Magdalene, Susanna, myself and Jesus when I was told that since I was buying four, I could have another by paying about three shekels or so more. Therefore, I purchased five, one of which was for you."

Peter broke in impulsively. "Doesn't the prophet say 'The Lord loves mercy and not sacrifice'?"

Judas dumped his bag from his shoulder violently. He spat upon the ground. "What do you intend to do about the temple—ignore it? Destroy it? Or do you intend to make use of the existing strength embodied therein for our cause?"

No one answered, but, Judas saw, he had the attention of them all.

"The other night," he went on, "when Jesus said he would go to Jerusalem and be crucified, Peter said to him, 'Teacher, you must not!' What happened? He was rebuked. But I agree with Peter. Such a thing must not be allowed. We must reach some agreement with the Pharisees and the Sanhedrin. We must make allies, not enemies. Only thus can we oust our common foe, Rome, and make our Master ruler of Jerusalem."

Simon the Zealot cried disdainfully: "What is the Sanhedrin? Only the puppet of the Roman governor! Who is its ruler? Caiaphas. And what is Caiaphas? Head of the new Roman party."

John said slowly: "That's true. All the corruption in Jerusalem today can be traced to him."

"And did not Jesus go to Jerusalem immediately after his baptism and cleanse the temple?" put in Andrew.

Judas faced them defiantly. "I, for one, consider that a mistake on Jesus' part. I don't defend Annas, of course, but nevertheless he's an Israelite as we are and Israel must be united."

Thomas said mockingly: "Feeling that way, why don't you return to Jerusalem and become a porter in the high priest's palace?" His prominent eyes, bloodshot with journey dust, rolled at Judas.

Judas shook with fury. He wanted to smash his fist into Thomas' round face, to feel those small even teeth against his knuckles, to see those pale eyes purpling at the rims. All of his anger against fate, all of his fear of Eliab and the debt, all his protest against Jesus' prophecy, rose in him. Were these men going tamely on as before, hanging upon the Master's philosophical sayings like women, watching him heal and save and reassure multitudes when he had admitted his own inability to triumph himself? He must rouse them. He must lead them—show them how to overcome the odds against them.

"Fools!" he shouted. "Every moment matters. We can't afford to antagonize the powers at Jerusalem. We must work so that when we are ready to declare ourselves, the high priest and Jesus will be aligned together." He shook his fist in Thomas' face. "For I tell you—unless we can borrow the power and influence of the high priest, our plan will never succeed."

He looked from one to another. His words were not without effect, he saw exultantly. John looked thoughtful. Philip nodded slowly. Matthew rubbed his chin, a gesture of his when stirred to a change of opinion. Peter's eyes looked at him sharply. Even Thomas appeared partially convinced.

"Knowing in advance what may happen, shall we not

try to prevent it? Shall we go down, without struggling, to defeat? Will you not strive to defend the Master?"

Thaddaeus said slowly: "Truly, if Jesus should leave us, what could we do? What would be left for us?"

"We want to win," nodded James the Less.

"By all means," said Simon the Zealot, "we must prevent the Master's death."

"Yea," said Peter fervently, "we are all agreed on that, I think."

"Since Jesus is opposed to violence, an armed rebellion is out of the question," said Judas. "Therefore, only one way remains. To take Jerusalem or to win Caesarea or Tiberius to our side."

No voice was raised in opposition. Elation brightened Judas' aching eyes. He breathed deeply and thrust out his chin. He had moved them. He had persuaded them. His words carried more weight with them now than those of Jesus himself.

He took a step forward. "Now—who is to be the leader?" Looking affectionately from one to another, he waited, his confidence mounting.

James broke the silence. "Such a great problem ought not to be deferred until we reach Galilee. Let's sit over there on the grass, under that oak tree, and discuss it."

All except Judas settled themselves among the blue corn flowers by the roadside. He remained standing, facing them. Could they fail to see in him, standing straight and tall before them, their rightful leader? Could they miss the keenness of his eyes, the firmness of his lips, the intelligence evident in every feature?

James the Less said: "I should think that Peter would naturally be our leader."

Judas swallowed. Then he shrugged laughingly. "Peter

is good at taking fish. That I admit. But I don't think he looks like a man capable of taking a castle!"

The disciples laughed. Peter's eyes flashed indignantly, but he said nothing.

Thomas suggested Simon the Zealot, but James was opposed.

"That might be dangerous, considering the recent trouble in Jerusalem. Doubtless he could lead well those who object to paying taxes, but I doubt that he could attract the average citizen."

Simon the Zealot proposed Philip, but Judas scoffed at the idea. "As I said before, unless we have a strong man who can unite us with the present powers of Jerusalem, it will be useless."

Matthew said, picking a corn flower and holding it between his fingers meditatively: "I still think Peter ——"

"Nay!" said Judas vigorously. "Peter is too excitable." He shifted from one tired foot to the other. "A Galilean doesn't understand Judea and wouldn't be able to accomplish enough in Jerusalem."

Were they blind, these men? Their leader stood before them, waiting to assume the great responsibility—and they —they could not see him for looking at one another. Fishermen, publicans, peasants—Galileans all. Only he, Judas, had been born in Judea. Only he knew Jerusalem, and how it might be taken.

"Why not make me the leader? It was my plan."

Thomas, chewing upon a grass blade, spat it out laughingly. "What! A leader—you? A man who couldn't even cure a dumb child?"

Judas smiled thinly. "That's an entirely different matter."

The hot rays of the summer sun splashed through the branches, and burned into his cheeks. Through his worn sandals he could feel the warm road pebbles. His feet hurt. His head began again its incessant throbbing. He listened to the disciples arguing, and all at once was so weary he could no longer remain upright. He sank down beside Peter and put his head in his dusty hands. The voices dimmed. His head lolled. Consciousness faded.

A voice awakened him. A clear pleasant voice. He looked up.

Jesus stood a little distance away. He had apparently come back to see what was detaining them. His eyes were quizzical, smiling.

"If you are rested, shall we journey on? We are still far from Capernaum."

Peter sprang up at once, murmuring apology. The other disciples followed, gathering their packs, putting on again sandals which had been taken off.

Judas was last to rise. He did so wearily, unrefreshed by his short sleep. From the woods to the left came the loud cawing of a crow.

Thomas looked over his shoulder nervously. "That sounds like an ill-omen."

CHAPTER XIII

AROUSED by noises down along the shore, Judas dressed and made his way outside. It was not yet dawn. For a moment he stood, trying to clear sleep from his mind. Resentment at being disturbed so early was sharp in him. Fishermen had no thought except for themselves, he thought. Simple folk, it was said of them, but he knew better. Their seeming simplicity was a kind of animal cupidity. Selfish and quarrelsome, in the dark hours they came awake to be first out to the fishing grounds. Jubilant when their own nets were full, they were jealous of others. A division of fish among them was always cause for haggling and dispute, often blows.

Why Jesus favored these men as a class, considered them morally superior to others, Judas could never understand. He wondered if there might not be a secret side to them he had not seen, some unusual virtue that was hid. They were without learning, surely. Their language was simple and flavored of the sea. They had no political knowledge. They paid their taxes with naive acceptance of hard conditions.

Turning from the path, Judas walked toward the beach. Sand gritted under his sandals. He stepped around fishnets, spread out to dry. Boats were being loaded with tackle. Lines creaked through pulley-rings as three-cornered sails were furled. There were sounds of scraping and bumping and splashing, and the sight of vapor rising over the water in such volume that it obscured all sight of Gennesaret opposite.

Another day, thought Judas, and clutched tightly the cloak he had thrown around him, feeling an ill taste in his mouth and heaviness within. Why and wherefore was man so forced to live that each rising was but to the old awareness? Yesterday's specters returned to the same couch they had left at eventide. One saw the same sun tipping the horizon, the same clouds gathering upon the earth's rim and the same grass growing green upon the ground. The rains and the winds, the shining of the stars, the wanings and waxings of the moon—all constituted an inescapable and monotonous routine. Like the maze in Herod's garden, the entrance was also the exit. The beginning was the end. And, in like manner, one's thoughts circled back, one's deeds, one's sins, one's short-comings, one's problems—everything returned to the entranceway that it might again go forth and return defeated.

Last night the crow's cawing had been an omen of evil to Thomas, and he had so proclaimed. He was fearful for the Lord, whereas Judas had read into it a more personal meaning. In his accounting of funds there had been no attempt to deceive anyone. He had borrowed small amounts to pay the interest on his debts. He had had, of course, no authority for purchasing the lambs from the priest for sacrifice—yet his motive had been unselfish, he felt. Also, he was constantly paying back borrowed money in savings to the disciples—savings represented by reduced prices of food and clothing, and not without a great amount of shrewd bartering on his part. Every penny thus saved he had personally earned. Couldn't they see he was entitled to a commission? It was the custom in Jerusalem. Hadn't the disciples themselves visited the market places, where competition forced all purchasers to save a penny here and a penny there at the expense of the sellers? Such savings were not to be won easily. One must be adroit and have a knack of reading character. One must know how to handle men.

Judas wandered on, following the shore. Incredible that there were so many fishermen for so few fish. The commotion they made in embarking would raise the dead. What a filthy business to be in! Cold, snake-like mists crawling over the water, the maddening thumping of the waves on shore, the foul smell of rotting weeds, and the nauseating sight of little finny bodies, white and putrid in the shallows.

The disciples, Judas thought, would soon, very soon, attempt to expose him to Jesus as a thief, a juggler of accounts. They were jealous of him, probably because he had the qualities of leadership. He was a city man, while most of them were peasants. He could read and do sums in Arabic, and speak fluently in several languages. He had an understanding of science and the law. He could expound doctrines and speak with certitude upon the problems of government and political economy. Self-taught, he was, a made man of many gifts—only poverty and his debts held him down.

He a thief! Judas turned eyes toward the sea in supplication and paused to watch the reddening east. He a thief! The sails of the fishing fleet were white moths flitting across the water. The day had begun, another circling back from the entrance to the exit, ceaseless returning and advancing—an inane and senseless destiny. They had not said so in words, only by implication. He a thief! Thomas with his dull, doubting brain. Peter, Matthew, Andrew, John—all of them piously accusing him. Eyes, expressions, manners rebuking him. Strange to be thus doubted by his fellows. He a thief! It was preposterous! Had they a grain of proof except for the slight shortage in his accounts, money he had borrowed, not stolen? A thief! In their little minds and with their shallow intelligence they believed it, actually. Fools. He who had bargained for them, fed them from a purse of penury, kindled their fires, clothed them, cooked for them like an obedient slave—a thief. . . .

In a rage, Judas flung about and now strode along quickly, ever more quickly, his breath short and broken. He a thief! Fools! He had borrowed the money. He ran. It would be paid back—all of it, to the last coin and with interest added.

He stopped. Why did he run? Surely he was not running away. He felt no guilt, only anger. He was not afraid of them and there was no need to run. Fishermen dipping their nets in a salty, stinking sea had little understanding, and that was what the disciples were, fishermen. Jesus had said once, "fishers of men." They were fishing for him now with bared hooks and a sinuous net of suspicion. But he would not be caught. He would struggle, he would elude them. He would jump out of the net, he would slip past the bared hooks—he would swim to the deeper waters beyond their reach.

Would the Master accuse him also? Judas, meeting Jesus' glance unexpectedly upon the wave-crests, finding it in the shallows and unwatered sand of the beach as the morning sun first blazed across the earth, groaned and sat down. The rock upon which he sat was near the water, where beds of reeds ran out a short way to be submerged in the high-running surf. Beyond were the fishermen, bobbing at anchor with lowered sails, leaning overside tugging at their nets.

Judas said aloud, his face lined with anguish: "Master,

I borrowed the money to pay interest on a debt. It was not stolen."

Jesus was not there, of course. He, Judas, was rehearsing the words it might be necessary to speak later. They would accuse him, of course. Their looks said so, their manner belied it not. This morning they would go straight to the Master.

"Master," said Judas, "I am falsely set upon by these, your followers. Believe me, I beseech you."

Judas shut his eyes. He could gaze no longer at those glinting crests, at the bright sand, nor at the ripples close inshore. Jesus was not there, of course. Only the sharpened rays of morning light. Only the shooting beams of the sun. What if they did remind him of—well, of the Master, of his certain clear look? Was that unusual?

"I would betray no trust," Judas went on, rehearsing his defense. "The sum is in itself insignificant. I have already more than repaid it in extra service to you, Lord."

Judas heard steps. His eyes sprang open as he turned his head, startled. Jesus approached, surrounded by wives of fishermen and their young, a score of children of all ages. Nurslings in arms and little ones measuring short insecure steps upon the sand to keep pace with their elders. Laughing, shouting children, large and small, making a ring around the Master, except one whom he carried in his arms. Bringing up this not unusual cavalcade, in more sober array, marched the disciples.

As Judas watched them, he could see by the expressions on the faces of the disciples that they would have word with Jesus, but were hindered by the presence of the children. The older ones were shouting and pursuing one another. There were some who purposely fell down and rolled over in the sand. Others found shells and bright stones and shrieked with pleasure as they showed them to their mothers.

The disciples quickened their pace to overtake the Master and immediately they were pummeled by many tiny hands and made the objects of a new attention. They were invited, with innocent, wide-eyed seriousness, to join in the games. On hands and knees, a boy crawled between Peter's legs. A small girl tugged at Nathanael's gown and begged to be taken up. Thomas stumbled and nearly stepped upon an infant who sat sucking its thumb.

"Brats!" he shouted. "Begone! You are but in the way here. Cease your clamoring."

Irritably, Nathanael pushed the little girl away, to Judas' amusement, and turned sternly to its mother. "Can you teach your child no manners?"

Judas could see that Peter, too, had grown angry. One could read his face and find resentment there against the mothers for bringing their children, and against the children for their clack and noise. As Peter advanced in the center among them, his manner said: "Time is too precious to be wasted thus. Here, I shall put an end to such nonsense."

Suddenly raising his arms to draw attention, he shouted: "Disperse, all of you disperse, I say. The Master will confer with us on more important matters."

In the silence which came then, Judas rose and walked toward the group. Jesus still had the child in his arms and he drew it closer to him. The child's head rested upon his shoulder. The child's face was upturned to his.

"Rest ye here a little while," he said tenderly and kissed the round cheek.

Peter lowered his arms in resignation. "But Master ——"

Jesus placed his own cheek against that of the child, and once more Judas beheld upon the countenance of his leader the same light that sparkled in the shallows of the sea, upon the wave-crests and in the glinting sand. And he heard Jesus' voice, as though waves reverberated through it with a deep and solemn warning.

"Let the little ones come to me, and forbid them not, for of such is the kingdom of heaven. Despise not one of these, for I tell you truly that in heaven their angels always behold the face of my Father."

Peter bowed his head and plucked his robe in embarrassment. But Thomas advanced stoutly and with a resolute tread. Then Judas saw that the eyes of all the disciples were cast his way.

At last and at length, he had been singled out for their accusations. His integrity and motives would be assailed. These men, all of whom he had served—and with whom he had broken bread, had come here, purposely, and with intent perfidious and vile, to place upon him the mark of a thief and the name of a thief.

No sooner did he realize it, than Thomas spoke.

"Master, there is one here who has kept false accounts." He turned his prominent eyes and stared at Judas.

Judas could feel a prickling at the roots of his hair. The white light of morning came as though filtered through a dark cloth. His temples were throbbing. His throat was dry. The words he would speak had become lost in the blank and tortuous spaces of his mind.

From afar off, he heard Jesus ask: "Who is this man?"

"He is one of us."

"If he is one of us, how then can he be such an one?"

Thomas' voice sounded bewildered and now he spoke with less assurance.

"We had occasion to examine his ledger and count the money left over after certain purchases were made. The amounts do not balance. Also there is a certain false entry."

"Was the money stolen or was it borrowed?"

"In either case," said Thomas stubbornly, "a wrong has been done."

"Did you wash your own hands and those of the other disciples?"

Thomas choked. "I know not what you mean, Master."

"Do you rend your own garments when another's is rent?"

"No, Master."

"Then say no more. Wash your hands and guard your cloak. Forgive, that you may be forgiven also. Love in order that you, too, may be beloved. For I say to you that in the courts of God there are none to witness against you, or bear testimony, either for or against."

Jesus' hand was gentle upon the child's soft hair. A tiny arm stole around his neck.

"But, Master," protested Peter, "how many times must one forgive? Seven times?"

The Nazarene smiled but his answer was emphatic.

"Not seven times, Peter. Seventy times seven."

Silence fell upon the disciples. They no longer looked at Judas. Scarcely believing, he stepped within the circle gathered around Jesus. His lips trembled and he, too, plucked at his gown.

The Master had absolved him!

CHAPTER XIV

JUDAS left the still, stifling heat of Peter's house to stand by the back door. It was no cooler here. The slight relief he felt lay in the change from hot air that was motionless to hot air that moved. A dry, dust-laden wind blew along the almost deserted beach. The earth's warmth came up through his sandals.

Thus, ever, were summers beside the Sea of Galilee, six hundred and eighty feet below sea level, and this, too, thought Judas restlessly, was a typical July Sabbath. Far better to have remained in Caesarea Philippi.

With his sleeve, he wiped sweat from his eyes. "It is more than I can stand." The words came from cracked lips.

The rest of the disciples were Galileans and so inured to the wretched climate, but used as they were to hard outdoor labor, they fretted at this continual confinement nearly as much as he. Now and again, Andrew, Philip and Peter stole away to catch fish for meals, but after the first time, they had not asked Judas to go along. He had been, he realized now, somewhat too disdainful. He was a business man, he had said, not a fisherman. But at this moment, he would have given much to trail his hands over the boat's edge and feel the cool of waves over his fingertips. Even the memory of the torrid reflection of sun on water burning and blazing against the skin, did not slacken his longing. Enviously, he looked out across the lake to the dot which was Peter's craft.

Inside the house, all was quiet. Matthew and Nathanael were napping. James the Less had not returned from the morning service at the synagogue. Simon the Zealot had gone to the bake shop for bread. Thomas and Thaddaeus he had left in the room adjoining that of Jesus, exchanging low-toned but fervid complaints ranging from the weather to Herod. Their voices had rasped Judas' nerves and he wondered if the murmur might not prove disturbing to the Master, sitting cross-legged in meditation in the next room.

Judas sighed and looked along the lake shore to the street which led to the house of the sons of Zebedee, John and James. Would it be a shade cooler there, perhaps? He doubted it, but Salome, the disciples' mother, might have something agreeable in the way of refreshment. She was a good cook and a generous hostess. There were times when Judas had wished he had been quartered there with James and John, but of course the house was small.

He leaned against the wall, undecided. Even the thought of putting one foot before the other was wearying. If he went, he would doubtless stay the afternoon and not return to Peter's until late. By that time, even the wind would have died down, as it invariably did at evening. He would be none the cooler and possibly warmer for the exertion.

Thomas came out and stood beside him. "The air a man breathes is hotter than body temperature," he said.

Judas made no reply. He turned his eyes from Thomas. To look at the stocky little disciple was to behold heat itself personified. Perspiration dripped from disheveled black hair, trickled into his veined protruding eyes, threaded the grooves from nose to mouth corners. His damp tunic clung to his body, and from it rose like invisible steam the odor of unwashed flesh and its excretions.

Judas started. A man was coming along the beach—a man hurrying! He could hardly believe it. Haste on such a day?

" 'Tis John!" Thomas stared in dull amazement.

When the disciple was within hail, Judas shouted: "Greetings, brother! What brings you here?"

John covered the last yards to Peter's dwelling without answering. He was short of breath. "Great news!" he panted finally. "I must tell the Master."

Always, first, John must tell the Master! Annoyed, Judas followed him to Jesus' room. John knocked upon the door.

Composed and gentle, Jesus' voice came from within. "Enter."

The Master sat in an easy, comfortable position upon the floor. His hair, curling at the temples from the moisture, and the sunlight, spilling in a bright pool at his feet, seemed to have borrowed from the same source, for they differed only in shade. His blue eyes, so dark that at times they looked black, were clear and warm with welcome. For John, the beloved, they were always warm, Judas thought bitterly. Tall, long-faced John, who drank at knowledge like a thirsty sheep and followed the Master with the same animal-like devotion. Without discrimination or question. Simply accepting, glad of what proof there was, but demanding none. A gullible fisherman.

"Master," said John, and wet his finely carved lips, "the Roman soldiers have captured Barabbas the Zealot in Lachish!"

Behind Judas, Thomas breathed: "Barabbas—taken!"

Slowly the meaning of this event came to Judas. With the leader of the insurrection out of the way, Jesus and his disciples would be able to move about freely again. The danger of being linked with the rebels and under similar suspicion of intrigue was over. No more cowering in a fisherman's cottage. No more need to hide while time crawled by. No necessity, praise heaven, to swelter longer on the Galilean coast.

He looked at Jesus, relaxed and motionless upon the floor, one foot tipped with sunlight.

"Where did you hear this?" he asked John quietly.

"Mother heard it this morning from a Pharisee at the synagogue."

The voices had roused the other disciples. They crowded into the room, questioning John excitedly.

"That means the Zealots will lose their strength," said Thaddaeus.

Thomas asked: "How was he taken?"

"Mother heard that he had gone to take a drink at Lachish, and there the waiting Romans seized him. The Zealots were starved out, apparently."

"Who else was arrested?" asked Matthew.

"Onesimas, probably," said Judas. "And perhaps those disciples of John the Baptist who came to see the Master —what were their names?"

Matthew rubbed his cheek, "You mean the two, Akkub and Baasha?"

"Yea."

"Akkub, in particular, seemed an intelligent, decent man," said Matthew. "I remember thinking he might, with some encouragement, become a follower of Jesus. A pity he went over to Barabbas."

"If he's been caught," said Thomas, "he thinks so, too, I imagine."

Nathanael shook his head sympathetically. "A Roman prison breeds penitence."

Jesus sat still upon the floor. He asked no questions. He seemed not to listen to any, nor to the answers given by John. The Master was like a rock in the sea, Judas thought, around which waves washed, but could not climb. Yet, he must know what this happening meant to them, to their cause. Surely, he must know.

There were voices at the back door and almost immediately Peter entered, followed by Philip, Andrew and James, John's brother. By their faces, Judas saw that they had heard the tidings. A moment or two later, James the Less and Simon the Zealot came in with Jairus, the ruler of the synagogue.

Peter greeted Jairus, and asked at once if the report of the recent arrest were true.

Jairus said: "It appears to be. I heard it this morning from a Pharisee named Melech. He had just come from Jerusalem."

Jesus did not rise. The disciples sat down in a circle about him.

"As long as Barabbas and Onesimas were at large," said Philip eagerly, "our cause was in danger of being mistaken for theirs, but now ——"

"But now that's past," broke in Peter exultantly. "All is well again."

Jairus leaned his turbaned head back against the wall. "It is but another tribute to the Master's wisdom that he did not join those others. Had he done so, no doubt he too would be in custody."

"But instead," cried Peter, "he's free!"

Jesus' eyes were steady and a little sad. "Think you the Son of Man is free? Do you forget so soon those things which I have told you must first come to pass?"

Peter's eyes clouded. "But Master ——"

"I tell you that in men's eyes Barabbas shall yet go free

upon the earth, but a cross awaits the Son of Man, and he must lift it and be lifted by it unto heaven."

Jairus looked around the subdued circle uncertainly, his glance going from one sobered countenance to another. He said uneasily: "If this be a parable, I understand it not —and like it little."

A smile flitted across Jesus' face.

Jairus laughed, relieved. "You spoke thus to test my faith."

"Nay, Jairus. Because I smile you refuse to believe me, but before long the Son of Man shall be seized by the Romans, as Barabbas has been, and shall be questioned before the high priest and be made to suffer much at men's hands, and in the end, shall be killed."

Horror swept the ruler's face. "Master!"

Judas felt again that peculiar emotion which made a tightness in his chest. Fear for Jesus? Not all. The feeling was too personal. His own mind was agonized; his own flesh suffered; his own vision threatened by blackness. It was as if he leaned for an instant over the edge of an abyss, and might have no choice but to plunge headlong into gloom. Nay, this unique and sharpened dread struck at his own being. Judas stared at the floor. He clenched his perspiring hands to still their shaking.

Jesus was speaking. "But I also know that the Son of Man shall rise again upon the third day." His voice rang with conviction. "Therefore, fear not, nor be dismayed."

The disciples were silent. Thomas wiped sweat from his forehead confusedly. Peter sat aggrieved. Andrew stared out of the window. No one, except John, looked at Jesus and in his eyes was steadfast loyalty, but no understanding.

Nathanael said in a low voice: "The Master speaks too

much of death these days. Lord, speak rather of life eternal!"

"I tell you of these things, not to bring you sadness," said Jesus tenderly, "but that afterward you may remember and rejoice."

Jairus cleared his throat. "But Master—about this news. Are you not relieved that you may go about freely again and continue your ministry?"

Jesus smiled.

The ruler went on as if eager to remain upon ground which he understood. "I wonder if you knew that the Galileans resented it because you would not join Barabbas." He waited nervously, but Jesus merely inclined his head. "Until that objection to your group died down, I for one could not foresee success for your teaching."

"But now," put in James the Less, "most of the disturbers have gone to Judea, Master, and all the leaders have been captured, they say." His tone was hopeful.

The heat of the afternoon was growing intense. It was hot enough, Judas thought irritably, to scorch a pot. Were they to go on like this, day after day, enduring it? Was Jesus yet going to delay all action? Frowning, he glared at the floor, at the patch of sunlight, at the feet of Jesus.

Then he was aware of eyes upon him. The feel of them was like a touch upon his lids. He looked up. The Master was studying his face. There was a smiling compassion in his glance, but back of it lay a sorrow which caught at Judas' throat. Passing by, the Nazarene's gaze went slowly around the circle, dwelling on each disciple in turn.

He said at last: "The time approaches. Shall we go now from village to village, teaching and saving?"

The disciples straightened. Drooping heads lifted. Discouraged eyes cleared, grew brighter.

Thomas cried: "Yea, Master!"

The disciples got up quickly. The heat was forgotten. They crowded around Jesus, who also rose, smiling at them all affectionately.

Judas, too, stood up, laughing. But, to his surprise, his vision blurred, and he coughed chokingly. He sank down, sobbing, his head against his knees.

Peter touched his shoulder. His voice was concerned.

"What is it, Judas? What is it? Are you not glad that our long wait is ended?"

Judas could not answer. Was he glad? He should have been, certainly. But now—now there was a loudness in his ears. Words throbbed in his mind. Over and over. Jesus' words: "The time approaches."

BOOK THREE

WHO FOUND ONE PEARL . . .

CHAPTER XV

THE morning was glad with sun—all the land and the water and the shining housetops of Tiberius. Heat had not yet gathered in sultry pools in the streets nor come sweating across the flagging of the inner court of the palace. There was not, as yesterday, the wind strong from the desert. The air had become still, Joanna perceived, and clean of dust, easy to breathe again. It was so clear that across Galilee the sheer cliff of Gerasa was deep marked upon the horizon. To the left, looking toward Capernaum, small mountains were like the rounded breasts of young maidens. To the right, in the direction of Emmaus, they were sharp and angular, grooved by rains and washed by floods.

Joanna crossed the court and went up the stone steps to the reception hall, and made her way timidly inside. As it was too early to receive visitors, Herod Agrippa lounged on a deewan, talking to his wife, Cypros, who sat near him. The prince's eyes were puffy and bloodshot, his long hair was rumpled, but otherwise he looked neat and cool in his loose-fitting morning robe gathered at the waist with a bright sash. Like all the Herods, he was subject to dark moods, especially of a morning. The fact that he had not rested well last night could be attributed to two causes, his continued brooding and drinking. During the night, Joanna had heard, he often called the steward for sleeping potions, and, when these failed, would leave his couch and go stamping about the palace, moaning and groaning, summoning servants and irritably dismissing them, then awakening his wife on the pretext that he was very ill.

He was a problem for Cypros, truly, but she was of a practical mind and usually could find some way to soothe him. Although her sympathy for him was neither very real nor very deep, it was successful. She had been known to put a drug in his wine to sicken him of the taste of liquor. On other occasions she would encourage him to intoxication, often sitting up to drink with him.

Long ago, Joanna had ceased to try to understand the motives of either husband or wife in doing what they did or continuing such a curious relationship. In many ways, they were more like sister and brother. She was rarely jealous of him, though often she had good reason to be; his escapades in Rome had been common gossip in every corner of the Empire. She had never, as far as Joanna knew, held anything against him, either his temper and drinking, or his affairs with women. His uncle, Antipas, had once said in Joanna's presence: "She keeps her mouth shut, wisely, that woman. If she undertook to reform him, and he did, it would but focus the light on her own milder intrigues."

Antipas had no reason to say this, as everyone knew. Cypros was unemotional, a frigid, calm creature with few wifely instincts and a secret distrust of all men. Joanna decided that the reason she clove to her husband was because she was ambitious. Agrippa had influence in Rome and, though lately he had suffered losses, would recoup them all and more, too, in spite of the plotting of former friends and present relatives.

Agrippa and Cypros were the only ones in the reception hall with the exception of Mazzahab, a guard, and the queen's personal slave, Rahel.

Cypros raised her slim white hand, and said graciously: "Come and be seated, Joanna."

Joanna obeyed, smiling. Agrippa gave her one quick impersonal look and then stared at the floor.

Cypros asked curiously: "Have you been out?"

Joanna straightened a fold in her skirt, feeling uncomfortably close to so practical a woman. "Yea, I went for a walk."

"But the heat ——"

"It is cooler this morning."

"Hotter," contradicted Agrippa. "Why we stay here, I don't know. The dust chokes me. It's intolerable!"

"There is a cool breeze from the sea," Joanna ventured. "It looks so pretty out on the water. The sails of the fishing fleet and the blue rocks on the far shore."

Agrippa sat up straight, scowling and muttering. Again he looked at Joanna for a brief space, as if she were the cause of his misery.

"You're tired, dear." Cypros reached over and patted his hand. "You must be quiet."

"I won't be quiet," snapped Agrippa. He got up and began pacing the floor. Suddenly he stopped directly in front of Joanna and stood, towering and raging.

"I said it was hot!" he shouted. "It is hot!"

"Yea, my lord."

"Plague such a situation. I ought to be in Rome or, better still, Tarshish. By heaven, a man can breathe there!"

"Yea, my lord."

Agrippa strode the length of the hall and back, then threw himself down and covered his eyes. Joanna decided to say no more. Rahel had come forward at the bidding of her mistress with a small phial of aromatic salts. Cypros sniffed from the bottle first with one nostril, and then the other.

She said: "I think it's hot, too. My head is bursting."

"I'm glad someone agrees with me!" Agrippa snorted through his fingers. "Why don't we go on the roof?"

Cypros rose at once. "Very well, we shall."

It was better upon the height, less stifling, Joanna thought, with the sea rippling off into the distance below and a slight breeze gentling one's brow. It was good to look out and see the humble fishing boats, and the men in them intent upon their tasks.

Agrippa flung himself down, blowing air from his lips. "This is better." He frowned at Joanna, amended testily: "Somewhat."

"We must go down again for the conference," Cypros reminded him.

"Conference. With whom?"

"Someone from the military, I think. There have been some queer rumors."

"Plotting, you mean. I'm aware of it. He won't tell me anything new. If I numbered the hairs of my head and gave each a name, I couldn't possibly know them any better than I know these plots and the men who think they're well hid behind them."

Agrippa sat up and stared at Joanna, this time with his eyes wide open and in them the smoke of battle. Joanna felt a sudden chill for she knew the talk at the palace of Antipas; knew all the rounds of gossip there; the stories drifting around the banquet tables from one whispering behind-hand to another. Even the kitchen maids and the garden servants heard them. Words were snatched from Herodias' lips on the most secret occasions by palace spies and even the thoughts most privy to the king were drawn from Antipas by experts in indirect questioning.

"Our guest must also know something of these matters," said Agrippa, turning to his princess.

Joanna flushed. No one could make her tell what she knew. Not anyone. Her husband had warned her. Their own position at Machaerus was none too secure since the death of John the Baptist. Nor had Antipas looked with approval upon their more recent conversion to the precepts and teachings of the Judean carpenter, Jesus.

Antipas had said: "The man is a rabble rouser. He secretly conspires to overthrow me."

Joanna breathed relief as Manaen entered from the balcony, and came striding along, dressed in a white toga, after the custom of the Romans, his handsome gray hair falling to his shoulders. Always his appearance in any company precipitated a freshening interest, for he brought with him, probably unconsciously, a sort of flowing radiance that was not easily withstood. Joanna had always greatly admired him, his good nature, his gentle manners, his unstudied naturalness. She had seen much of him at Machaerus and had never heard anyone speak ill of him. Antipas, of whom he was a foster brother, held him in the same esteem as had his father, Herod the Great, held Manaen's venerable sire. That Agrippa should like him, too, was most unusual as he seldom trusted anyone who was a friend of his uncle's.

But now he rose and went forward to meet him. The beginning of a smile touched his lips. "I'm horribly bored," he said, "and tired and sleepy. I was wishing you'd come!"

Manaen thrust his arm companionably around Agrippa's shoulders and they came forward and sat down upon a deewan.

Manaen said: "You look very well, I think. All you need is cheering up. What's wrong with you?"

"Not with me," said Agrippa. "It's my affairs. My debts. I owe everybody. I'm stuck here like the stones in the street."

"Pleasant place to be stuck in." Manaen glanced around approvingly. "As for your debts, who hasn't them?"

"My uncle."

"Don't you ever think so!"

"Is that official?"

"I'm not saying."

"You like him better than you like me."

"I do not say that, either."

"I have estates and principalities and certain influence with the Emperor, but I'll be damned if I can claim a penny that isn't mortgaged to someone."

"You lived too affluently in Rome, my pretty fellow."

Agrippa grinned. "Well, perhaps I did."

"Why don't you reform?"

"I'm thinking about it. I wish I could, and then I'm glad I can't. I was once truly an Epicurean and it was amusing while it lasted. If a man's stomach and purse were only as strong as his desires, life might be worth living. When he discovers that they are not as strong, then he is wholly disillusioned. In my disillusionment, I, for instance, tried to cut my throat."

"I heard about it."

"And, did Antipas, my own uncle, help me then? Did he offer to pay my debts? No. Did he encourage me when I came home suffering, ill and wanting to die? No!"

Manaen stroked his lean jaw and seemed, for a moment, in doubt. Joanna sympathized with him. Like herself, he had no wish to offend anyone.

"And Herodias," Agrippa went on bitterly, "has she

made matters easier for any of us? Can you placate the Jews by serving their heads on platters? Disgusting whim in a woman, and I'd tell her so to her face."

Manaen shrugged his shoulders. "I, too, deplore what she has done. My father, Manahem, as you know, was of the Essenes, and my whole thought has been colored by his teaching. To kill is a sin, whether in peace or in war. To believe that position, title, money or possessions have any real value in life is foolish. We are strongly convinced that only in lives of service and labor for the glory of God does one find real happiness."

"But that is difficult, Manaen."

"True. It is not easy to be good."

Agrippa shrugged. "Who wants to tend sheep in the fields from dawn until dusk and thereafter? Why waste one's days ministering to the sick? There are so many more pleasant things to do."

Manaen smiled slowly. "There are those who can find pleasure in being helpful and of service to others."

Agrippa laughed, without mirth. "Yea, and those you help and serve may be the first to cast stones upon you."

Manaen admitted this with a nod and placed his two strong hands on his knees and looked across the room at Joanna. His eyes seemed to say to her, "I have hope even of him." He turned to Agrippa. "Service may go unrewarded by man. You shouldn't expect it or even think about it. All you need know is that when you serve man, you serve God."

Agrippa stared blankly. To Joanna it was evident that Manaen's meaning was not clear to this Herod who abode in the flesh, and who viewed life from the road's dust and mud. He was, and the simile that occurred to her seemed very apt—he was as a chariot wheel. Forever turning upon the ground and being conscious only of the earthly contact. The weight always upon the ground—always the movement through the mire and grit and gravel—striking useless sparks upon dull stones.

But suddenly she heard him speaking.

"Is it wrong, then, to seek happiness and pleasure?"

"Nay, not real happiness and pleasure."

Agrippa closed his eyes and opened them. Then he gestured impatiently. "No one ever finds either one."

"I know of such a person."

Agrippa snatched at the words. "Who?"

Into Manaen's voice there flowed a new quality. Unconsciously, he spoke softly. Joanna thought, reverently. "A man of very humble origin. Jesus, the carpenter of Nazareth. I can't truthfully say that I met him or know him. But I saw him, and felt him. It was in the spring. Near the Jordan. There was a multitude of people there. They were around him and he talked in simple language of very simple things. But in that simplicity, Agrippa—if you follow me—was profundity beyond the power of ordinary man to know. I never realized before that little words could be so big, or that the commonplaces could be so unique."

Yea, thought Joanna, her heart stirring within her, she knew. What Manaen had experienced, so, too, had she.

"It was as though you gazed upon a hill," Manaen said and seemed unconscious that he spoke, "and suddenly it rose high to the proportions of a mountain. There I stood apart from the crowd, some distance from the speaker, possessed by the curious feeling that if I could walk a full furlough away, I would still be approaching and not departing from him."

Agrippa snorted. "What utter nonsense!"

Interrupted, Manaen seemed to remember his audience. But he was not embarrassed. "Believe it or not. The point

I would make," he said, "is that Jesus gave, as from a deep sweet well of water, all the pleasure and happiness one could drink." He smiled at Joanna.

Within the folds of Agrippa's too-tired face ran dark lines of suspicion and irritation. He said: "You are commending one who is plotting a rebellion."

Manaen shook his head. "Not he."

"One of our slaves," said Cypros, "told us he was."

"Wrong."

"There are fools," growled Agrippa, "who actually believe the fellow is the Messiah. They believe and say he is preparing to depose Antipas. But I tell you, before many days have passed he will be arrested like all the rest and be put to death by the Romans."

"Nay," said Manaen with prophetic somberness, "by the Jews."

Joanna shivered, despite the day's heat. But Agrippa went on: "Manaen, you well know how exceedingly my grandfather feared the words, 'Coming of the Messiah.' I remember that when I was about five or six years old there was a strange rumor that the Messiah was born in Bethlehem, and my grandfather ordered that every boy baby in the whole district be killed." He yawned. "But, of course, there was no Messiah born."

Joanna could keep silence no longer. "Your Highness!" She clasped her hands tightly together. "It is said that this carpenter Jesus of whom Manaen is speaking, was one child who escaped the sword of Herod the Great. His family, being warned in a vision, fled into Egypt taking the child there for safety. They say that he belongs to the lineage of David. That he—that he—is the Messiah!"

CHAPTER XVI

AGRIPPA paled. "What? Is that true?" He looked nervously about, then forced a laugh. "Doubtless it's only talk, another fraud." He stretched his legs out, flexing the muscles. "I remember that my grandfather's brother Phasael and his sister, Salome, were once part of a movement which looked for the Messiah. At that time, a false prophet named Bagoas used to come often to the palace."

"I remember your telling about that," nodded Cypros, amused. "Was he not the one who preached that the Messiah would not be defiled by being born of a woman, but would instead issue from his own loins?"

Agrippa snorted. "My great aunt Salome really believed him! But now—" he yawned, "—now it is only something to laugh about." His manner was tolerant, the tone that of a father to a fanciful child.

But Manaen, who had listened quietly to Agrippa, neither interrupting nor opposing him, now spoke thoughtfully.

"Belief in such a saviour was nonsense indeed, I agree. But we of this time are degenerate. We need a true Messiah to turn our spirits to God." He looked at Herod levelly. "I believe this carpenter from Nazareth is he."

"I, too!" broke in Joanna eagerly. "And we are but two among many. Roman soldiers, Zealots, tax gatherers, prostitutes, Pharisees, Essenes, anybody and everybody, regardless of religious or political affiliations, learn of him and are spiritually reborn."

She stopped, abashed. Cypros' long eyes were upon her, darkly derisive. Agrippa stared out over the water, his mouth a cynical twist. If they would only believe! What a blessing for them—what an impetus it would give the cause of the Nazarene!

Joanna clasped her hands to still their sudden shaking. "Truly, he is a man sent from God."

Herod's eyes flicked her. Agrippa was not a wicked man, she thought. The vicissitudes of his life had embittered him, certainly, but he observed the Law strictly. If the hard justice he meted was untempered by mercy, still he had shown many times his desire to win the favor of the Jews. How better than to receive one of them as the Messiah?

"Your highness," she said boldly, "will you not arrange to meet Jesus of Nazareth and judge for yourself?"

Swiftly, Cypros stood up. "But sister Herodias heartily dislikes the man. Someone told her that this Jesus is the resurrected John the Baptist and she detests the sound of his name."

Her words, her expression were final. Joanna lowered her eyes. Her white knuckles were sharp under the tense pressure of her fingers. They did not believe. They would not. To accept the truth would be to acknowledge a greater power than human authority and wealth. To believe that the humble Nazarene was the Messiah would be to rend the glittering fabric of their lives. To believe— to believe—nay, they dared not. For them it was impossible.

"What's that?" asked Herod abruptly.

From below came the sound of voices, of singing, and the tramp of many feet. Joanna saw upon Agrippa's face a familiar expression. She had beheld it often upon the countenance of Herod Antipas. Indeed, since the death of John the Baptist, it was rarely absent. Suspicion and controlled fear which crumbled in a crisis to an angry kind of panic. Crowds brought that look to rulers' eyes, and because of it distrust of the multitudes grew. But in the beginning, here and there, firebrands of hate had been kindled individually in the throngs. A wrong here. A persecution there. A seizure of property. A crucifixion. Debasement. Yea, thought Joanna, and yet could feel compassion, the Herods feared a hate which they themselves had engendered.

A slave dispatched by Cypros to find out what was happening, returned on a run with the news.

"A great crowd passes the palace gate. They go to meet the disciples of the prophet Jesus."

Herod sat back, relief smoothing his face. "So. It was naught."

"But why come they?" asked Cypros irritably. She slapped the slave smartly on his bare shoulder. "Come—why?"

The man's dark eyes rolled. "I think someone sent to Bethsaida for them to come and cure some of the sick in the town. Many of them thought Jesus himself was coming, and so went forth to meet him."

Cypros dismissed him. "Fantastic—these tales of cures!" She shrugged, and went to stand beside Agrippa, watching the fishing boats as they drew up on the banks beyond the palace.

"Fantastic, if you will," said Manaen quietly, "but true."

Cypros sniffed, her gaze on the fishermen putting their catch into baskets.

Herod said: "He's very popular, that carpenter Jesus." His voice was soft. "Perhaps too popular."

"You mistake," said Manaen. "Had he dreams of an earthly kingdom like Simon of Perea, or the brothers Athrongeus, or Judah, son of Ezekia, I, the son of my Essene father, should have no interest in him."

Herod said mockingly: "Continue. The man sounds as strange as his cures."

"Given your leave, I shall," said Manaen promptly. There was conviction in his manner, assurance in his lean, scholarly face. "Mark you, this man of Nazareth will be longer remembered in the hearts of men than Socrates, Plato, or Aristotle."

Cypros smiled. Her fingers caressed Agrippa's shoulder. "Say on. We are fascinated."

Joanna leaned forward, listening to Manaen. Her heart beat proudly. Manaen was defending Jesus. He was speaking of that which lay in her own heart, inarticulate. He was confirming her faith, and in the presence of this worldly minded prince and his wife, it was a good thing to hear.

"Truly, the populace exalts Jesus," said Manaen slowly, "but he makes no bid for shallow approval. He has enemies, too."

Herod took his eyes from the fishermen and his lips smiled wryly. "A bad sign. I am beginning to be convinced of his greatness, Manaen. All the great abound in enemies."

"His enemies," said Manaen, "*are* the great. The chief Pharisees. The high priest Caiaphas, and Annas, the former. The wealthy. The powerful." He walked the floor, turned and came back, his hands clasped behind him. "He denounces them as hypocrites."

"Amazing!" Cypros' cool voice was polite but indifferent.

"When I was in Caesarea a short time ago, Pilate's wife and I were speaking of that very thing."

Cypros lifted her brows. "Pilate's wife?"

"She is much interested in Jesus and his teachings," said Manaen.

"But," said Herod, "was not that Barabbas, the ruffian who started the insurrection which the Romans put down, a follower of Jesus? I can't understand ——"

"Nay," said Manaen quickly, "Jesus had nought to do with the uprising."

Joanna rememberd briefly the story of that ill-fated revolution. Barabbas and Jehu the Zealot had been imprisoned. Baasha, the disciple of John the Baptist who had reviled her at Capernaum as one of Herod's household, had been slain upon the altar in the Temple where he had fled for refuge. Also killed there, his blood staining the holy place, was Nadab, father of Onesimas. One Jeriah, they said, had escaped with Akkub, another disciple of John the Baptist, to a lonely desert town. Thus violence had been met with greater violence, and Joanna blessed the day the Nazarene had chosen the way of peace.

Manaen was telling a story. "They brought to him, in the midst of the temple, a woman taken in adultery, asking whether or not she should be stoned according to the Law. Had he said "Yea," they would have condemned him as cruel, since the woman had been given to a husband thirty years older, in payment of a debt and thus, some said, might be excused for her sin."

"I agree," said Cypros languidly.

"But if the Master had said she should not be stoned, he would speak contrary to the Law and thus give his enemies grounds to seize him."

"True," nodded Herod. "A dilemma, indeed, for the young carpenter."

"How then did he answer?" asked Joanna eagerly, for this was the first she had heard of the incident. All the sayings, all the acts of the Nazarene were to her like shining jewels to be treasured and held before the mind, so that the inner vision might delight in their beauty.

For a moment, Manaen stood silent, looking out over the water. Then he lifted his eyes, watching a feather of cloud drifting in the sky above. "He said to those gathered around: 'He that is without sin among you, let him cast the first stone.'"

Agrippa looked blank for a moment, then, slapping his knee, he roared with laughter. "By heaven, the man is a diplomat. An excellent answer!"

Cypros stared down at her pale ringed hands. "Without sin," she whispered. "No one—is without sin." She moved restlessly, and stood up, her eyes fast upon a fishing boat which had just come into view.

"Well, Manaen," said Agrippa, "no doubt he's a shrewd fellow, this Nazarene, but he is not for us. We cannot become Essenes now."

His wife lifted her head dramatically. "It was our fate to be born in the king's palace, and we know nothing but a life of authority. We cannot change now."

It was true, Joanna thought. They could not change. Luxury had weakened the will. Pride of power had deadened the spirit. Fear and ambition possessed them as, in midsummer, the arid winds of the desert possessed the land bordering Galilee. Not the smallest seed could find life-giving moisture here.

Joanna sat suddenly very still. A new thought chilled her. Did she not, in a measure, share their way of life? Nervously her fingers smoothed the fine texture of her purple robe, outlined the rich embroidery. Imported from Phoenicia, and very costly, it had been a present from her husband, Chuza. With what delight she had first beheld it! What gratitude she had lavished upon Chuza! Yea, had she not even wept tears of joy? Remembering now, she was hot with shame. For was it not but perishable cloth, woven by mortal hands? Yet, in its possession, what harm?

Cypros spoke to a slave. "Bring my octachord." She smiled graciously at Manaen. "As a farewell for you, Manaen, I shall play 'The Fall of Troy.'"

The song was one which Cypros had learned in Greece, and was played not so much for Manaen's pleasure, Joanna felt, as to divert Agrippa who sat scowling at the waves of Tiberias. Wind, suddenly risen, tore at the water and the sky, nearly clear a short time ago, was darkened with rolling clouds. Fishing boats pulled for the banks, rocked and tumbling in the pitching sea.

Cypros' long fingers plucked expertly at the stringed instrument. The plaintive tones were like articulate tears, Joanna thought, like the sobbing of an anguished world. Her throat choked, though she had often heard the song before. She looked at Cypros, wondering that she thought such melancholy music might soothe her husband and please Manaen. Cypros' head was bent with studied grace above the harp, her profile a thing of finely chiseled beauty. But her long, half-shut eyes were expressionless and no inner feeling, artistic or emotional, softened the set scarlet of her lips.

The creak of chariot wheels sounded at the gate. The tetrarch's wife looked up, but went on playing. Joanna stirred, hopeful that some visitor might put an end to Cypros' music. She found it depressing. Manaen, too, looked toward the gate.

Almost immediately, a young woman accompanied by a slave appeared.

Cypros stopped, her fingers trailing the strings. "Salome!"

She placed the octachord upon a nearby chair and went swiftly to meet her. They embraced. Agrippa nodded in surprised and genial welcome, but did not rise.

"Did you come alone?" he asked, and looked beyond her as if half-expecting to see his half-sister Herodias.

"Yea, quite alone," said Salome. She laughed and looked around at them all vivaciously. She was slim and supple in a lovely damask robe and her hair was becomingly arranged in the Greek style. At the question in Joanna's eyes, she shrugged arrogantly.

Since that night when Joanna had shut her eyes against the sight of Salome bearing John the Baptist's head to her mother, there had been friction between them. Defiantly, Salome had mocked Joanna for her weakness. "A prophet's head bleeds like any man's," she said. Her laughter was brittle and, Joanna realized, since that night, joyless. As a small child, Salome had had moments of sweetness and normal affection. As she grew older, her temper became uncertain, and her bewilderment at life's changes was cloaked in haughtiness. These last years, growing to beautiful young maidenhood, she had hardened. Recklessness brightened her brown eyes, brought frequent restless laughter to her lips. Never, for a moment, was she at rest. Even in her sleep, Joanna knew, she moved and murmured.

"Mother thought I might bring you cheer, uncle," she said, moving to Agrippa's side.

"Most considerate of my sister." Herod took Salome's small, almost boneless hand and held it caressingly. "I'm sure you will." Then, conscious of Cypros' slanting eyes, he let it go.

Salome walked, with the smooth rhythm of an accomplished dancer, to the balcony. "I had no idea Tiberias was so beautiful," she said.

"Your first visit?" asked Manaen.

She nodded. "That's one reason why, when mother suggested it, I was eager to come." She looked down at the lake, boisterous now with white-crested waves. "Is all this water fresh and good for drinking?"

Joanna knew she was thinking of the scarcity of water in Judea.

Herod boomed. "Yea—all of it."

"You may bathe seven times a day," smiled Cypros.

Salome lifted her arms, stretching her lithe young body. Her back was toward them all. She was a slightly swaying figure etched against the storm.

CHAPTER XVII

THE royal party arrived at Caesarea at noon on the day
of the quinquennial gladiatorial games. They were a smart
cavalcade as they marched into the city, flying banners
and blowing trumpets. Housetops were thick with spectators and the streets had to be cleared. As usual, Herod
Antipas and the Roman governor, Pontius Pilate, had
come in style. It was a longer procession than last time.
More color, music and pomp. Ordered ranks of foot soldiers ahead, trumpet and cymbal players and harpists following. Then slave girls, carrying baskets of flowers; girls
with jet-black skin and voluptuous forms; white maidens
with flowing streamers of vari-colored cloth; pipers blowing their odd-looking instruments; youths in white robes
and green head-garlands.

And still they came, Joanna saw, as she turned to look
back. Magnificent steeds from Arabah and Egypt ridden
by officers and officials. Camel trains. Then drawn chariots
with silver or gold mountings and more foot soldiers, and,
presently, the king's personal bodyguard and the governor's own magnificent escort and entourage.

They made a great noise, marching and shouting. The
earth rumbled under their feet. Wheels jolted in the ruts.

"Hail, the king! The king!" shrieked the crowds.

Such tribute, such display, such mummery, Joanna
thought, was what Antipas loved. Did he care that the

soldiers were weary, that the feet of slave girls burned and bled? These lovely creatures, coveted on all sides by men's eyes, were in torment, that Joanna knew. She had seen some fall in the ranks from exhaustion, only to be purposely trampled underfoot. It was part of the accepted ritual that at least a score or more of them should be run over by chariot wheels or stamped down by horses. The weaker ones never managed to survive the trip.

"Slave down!" the cry would echo back.

"Forward!" The cry was answered and a great shout of derision arose as another screaming body was blotted upon the road.

Once Joanna had been able to witness such a sight without becoming ill. Even then, it was not easy, but one schooled onself to a point of view that did much to smooth and soften the indwelling consciousness of wrong. It was that the poor slave was probably better off dead. And one kept repeating over and over, "Far better off dead." And one looked at the other slaves who had not been trampled upon. "Far better off dead." Why couldn't something happen to them, too? Life was too evil to them. Suffering could so quickly be gotten over.

Joanna turned for her first close view of the Mediterranean. Here was Caesarea, 600 stadia from Jerusalem, the seaport King Herod the Great had built to compete with Tyre and Sidon for Rome's opulent commerce. Here was Caesarea, rising in shining gray-white from the green coastal plain. More Roman than Jewish, Joanna thought, more foreign and barbaric—more unreal. It was as though she looked upon a mirage, but—a mirage only in part. The city, she could well believe, was phantom and ghostly, but the coast and sea were real, a coast and sea she could remember from her earliest childhood. In those long-ago days she used to think that the waters leaving that coast

had fallen in some unaccountable way from the spring
sky, bearing along in their descent particles of the sun also.
Who could doubt it should but proceed to its shore
and let his eyes be as ships upon its moving surface, sail-
ing through the glints on the lazy combers to the outer
interminable reaches of blue.

The Mediterranean she loved and this green, green
coast, but the city—she had a fear of it. Now as the procession entered Caesarea, she decided that she had been
foolish to feel so, and would feel so no more, for to her
heart had come the gentle ministering of the Nazarene,
and the doctrine of fearlessness, whether of men or of
cities. "Fear not," he had said.

But today, inexplicably, the fearlessness was not in her,
nor the calm to look again upon those gray-white streets
and those stark houses and the polyglot assemblage, come
from far and wide to watch the contests. Antipas and his
new queen, Herodias, would be guests this night at the
governor's palace, as would also Agrippa and Cypros, and
the king's half-brother, Philip.

Agrippa, Joanna had heard, had received an invitation
of a more pressing and personal nature than any of them,
to his uncle's great mortification. It piqued Antipas that
his profligate kinsman should have become a favorite of
the Emperor Tiberius. Pilate's wife was the Emperor's
niece and she, too, gossip said, favored him. It was she,
at any rate, who had inspired Pilate to send to Agrippa
by special messenger not only one invitation but three.
Gossip had it that the last one, a perfumed note in a lady's
handwriting, had not borne the official seal of the governor, but the more unofficial seal of the governor's lady.
Gossip said, and said it wickedly, that Cypros was a fool
if she did not sleep those nights in the palace with her
arm chained to her husband's.

These things Herodias had told Joanna, a certain look of triumph in her calculating eyes, then had added: "But I doubt if it be true. What think you?"

"I think it's preposterous!" Joanna had said, and could feel crimson on her cheeks.

Salome had come with her mother and was still warming in the glow of notoriety that had shone upon her since her infamous dance. Joanna, not wanting to, hated her and, wanting to hate Herodias, the real culprit, only succeeded in a half-torpid dislike, a sort of sleepy resentment. After meeting and hearing Jesus, Joanna tried to like both of them equally, but could not. On the journey from Jerusalem, Salome had ridden in the same chariot with her. Here she now was, sitting beside her. And feeling the old hatred anew, Joanna would whisper to herself: "Judge not lest ye be judged."

"Because of our late arrival," Salome said indolently, "the games will not commence until two o'clock. Even so, there will be scarcely time to refresh ourselves at the palace before we go to the stadium."

"Yea," said Joanna politely, "that is true."

"I would stretch my legs and bathe my face and feet," said Salome. "The dust parches my throat, and I would have some wine."

"Yea," said Joanna.

Salome half-rose from her seat. "Look! The handsome centurion. Look quickly, but covertly, Joanna."

"I see him."

"Is he not sweet?"

"His eyes are bold."

"I like bold men."

The centurion eyed them steadily. It was Man challenging Woman. Every quiver of his full lips was an unspoken word of avowed intention. His desires were written in the bronzed skin of his lean face and in the bulging knots of his magnificent shoulders. Flesh and bone and blood were visible conveyors of his deep-seated, worldly instincts. Joanna turned her head and blushed, feeling her thoughts sullied, but Salome made a face at the soldier and laughed recklessly.

"He's flirting with us," she said.

Joanna nodded, but answered nothing. They were turning into a wider thoroughfare, bordered with palms and olive trees. Ahead were the walls of the governor's palace raised flush, on this side, with the street, three rows of columns guarding the entrance to an open court. The court, like everything else about the palace, was unsmilingly formal, in spite of grass and flowers and a shining open pool. Balconies looked down upon it from three sides. Up a flight of stone steps one passed under a high-arched entrance to the reception hall of the palace, and then to the great court, imposing with its central altar and plotted grounds.

The governor himself, preceded by his own bodyguard, escorted his guests within and Joanna was glad to continue on with the ladies and their servants to the special quarters provided for them. Here, off a shaded inner court, she rested while a Nubian slave girl brought water in a large stone bowl, towels folded neatly in a wicker basket, and a silver flask of sweet cleansing oil. On a marble table were fresh fruits, a jar of fish-cakes, bread that had been kneaded into flat tiny loaves, a jug of milk and a bottle of wine.

"For madam," said the slave girl, "unless she prefers the luncheon table, spread in the inner court. It may be cooler."

"Nay, thank you," said Joanna. "I prefer this."

She wanted to be alone, she realized now, more than

she had wanted anything. Just to be alone—to be quiet! To seek that inner calm that somehow she always associated with the Master, Jesus. Certainly any sort of rest, mental or physical, had been impossible on the journey hither.

"Is madam comfortable?"

"You may fan me if you will."

What a precious servant, the little black girl! So very black and nimble and—and, yea—poised. Joanna felt a stirring of air from the long plumes of the feathered fan, but she could not hear the fan itself. The girl's too-thin arms wielded it as one who administers a ritual. There was rhythm in the movements, an up and down slow sweeping of the plumes, a graceful bending and straightening of the jet-black body—on and on, but neither tiresome nor tiring.

Joanna smiled at her. "You do well," she said.

"Thank you, madam."

"Are you happy here?"

"Yea, madam."

They heard the sound of steps. Salome came into the room wearing a daring dress and headdress of gold leaf. Her sandals were gilt, ornamented with gold buckles set with precious stones. Her hair had been so arranged that it looked like a crown upon her small head. Her whole body had been delicately sprayed with an exotic perfume that Joanna could not identify. It was suggestive, somehow, of the evening scents arising with the first dew over an oriental garden.

"What think you—is my appearance pleasing?" Salome advanced and then turned around slowly, languorously. "Philip is to be my escort. Just think—Philip!"

Before Joanna could reply, she heard the little Nubian cry out in admiration. Whether it was the perfume or the dress or the combination of both, she did not know. But the slave girl had lost her calm. She stood staring and gulping. The feathered fan had fallen across Joanna's shoulders.

"You are beautiful, Salome," Joanna said ungrudgingly.

Salome raised herself with the grace of a dancer to the points of her toes. Suddenly, she threw both arms outward and back, her lovely chin outthrust and her full young breasts swelling under their gold sheaths.

"Many thanks," her voice tinkled. "Joanna, you darling!" Her eyes grew pleading. "And you won't tell mother that I stole her perfume and appropriated some of her jewels, will you?"

Joanna laughed. "Why should I?"

Salome ran forward and gave Joanna a quick impulsive kiss. "You're a dear—so reasonable and good. I wish you liked me. Why don't you, Joanna?"

Joanna felt her cheeks grow hot. "Everyone likes you, Salome. You're—lovely."

"You're just saying that," Salome pouted. A jeweled hand moved ingratiatingly toward Joanna's shoulders, then was snatched back hurriedly. "You!" she said, choked with anger, eyes blazing at the slave girl. "Take it away— that fan, you dirty wench!"

The plumes dropped to the floor.

"Don't scold her," Joanna said gently. "She's really very nice."

The Nubian mumbled an apology, the whites of her eyes glistening. She picked up the fan and held it to her, as one might hold a shield. She was trembling, but still admiring. All at once, Joanna realized that it was the girl in her, the budding womanhood. Generations and ages of girls and women of all lands and conditions worshiping personal adornments, finding glamor in some new trinket or arrangement of dress. The way a necklace shone and comforted a bare white throat; the neat turning or cut of cloth; the draping or clinging of soft fabrics. The feel of silk upon skin, the radiance of gems—the allure of scented water, paint and powders.

The love of those things, inherent in every one of them —too powerful to be withstood. A black Nubian slave no less than a princess—than Salome.

"Sorry," Salome said, and with a great show of benevolence plucked one of the lesser ornaments from the folds of cloth at her waist and tossed it to the girl.

The little Nubian wept. She sank to her knees and groveled. Joanna turned her head so that she might not see.

"We'll be going to the stadium soon," she said, rising. "Have they arranged for our departure?"

Salome nodded. "That is what I came to tell you, actually. Everyone is ready. The governor is impatient to be off. But are you sure that I look all right?" She revolved slowly, posing and posturing.

"You're perfect," Joanna told her. They made their way to the inner court. But in her mind she still saw a black, undernourished little bundle of spindling arms and thin shanks sprawling on the floor of her chamber, clutching the shining gift Salome had flung to her.

CHAPTER XVIII

D IRECTLY in front of the royal box, a great eagle, symbol of Rome, spread its golden wings and looked down upon the grounds. Row upon row of spectators were already in their seats. The governor and his wife had entered, followed by King Herod and Herodias, then Agrippa and Cypros, then Philip and Salome. The salvos and cheers from the composite throat of the thousands there assembled echoed and re-echoed to the arena, a massive and mountainous roar.

Entering upon Chuza's arm, Joanna experienced the old feeling of not belonging here. The contests had never interested her or her husband and often it was painful to sit and pretend to like them. The crowd was gay and the sun shone obliquely across the high walls of the stadium, producing a colorful effect by highlighting the imperial banners and streaming brightly across the canopies raised over officialdom and royalty. The commoners had no protection from the glare but did not seem to mind it. They were here for quite a different reason than that of the socially elite. Not a man or woman of them was on exhibition; cared one jot what they were, how they acted or what other spectators thought about them. They, not the king, the governor, or the ladies of the court, witnessed every event and enjoyed it. What the king enjoyed was the occasion itself, the homage, the tribute he received.

And Joanna knew what made it all very exciting, if not thrilling, for the women of the court. They, too, were on parade. It would have been incredibly stupid of them not to come beautifully and exquisitely gowned or properly attended. This day was not merely a holiday, she thought wearily, it was a style show, a competition in deportment and manners, a race for social leadership. Every woman was every other woman's judge, and, if needs be, her murdering executioner. Reputations were won and lost at the gladiatorial games.

Chuza pressed Joanna's arm as he helped her be seated, smiling at her from his expressive eyes.

"It's an ordeal, but we must go through with it," his manner said. Then aloud, but not too loud: "You can shut your eyes when you see suffering or feel you're becoming ill."

Joanna inclined her head, grateful for his understanding. "Yea, Chuza."

She was thinking: "I can't look down there. I did last time, and the pictures still torture my mind. I must keep my thoughts away from the arena. I must shut my ears to the snarling of the lions and the cries of the gladiator."

Yet, against her will, she was forced to look. As she did so, the trumpet signal sounded. A blare, repeated thrice. The echoes of it seemed to swing forth and back on wires of brass. Suddenly the crowd was on its feet, screaming and cheering. Inexplicably in the center of the arena, men were lowering a caged lion from a chariot. Across from the royal box, far across the arena—as far as one's dazed senses could see—the gladiator and his attendant were emerging from the shadowed exit into the light. A Roman helmet on his head, a javelin upright in his grasp.

"Bravo! Bravo!" shrieked the crowd.

He forced a strut, as gladiators do who would be brave, whose stomach walls are tottering and whose blood goes roaring out of their heads.

"Bravo!"

Why did they cheer him? More vociferous applause would be reserved for the lion. He was the real hero. They would go frantic over him, these plebeian blood-hungry dolts, and rise en masse to thunder their joy. They loved him and wished him victory—he, the living symbol of fearlessness. For he was king by the same right as Herod. By the same law of ruthlessness he ruled.

Chuza leaned toward her. "Joanna," he said, "you're trembling."

She wouldn't look at the lion. She looked at the gladiator. He was walking very erectly, feigning coolness while the strength ran out of his fingers. With him, it was a matter of personal pride to show courage even though every muscle was being tied in quivering knots. Proceeding to the chariot, he mounted and drove over in front of the royal tier of boxes, saluted the governor, Pilate, and the king, and returned at once to the center of the arena.

Joanna shut her eyes. It was much too soon to shut them, because nothing had happened yet. The lion still crouched in its cage, growling and roaring and the gladiator was safe. Obviously he would be safe until the cage door opened. It would be his duty to open it after he had gone through the usual preliminary of strutting and posing, infuriating the lion by pricking him through the bars with his javelin. Every time the lion felt a jab of pain he would jump and bellow with fury. The cage would shake and the crowd would rise to its feet shrieking its delight. The whole stadium would be noisy at such a time. Frequently the individual shrieks of some of the spectators would rise out of the concerted tumult like the higher notes in a score of music. Women's shriller screams made a nerve-tightening complement to the tenor and bass clefs of men. One man in that great crowd of thousands always managed to hold off his own guttural yell until the combined cheering had begun to thin. The effect was weird, a lost voice trailing grotesquely along behind other voices and straining to overtake them. His efforts caught the humor of the crowd, and it would either applaud or jeer. Other spectators had brass cymbals which they sounded at unexpected moments and there were a few who rang bells attached to short sticks.

As the clamor increased, Joanna decided that it would be far more sensible to shut her ears than to shut her eyes. Everyone was trying to make more noise than his neighbor, with the exception, of course, of the gentlemen and ladies of the court, and the governor and the royal party. It was not considered polite to raise one's voice with the rabble, though applause was not prohibited. Even the king applauded occasionally.

Joanna noticed that Salome was receiving all the attention she might wish. The court ladies were envious of her, always certain evidence that one was doing very well indeed. Today she could claim the double triumph of being not only the most alluringly gowned young woman there, but the most fortunate in escorts. She sat very close to the young bachelor, Philip, and spared no effort to impress upon him her physical charms.

Chuza said, lips amused: "She's doing very well, little Salome. Breaking a few hearts, and justifying Herodias' pride in her."

"That's gossiping, Chuza. We said we wouldn't."

He patted her hand. "Sorry."

Joanna stole a look into the arena through half-closed lids. She started in her seat and caught at her husband's arm. She knew that her fingers must be hurting him, but she also knew that he probably wasn't aware of the pain, for the cage door was open and the lion had bounded out. A huge beast—massive head and thin flanks, a body long and sleek and powerful. Even from here one could count the brown stains on his tawny sides, blood-marks made by the gladiator's javelin.

"The man hasn't a chance!" Chuza exclaimed. "They say the lion is the largest ever brought to Caesarea. They've been starving him and his disposition is vile."

Free—and aware that it was free—the lion ran to one end of the arena. The gladiator, his javelin leveled, followed. The crowd, after a great burst of cheering, was silent. The moment of greatest expectancy had come. Spectators either shrank down in their seats or else half rose, faces turned irresistibly toward the coming scene of combat.

Joanna, deciding she wouldn't look, could no more resist opening her eyes from time to time than she could stop breathing. And always her gaze was there in the arena—there with the gladiator and the tawny beast crouching and slinking toward him. No attempt now on the part of the man to pose, to pretend he had no fear; nor could it be said that he seemed in haste to meet the lion as he had at first. His walk had slowed. Each step forward he begrudged, for obviously it might be his last. The shaft of the javelin was clutched in a too-tight hand, Joanna saw. The arm was visibly shaking. Perspiration poured from the gladiator's face and its salt must have stung his eyes.

"Lord God Jehovah!" cried Joanna in a stricken voice. "Save him!"

Measuring his steps against death, the gladiator went on. Ever so slowly now in stiff-legged, straight-backed tension. He should have gone with his muscles flexed. He should have gone with his hand light upon the weapon. He should have gone with alertness in his eyes. Probably, too, he should have gone swiftly and confidently for, Joanna reasoned, a lion, as no other beast, is quick to detect courage or fear and choose its course accordingly. This gladiator, who had little knowledge of such things, might have profited by the advice of those who had gone before him. But, of course, there was no one to tell him. No one, Joanna thought bitterly, cared whether he lived or died. He alone cared, and he alone had his life to lose or to save. If he killed the lion, he would be made a free man. If he did not. . . .

Joanna shut her eyes. So the rules had been made and this slave had but this one chance for freedom.

Suddenly, her eyes open involuntarily, Joanna saw the lion sprinting forward and leaping high into the air. Over the stadium sounded a quick fluttering gasp and then silence, thick and intolerable. It was as though a carpet of dust had fallen over the tiers of seats, row on row. It was choking and blinding everyone. It poured into the open mouths of the crowd, and spread aloft in a smothering cloud. Joanna could hear the sound of her hand drawn despairingly across her bosom. She could hear Chuza clank his teeth and stammer,

"G-God, he missed him!"

It was the gladiator who had missed, not the lion. The lion would go free. In Libya he would find his old haunts again and continue to be a king as he scoured the desert for deer and antelope—and sometimes men.

Chuza said: "Well, it's all over with until tomorrow. How do you feel?"

Joanna couldn't answer. The horrible sight down there, though she didn't look, she could visualize. Everybody, indeed, had expected it. It was part of the games and to certain lowly, unspeakable minds, the most thrilling part.

"They shouldn't starve the lions," Chuza muttered. "Savage enough without that."

"Please—please take me out of here," Joanna whispered hoarsely.

She hardly realized she was being led away. The crowd, still thundering approval of the spectacle, was hurrying to the exits, pushing and trampling like swine. There would be feasting and revelry this night. Pontius Pilate, Joanna knew, would give his usual banquet for his royal guests. There would be the usual ceremonies, the usual superficial speeches masking mutual hatreds, the usual drunken toasts. The usual expensive dresses, some of them worth a dozen such slaves as the unfortunate gladiator, would incite both comment and criticism. Jewels would sparkle to be admired and envied. If anything new or different were to be added—and it began to appear as though it would—Salome, daughter of Herodias, would be responsible. For everyone could see how protectingly Philip watched over her. Already it had been whispered that Salome had won her man. She had played a much better game than the poor gladiator.

Yea, Salome and the lion were both victorious.

CHAPTER XIX

THE morning after her return to Sepphoris in Galilee with Herod Antipas and his retinue, Joanna awakened with the feeling that someone had spoken her name. Yet, obviously, no one had. She was alone in her chamber. As sleep thinned, she felt no joy in the new day, nor any desire to rise from her couch. Her lids fell, shutting out the sight of the ivory bed, the fine linen coverlet, the pillars and canopy. Trappings of her life in Herod's household—symbols of pomp and restriction.

It was early. The sun was pale and young upon the high windows. Drifting into slumber, again Joanna heard—or felt—that someone called her. A voice, gentle but persistent, seeming to come as much from within as without. She sat up then. What had roused her? What strange compelling urge? The answer was very near the surface of her mind, but dreading the decision it must bring, she turned from it. Not yet. Not yet. . . .

Outside the door, she heard the running feet of a slave. Summoned, perhaps, by Herod in a vile humor for one or several reasons. A sensual night. A quarrel with Herodias, increasingly ambitious for higher place and greater power. Sleepless hours, cursing the huge sum bet on Pilate's gladiator and lost by his death to the Governor. Herodias, too, had gambled and lost, Joanna remembered. Her temper, never strongly anchored, snapped at the most trivial provocation.

Sighing, Joanna pushed her hair back from her forehead wearily. Yesterday, Chuza had warned her not to give either Antipas or his wife cause for anger. "Keep your own thoughts hid, Joanna, and speak not of controversial matters." He had looked at her gravely, his face lined with concern. "I fear you were too outspoken about the Nazarene upon your visit to Agrippa and Cypros. I heard the prince speaking of it to his half-sister during the banquet in Caesarea."

Summoning a slave, Joanna swung her feet to the floor. It was ever thus. Hide your thoughts. Keep your own counsel. Be controlled. Be careful. Be—Joanna smiled wryly—be hypocritical! Only thus might one gain and retain position and a life of luxury. For the body one did this. That it might be well-fed, well-clothed, well-cared for. That it might be shielded, indulged, caressed. That others, beholding it, might find it pleasant in appearance and give it due homage. But as for the soul, it could wait upon the leisure of the flesh.

The fingers of Azubah, the slave, were quick and skillful on Joanna's hair in which, here and there, silver threaded the dark. The odor of sweet oil which gave gloss to the coiffure was pleasant to the nostrils. Joanna watched Azubah's intent young face, the lips earnest, the soft hazel eyes anxious to please.

"Azubah," she said, "would you like to be free?"

The maiden's hand, poised to apply more ointment, began, very slightly, to tremble. Then she went on with the work.

"Free?" she said, her voice reverent upon the word. "Nay, I cannot think of it. But eight seasons have passed since I was sold into this household, and sixteen more must run their course before I may be free, according to the Law. Nay, Madame Chuza, I cannot think of it."

Joanna said no more. Her own decision was not made.

But she remembered the words of the Nazarene: "He that would be greatest among you, let him serve."

Scarcely was her toilet completed when her husband appeared. His face was apprehensive.

"We are summoned before the king," he said.

"I, too?" asked Joanna. Her eyes sought his questioningly, but he looked away.

"Best make haste," said Chuza.

Herodias, carefully groomed and perfumed, sat beside Antipas. In her face were lines of irritation. Her full red mouth was sullen. Her slanting eyes smoldered, a hundred little grievances lurking in their dusky depths. There was about her the unpredictable quality of fire which flares, dies, and, when additional fuel is added, flares again.

Next to her, Antipas was a flabby dissipated mound of flesh. His jowls quivered when he moved or spoke. The skin under his bloodshot eyes was baggy and discolored. He wet his lips frequently, his tongue lingering over places where the skin was broken and rough. Everything about Herod Antipas, except his darting eyes and hard beak of a nose, was loose. Flesh, mouth, muscles.

He stared at them without greeting, and barked: "I can no longer support Agrippa's extravagant mode of living!"

Chuza bowed. "Nay, your highness."

Antipas was annoyed, Joanna realized, because the younger prince had gambled and won a considerable amount at Caesarea, whereas he and his wife had lost. He had apparently quarreled with Herodias over the matter, for she sulked and had no word to add to his. Her fingers played restlessly with the ornate gold chain about her neck while Herod delivered a tirade upon Agrippa and his wasteful expenditures.

Chuza, the respectful steward, bowed at the proper in-

tervals, and inserted "Yeas" and "Nays" when Herod
paused for breath. This proceeding was a familiar one to
Joanna, but now, quite suddenly, it became unbearable.
Why should Chuza, just, honorable, kindly, appreciative
of the things of the spirit even as she, scrape and abase
himself before a man who, seeking control of others,
could not control himself?

Herod finished the subject and sat back, puffing. Thinking the interview over, Chuza and Joanna prepared to
take their leave. It would be good to escape to the com-
parative peace of their own apartments.

Antipas lifted a fat hand. "Remain, Chuza! I would
speak to you of another matter."

The steward bowed, his face set in wary lines.

"I want information concerning Jesus of Nazareth
who they claim is the resurrected John the Baptist."

Herodias shivered as if with chill, but the morning was
warm and Joanna knew that her own thoughts had caused
the tremor.

Chuza swallowed. "What information, your highness?"

Herod's eyes stabbed into him. "You know him, don't
you?"

Chuza inclined his head.

"I heard of him on every hand in Caesarea, and now
they say he has gone to Perea." He raised his voice and
said harshly: "How think you, will he stir up the populace as did the fanatic, John?"

Joanna's hands gripped the folds of her robe. How
would Chuza answer? How answer to please Herod and
yet defend the Master?

Before the steward could formulate a reply, Herod
thundered: "Now is the time to investigate and punish
offenders, before it is too late."

Now Herodias, whose shrewd eyes had been watching

Joanna, spoke. "Agrippa was telling us that your wife, too, has lately been fascinated by this carpenter prophet." She laughed and her laughter was as hard as her expression. "Do you not fear, Chuza, that she may become so enamored that she will leave your bed and go to his?"

Tighter, yet tighter Joanna's fingers twisting in her dress. As through a mist she was aware of Chuza's warning glance, of Herod's mocking glare, of the long fingers of Herodias upon the Roman necklace. She could not, she could not endure the implication of Herodias' words. Unclean they were, and issuing from an unclean mind. "I will speak," she thought, "I must speak, though it may mean my life and Chuza's life and even that of Kish!" Kish. It was the thought of him which stayed her. Kish, her only son, born after nine years of hoping, praying. Kish, who, about to die, had been restored by Jesus. Nay, she could not jeopardize him.

It was then she heard Jesus' voice, and it was like the voice which had that morning waked her. These words were so clear in her mind that they seemed even to possess sound.

"Return not evil for evil. If your enemy compel you to go with him one mile, go with him two. If he demand your robe, give him your cloak also. By this you will show yourselves children of your heavenly Father."

Thus, she had heard the Nazarene teach once beside the Lake of Gennesaret. Joanna was suddenly calm. The unclean might speak the name of Jesus of Nazareth, might revile him and make light of his great goodness—but nothing could soil him, nor quench the heavenly Light come down from on high. Defense—he needed none. He bore it always with him—a shield of shining and impenetrable purity.

Red spots on Herodias' high cheekbones brightened.

Her breath came short. Her hands clenched into white knobs. She jerked to her feet and came to stand before the silent Joanna.

"Do you not speak, Joanna? Do you stand before the queen and refuse an answer?"

"Nay," said Joanna quietly, "I refuse no answer, your highness. I heard no question."

"Then," said Herodias shrilly, "I will ask you one. Cypros informed me that, about the time the ranting John was—killed, you sought out Jesus and his rebels to plead for our lives. Is that true, Joanna?"

Joanna dropped her eyes. "It is true." She put forth her hand pleadingly. "I feared Heaven's wrath."

"What made you think you needed to do that? Think you we depend for our lives on such as you? Have we not swords and chariots and strong men to fight for us?" Her glance raked Joanna scornfully. "Remember, all you possess upon this earth is due to our benevolence."

Not all, Herodias. Not the important things of the spirit. Not high moments, when one remembered the sayings of Jesus and felt God very close. Not Chuza's integrity. Not Kish, nor his blessed return to health. Five years ago she might have believed that Herodias spoke the whole truth. Now she knew it was but half-truth, and that, ultimately, half-truth is no truth at all.

The voice of Herodias screamed about her ears like a desert tempest, but she no longer listened. Half-truth, ultimately, is no truth at all. That thought, recurring, led to deeper and more challenging knowledge. Half-life, then, half-devotion, was no life, no love, at all. There could be, she realized, no compromise.

Again, as she had once heard them, Jesus' words thundered in her mind. "No man can serve two masters: for either he will hate the one, and love the other; or else he will hold to the one, and despise the other. You cannot serve God and mammon."

It was past midday when, at last, Herodias' fury had spent itself, and Joanna and Chuza were permitted to withdraw.

In silence, they walked together through the courtyard and paused, as if with one accord, beside a fountain tossing silvery spray.

For a long moment, Joanna stared at the sun-made diamonds in the lacy water.

Then: "I have made my decision, Chuza." Her voice was low and steady.

He looked at her, startled.

The lines in Chuza's kindly face grew deeper. "Think well, Joanna. Consider what it will mean to you, to me—to our son."

To our son! To Kish, even now playing about the inner gardens, strong-limbed, light-hearted, swift to laughter and intelligent beyond his years. She had been married nine years before he was born. She had prayed for a child and Kish, to her, was the answer of God. When it seemed that he might die, Jesus had restored him to life. Could she now, by her own action, however right it might seem, endanger him again?

She looked at Chuza, moisture on her forehead. "I am considering, Chuza."

He said, his eyes dark and grave upon her lifted face: "Whatever the decision, Joanna, it is yours to make. I shall use no persuasion."

Tears trembled on her eyelids. "Bless you, my husband!"

It was nightfall before she came to a decision. She had known long hours of agony, of uncertainty, of fear and, finally, of exaltation.

She went to her husband. White-faced and still, he waited for her to speak.

"I want to sell everything," she said. "Our property, our expensive robes, our jewels. I want to give the money to the Master."

Chuza said nothing. She saw that he could not. He could see a lifetime's labor crumbling. He could see the existence of comfort—yea, luxury—which he had attained for his wife and heir, thrown away in a moment. It was not, she understood, an easy thing for a man to witness. Only such a man as Chuza was, fortified by the belief that the Kingdom of God was at hand, could stand silent and not lift his voice in protest.

"I should like, too, to free our slaves," said Joanna. "I have grown fearful of using people. It will be better, as Jesus has said, to be the servant."

Chuza said: "I will remain and attend to these matters." His jaw was set, rocklike. "Herod will be exceedingly angry."

Joanna knew what he was trying to say. Herod might vent his wrath upon husband and son. She trembled suddenly at a never-to-be forgotten memory. John's bloody head upon the platter. The triumph in the eyes of Herodias. Yet, surely, she could not turn back now. To do so would be to become a weakling, fleeing always from truth and reality.

Late that night she stole into the room where Kish lay sleeping. The moonlight fell in a white path across his bed, touching the dark hair to an ethereal gloss, making his face to shine.

Joanna knelt by his side. Her heart was moved in prayer for him.

Dreaming, the boy moved in his sleep and smiled. Joanna's throat ached. She wanted to throw her arms about him, to cover his hard brown cheeks with kisses, to weep . . . to pray . . . to weep. He was more precious to her than her own eyes. How could she leave him? Father in Heaven, how?

"But," she thought, "it is really for him that I go now, ahead of him to Jesus. It is to keep Kish from going the way of Salome and others reared in king's palaces that I, his mother, leave now to fashion a different life for him."

Placing her hand gently on Kish's brow so as not to waken him, she prayed softly. "God in Heaven—I pray you to guard my Kish. Even though his mother be taken from him, may he be kept from evil and wicked ways."

Her thoughts turned to Peter's simple happy household, as she had seen it on her visit to Capernaum. In comparison, power and position were worthless.

Her tears fell upon the linen coverlet. Yea, it was true. More happiness came from walking, in love and patience, the road to the Kingdom of Heaven than in sitting in high places consuming the service of others. Convinced of this, there was but one course to take. She must make a sharp cleavage between past and future. The present was a knife and she must wield it with quick strokes.

She rose to her feet, dried her tears, and tiptoed gently from her son's room.

It was still a little before daybreak. Chuza had fallen at last into troubled slumber. Joanna rose, dressed herself as a country widow, and stole from the room. How loud her footsteps sounded in the shadowed court! How the dark trees and shrubs whispered as she passed! How the fountain seemed to roar and gurgle like a waterfall!

Quietly, Joanna slipped out the palace gate. She stood, for a moment, looking back. Then, with quickening feet and an eager heart, she hurried on to the outskirts of Sepphoris where a servant joined her.

It was done. She had chosen the way.

CHAPTER XX

IN SUCCOTH, on the eastern bank of the Jordan, Joanna dismissed her servant and made her way alone to the house of Elihu, a tax collector. Jesus of Nazareth was there, the townsfolk said, and eyed her curiously.

Jesus was there! Outside the dwelling at last, Joanna paused. Strength seemed to ebb from her body, as if the ground on which her weary feet were blotted it up. Tears trembled on her lashes. What sort of tears they were she knew not—whether of joy or some strange sadness. Only that they came without her bidding.

She took a step forward—stopped. The early autumn dusk lay like a gentle caress upon the land. Sheep grazing on the shadowed hillside were blurs. Men and women, pressing past her as they went in and out of Elihu's house, were but vague shapes.

Out where she stood, it seemed to Joanna, was no substance nor reality—nay, not in the darkening streets of the little town, nor in the dwellings where candles bloomed with their evening's flame, nor yet upon the hills rimmed with the last of that day's light.

She drew a deep breath. But within—where he was—all was real. Once inside, she prayed, let the memory of Herod's sunken eyes and flabby flesh fade. Let the memory of Herodias, fury-possessed, be erased. Let the memory of Chuza, left behind to face the storm, cease its harrowing of her mind. And, dear God, let the memory of Kish innocently asleep in the moonlight, lose its power to pierce her heart with terror. Let peace come, Father, and sweet assurance of the way of Life. . . .

She went in then.

Mary Magdalene, bearing a tray of food, passed her without recognition. Joanna reached out and caught her by the sleeve.

"Mary!"

Mary Magdalene turned. She opened her lips, closed them. Her eyes went wide upon the subdued garments of widowhood.

"Joanna," she said, "is it truly you?"

Joanna smiled tremulously. "Yea, truly."

"But—Chuza?" Mary's face was concerned.

Joanna looked down at herself. Her fingers smoothed the rough unfamiliar fabric of her tunic.

"Nay, be not concerned," she said. "I left him well—and Kish, also."

Relief softened Mary Magdalene's mouth. "But—your dress?"

"I wore it to escape notice as I traveled." Joanna's eyes went past the other woman, seeking out Jesus. "I have come to be with the Master."

It was such a simple thing to say. "I have come to be with the Master." In it none of the agony and struggle which made the words possible. In it none of the love or fear or humility. As simple, that sentence, as the phrasing of the Master's parables. And, like them, as meaningful.

To Mary Magdalene, there was no need to explain further. Amazement, compassion, understanding—finally admiration in the clear brown eyes meeting hers. Joanna felt warm young arms about her, another's tears mingling with her own upon her cheeks.

"You will not regret it, Joanna," Mary Magdalene said over and over. "You will not regret it." Then: "But your courage—that is what makes me weep. You have given up so much more than I for God."

"Nay, not so!"

Mary's eyes were sweet and serious. "I gave up only sin and pain. I was glad to leave them. But you—you have denied all that the world holds most precious, pleasure, family, position and wealth."

Joanna swept the tears from her eyes with one hand, and was aware that others were gathering about her, some of the disciples, exclaiming, questioning. She heard Mary Magdalene speaking to them and was embarrassed at the fervor of her praise.

Suddenly the group quieted, as if upon the babbling mouth of a child a hand had been placed. It was that Joanna always noticed first when Jesus approached—that quietness. Vital flowing peace. She felt it now, and was reassured and comforted even before he spoke to her.

"Joanna, fear not that your sacrifice has been in vain. Fear not!"

The first sentence was one of tender encouragement. The second, Joanna realized amazedly, was command. Fear not! She felt like a child learning to walk whom someone sets upon his feet, then deserts, bidding him make his way to his father, waiting across a far formidable stretch of room. With his clear discernment, Jesus had seen in her the apprehension she felt for Chuza and the boy. A fear she could not shake. And suddenly she saw that she must rid herself of fear as one must turn from sin. Swiftly. This in itself would mean the saving of her husband and her son. Fear not! She knelt at his feet.

Jesus, looking round about at them all, placed his hand upon her shoulder.

"No one who has left house, family, property, or wealth for my sake and the gospel's, shall lack. Nay, rather he shall receive an hundredfold now, in this time, houses, family, lands—with persecutions; and in the world to come eternal life."

Fear went from her. She rose. From her bosom she brought forth her purse.

"Master—I have my husband's permission to give you this."

Judas Iscariot drew in his breath. "All that—money?"

Jesus made no move to receive it. He said gently: "It is the lesser gift, Joanna. I have already received of you the greater."

"Yea, Lord," she said humbly. "But receive this also, I pray you."

Judas, drawing close to her, thrust out his hand. "I know just the use for it, Joanna ——"

But Jesus called Simon the Zealot to him. "Simon, the night before last, there was a woman weeping in the kitchen. Where did she say her daughter had been sold?"

"I remember, Master," said Simon, "it was the wife of Jehu who has been imprisoned in Jerusalem since the insurrection. Her daughter was sold to a house in Ramoth Gilead."

"Jehu." Jesus' tone was meditative. "Jehu."

"A rough, reckless fellow," said Simon, "but kindly at heart. I knew him of old. He was with Barabbas and those others at Capernaum."

"And his daughter's name?"

"Drusilla."

Jesus looked at Joanna, his eyes deeply shining. "Mary Magdalene and Simon will go with you to Ramoth Gilead."

Behind, Judas gave a quick exclamation. Joanna was

scarcely aware of it. Tides of bewilderment and disappointment swept over her. How she had expected the money to be used, she did not know. A new and glistening robe for the Master, perhaps. A banquet for the needy. Distribution among the disciples. Furtherance of the cause in some significant way. But—instead—the wealth obtained and bestowed at such cost was to be used to free a harlot whom she, Joanna, had never seen!

Resentment clouded her eyes, choked her. Then, through it, she beheld in Jesus' face a sadness, though his lips still smiled.

"Joanna." His voice was gentle. "Know you not, that what you have done to the least, you have done to me?"

In part, she understood. She bent her head.

"When are we to start for Ramoth Gilead?"

The wind changed to the south. Huge clouds lowered in the western sky. The autumn rainy season was drawing nigh, thought Joanna. No word yet of Chuza or Kish. Yet she was, oddly, no longer worried. All was well. She clung to the thought. All was well.

It was the fourth day since she had come, with Simon the Zealot and Mary Magdalene, to Ramoth Gilead. This morning, after three days of negotiations, Jehu's daughter had been freed. Joanna looked over at her now, crouched upon the floor. Mary Magdalene sat beside her, an arm about her shoulders, her voice low and comforting. What was said, Joanna could not hear. But she could see the slow tears falling upon the fringe of Drusilla's robe. Tears that, having their source in the deep fount of bitterness and despair, could not be dried in a moment nor in a day. Not by words nor, even, by an act of compassion. Shame welled up in Joanna's heart, shame that even for a moment she had resented such a use for Herod's brittle coins.

Simon the Zealot stood at the door, his eyes watchful and expectant. They were waiting at the house of Simon the Pharisee for Jesus. As they prepared to return to Succoth, word had come that the Master was in a nearby village where Drusilla's mother lay ill. He was to come here, this evening, to be the guest of the wealthy Pharisee.

Joanna's gaze left Simon the Zealot and returned to Drusilla. How young the girl was! Younger, even, than Salome and, because of her country breeding, no doubt, seeming younger still. Under her robe her breasts were small and round. Her hips were slender as a child's. Her features, half-hidden by dark silky hair flowing nearly to her feet as she drooped upon the floor, were open and intelligent. She was growing quieter now, Joanna thought, beginning to be conscious of Mary Magdalene's compassion, beginning to realize faintly that the dark nightmare days were miraculously at end.

Joanna wanted to go to her, too. But Drusilla, learning who she was, had drawn away from her timidly. It was better, she had thought, to leave her with Mary for a bit.

"I hear the Master's voice!" Simon ran from the house and returned almost immediately with Jesus.

The Nazarene's eyes rested for a moment upon Joanna. He nodded slightly, then turned toward Drusilla. Mary Magdalene drew the girl forward with her.

"This, Master, is Drusilla, the daughter of the patriot, Jehu."

Drusilla did not lift her wet eyes to his, but slid into a little heap upon the floor.

Jesus said tenderly: "Grieve no more, Drusilla. You are free."

Her hands clasped Jesus' feet in mute gratitude.

"Your mother, too, is well again," he said.

Her great tears splattered upon his sandals. "Master—Master—I know not what to say."

Was there ever such warmth, such deep and tranquil understanding as in Jesus of Nazareth, wondered Joanna. She heard him say: "The words are in your heart, Drusilla, and behold, I hear them."

"Master! Master!" Simon the Pharisee, their host, hurried in, perspiring and panting. "I did not know you were here, until I heard. I waited for you with a carriage at the edge of town." He mopped his brow with an embroidered sleeve. "I cannot think how I could have missed you."

Jesus smiled.

Simon stood with his short legs apart. He beamed from one to the other. "I have prepared a great feast," he said, rubbing his hands, "a great feast so that everyone may meet the Master. I must hurry now. My guests will be arriving, and I must see how things are going in the kitchen!" He went out, still puffing.

Drusilla looked after him, then at the Master. In her eyes was an inexplicable emotion.

There were voices, many of them, in the street outside. Simon the Zealot came to Drusilla, and took her arm.

"Come, it is best we go to the inn. Guests are arriving for the feast, and you must not be here."

Drusilla drew back, her narrow face turned up to Jesus, her dark eyes puzzled and questioning.

He touched her shoulder. "Until later, Drusilla."

She went out, then, with his disciple. On an impulse, Joanna ran after her and pressed some money into her hand.

"Buy something you want very much with this," she whispered. "Something that will make you happy."

Drusilla's fingers closed on the coins tightly. "I will!" she said eagerly. "I will!"

Smiling, Joanna watched her go. The child would buy herself a trinket, perhaps, or a savory meal.

When all the guests had arrived, they went in to Simon's feast. A feast indeed. Tables laden with every good thing. Breads browned golden in the ovens. A yearling lamb, roasted and garnished with spices. Fig cakes, lentils, onions and leeks, and honey like thick prisoned sunshine. The finest wines in great earthen jars. Nearly as sumptuous a banquet, Joanna thought, as those of Herod.

Simon the Pharisee, hearing who she was, had placed her near Jesus. She watched the Master curiously. It was the first time she had dined with him. Was it true what they said, that he was a glutton and a wine-bibber? Nay, truly, the words were false, for though he ate well and seemed to find the food good to the taste, yet he did not eat as if the process were particularly important. He spoke to those near him, answered their questions, entered freely into conversation. Nor, to Joanna's surprise, did he always speak of the things of religion and God. Often his stories were merry little anecdotes, suited to the understanding and appreciation of his hearers. When others laughed, he joined whole-heartedly. Only when the conversation took an unpleasant or pessimistic turn, did he, gently but insistently, steer it into more wholesome channels.

Joanna was suddenly conscious of a disturbance near the door. To her astonishment, she saw that the girl, Drusilla, had entered and was approaching the Master carrying an alabaster box of ointment. She stumbled a little as she walked, for tears blurred her vision.

Joanna half-rose, to admonish her, then sat back. Nay, it was not her place to rebuke.

Drusilla knelt by Jesus' feet, and, breaking the box, poured oil upon them, mingling with it her tears. Jesus, having become aware of her, went on speaking with another guest as if he did not see.

Those at the table were stiff and tense. Whispers began. Harsh. Critical. Eyes hardened. Lips thinned. Talk died away. All stared at Jehu's daughter who, having anointed the Master's feet, now dried them with her long tresses.

Simon the Pharisee sat at the head of the table, hearing the murmuring undercurrent of disapproval, his eyes moving restlessly from one to another of his influential guests, glaring occasionally at Drusilla.

Beside Joanna, someone said: "Isn't that a woman from the harlots' house? Your prophet teacher has strange friends!"

Joanna felt herself flushing. She looked at Drusilla's face, intent, worshipful, glowing with love and repentance. Of course her appearance here was unconventional, yea— but could they not see—could they not see the transformation in her? Could they not sympathize and rejoice in it? What manner of men were these to stand in judgment?

Jesus spoke to Simon suddenly. "I would ask you a question, Simon."

Simon coughed. "Say on, Master," he said.

Jesus' glance, meeting his, was sharp and arrow-true. "If two people had debts—one, five hundred denari, and the other seven hundred and fifty, and both were forgiven, which would be more grateful?"

Simon pursed his lips, said smoothly: "Why, Master, the answer is very simple. The one who was forgiven most, of course."

"Behold this maid!" Jesus said. "When I came into your house, you gave me no water to wash my feet, but this woman washed my feet with her tears and dried them with the hairs of her head. You gave me no kiss of greeting, but this woman has not ceased to kiss my feet. You did not anoint my head with perfume, but this woman has poured oil upon my feet."

Simon cleared his throat, drew in his belly. "Well, Master, I was busy with preparations for this feast. I ——"

Jesus' voice was quiet, but in the silent room seemed loud as music. "To whom little is forgiven, the same loveth little." He turned to Drusilla who stood trembling at his feet. "Your sins are all forgiven, Drusilla. Worry no more concerning them."

The fragrance of the precious ointment lingered in the room long after Drusilla, with a light step and shining face, had taken her leave.

CHAPTER XXI

JOANNA sat on a low stool and watched Drusilla and her mother move about their evening tasks. Darkness was falling but there was no light in the little house and since there was no wood, no attempt had been made to light a fire under the kettle. Joanna had offered—yea, begged—to help with the work, but Drusilla and her mother would have nothing to do with such a suggestion. Was it not enough that she had deigned to shelter herself under their lowly roof?

Drusilla, in passing, threw her a shy smile. The change in Jehu's daughter was very evident. She had taken off the cheap brass earrings, the gaudy bracelets and clanking anklets. Once again she was wearing the plain blue frock of a country girl and her only ornament, surpassing all artificialities in Joanna's opinion, was the happiness which welled up in her dark eyes and gave lilting rhythm to every movement of her body.

Joanna and Simon the Zealot had escorted the girl to her mountain village home, one of a dozen small houses built in caves hewn in the side of a sheer cliff. When, after an arduous journey over rugged countryside, Drusilla had pointed it out from a deep valley, Joanna had gasped.

"There! Surely none but the martins could build their nests there!"

Some of the delight of homecoming had gone from the

eyes of Jehu's daughter. She answered quietly. "We live a little like the birds."

Simon the Zealot explained it to Joanna. These men, he said, lived thus through fear of enemies. They were leaders of seditions, robbers by necessity, outlaws wanted by Herod and the Romans. Joanna, thereafter, had made no comment. In silence, she had climbed with the others to the high-perched settlement. She had met Drusilla's mother, rejoicing in her healing by Jesus, the twelve-year-old brother and sister of eight who tended sheep. Dark skinned, sturdy children, more self-reliant in the manner and method of life than the queen's daughter, Salome, years their senior or—yea—even her own beloved Kish. The boy, Jotham, reminded her a little of her son and brought memories both sweet and painful. Still no word from those two her heart held dearest, Chuza and Kish. But, she reassured herself, had not a wise man said that no word was good, since bad news always traveled fleetly?

The sun had disappeared and it was so dark that faces were barely distinguishable when the two children entered the hut carrying a plain crockery jug full of goat's milk. Their mother took the burden from them, and they came to a halt beside Joanna, abashed but curious, although she had been with them now five days.

"I will fetch the firewood now, mother," said Drusilla, and tucked her dress up about her waist. She left the house, and Joanna, looking after her through the low aperture, saw her spring up the hillside with the grace and sure-footedness of a young deer.

A moment later she heard Simon the Zealot calling Drusilla's name and knew that he had gone, as was his custom, to help her gather the fuel. They returned shortly together, arms heaped with sage brush branches.

A fire soon blazed under the great caldron. Joanna

watched the light flicker upon the face of Drusilla's mother and saw both anxiety and anticipation mingling there. The reason she knew.

Only an hour ago, word had come that Jesus was on his way to the village, and that evening would be a guest in Jehu's home.

Now Drusilla's mother wrung her hands. "There is no bread!"

Drusilla's eyes clouded. "No bread for the Master?"

Joanna said quickly: "I will go and buy ——"

"Nay!" Drusilla lifted her hand in quick protest. "He shall have more and to spare. I will go and spread the news of his coming among our neighbors."

She had been gone but a few minutes when a procession began to file through the low doorway. Friends were responding. Some brought bread, some goat's meat. Others brought cakes and jugs of olive oil. Each, Joanna saw, gave of his best and faces were glowing with joy at Drusilla's news.

Drusilla's mother was tearful in her gratitude. "Yea, the prophet Elijah gave an unfailing cruse of oil to the poor widow. Surely it was something like this!"

None left without an invitation to return and dine with the Master.

Jesus was in the village three hours before he came at last to the cave house of Jehu's family. The cliff was so steep that it was difficult to carry the sick over the paths. Jesus, therefore, had gone from house to house to care for them.

Joanna had begun to believe that he would spend the entire night in ministering thus, when she heard his approach. Heard rather than saw. Voices of rejoicing villagers made a great happy symphony as they followed Jesus to the little hut.

"Quickly now!" said Drusilla's mother. "Light the candles, Drusilla. He comes!" She hurried about the room bearing food, rearranging the few pieces of furniture, calling orders to the scurrying children.

Joanna sat quietly in the corner, her hands clasped. Jesus was coming. Peace was coming. Life, an endless river, warm as sunshine, refreshing as air on a mountain top. In a moment she would see her beloved Master, stooping as he must to come through the low entrance, then straightening to his full vigorous height, candlelight and firelight gathering in his hair.

But when Jesus came, she felt more than saw him. How he looked was less evident than what he was. Others crowded into the house behind, so that bodies pressed close, but yet, oddly enough, there was no feeling of friction or irritation. Jesus had brought spaciousness with him into the humble dwelling of Jehu's family. Each found his place easily. Drusilla's mother lost her fretful anxiety and grew calmer. Drusilla herself moved in and out among the invited guests, unobtrusive as a mountain breeze.

More than twenty villagers had come to the feast. Eyes looked hungrily at the food which Drusilla and her mother passed to each in turn. Bread and meat were snatched in unwashed hands, and gulped down noisily. A little new wine which someone had brought in a new goat skin was hailed as a rare treat. Water, whispered Simon the Zealot sitting beside Joanna, was scarce in that steep village of cliff dwellers. As for wine—he spread his thin hands expressively.

All sat upon the floor in a circle around the Master. Joanna, listening with interest to their talk, learned that every man over forty years of age had either had a part in the sedition incited by Juda, son of Hezekiah, or in the revolution fostered by Simon who called himself the King of Judah.

"But," said a strong-looking sun-tanned man, chewing as he spoke, "Simon the Zealot here has been telling us of the Kingdom of God. He says we must repent and believe the gospel." He took a swallow of wine, smacking his lips: "Now what think you, Master, could heaven come to this place which is fit only for martins?"

There was laughter, the full unrestrained laughter of the child-like. When it had quieted, Jesus spoke: "Deny yourselves. Think first of those around you, and their needs. Only thus can you become conscious of the true Life. Be kind and considerate, even as your heavenly Father who sends rain upon the just and the unjust. Then be assured you will find your own needs supplied." He looked about at them all, smiling gently. "Verily the Kingdom of God is within you. It is here now."

Drusilla's mother said chokingly: "Heaven has come to our poor house. Behold, my daughter freed from her hateful bondage, and myself well and strong once more!"

"And more than that," put in Drusilla in a shy, yet ardent voice, "the son of David has come to us, is even now supping wine in this dwelling. Yea, truly, this is heaven!"

A bald-headed old man, whose countenance was grooved deep by the chisel of time, said gruffly: "It is just as the prophet says. Juda ordered us to steal—but that is the part of dishonesty."

Jesus, sitting tailor fashion on the coarse goatskin rug that covered the earthen floor of the cave, looked out at the stars in the southern sky, and said nothing.

Little by little silence passed like an unseen cup of wine from one to the other about the circle. Joanna, hearing a cough and sudden movement on her right, looked up to see that the man who had first spoken of the Kingdom had risen awkwardly. He stood before Jesus, his cheeks slightly red. His head was bowed and his eyes glistened with tears beginning to drop. The sight moved her oddly. Such a great strong fellow he was, rough-hewn of form and face, hands twice the size of the average man's—yet now he wept like a repentant child.

"I have done ill most of my life, Master. I have been in prison often for theft, robbery and—yea, I will admit it—murder. I thought myself justified. Can a man give back to life more than life has given him? We have so little here —or had, until you came." He lifted his head, unashamed of the shaking of his lips or the tears which caught the candlelight as they fell to the matted rug. "But now, since your coming, I feel—I feel that I have been born again. I would be your disciple, Master. I, too, Jose, son of Asa, would become an heir to heaven."

It was a long speech, slowly spoken and with great effort. Joanna could see by the man's struggle to express himself that words did not come easily to him—words of deep meaning and emotion. How different from the oily flow of pretty phrases in the household of Herod!

His friends, hearing his moving words, set down their wine cups, and Joanna saw that in their eyes, too, tears were gathering. Her own throat choked in sympathy. Truly, the coming of the Nazarene was making their desert life to blossom as a rose!

Jose was not yet finished. It was as if a powerful mountain stream, long dammed, had been released at last.

"Master, we are gathered here in the home of Jehu, who now lies imprisoned in the tower of Antonia in Jerusalem. With your great power, you could save him, so that he, too, might rejoice in the advent of the Kingdom of Heaven."

Joanna, watching Jesus, saw his eyes close. He did not

move nor speak, but seemed to have retired to some other
world whither they could not follow.

Jose went on. "If with your aid, he is saved, I swear to
you that we will sacrifice everything. Master, rescue Jehu!
In exchange for that, our band will promise to avenge the
slightest harm that may come to you. We care not whether
it be the Roman government, or Herod, the Pharisees, or
the followers of Annas who are congregated in the temple
at Jerusalem."

Gone was the humble Jose of a moment ago. He stood
now, great legs spread, feet as if rooted heavily to the
ground. Muscles rippled like silk in his flexing arms.
Sinews of his thighs bulged glistening in the flickering
firelight. He looked—Joanna gasped—he looked like the
brother of Barabbas himself!

"Master!" Jose raised his voice. "I pray you, save our
leader, Jehu! I tell you he is in danger of the cross!"

Joanna saw the sweet mouth of Drusilla twist suddenly.
From behind, Jehu's wife uttered a strangled cry.

"Not the cross for my Jehu, Master! Ah, who could
bear the agony and shame of it?"

A breeze, strong and cutting as a spear, blew in from
the south window, and the lights of the few candles bent
and swayed, so that shadows darted eerily upon the walls,
and made dark patterns on faces.

Only upon the face of Jesus of Nazareth, no darkness
was. Starlight fell upon it, as he opened his eyes and
spoke quietly to Drusilla and her mother.

"Fear not. I tell you, the feet of Jehu, even now, are
set upon the narrow way which leads to the Kingdom of
God."

BOOK FOUR

WITH WHAT MEASURE YE METE . . .

CHAPTER XXII

CAIAPHAS' bare feet padded over the tiled floor to the balcony entrance. There they paused while he, the high priest, loosened his girdle and let his cassock fall more freely about him. Under the colored awning he had a view of the street to the gate called Beautiful. All the fretting business of the morning was over, the chants, the sacrifices, the prayers, the conferences. For a few moments he would be alone. Here on this balcony he had given orders not to be disturbed. He would try to rest. The closeness of the inner room had chafed him and his thoughts.

He, Caiaphas, high priest and chosen of God, wanting little of men except obedience and service in the true Faith, had need of quiet and composure of mind. This must not be denied him, especially today when he would seek divine guidance in a matter that could no longer be put off.

It was a pressing and irritating matter, this case of the Nazarene, Jesus. Nights he had lain awake, days he had been disturbed. Patience had been his in the face of the most exasperating acts of that blasphemous pretender. Evidence growing had proved the guilt of the man, yet he had been lenient. In quiet he had watched the ambitious attempt to wrest authority from the priests, discredit the sacred ministry, abolish the ceremonies and seals of high office of the Church without doing more than trust that the various overt acts and conspiracies of this common carpenter, Jesus, would become entwining lines to trip his feet.

How patient indeed he had been, listening in silence to the murmurs come up from Galilee of a mad man who claimed kinship with God, who was, he said, himself a god, one with the Father.

Caiaphas strode out upon the balcony and sat down. More temperate here but not cool. It was the hour when the sun, at its zenith, tore off its veil to show its burning face. It was the hour when the street languished and breathed dust; when the glare polished all the stones and bricks on the façades of the houses. Not, by any means, the best time to be out on a balcony, but the only time today when he could be alone.

One had need for solitude these days. He had marked the change coming years ago. A strange unrest growing as a garden with weeds, sprouting through the soil of unbelief—oh, wayward people of Israel! New gods for Jehovah, the divine and unconquerable Spirit, were taking the thoughts of the chosen. The established orders and ceremonies of the Church were being neglected for the rantings of the soothsayers and the teaching of the mystics. Even the more devout had grown lax in offering up prayers and sacrifices to God. But of all the harmful influences today, there was none more devastating than the preachments and so-called miracle-workings of him who daringly called himself the Christ, the Son of God come to redeem and save man.

His dastardly presumption and bigotry were without precedent in this or any other generation. He, of plebeian stock—an uneducated, unmannered fellow, more to be found in the company of peasants and fishermen than intelligent men—had proclaimed himself the Messiah. Son of a lowly Galilean builder—a god! Ridiculous indeed, but the rabble believed him. And by tricks of healing and dexterous magic, he had convinced them.

Caiaphas scowled and blinked down upon the almost empty street. A fish stall had several customers. In the shade of a high wall, a street hawker drowsed among his wares, head reclining upon bare, skinny knees. Even at this distance one could see his skin glistening with perspiration. Flies buzzed everywhere, the only active things in this heat. Torpor and stupor were both here, lying upon the same slumberous couch, Caiaphas thought, and would not awaken for another hour.

Again his mind reverted to the pretender, the man Jesus. His rise had been phenomenal, one had to admit. This was due to his shrewd understanding of the crowd and his knowledge of the tricks of the magi and the black art of street fakirs. By sleight-of-hand he could produce money from the smelly clothes of a mendicant. Roses could be made to bloom in the air simply by mutterings and exhortations. Paupers could become happy over the recital of some fortune awaiting them in the stars. Lepers could be deluded into believing that their stinking sores were healed. The blind, who would never see again, were excited to behold within the confines of their heads and staring eye-sockets the illusion of reality.

Yea, he was clever, this Jesus. He turned water into wine, it was said, and walked upon the sea with dry-shod feet. And now had come the incredible report that a man, Lazarus of Bethany, dead for four days, had been made to breathe again—to live, free of all his former ills.

It was this—this last preposterous deception that had brought matters to a head. Caiaphas remembered how, when the news had first come, he had dismissed it forthwith, for rumors were flying everywhere. Indeed, the most amazing stories had grown through the process of retelling, each repetition adding something until, when last told, one heard the lies and distortions of perhaps an hundred persons.

The damaging effect of it all was that people were credulous. They believed what they wanted to believe. No one knew this better than the pretender. He never repudiated or denied anything that would cast glamour over him or add to his reputation as a mystic. In the case of Lazarus he had gone even further, boasting: "He was dead and I raised him up. He was gone and now he has returned among you—and lives. Glory to our Father in heaven."

Caiaphas felt something more than heat tingling in his fingers at the memory of that flaunting blasphemy. He looked off toward the gate Beautiful and it seemed to him that in the pulsing air it was moving—dancing lewdly and mockingly. Down in the street, the sleeper slept, the flies buzzed and the stones glistened. Above him, the canopy was slack in the stillness, drooping through its frame. As he breathed, Caiaphas detected a burnt odor like that from the sacrificial altars. From habit, he glanced down at his hands, forgetting that they had been washed. The diffused light through the canopy, mingling with the refracted glare coming under it, put upon him a brownish stain as of dried blood and involuntarily he shrank back, feeling the repugnance he sometimes felt, despite long habit, in the slaughtering pens. Angrily he smoothed out his cassock, aware that the constant nagging of his thoughts about the pretender had made him nervous and emotionally unstrung. The alleged raising of Lazarus had thrown down a challenge which must be met else he, of the Sadducees, of the sacred order of priesthood, chair-

man of the Sanhedrin, could not bare his face nor raise
his heart to Almighty God.

Caiaphas fanned himself with one hand until his arm
tired, then with the other. He still looked down into the
street, but the glistening light on the walls of the house
fronts was no longer a conscious impression, nor was he
aware of the sleeper, nor could he see the quiverings of
the intensely hot air thrown off the paving stones. The
range of his sight had not lessened as he looked, but it
could not register in a brain inwardly seeing, going back
over the long journey of events that had to do with the
false Christ. Always in his thinking he reverted to begin-
nings and basic causes, and it was his habit to be orderly
and logical. Often he acknowledged this to himself, especially his faculty of retiring from the world without to
the mind within. Indeed he could so live in his mind as to
be unaware of all outer sensatory impressions. In the temple of his thoughts he could feel, see and hear again what
had happened even years before. No detail was ever lost.
He had a prodigious memory. He could journey within
it, not as one going aimlessly hither and yon, but as a purposeful traveler to a definite objective.

Caiaphas opened his eyes inwardly and looked out over
the great "Hall of Hewn Stones." The Sanhedrin had
assembled in good order and its members were now
seated, each behind his desk in that sacred semi-circle. The
Sadducees at his right were grave and silent, and the
Pharisees at his left had the appearance of piety and
decorum, though there was some whispering among them.
Caiaphas counted the places not occupied and drew his
hand through his beard, then slowly composed himself for
prayer.

He began the meeting with a benediction which he
chanted more loudly than usual, more sonorously, for he

thought: "I will impress upon them the significance of this day and decision to be made here. We will exalt the Lord. My voice will be both a sounding board and a trumpet to praise the Most High."

There were ten empty seats and Caiaphas glared at them as he chanted. Joseph of Arimathea was away. The Pharisee scholar, Gamaliel, was also absent. Seventy-one members of that august and holy body should have been present, but today there were only sixty-one. He wished he could remember who were the eight not accounted for. The two he could account for, Joseph and Gamaliel, he suddenly despised, feeling the cold, clear flame of his hate inwardly burning. For here was a responsibility they had brazenly ignored. Gamaliel, especially, had, by his absence, shown a most amazing and intolerable disregard for the dignity of his position. It was quite obvious that he had stayed away because he secretly admired the Nazarene and would have no part in pressing charges against him. A weakling was Gamaliel in this respect—an example of the bad influences of the times, dabbler in unorthodox theologies and preposterous credos. He posed as a scholar and an advanced thinker. He consorted with dabblers in art and silly poets and muddle-headed fools. It was said that he often quoted the carpenter from Nazareth, declaring that the man had literary qualities quite apart from his somewhat irrational views on religious doctrine. If he kept on, Gamaliel would be forced to renounce his orders and suffer public disgrace. How unlike he was to Benezra of the long thin face who would no more split hairs with upstart theologists than he would attempt to desecrate the temple. He was here now, one could depend on that. And so was Nicodemus.

The benediction ceased. Caiaphas, in the silence which

followed, sat down. He whispered to Malchus, his scribe: "Make a list of the absent ones."

"Yea, your Holiness."

Malchus' bald head was pink on top like a baby's and his eyes were two round wells of interrogation. He began scribbling.

"You might also make a note of the fact that tomorrow at the conference hour I would speak privately to Gamaliel. Have him summoned."

In a moment more he, Caiaphas, would rise and speak. But, strangely, he felt in no mood for it. He would have preferred his couch and a bottle of wine. He could sleep from sheer weariness. He could sleep if he were not so angry. He could sleep if the Nazarene would let him. If he could forget the man's insolence, that is. All the maddening slights and petty taunts and subtle conspiracies had combined to mock him. But soon, very soon, there would be retribution and God, declaring himself through his most high and holy servant, would be avenged.

CHAPTER XXIII

CAIAPHAS cleared his throat. He had a way of clearing his throat that was portentous. A gruff, rumbling sound, silence and then—every movement deliberate and timed—a slow rising to his full broad height with the consciousness in him of a God-given self-mastery. He, Caiaphas, high priest of Judea. He was proud of his strength, for it was both mental and physical, and, whether one was considered or the other, it was impressive. And, too, he was proud, justly, of his high office. He was proud of the quick dispatch of his duties. He was proud of his body, envied by men and loved by women—for that body was the symbol of his greatness. On the sacrificial altar it was not uncommon for him to seize a bullock by its horns and, unaided, send it crashing and struggling to the floor while the suppliant stood gaping admiringly.

Now he said in a clear voice that rang back against the wall: "You all know the purpose of this meeting. You have come to bear witness against one whose words and deeds are blasphemy against the Most High, the carpenter, Jesus of Nazareth."

He paused, purposely waiting for them. He wanted their assent, their acknowledgment of his statement. He wanted to hear their vigorous "yeas" beating up against the front wall as his own words had beat against the back. Yet of all that group, three score and one, sitting there with their faces square in his eyes, lids blinking and features expressionless, only one voice, that of Benezra, sounded through the hall. It did not "yea," it snarled—while a black frown and thin lips grew blacker and thinner, and on the table's edge, fingers crooked in a spasm of rage. So typical of Benezra to conceal nothing, never to wear a mask of indifference as did so many of the others. He was more frank than they, more basic and fundamental. Although Caiaphas did not altogether approve of him, he admired his honesty.

Caiaphas went on: "Members of the Sanhedrin, we have met here to consider the activities of the Nazarene, in Galilee and in Judea. A most unruly person, a revolutionist connected with Barabbas and his group who were recently captured by the Romans and cast into prison."

"A political offender," someone said. "Let the governor attend to him."

Benezra leaped to his feet, raging. His small eyes were like two shining black stones in the puckers of his face.

"I object!" he shouted, appealing to Caiaphas. Then he turned, fuming, to the one who had spoken, a Pharisee named Achim, a docile-looking little man who sat with his huge paunch almost resting on his knees. Benezra shook his fist at him.

"You're too evasive for me, curse you. You're gilding this thing over—trying to protect that bastard—that's what you are!"

"Bastard?" The other man was calm. "You have no reason to say that, nor to call me evasive. Nor for using such language in this hall."

Benezra's hands were flung out in front of him. On each, the fingers were coiled so that the nails showed like an eagle's talons. For a moment, Caiaphas had the strange impression that Benezra was really an eagle. He could see him soaring aloft, preparing to swoop down upon Achim, the fat lamb. So strong was his imagination that he could see them both ascend, Achim struggling and bleating, and Benezra croaking his victory through a hard curved beak.

Benezra shrieked: "I said bastard and I say it again— and again! Joseph was not his father and admitted it. The mother, Mary, was not impregnated in this case by her husband, and she admits it. Are you, fool, credulous enough to believe that the conception was by divine spirit?"

A roar of laughter rose from the assembly. Caiaphas rubbed his hands together and smiled at his scribe who was busy taking notes. When the commotion was over, Achim said in a choked voice:

"What of the prophecy?"

Benezra glared. "Think you for one moment that such as he could fulfill the holy prophecy?"

"It is possible," Achim said firmly. "It is even very probable."

From the right where the Sadducees sat, Eleazar, the high priest's brother-in-law, arose. He was the younger brother of Caiaphas' wife and had served as high priest for about a year prior to Caiaphas' predecessor. He spoke now as a representative of Annas, his father. He, too, stared angrily at the fat little Pharisee, Achim. Caiaphas, himself, was stirred to arise as well, but decided against it for the moment. Everything was going very well, he thought, better than he had expected—ah! Very much better than he had expected.

Eleazar had a thin long face but a short thick voice that grew huskier and more abrupt the longer he spoke. And he spoke, as champion of Benezra's cause, for a half hour, thumping the table and barking. When, finally, he sat down, there was no one who knew exactly what he had said, or could have quoted him. Yet the implication of all he had said was a brand burning upon Achim's bared head. Immediately, Benezra went on with it, as though a single mind spoke through two separate throats.

"Resign!" he thundered. "I appeal to this assembly. I appeal to every right-thinking person here. To hold Achim's views is to be a traitor to Israel and to the Lord God. I say death to the false prophet. I say death to any common man who asks us to believe that he was conceived by spirit, is one with God and has the power even to raise the dead."

"He raised Lazarus," Achim said.

"A lie! A lie on the face of it. The man was only in a trance. Or else it was a cheap trick in which both Lazarus and Jesus connived."

The time had come, Caiaphas perceived, to take full charge, to throw into the scale the weight of his superior knowledge. Benezra had done very well for the cause of God and the holy priesthood, but he lacked experience and poise. His rough speech and wild bursts of anger did not always have the effect he hoped for. Often he antagonized members of the Sanhedrin quite unintentionally by profane words and indelicate reference to matters more or less sacred. Just now, however, he had made a sharp point upon which to impale the story of the raising of Lazarus by the so-called miracle-worker, Jesus.

Caiaphas rose amidst a heavy silence. Every face turned toward him and everyone there, he felt, secretly breathed relief that he was upon his feet at last to guide and dominate the gathering. Benezra, the only possible exception, sat down as swiftly as he had leaped erect, almost shattering the chair under him.

"Devoted members of this exalted assembly," Caiaphas said, "it is God's desire that you hear from me the true facts of this Lazarus story. One of our colleagues has just told you that he believes that Lazarus was actually raised from the dead, and another, who has just spoken, holds a contrary view."

"That I do!" roared Benezra.

Caiaphas frowned slightly at the interruption. And while he was frowning, his gaze upon Benezra, Achim slid timidly off his chair.

"Your Holiness," he said, "it is quite apparent that nothing that I can say will be given consideration by anyone here. I had hoped otherwise. I had hoped that Joseph of Arimathea would attend this meeting, or Gamaliel the renowned scholar, but they are both absent today. However, I understood that this was to be a free and open-minded discussion. I had—er—thought ——"

"Sit down! Sit down!" Voices shouted all around him.

"Sit down," said Caiaphas.

Achim did not sit down. He stood, blinking stubbornly. The meeting was getting out of hand. For a moment, Caiaphas felt a black, towering rage rising in him as it had risen in Benezra and Eleazar. Then, as suddenly, he relaxed, for a form was creeping up behind Achim, making a moving shadow across the floor. Caiaphas, alert now to the possibilities of the moment, smiled and half-glanced at his scribe, Malchus. Malchus wrote upon his parchment with nimble strokes while he bowed his head so low that no one else could have seen, much less read, anything he wrote. Malchus' eyes were moist from weakness, and now and again wet drops fell spattering upon his handiwork.

The moving shadow was near Achim's table. The fat little Pharisee turned, fright distorting his face. He saw Benezra and Benezra's raised arm, and the stares of the startled assembly. He saw a knife glinting in the light from a high-up window.

He was quite dead even before he fell crashing against the chair and then prone upon the mosaic pattern of colored stones. The knife, Caiaphas observed with a start, had not descended. Benezra's arm had not fallen. He swallowed his relief and licked his lips, murmuring a prayer of thanksgiving to God for His consideration. It could not now be said that within the holy confines of that chamber a blow of death had been dealt by one member upon another. Truly his holy reign as high priest was well-favored by the Most High.

"Take him out," said Caiaphas, amazed at his own calmness, "and the meeting will go on."

Benezra walked back to his own place again, strangely puzzled, but hot and shaken.

"He fell before I had a chance," he mumbled to Eleazar, and he sat down, his face twitching and his limbs trembling as with the ague.

Eleazar stood up, and his husky voice broke the frozen quiet of the hall.

"It is the judgment of the Most High," he rasped. "He was a traitor to the Almighty and, as such, could expect only what came to him—God's sudden and righteous fury."

Jehoiada, chief of the temple guards, intoned: "Yea, the judgment was upon him. So death to all such traitors!"

"And death to this Jesus of Nazareth!" yelled a Pharisee.

"Nay!" Nicodemus stood up suddenly. "I object. Let us not make such a decision without due deliberation. I suggest——"

"Death to the Nazarene!" chanted three Sadducees in unison.

The face of Nicodemus was determined. "I suggest further investigations, inquiry without bias and calm judgment. I beg of you——"

"Death to the Nazarene! Death to the carpenter-magician!" Voices drowned his. Eyes glinted hate. Andronicus, usually a supporter of Nicodemus, arose uneasily and made an excuse to withdraw. Caiaphas inclined his head benignly. Now, he reflected with triumph, only Nicodemus remained, of all that august body, to defend the false prophet. And what was one voice among nearly three-score?

Nicodemus was looking after his friend, his face swept alternately with bitterness and sorrow. The assembly rose now as one man.

"Death to him who would upset the tables of our money changers. Death to him who would blaspheme our God, who brazenly declares he would destroy the holy temple. Death—death—death to the Nazarene!"

No longer was there any need, Caiaphas perceived, for a mere human discussion of a matter that had already been settled by a Tribunal higher than their own. Raising his arms for the benediction, he gave it while tears of thankfulness streamed from his eyes and, like Malchus' wet drops, fell from him unheeded. He saw Nicodemus, refusing to participate in the voting, stride angrily from the great Hall of Hewn Stones. In his mind, he saw already the black-lettered proclamations posted in towns and villages near and far. He saw the words, soothing to his eyes as the delights of women: "A reward of thirty pieces of silver will be paid the person who first reports to the high priest, Caiaphas, the whereabouts of Jesus of Nazareth."

Near the center of the room, Benezra covertly returned the knife he had borrowed from Eleazar and, turning, the two walked from the assembly, arm-in-arm.

CHAPTER XXIV

THE meeting of the Sanhedrin was over. Caiaphas, dressed for the street, directed his steps toward home. It was nearing the evening hour. Jerusalem had thrown off the torpor of another day. Air now flowed in cooler currents through the narrow valleys between broken rows of houses and over the clustered rooftops in the humbler sections of the town. Children had left shadowed walls for the more open lanes and alleys to play before-supper games. They even came streaming out upon the more frequented thoroughfares, whooping and shouting, much to Caiaphas' annoyance. For they were always getting under his feet, or brushing against his clean robes. Among them were street urchins wearing saucy caps over hair matted in hopeless disorder, thin dark faces streaked with grime and little hands scaly from lack of attention. From every passerby they begged alms and, being refused, shouted insults.

"May your fat carcass boil in oil," one of them said to Caiaphas, and spat contemptuously upon the ground. "Holy priest, your father was a pig."

Caiaphas struck at him, but the child leaped back to safety and stuck out his tongue.

"You can't catch me," the urchin taunted. "Your legs are like columns, your feet are heavier than building stones."

"Begone!" Caiaphas snarled. He regretted now that he had dismissed the guards whose duty it was to protect his holy person from such incidents. He was tempted to retrace his steps, but would not permit himself the indignity of retreat.

The child stood his ground, while he pulled at a greasy forelock and screwed his mouth into a contemptuous pucker.

"Your bosom rattles with gold, yet you refuse me one mite. Down on the next corner from here, a leper named Jonas sits in a niche in the wall nursing his many sores. But he's a better man than you. He has little, yet he gives me bread. You have much but give me nothing."

Caiaphas flung a coin at him and went on in a rage, thinking about the leper and this child the leper had fed —both social outcasts, unworthy of the life that sprouted in them. They were better off dead and the world better off without them. The governor would do well to drive beggars from the city. Of late they had increased at such a rate that no man could walk a house-length even in broad day without finding his progress barred by mendicants of every age and nationality. Often they walked together in packs like wild dogs. They would seize upon a stranger and literally wrest from him his purse and divide it among them. Such division was achieved only after many struggles and blows. He had seen as many as eight or ten of them diving into the dirt of a roadway for a single copper. They begged by day and robbed by night. Always, at any hour, they could be seen slinking from doorway to doorway or popping out unexpectedly from alleys whining that they suffered from hunger, or perhaps drawing attention to their stinking rags or numerous infirmities.

They were halt and lame and blind; legless, armless

men, women and children; rogues, fools, idiots—and these were the motley class who made up the following of the man, Jesus. Of such materials he would build a new kingdom upon earth, teaching them his impossible doctrine of social equality, the while claiming his kinship with Almighty God!

Caiaphas smiled sourly at that, and proceeded on his way. He thought again of the meeting of the Sanhedrin and rubbed his hands together in satisfaction. Soon, very soon, the pretender would be arrested. Sufficient pressure put upon Pilate would be certain to bring results. The Pharisees, and Sadducees, the publicans, the merchant class, the traders and buyers, the military, the courtiers and even Herod, the king, were all united in their desire to see him, the elusive Nazarene, in the dungeon of Antonia or, better still, executed.

Tonight Jonathan, his own brother-in-law, youngest son of Annas, would bring a full report from Galilee of the origin and activities of the mad carpenter. He had gone to investigate rumors concerning him that had come to the city by devious routes. He had said before departing that he would soon learn the truth by mingling with Jesus' followers. He wanted to secure first-hand the evidence that would surely condemn him. For he, Jonathan, devout member of a religious family of much consequence, would not be tricked by the man's pretenses. Seeing through all the shallow artifices and devices he used to impress the ignorant would be easy for him. He would have, and Jonathan had laughed in saying it, an interesting tale to tell them.

Caiaphas smiled as he turned from the street to the cool enclosure of his garden, and then up a low flight of steps to the hall leading to the inner court. The breath of flowers agreeably stirred his nostrils. Behind him sounded the splashing of a fountain and the noise of the gardener's shears clipping the grass. Within, there was the quiet of a household ordered for the special comfort and peace of mind of himself, his family and his guests. No clattering and confusion was ever permitted here, a decree he had himself laid down. Servants went barefoot about their tasks, careful never to bump or crash into things; learned to cook over charcoal fires without unnecessary sounds; communicated together without talking, or, if forced to speak, did so in undertone or in guarded whispers.

On the balcony, Caiaphas found his young brother-in-law. Jonathan was alone there, wrapped in the deepening shadows. At the sound of Caiaphas' heavy steps, he turned as if startled, but gave no word of greeting.

Caiaphas rubbed his hands. "Well, Jonathan, you are returned at last."

"I am returned."

The high priest settled himself comfortably in a chair, stretching his legs and smoothing his cassock. Below him were the flickering lights of Jerusalem. He liked to sit here upon his balcony at night, looking down upon the holy city whose spiritual welfare the Lord God had given into his care. Above him, growing brighter in the darkening sky, were the eternal stars of heaven. He expelled a long breath. The day had been one of satisfaction and accomplishment. Aside from the unfortunate incident of the mild Achim—which had eventually helped rather than hindered his cause—all had transpired according to his pleasure. Already the proclamations announcing the reward for the capture of Jesus were being readied for the posting, and in a day or so the arrogant fellow would be harried from town to town.

Now, Caiaphas felt, he needed only one thing to complete his contentment. Jonathan's report. Jonathan's confirmation of his own deep-rooted convictions.

He said now, with a touch of impatience: "Let us have it—the whole story. You have no doubt many things to tell concerning the Nazarene."

"Many things," said Jonathan. "But first I will ask you a question."

"Ask, then," smiled Caiaphas. There was a cool breeze, sprung up at sunset, against his face. Tonight he would dine sumptuously with friends and relatives who held him in esteem. He would eat and drink. He would listen to soothing music. He would, finally, retire to the softness of his bed. He frowned slightly. Rachel, his wife, was growing older and the warmth he felt to be the proper tribute to his manhood was lacking in her of late. Yet, in marrying her he had made a good alliance, and the children she had borne him were well-built and ruddy. He was, withal, fortunate. He would make no complaint.

"Why," asked Jonathan, his voice oddly unsteady, "did you not wait for my report before you brought up the matter of the Nazarene before the Sanhedrin? So it was agreed."

Caiaphas stared. "Do you question my authority?"

"Nay, yet I——"

"The time was ripe for a decision. You were too long at your investigations." Caiaphas allowed himself a bit of humor. "I had begun, indeed, to think that you had renounced your vows and become a follower of the carpenter."

Jonathan said nothing.

"Besides, the members of the Sanhedrin were of one mind, or nearly so, in condemning the heresy of the Nazarene. What, actually, could you have added to the weight of evidence against him?"

"Against him? Nothing."

Jonathan came to stand before Caiaphas, the high shape of him towering against the star-sprinkled sky. The priest was startled and drew in his legs, scowling.

"What do you mean?"

"I mean you must stop your persecution of Jesus."

There was a sudden roaring in Caiaphas' ears, a dryness in his throat. What nonsense was this? If this were a jest —yet Jonathan had always been a serious young man, little given to merriment. . . .

"You must take down those proclamations. You must persuade the Sanhedrin to reverse the decision. Jesus is a good man—a teacher of great and holy wisdom."

Caiaphas stood up. The great carved chair, unbalanced, crashed upon the tiling.

"What foolishness is this? What mad babbling?"

Tall as Jonathan was, the high priest over-reached him by a hand's span and he was by far the stronger. Nevertheless Jonathan did not move away.

"I tell you the truth. From what I have learned, this man Jesus may well be the Son of God as he claims—the Messiah!"

Such a rage gripped Caiaphas that he wanted to seize his brother-in-law by the throat, to throw him as he would a young bullock, to drive him back, back over the balcony until he hurtled to the black street below. He felt now as he knew Benezra must have, faced by the insubordination of Achim—Achim so gently, maddeningly stubborn. Caiaphas, his whole frame shaken by his intense fury, became aware that his own powerful fingers were stiffly curved like talons, and that his voice, completely out of control, was crying out shrill denunciations.

Jonathan was calling out, too, pleading, petitioning for the high priest's ear. "Only let me tell you what I have heard—what I have seen. Do you condemn me without a reasonable hearing, my brother-in-law?"

Little by little, anger ebbed from Caiaphas—not entirely, but enough so that the tenseness left his muscles and he regained mastery of his speech.

"Very well," he said hoarsely, "I will hear your account."

There were steps behind him, heavy breathing and the rustling of skirts. He turned. Annas and Rachel stood close together in the dimness of the entrance. He could feel, rather than see, their frightened stares, Annas' wrinkled face flushed from the swift climb and Rachel's blinking eyes and nervously twitching mouth. Back of them huddled dark shapes, drooping like willows over the Jordan, the servants alarmed, Caiaphas realized with renewed resentment against Jonathan who had caused it, by the unwonted noise.

"What—what happened?" asked Annas, coming forward. Rachel slipped quietly toward the overturned chair and set it upright again, then back a little to one side. Her wariness increased his irritation. As the years went by, the gaiety and boldness which had attracted him to her gave way to timidity. As her beauty faded, so her voice, her gestures. Finally, he thought, his exasperation deflected to her for a moment, she would be but a shadow blurred in mind and body. So anxious not to displease that she could never hope to please. Why was she not happy? She had everything that the world could give. Yea—everything.

"We had a little argument," Jonathan was saying to his father. "We are about to continue it—more quietly, I hope."

"Shall I bring some light?" breathed Rachel attentively.

"We need none!" barked Caiaphas. Then, with irony:

"I am hoping that my brother-in-law's words will be illuminating. If not, however, I am content to sit in darkness."

After a little silence, Jonathan began. "I went first to Bethlehem in Judea, for it is there that he was born about thirty-three years ago. I talked to several shepherds who had witnessed strange things the eve of his birth. They remembered well the night and have never ceased to speak of it. They were keeping watch over their flocks when the heavens were filled with a great glory of light and the singing of the angels——"

Caiaphas snorted. "And you believed that? They have been paid, no doubt, to tell the tale."

"I believe they spoke the truth," said Jonathan.

"Fool!" said Annas sharply. "You are a fool, my son."

"And about the so-called virgin birth," put in Caiaphas derisively, "do you accept that, too?"

"After I left Bethlehem," replied Jonathan steadily, "I went to Nazareth where Mary, the mother of Jesus, lives with his brothers and sisters."

"And were they, too, conceived without benefit of the father? Or did Mary, perhaps, not bare them at all, but pluck them instead from a magic tree?"

"Joseph fathered them," said Jonathan.

He paced the length of the balcony and back, restlessly as if cramped for space, and he spoke in the same manner. As if words, needing to be so carefully weighed, hampered his thinking. He was a different man than the one who had left Jerusalem a month ago, thought Caiaphas dourly. The Nazarene, borrowing influence from Beelzebub, had cast some sort of spell over him. It had been the same with Gamaliel, with Joseph of Arimathea, with Nicodemus. The high priest praised heaven that he had not waited for Jonathan to give his report to the

Sanhedrin. Now it was too late. The proclamations would be posted on the morrow.

"But Mary was *almah* when she conceived Jesus," said Jonathan. He spoke with conviction.

"But how—?" Rachel's half-credulity infuriated Caiaphas.

"Have you no duties to perform?" he roared. "Be about them. This discussion is not for women."

She left the room immediately, like an alarmed animal, but her going did not cool Caiaphas' forehead, nor stop the perspiring of his palms and feet.

"They said in Nazareth that Jesus had been an excellent carpenter, choosing carefully the foundations for his houses and the materials which he employed for them. All that he did, he did well, and was a devoted son and brother before he left his business to the care of the others, so that he might be baptized by John in the Jordan. Thereafter, he was home but rarely, and then without the approval his neighbors, for they said he gave himself airs."

"That," said Caiaphas, who had been poised during the entire speech for such a pounce, "I can well believe."

"Thereafter," went on Jonathan calmly, "I sought out Jesus' followers and learned much from them of his wonderful works. I talked to those he has cured, to a man crippled from birth, a woman who was maimed, a blind man—even a man who had been dead and was raised again to life."

Annas sprang to his feet. "Enough! Enough of this blasphemy. No son of mine shall league himself against the Most High ——"

"I league not myself against the Most High," cried Jonathan, his voice full and passionate. "Indeed, for the first time, I begin to understand how to find Him."

Caiaphas snatched at the opening. "For the first time! All your life you have studied holy writ. You have learned from the prophets of Israel. Now, from a man who claims he is better than Abraham or Moses, you say you learn!"

"Tell me," rasped Annas, and pointed a long shaking forefinger at his youngest son, "what tricks did you see this Nazarene perform?"

"None."

"None!" shrieked Annas. "You admit it—you ——"

"There was no trickery in what I saw. I saw the lame leap and run. I saw the blind become aware of a world they believed forever lost. I spoke to a man who had been deaf and he heard me."

"You don't know what you're saying!" shouted Caiaphas. He clapped his hands over his ears. "I will listen to no more of this, I tell you!"

But Jonathan stood facing them in the darkness, unperturbed.

"Moreover, I saw those he had healed laughing and weeping for the joy that had come to them. And I heard him speak to the multitude that thronged him daily—yea, I heard him speak." His voice fell to a whisper, awed and humble. "Never heard I a man who spake with such power—and with such love."

Caiaphas could manage his hands no longer. They closed upon Jonathan's throat, or was it the throat of a sacrificial dove? He knew not. He cared not. . . .

Annas pulled him away. He heard Jonathan coughing and strangling.

In the doorway, Rachel wailed: "The guests are arriving. The banquet table is prepared!"

Caiaphas swallowed once, twice, thrice. Great aching lumps in his throat. His body felt weak and flabby, almost old. His eyes watered.

"We are coming," he said.

Tomorrow, between them, he and Annas would find a way to stop Jonathan's traitorous prattling. They would threaten, or plead. Let him disturb the peace of the high priest's family, if he must—if he had no more reverence for God's high office than that—but no word of this must trickle into Jerusalem's streets nor weave a web of whispering in the temple.

CHAPTER XXV

Abruptly, Caiaphas returned from those inner journeyings to the place and time of recent events and once more became conscious of the white glare in the street below. Over his head, as he sat there on the little balcony, the canopy, woven with bright threads of sun, began softly to flutter in a freshet of wind. It was cool, strangely, for it came from the desert of the East Country, land of the Arabs, and at this hour should have been hot. Why it was not, however, he would not question in his gratitude. Enough to feel the delicate fingers of air caressing his face and breathe, for a few moments at least, without that taste of brass in his throat and pricking in his nostrils.

To his amazement, the breeze drooped a little, then grew stronger. The turgid, held-in smells of the street whisked off, and the street itself came drooling out of its doze. The sleeper raised his head, Caiaphas saw, and slowly came to a standing position, blinking and sniffing. A dog, stretched out in the shade, rose and growled. One could hear the sound of shutters being opened. There were voices, and Caiaphas shuddered slightly, of small children mingled with the squalling of infants and the fretting and scolding of mothers. Two Roman soldiers stepped from an open doorway and stood, tipsily, gawking at the sun to determine the time. All day they had been inside drinking, Caiaphas surmised, and now would return from the house of this wine merchant to their own cohort, fuddled in mind but still high in spirits, carrying a jug between them.

From contemplation of the soldiers, Caiaphas' attention was suddenly drawn to the gate. It had swung open, to the accompaniment of furious shouting. What appeared to be a column of the military, in broken rank, began pouring through. Then Caiaphas saw that it was not the military. As many women as men, and youths, too, of both sexes—a strange polyglot crowd dressed for the road in strong garments and sturdy sandals, some of them— others barefoot and ragged, still others in holiday dress, colorfully and fantastically out of place in such a mob . . . and children, each with a basket, in some cases filled with food; in others with wilted flowers which they scattered underfoot.

On they came, clamoring and singing, and making a great uproar, shouting at the top of their lungs: "Hosanna! Hosanna!"

"Hosanna to him who cometh in the name of the Lord."

"Hosanna—the Messiah is here!"

In his excitement, Caiaphas leaped to his feet. They were surging through the gate. Not hundreds but literally thousands and the great chorus they made was like rumbling thunder between bulwarks of mountains.

"Hosanna! Hosanna! Blessed be the King that cometh in the name of the Lord: peace in heaven, and glory in the highest!"

"Hosanna to the son of David!"

They walked, they rode, they ran—scores upon scores passing through the gate until the street was wild with clamor and moving with human forms. Soon they would be taking over the holy city itself, Caiaphas thought, and his throat constricted with fear. In apprehension, he looked down at the temple gate. Here they might even attempt to force an entrance, but just as he considered the possibility, Jehoiada, chief of the temple guards, rushed out with some of his men to close it. Caiaphas heard a swish of garments behind him and turned to face Benezra, who was panting from running and from climbing stairs. His dark eyes were gleaming queerly. He kept rolling his tongue in his mouth and snapping his fingers and saying, whenever breath permitted: "Ah, I might have known. I might have known!"

"Known what?" Caiaphas snapped. "Speak, man!"

"That it was Jesus, the carpenter."

Caiaphas muttered an oath and stepped closer to the balcony's edge. He was scanning the crowd below. Fury made the iris of his eyes red. He had to shout to make himself heard.

"Which one?"

Benezra pointed a shaking forefinger. "There—the fool riding the donkey."

Caiaphas' eyes bulged and his fists clenched and unclenched spasmodically. There he was indeed, the insolent Nazarene. Two of his disciples were clearing a path for him. "Make room! Make room! The Messiah seeks to pass." His followers were strewing their head dresses and cloaks before him, weeping and cheering. Judas Iscariot, Benezra told Caiaphas, was the man leading the donkey on which the carpenter sat.

"Hosanna!"

"Hosanna to the one who cometh in the name of the Lord!"

Caiaphas' eyes sought the face of the upstart carpenter. To his amazement, though the crowd continued to cry hosannas, Jesus did not smile. His gaze rested steadfastly upon the golden dome of the temple, turning crimson in the setting sun.

"This is terrible," rasped Benezra. "Another riot is being born. We must do something to stop this idiotic demonstration."

Yea, thought Caiaphas, they must do something. The priests, the Pharisees, the followers of the one true God, Jehovah, must rise in righteous wrath against this pretender. They must grind him and his doctrine to nothing. Yet—how? And when? Always, as now, he was surrounded by the untutored multitude whose fancy he had snared. Those sent to take him in the temple or in the streets of Jerusalem returned, pleading that they dared not. His followers were too many, and too zealous. Daily he drew more to his cause.

Benezra was saying violently, over and over: "Do something—do something! Seize him!"

The high priest whirled. His fury must find an object. Suddenly he hated every harsh line of Benezra's face, his drawn-back upper lip, his claw-like fingers. Most of all he despised his headlong thinking. No one, not even the high priest of the temple, could check that crowd below. What would Benezra?

"Fool!" he said. "Can you stop a bolt of lightning? Can you pluck the wind from the trees?"

Benezra stepped backward. "You will do nothing?"

"I can do nothing!" Caiaphas spat out the words, hating Benezra anew for having forced the humiliating admission from him.

"Then I will send out a call for the Roman soldiers." There was venom in Benezra's narrowed eyes. "Perhaps," he said, "Pilate will prove more zealous for Rome than the high priest is for Israel!"

Before Caiaphas could answer, he was gone. The high

priest stood far back on his balcony, seeing but unseen. Every cheer for the Nazarene, he felt, was a stab at his own heart, a blow at the hallowed religion of Abraham and Moses. Every look that his bitter eyes cast at the pretender prophet was a torture. Yet he could not leave the balcony. A terrible fascination made him an onlooker at the triumph of a man whom he had grown to consider his deadliest enemy. Jehoiada came, shouting irate phrases in his ears. Caiaphas waved him away. Annas came, his voice shrill with emotion, his hands cutting the air with wild gestures. Caiaphas hardly heard him. He was watching Jesus dismount and walk upon the outspread garments. He was following that hated figure as it entered the temple—his, Caiaphas' temple!

When the Nazarene had disappeared, then and then only, would Caiaphas leave his observation post. The day had ended. The holy light of the seven-sticked candelabra burned dimly in the temple.

Caiaphas, on his way to his inner office, met Benezra. The latter's face was dark.

"Where are your Romans?" asked the high priest.

For a moment, Benezra made as if to pass without answering. Then he muttered: "They came at once, but when they saw the mob, they declared it would be useless to try to capture Jesus now. It would only cause an uprising, they said."

Caiaphas nodded. "They returned to the tower of Antonia?"

"Yea, they returned. Cowards like all the rest!"

The high priest, continuing on his way over the polished marble of his holy domain, felt despair well up in him. Even the Romans dared not touch the charmed carpenter. Could he, Caiaphas, with all his scheming, hope for success?

CHAPTER XXVI

FOLLOWING the ceremonies of the Feast of the Passover, Caiaphas sought the silence of the inner rooms, conscious of bodily fatigue and bewilderment of mind. Was he—and the thought plumped down with sudden weight —losing that certitude of purpose he had always known? What of his self-assurance that had in itself been so reassuring when difficulties arose or problems came up? Was he getting old as men sometimes do while yet counting the blessings of their rich maturity or contemplating their strength?

Life was still the mother of all mysteries—strange, unknown, unconquerable—a thing you had reason to believe in your youth could be dominated and held in thrall forever. It was yours to do with as you would. It obeyed your whims and brought you gifts of friends and money and high position, gave countless opportunities for advancement and pleasures, and blessed you with health and children.

In time, reasoned Caiaphas, your acceptance of its state of servitude had become so fixed that you gave no thought to the pleasant arrangement existing between you. That you would continue to rule was, of course, instinctive within you, a realization that you had no occasion to doubt, for it was always there within, like a friendly warming fire upon a hearth. If you ever paused to reason

at all, you would say proudly: "Life is my obedient servant, whereas in some men, who are less strong to command, it is but a companion, and, in others, a master."

So Caiaphas thought, treading his way barefoot along
the corridor. He was aware for the first time of the need
to summon his will, to drive his steps forward. Each muscle seemed to require a special urging. He could not order
the thing done, and then forget about it until its consum-
mation. Each time he would bend his knee to advance, he
must send his desire from his brain to the seat of opera-
tion and then hold his consciousness there for the period
of its accomplishment.

Was that, then, a warning of approaching age, or was it
merely the effect of yesterday's crashing experience? He
could not be sure, of course. More and more, doubts were
rising in him to tear at the citadel of his earth-body in
which life had once served him so well. As he saw it now,
there could be no surcease until the man, Jesus, was destroyed. There would be, he suddenly realized, no hope
of any compromise with life or expectation of God's in-
dulgence until the evil power of such an one was broken.
Indeed, perhaps, here was the mission to which all of his
life had been dedicated—the supreme test of holy power.
He must not fail. . . .

Caiaphas paused, listening, for the sounds entered the
corridor through the door from Jehoiada's office. He heard
a stranger's voice, then that of the chief of the temple
guards. They were talking quietly, almost too quietly.
These were the careful tones men used when they did not
wish to be overheard, nor yet attract attention to themselves by whispering. Caiaphas had long known that
Jehoiada had plans for himself. He coveted the honor and
power of the office of high priest. He would not hesitate to
do anything that would advance his own stupid interests.

On several occasions Caiaphas had uncovered little intrigues and minor conspiracies against his own authority that could be traced to the man; and, lately, there had been a much bolder attempt on Jehoiada's part to oppose him openly.

Caiaphas moved quietly forward and stationed himself near the door. The other man was speaking.

He said: "I am really not worthy of your confidence. But I sought you out because I felt that you might be interested in learning more about our leader."

"This Jesus of Galilee?"

"Yea."

"Tell me about him," Jehoiada said gruffly.

It was obvious to Caiaphas that Jehoiada's guest was embarrassed, possibly even somewhat afraid. He wanted to think his words carefully before he spoke them. He did not wish to commit himself too far. The interval of his silence grew so prolonged that Caiaphas felt his own patience dwindling.

"Talk, man!" Jehoiada snapped. "What would you tell me?"

"Of my Master," choked the man. "I am on intimate terms with him. If you doubt this, let me repeat that I am Judas Iscariot, one of the twelve chosen by Jesus to be personal advisers and, in a manner of speaking, his bodyguard."

"Yea—yea, go on."

"The motives of my Master are not generally understood," Judas continued. "Even we who are very close to him do not always understand him, nor can I say that we always approve of him."

Upon hearing this remarkable statement from one of Jesus' own disciples, Caiaphas stepped to the threshold of the door. He would, in the line of holy duty, take charge of this man himself. It was an opportunity he had not even hoped for, and, certainly, he had no intentions of permitting Jehoiada to have the personal satisfaction of taking such important matters to himself. The time had come to assert the rights of his office and put down all insubordination.

He frowned disapprovingly at Jehoiada, then bent the full strength of his gaze toward Judas. Consciously he drew himself up, straightening and broadening his shoulders and raising his chin. In his holy robes, he knew the impression he made, just as he sensed the discomfiture and secret annoyance of the wily Jehoiada. Judas got to his feet hurriedly and bowed low.

Caiaphas strode into the room with a dignified measured gait, and made a brief gesture to Judas to be seated.

"I overheard you say that you did not approve of your Master, my good man. Why?"

Such abruptness had its immediate effect. Judas flushed. He lowered his eyes and clutched handfuls of his gown until he almost rent the cloth. The heavy odor of some scent he wore flowed to Caiaphas' nostrils. It was as repulsive as the smell of warm blood.

"Why?" he repeated impatiently.

The Nazarene's disciple made his tongue go around the walls of the cavern of his mouth, puffing out his cheeks and blinking. With an effort, he sat straight.

"I had not expected so to be honored," he said, "or privileged to speak to your—to your Holiness, for I am a humble man."

Caiaphas smiled reassuringly. "Be at ease. We're glad to have you come. What you have to tell will be treated confidentially."

Judas thanked him and looked relieved. "Then I'll tell you. You may or may not believe it, but this takes courage." He thrust out his chin and his red beard was like a wind-ripped torch.

"Then he has threatened you?"

"Not directly—nay. But he has asked us, also indirectly, to have no dealings with you. By us, I mean his disciples, his—followers. I think that if he had his way he would destroy this temple utterly. Why he should take such a violent attitude I do not know."

"I know," said Caiaphas grimly.

"He preaches the Kingdom of God," Judas said on a higher note, "and yet he would destroy its temple."

"That's well put. I see you are a person of some discernment."

"Thank you."

"This Master of yours," Caiaphas said, "must be a mixture of strange contradictions."

Judas nodded. He had gained confidence now, and seemed less ill at ease. He no longer even glanced at Jehoiada, who crouched in the shadows sulkily. In the momentary silence, they could hear a draft of wind sweeping down along the corridor and then, before a door far off could be closed, snatches of a pilgrims' song. A pleased expression came over Judas' face.

"Beautiful, isn't it?" he asked. "All the old customs that have come down from our fathers. Those chants and songs—the sacrificial ceremonies—all this we, the followers of Jesus, are asked to renounce."

He paused, sighing a little, and raised his narrow eyes to meet those of Caiaphas, and the priest inwardly exulted. For here was an instrument ready to hand, a clay lump he could mold in any form that suited him. But he must move with caution, else the fellow might become too frightened to talk. Fortunate indeed that he had come along before Jehoiada, with his blunt manner and crude tongue, had spoiled everything!

"I can see you have suffered." Caiaphas spoke gently.

"I assure you—though you believe me or not—I have suffered greatly." In his agitation, Judas' voice broke. "The grief of disillusionment. The knowledge that we had been tricked—ah, your Holiness, no one will ever know the extent of what I have endured since ——"

Caiaphas interrupted him. "You say tricked. Please explain."

"I mean that in the beginning Jesus gave all of us assurance of some material reward for our services. There was every reason to expect that he would accomplish something worth while. But he did nothing but preach a strange doctrine of love for the world's redemption."

"Incredible!"

"You may think so. Our reward is to be found in heaven, it appears, not here upon earth."

Caiaphas asked sarcastically: "And what about Jesus' reward? Will he, too, find it in the hereafter?" As a Sadducee, the high priest professed no belief whatever in life after death.

"Yea," answered Judas, "at least, that is his belief. He expects soon to die on the cross. He has stated openly that he is the Lamb of God who must bear the sins of the world."

Caiaphas felt his temples pounding. "What blasphemy!" he shouted. "Lamb of God, indeed! Well, we'll see. We'll see. Hah! Lamb of God. What God I ask you? Some trumped-up, fallacious god of sorcerers and devils. Not Jehovah!"

Judas trembled. "I know not. I know not."

"Of course you don't. In one respect, at least, the fool

is right. He will die on the cross! He will—I tell you—
and probably much sooner than he expects."

Judas once more began fuddling around with nervous
fingers. Drops of moisture glistened between the wide
arches of his eyebrows just above his thin, sensitive nose.

"Personally," he said, "I can't see how the death of one
poor carpenter would ever redeem the sins of Israel."

Caiaphas snorted. "You might also be interested to
learn that many of Israel's present sins have grown out
of the false teachings of this so-called prophet."

Judas gulped, and said hastily: "I shouldn't wonder."

"Do you think that he is all that he claims to be?"
roared Caiaphas.

"Nay, your Holiness! He doesn't keep the Sabbath. He
doesn't observe purification rites, nor yet fast, nor offer up
the sacrificial lamb." Judas shrugged. "So you can well
understand my position. You can sympathize with my
disillusionment. Perhaps that will explain why I have
come here. I am the sort of person who would obey the
laws, your holiness—all of them, and any departure from
the sacred, time-honored path of my forefathers is most
abhorrent to me."

Caiaphas glowed from an inner warming fire. The
worries of yesterday no longer fretted him. His old
strength had returned. Life was still his servant, not his
master. His servant! Glory to the Lord God! In elation,
his hand went up to smooth his robes of state of which
he could well be proud. They had been presented to him
by the Roman government at the request of Emperor
Tiberius. Titellus, the governor of Syria, had brought them
from the tower of Antonia and had given them to him as
a symbol of his high office.

Careful not to show his gratification, he turned once
more to Judas Iscariot.

"From what you say, you no longer intend to follow him."

Judas drew his face into long tragic lines. He spread his hands. "I have no other alternative, for I am quite penniless."

"Poor man. But it is possible that we may think of something. Very probably, I should say. So do not be discouraged."

Judas sighed. Caiaphas saw that he was staring as if fascinated at the jewels and rich embroidery that embellished his robes.

"You—you mean," he stammered, "that you have—that you may be thinking of a plan? A—place for me?"

Caiaphas smiled and rubbed his hands. "Undoubtedly."

"I can be sure of that?" Ambition flared in Judas' eyes, dyed his cheeks scarlet. He swallowed.

Caiaphas rose. "You can be sure. As a preliminary, may I suggest that you come to my house tonight for supper."

"To your house!" gasped Judas.

"And indeed why not? We haven't any special treat except a rather delicious wine from—of all places—Galilee."

BOOK FIVE

AND THE FLOODS
CAME . . .

CHAPTER XXVII

Venus, poised in the clear sky above Jerusalem, was luminous. There was a perfume subtle as mist in the spring air, the scent of green things reaching upward from the earth. Mary had been aware of it all the way from Bethany. The olive trees in the garden of Gethsemane had whispered of it. The brook Cedron had sung the full sweet song of April as she crossed it. She had come eagerly the two miles from Bethany to assist in serving supper to Jesus and his disciples who had gathered in the upper room of the house of young John Mark and his mother.

But when she turned at last into the narrow twisting streets of Jerusalem, the early darkness ceased to be a friendly and familiar thing. Instead, suddenly and inexplicably, it became a threatening presence. Or perhaps it was the city itself which menaced, and the shadows crouched crookedly before the houses and shops but shared the emotional coloring.

Mary of Bethany began to walk faster and faster in rhythm with the hurrying of her heart. What was it that brooded tonight over the holy city? What forces had gathered within its walls, that a village girl happily on her way to serve her Master, as she had done so many times before, must feel a choking in her throat and her breath coming short? Under this strange feeling of pressure, of a weight pressing down, down, she found herself running. Dear

God, she might be too late. The thought was involuntary, sprung of itself. Too late for what? She could not tell.

"Jesus! Master!" His name came in gasps from her straining throat.

Mary Magdalene and the mother of Mark looked up in surprise as she burst into the kitchen.

"Mary, is something wrong?" Mary Magdalene, reaching into the oven for bread, paused. Mark's mother stopped stirring the young herbs she was boiling.

Mary looked about her. The familiar scene. The smell of warm food. Two women going calmly about ordinary tasks. Nothing different. Nothing to fear.

She laughed unsteadily. "I was afraid I might be too late!"

The face of Mark's mother crinkled into a relieved smile. "Too late? Nay, you are come in good season. My son has not yet returned with the wine he was sent to buy."

"But—Jesus—is he ——?"

"He and the disciples are all gathered upstairs," said Mary Magdalene. She bent down again to look into the oven, her face flushed with the heat. Mary crossed to stand beside her, glad of the fire's warmth, as if somehow it might take from her a thin foreboding, like a physical chill, which would not leave her.

"Master! Is something lacking?"

She looked up at the sound of the anxious voice of the mother of Mark. Jesus had come quietly down into the kitchen.

"I would have a basin of water," he said. "My disciples are weary and their feet dusty."

"I will wash them," said Mary of Bethany eagerly.

Jesus smiled slightly, shook his head. "Nay, Mary, tonight that is my task."

She started to protest, astonished, but could not speak

against the gentle determination in his manner. Yet all the way upstairs with the basin she rebelled at the thought of Jesus ministering to those who rightfully should have ministered unto him in such a menial task. Certainly, they would not allow it.

She returned to the kitchen to find young John Mark entering from the street with a large keg of wine. He greeted her, pleasurable excitement in his young face, as always when the Master whom he so admired accepted the hospitality of the house. Simon Peter, Mary knew, was well-acquainted with the family, through a distant relationship, some said, and for this reason Jesus often came here to spend an hour or more while in Jerusalem, though rarely did he stay the night. He preferred their own more humble dwelling at little Bethany where he might rest and refresh himself away from city noises, smells, and other confusion. Mary never ceased to be joyous that this was so, that the Master passed by the splendid comforts of larger homes and the prestige of their owners to dwell with Martha, Lazarus and herself. Their tiny garden, even when he was absent in Galilee, was fragrant with the memory of his presence. Often, when she sat there alone in the cool of the evening, her mind would go back to talks they had had there sometimes far into the night while stars seemed to burn closer, while thoughts grew, stretched—and reached with confidence into eternity.

She took the wine keg from Mark. "I will carry it upstairs, lad," she said.

It was heavy, but she took no thought of that. Little enough burden to bear for Jesus, who continually bore so much for others. Jesus who had raised Lazarus, calling her beloved brother forth from the dismal tomb with sure authority, divine authority. This had been to her the final proof. Never doubting his goodness and humanity, that demonstration of power convinced her that he was more than a righteous mortal—he was, as he said, the Son of God. The Messiah!

In the upper room, she set the keg down with a bump. Jesus was indeed washing the disciples' feet. They were permitting it. Bewilderment, even consternation, sat on every face—but, yea—they were permitting it!

Jesus finished with the drying of the feet of Judas Iscariot, whose face alone was expressionless, and turned to Peter who was next.

Peter, unable longer to control himself, said violently: "Master, do you wash my feet?"

Jesus paused, looking at him quietly. "What I do, you do not now understand. But you will hereafter."

Peter pressed his lips together and said righteously: "You shall never wash my feet." He looked about at the others rebelliously, critically.

Jesus' answer was swift. "If I wash you not, you have no part with me."

On Peter's face the inner struggle was written in line and muscle. At last he said humbly: "Lord, not my feet only, but also my hands and my head."

Pondering deeply, Mary of Bethany went down the stairs. She told Mary Magdalene what she had seen. The latter opened her eyes wide, then nodded, but said nothing.

The bread and herbs were now ready, and Mary and young Mark took them upstairs. The washing of the feet was finished, and all were seated around the long table. Jesus was in the center with John on his right hand and James on his left. Judas Iscariot sat next to James. Peter, apparently still embarrassed because of the recent episode, had chosen to sit on the end seat at the left.

As Mary picked up the water jug and basin to take them down to the kitchen, Jesus was speaking gravely to the disciples.

"If I, then, your Lord and Master, have washed your feet; you also ought to wash one another's feet. For I have given you an example, that you should do as I have done to you."

Mary went downstairs again, grateful that she had heard these words, and came back shortly with vinegar for the herbs. This time, she became aware of a change in Jesus' expression and tone.

"He who eats bread with me has lifted up his heel against me," he said sorrowfully.

Mary stood still. She was halfway to the stairs, but could not take a step, nor lift her hand. It was as if all the evil, all the revenge, the lust, the greed of Jerusalem had settled like a great brooding shadow upon this upper room. Yet it was a feeling that came to her, as before in the streets, rather than the words he spoke. For often he spoke in terms not easy to comprehend, and what he meant exactly by these words, no one could tell with certainty.

The disciples looked around the table at one another, and back at Jesus, uneasily.

Jesus said: "I tell you this before it comes to pass, that afterward, when all is fulfilled according to the scripture, you may believe that I am he."

"Master," said Andrew, "speak plainly. We know not what you mean."

There was silence—thick and impenetrable. No voice ventured into the dark stream of it. Mary put her hand to her throat. In its hollow, she could feel the beat of her pulse, loud and swift.

Then Jesus lifted his head. "Even that I must tell you, that afterward you may believe." His eyes went slowly from one to another, dwelling at last upon Judas Iscariot looking darkly at a bit of bread which he was crumbling in nervous fingers. Then the Master's eyes lifted upward, away from them all.

"Verily, verily, I say unto you, that one of you shall betray me."

Immediately, there were protestations.

"Nay, not I!"

"Master, do not believe it!"

"Never!"

But Mary saw that each looked doubtfully at the others, suspicion and incredulity mingling in his countenance. While all talked, while all remonstrated, filling the room with words as if to drown foreboding, Mary saw Peter beckon John who leaned against Jesus' breast. His gestures were clear. Peter was asking John to find out from the Master who the traitor was.

Now, uncertainly, the disciples were asking, each in turn: "Is it I?"

John was questioning Jesus quietly, but she could not hear what he said, nor Jesus' answer. The Master, after a moment when he seemed to be in prayer, broke off a piece of unleavened bread and, dipping it into the vinegar, handed it to Judas.

Judas Iscariot, after a moment's hesitation, took the bread, crushing it in his fist. He did not look at Jesus whose eyes were upon him, stern—yea—but somehow compassionate. Later, with awe, Mary was to remember that look and marvel at it.

Jesus said: "What you do, do quickly."

None seemed to know what Jesus meant, save John alone, upon whose face a strange expression dawned, unbelief struggling against apprehension. Mary, trying to evolve some clear thought from her chaotic emotions, argued that no doubt Judas had neglected some important errand for the Master, as lately he was wont to do. Perhaps he had forgotten to purchase the lambs for Passover, or to make some distribution to the poor. This seemed plausible, for Judas rose at once and, brushing by her without a word, went down the stairs.

Mary followed, but when she reached the kitchen he had gone. Mary Magdalene was standing in front of the oven with a stranger, a young girl in rags with no sandals upon her torn dusty feet. Tears had furrowed, like spring freshets tumbling from the mountains, down her dirty cheeks. Her hair was a dark tangle and dry as baked hay.

Answering the query in Mary's eyes, Mary Magdalene said: "This is Drusilla, whose father Jehu is imprisoned in the Tower of Antonia."

The girl's mouth worked, and fresh tears trembled on her lids.

Mary Magdalene put a comforting hand on her shoulder.

"She has been tending sheep near the Master's birthplace of Bethlehem in order to raise the two hundred shekels necessary to release her father from the dungeon. At night her bed was a pile of dried grasses in a cave ——"

"But I didn't mind that!" burst out Drusilla. "Little by little I was saving money to save my father, and when the lambs are born this spring—ah, but then it will be too late!" She began to sob, the weary rhythmical weeping of one who has done much mourning, and sank down upon the floor.

The eyes of Mary of Bethany grew wet in sympathy. "What does she mean—too late?" she asked Mary Magdalene.

"She has received word that her father is to—is to be executed tomorrow," said Mary Magdalene.

"I have saved one hundred and fifty shekels," gulped Drusilla, lifting great drenched eyes. "Only fifty more— only fifty more would save him!"

Mary said swiftly: "My sister has gone to Ephraim with Lazarus to sell some sheep. There should be enough from the sale when she returns ——"

Drusilla looked at her, faint hope in her face. "You mean you will let me borrow fifty shekels from you? You will, really?" She got to her feet. "Then I shall not have to bother the Master after all." She came to Mary, plucked at her sleeve. "When will your sister return—when?"

"I expect her any time," said Mary reassuringly. "Of course, if the shepherd were out with his sheep she might have had a little trouble locating him—but she should be back soon now. Even if she were to come tonight, though, the prison wouldn't be open, would it?"

"Not after dark," said Drusilla.

"Then nothing can be done until tomorrow, I fear," said Mary.

Drusilla knelt suddenly and picked up the hem of Mary's tunic. She pressed her lips to it in mute gratitude. "Then I'll come back early tomorrow morning." She stood, her chin quivering. "I—I cannot tell you!" She fled from the kitchen, and out into the city darkness before either of the Marys could protest.

"But where will she stay the night?" asked Mary of Bethany in concern.

"Perhaps she will return to Bethlehem and her flock," said Mary Magdalene, smiling sadly, "or it may be that she knows of a nearer cave. Indeed, this daughter of the outcast, Jehu, is a little like the birds of the air which the Master speaks of. She will find a nest, and our Father will watch over her."

The eyes of the two women met in deep, sweet understanding. Mary felt reassured. Mary Magdalene was always so sure, so certain that God would take care of His own. There was in her a strength of conviction hard won and fast held to.

Mary, thinking she might be needed to serve, returned again to the upper room with young Mark.

CHAPTER XXVIII

JESUS was looking around the table, which boasted no lamb, although it was the feast before the Passover.

"Tonight," he said, "I am become the lamb."

The disciples, Mary saw, were more than ever mystified. She stood unobtrusively in the shadow by the stairway entrance, her heart beating fast again, and anguished she knew not why. Perhaps there were things she could do to help in the service of the meal, but she could make no move toward the table. She was aware that something of solemn poignant import was transpiring.

Although the disciples had eaten, Jesus now broke more bread and lifting up his eyes in thanks, said: "Take, eat: this is my body."

Strange words, and stranger still the gloom which pressed into the room now, thick as fog. Again Mary felt that tearing at her throat of withheld sobs. Never—never before had she felt thus in the presence of Jesus of Nazareth. Could it be that he had had some terrible forewarning of disaster? It was true that for many months now the priests and Pharisees had been plotting against him. She remembered the proclamations posted after the resurrection of Lazarus, when the chief priests feared his swelling popularity. Anyone telling the whereabouts of Jesus of Nazareth to Annas and Caiaphas was to have thirty pieces of silver. Jesus had retired then into a city called Ephraim on the edge of the wilderness. Disguised so that none might follow her and discover where he dwelt, Mary had gone to him at intervals to bring what news there was. Once she had come upon him tending sheep on a hillside and his face had been calm as the countryside bordering the Jordan, and in his eyes the vision of skies. Picking up one of the little shaky-legged lambs, he had held it in his arms lovingly, and said what he had just now spoken to the disciples: "I am become the lamb." He had talked to her about scriptural prophecies, but she had understood little of what he said, for her heart was heavy, fearing for his safety. On the way to Ephraim she had torn down all the proclamations she could find concerning the reward for Jesus' capture. She told him this, but he only smiled, saying: "My time is not yet come."

Relief had flooded her heart, hearing that. "My time is not yet come." But now—now was his time come? Nay, she would not believe it. Was not the power of one who could raise the dead, four days entombed, sufficient to conquer any mortal malice? Had not Jesus said: "I and my Father are one?" Yea, despite the hatred and plotting of the chief priests, the Pharisees and jealous scribes, the Master would, must, be victorious.

Jesus had taken the wine jug now and was filling the cups of the eleven. "This is my blood of the new testament shed for the remission of the sins of many." Silently the cups were passed to each in turn. Many hands trembled, Mary saw, spilling the wine. In the face of every man was the dark print of bewildered fear and sorrow. Seeing this, her own inexplicable despair increased.

Jesus said, his eyes going tenderly from face to face as if he, younger than many of his disciples, were a father and they confused children to whom only maturity could bring proper knowledge: "Drink you all of it."

Putting down his cup, Jesus lifted his eyes to heaven, "The time has come when the Son of man must be glorified. I tell you, I will not drink of the fruit of the wine until I drink it anew with you in my Father's kingdom."

Slow tears were falling from the eyes of John, glittering briefly in the moonlight pouring through the east window of the room. Watching, Mary stood motionless. Young Mark had long since gone down the stairs, but she had hardly been conscious of his going.

Again, Jesus' voice: "Little children, yet a little while I am with you. You shall seek me and shall not find me: and as I told the Jews, Whither I go, you cannot come; so I say to you now likewise."

Peter leaned across the table and said with loud, rebellious insistence: "Master, where are you going? Wherever you go, there will I go, also."

Jesus smiled affectionately. "Whither I go, you cannot follow me now; but you shall follow me afterwards."

"But, master, why cannot I follow you now? I will lay down my life for your sake." His tone was strained, but full of courage.

Jesus took up his cup, empty now, and looked for a long moment into the bottom. Then he raised his eyes, and in them was stark, clear discernment.

"Will you indeed lay down your life for my sake, Peter? Verily, verily, I say unto you the cock shall not crow, until you have thrice denied me."

Peter's eyes went wide with hurt. "Never, Master!" With one hand, he brushed away tears which glistened suddenly upon his brown hard cheeks.

The next words Jesus spoke took some of the ache from Mary's throat.

"Let not your heart be troubled: you believe in God, believe also in me. In my Father's house are many man-

sions: if it were not so, I would have told you. I go to
prepare a place for you. And if I go and prepare a place
for you, I will come again, and receive you unto myself;
that where I am, there you may be also."

Now he spoke, thought Mary, as of old. With courage
and with confidence.

"And whither I go you know, and the way you know."

Thomas frowned. "Lord, we don't know whither you
go; and how can we know the way?"

Jesus' voice was clear and firm. "I am the way, the truth,
and the life: no man comes to the Father, except by me."

Philip said eagerly: "Master, show us the Father."

Surprise and grief mingled on the Master's countenance.
"Have I been so long time with you, Philip, and yet have
you not known me? He that has seen me has seen the
Father; and why then do you say, Show us the Father?"

Philip dropped his eyes, although the rebuke was gentle.
His hands gripped the table tensely.

"Don't you understand that I am in the Father and the
Father in me? Indeed, the very words I speak unto you,
I speak not of myself, and the Father dwelling in me
does the works."

Silence for a time. And the white April moon, a little
past the full, illumined the dimly lighted chamber. Jesus'
eyes were on it as he spoke again. "The prince of this
world comes, but has nothing in me."

Mary pondered the words. Whether he meant Herod
or the authority of Rome, she did not know. Perhaps it
was neither, but Satan. If so, it was true that in the mind
of Jesus of Nazareth, Satan could find nothing with
which to work. He had no foothold there.

Jesus said gravely: "Greater love has no man than this,
that he lay down his life for his friends."

James, son of Zebedee, cried chokingly: "Master!"

Peter hid his face, and Mary saw tears trickle through his calloused fingers. Andrew and Thomas were weeping, too.

The songs of the pilgrims, gathered in Jerusalem for the Passover, echoed from all parts of town. Jesus was silent as if listening to the chanting voices.

But Simon the Zealot, who all this while had remained speechless save for his burning eyes which vividly expressed his thoughts, cried out now: "Lord, do not desert us!"

Jesus said plainly: "I tell you the truth. It is necessary that I go away."

"Nay, Master!" protested James the Less.

"If I go not away," said the Nazarene gently, "the Comforter will not come unto you; but if I depart, I will send Him unto you." The moonlight streaming through the window made a nimbus about his head.

Mary found herself upon her knees in the attitude of prayer—found, too, that her tears were falling slowly, one by one upon the floor.

"I have yet many things to say unto you," went on the Master, "but you cannot bear them now."

He had but to look at each face, torn by grief, fear, bewilderment, to know that there was not strength enough yet in these men to bear any further load of agonized knowledge, Mary thought. In herself, too, she was aware of frightened weakness.

Jesus' voice roused her again from the gloom which threatened to stop her ears and blind her eyes. She was possessed with the feeling of necessity. She must remember to treasure up these words for the future. . . .

"Howbeit when he, the Spirit of truth is come, he will guide you into all truth: for he shall not speak of himself; but whatsoever he shall hear, that shall he speak: and he will show you things to come."

No sound in the room but the sobbing of Thomas, and the torn breathing of the other disciples. The olive oil lamps were burning low. It was time, Mary told herself, to go below for the cruse to refill them. Her mind, blown like a bird in a windstorm, fastened with relief on something solid. A duty to be performed. A service for the Master.

She got to her feet, her limbs still trembling, and felt her way to the stairs. She was both loath to leave and eager to be gone. Halfway descended, she heard Jesus begin again to speak, but what he was saying she was too far away by then to hear.

Only the mother of Mark was in the kitchen, and her back was toward Mary. Mary was grateful. She wanted no one to be alarmed by the pattern of anguish upon her face. In haste, she found the cruse, stepping lightly to the shelf where it stood. When Mark's mother became aware of her presence, Mary had turned back, one foot upon the stair.

"Is there anything the Master needs?" asked the older woman.

Mary's throat hurt. Is there anything the Master needs? Dear Father in heaven! Food, drink, apparel, these things could be supplied. But what he needed now, no man could give him. From his own inner store he must provide himself. But that secret place held all the treasure of earth and heaven.

She swallowed. "He has everything, I believe."

Mary climbed again. Up, up the steps. Led by a voice speaking with sorrowful assurance.

"Verily, verily, I say unto you, That you shall weep and

lament, but the world shall rejoice: and you shall be sorrowful, but your sorrow shall be turned into joy."

Joy! Spoke he in this hour of joy? When, but a little while ago, he had foretold his own doom? When his disciples wept? When he had said plainly he must leave them? Surely it was a contradiction. Then Mary remembered. "The flesh profits nothing. It is the Spirit that quickens." Did he then weep for the suffering of the flesh, while at the same moment rejoicing in the everlasting strength of the truth which he so oft declared made free?

His voice faded, though she could tell that he still spoke. When she reached the room, she found that Jesus had left his place at the table, and was standing before the window.

When Mary entered with the cruse of oil, he turned and faced his disciples, huddled like sheep where he had left them.

"These things I have spoken unto you, that in me you might have peace. In the world you shall have tribulation: but be of good cheer; I have overcome the world."

One by one the grief-stricken men lifted their heads. Jesus, his hands clasped behind him, lifted his eyes again to the starry spring sky.

"Father, the hour is come: glorify Your son, that Your son also may glorify You: as You have given him power over all flesh, that he should give eternal life to as many as You have given him."

Eternal life! Mary stood still. He was still speaking, but now she heard not his words for joyful relief. Eternal life! He would not leave them, then. Surely the giver of everlasting life died not. What she had feared, what they all who loved him had feared, would not, after all, come to pass.

She was still standing and the lamps were still unfilled. Jesus said: "Let us sing an hymn."

It was their custom to conclude a meal with singing. One by one, the eleven straightened. John's voice was lifted first after the Master's, trembling a little, but growing stronger. Then Peter's. Then James'. Soon they were all joined in the harmony of praise, a chorus of untrained, yet well-blended voices. As they sang Mary saw, strain lessened.

When they had finished, there was silence. Moments stretched long and taut.

Then the Master lifted his hand.

"Arise, let us go hence."

CHAPTER XXIX

HE IS taken!"

Mary of Bethany and the mother of Mark looked up from their dish-washing. The door was flung violently open. Young Mark sprang into the kitchen. He was entirely naked. Blood, from a cut over one eye, was caked upon his temple. Upon one shoulder was a red angry welt.

His mother ran to him, moaning. "My son, what has happened?"

But Mary could neither move nor speak. Her hands and feet were cold. She could feel the moisture starting on her forehead. A dish slipped from her nerveless fingers, crashed to the floor. The boy, clinging wild-eyed to his mother, began to sob. Great gulping sobs of pure terror. Mark's mother was repeating over and over: "Son—son, what has happened? What has happened?"

"Jesus has been captured!" gasped the boy.

Mary cried out. Her fears were become reality. Her mind accepted it as one accepts, against the will, a blow. But her heart rebelled. Not yet . . . not yet! Despite the Master's prophetic words at supper, she had hoped that the time of fulfillment was not yet come, that there were days, weeks, perhaps years ahead. . . .

She wrenched at her apron. The cloth tore. She did not care. She was in a frenzy to get it off. She would not stand idly by—she would not! He was taken—but he should go free!

She ran from the house. Joanna, wife of Herod Antipas' former steward, lived but a few blocks away. She could help. She had influence with the great.

Crooked streets and crooked shadows. People jostling, impeding her progress. Every breath a pain. Oh, Jerusalem, Jerusalem, do your people now rejoice because the holy Passover is at hand? Weep, rather—weep!

Chuza's house was behind the palace of the king. Mary hurried around to the kitchen door, and asked a maid to call her mistress.

Joanna appeared at once. She was dressed elaborately, apparently for some important function. Mary was, for a moment, abashed. Rarely had she seen Joanna so attired. When she was with the other women serving the Master, her raiment was like theirs, simple. To Mary, blinking in the glow of the olive lamps hung from the ceiling, this was but another part of the night's strangeness.

Joanna moved into the light, her damask robes gleaming. "Why, is it you, Mary? Do come in."

Mary stumbled inside. "You—you haven't heard?"

The answer was in Joanna's puzzled face.

"They have taken Jesus, our Master!"

Joanna's face went white. "It—it can't be!" She took a step forward and shook Mary by the shoulder. "It can't be!"

Mary choked. Like the first bearer of the evil tidings, young John Mark, she wanted to throw herself into comforting human arms, and weep. She swallowed hard. No time now for tears.

"I had the news from Mark," she said heavily. "He escaped naked from Jesus' captors and ran home to tell us."

Joanna's fingers gripped Mary's arm painfully. "But who—where?"

Mary shook her head blankly. She had not waited to

hear the details. The main, stark fact had been sufficient
to send her flying here.

"I'm not sure," she faltered. "The Romans, perhaps—
or the chief priests. Probably in the garden of Gethsemane,
where he often goes for prayer and refreshment." What
did it matter, how or where? It was enough that he was
taken, the most loving and beloved man who ever trod
the earth. Mary said pleadingly: "Don't you know a way
to save him?"

"Just a minute," said Joanna quickly. "I'll go and speak
with my husband." A whisper of her skirts, like the chill
sound of wind, and she was gone.

Mary of Bethany was alone, more alone than she had
ever been before. In body and in spirit. She was aware of
her fingers clenching and unclenching, the ache of her
throat, the tremble of her limbs. But it was as if these
things were no part of her. They did not belong to her,
nor she to them. Only her rushing, headlong thoughts
were hers—and the terrible agony of her fear. She moved
his lips numbly. "Master . . . Master . . ."

It seemed a starless eternity before Joanna's return.

"We've just sent a messenger to investigate." Joanna's
usually calm voice was jerky with repressed feeling. "You
had better come in. Indeed, I think you should spend the
night here. It isn't safe for a young woman to be out alone
this late."

Before Mary could reply, a tall slave came through the
back gate carrying a letter. Snatching it from him, Joanna
hurried again into the inner room. This time, she returned
almost at once, and spoke to the slave. "There is no
answer. Greet your master, please, and give him our
thanks."

The slave bowed wordlessly and slipped like a shadow
through the rear gate.

Joanna turned to Mary, her face strained. "It is true. The Master has been taken to the high priest's house. That letter was from Jonathan, Annas' youngest son."

Almost, Mary had begun to entertain the wild hope that young Mark had had a terrible nightmare, which, in boyish terror, he believed to be true. But now—if Jonathan, an avowed admirer of Jesus, verified the report—she knew with heaviness that it was so.

What was Joanna saying? "They—they are planning to put Jesus out of the way."

"Nay!" cried Mary. Jesus—out of the way? Jesus, of the free step, the joyous laughter, the healing hands and piercing fearless eyes—Jesus out of the way? What insanity! "Nay!" she said again, and her voice was high and unfamiliar in tone.

Joanna smote her hands together in sudden angry violence.

"I, too, say nay!" But after a moment, she said more moderately: "Come in now, Mary. The celebration here is over and we can talk matters over. What shall we do?"

Although she was vaguely embarrassed by her rough working clothes, Mary allowed herself to be led into the guest room. Hardly were they seated, however, when there was a loud knocking at the front gate.

When the guest was ushered into the room, Mary recognized him as Nicodemus, a member of the Sanhedrin. Seeing Joanna, he began to talk excitedly, his fingers clawing his long graying beard.

"Madam, the prophet of Galilee has been taken by the soldiers and led away to the house of the high priest. I'm afraid they seek his life."

"We have heard," said Joanna. "It is a terrible thing!"

Chuza entered and, after a brief greeting, Nicodemus

went on in a strained voice. "I have just received a letter from Annas' son, Jonathan, who believes as I do."

Chuza nodded gravely. His usually kindly lips were tight, the lines about his mouth were stern.

"We, too, have had word of this from Jonathan."

"What a mistake, this arrest!" said Nicodemus in exasperation. "But it has happened, and now we must see what can be done about it. You are on intimate terms with the governor Pilate, and I implore you to use your influence with him. According to the law, only Pilate has the authority to send a man to the cross." Nicodemus' eyes gleamed anxiously between sparse lashes. "Will you not see him and beg him to return a verdict of not guilty?"

That was it! Of course, that was the solution, thought Mary. Without Pilate's consent, the priests were helpless to accomplish the worst.

Another visitor entered. He was Joseph of Arimathea, wearing a Roman toga, and princely in his bearing. He and Nicodemus clasped hands, their eyes meeting earnestly. Then, in the dialect of Galilee, Joseph spoke to Chuza.

"They are calling an emergency meeting of the Sanhedrin. Annas and Caiaphas, I am convinced, will force a decision to crucify Jesus." His lips twisted scornfully. "The prophet has interfered too much with their—business."

Joanna urged everyone to be seated. No one heard her.

"If they do this thing," said Joseph with decision, "it will but increase the sins of the people in the sight of God. There will be no alternative, save the destruction of the people of Judah. King Herod Antipas killed John the Baptist because of his condemnation of the adultery of Herodias, and now this year if the high priest, who in national life holds a higher position than king, kills the prophet of Galilee, the future of our people is black indeed." He sat down on the formal Roman chair to which Joanna directed him, but rose restlessly a moment later, and began to pace the floor.

Chuza said: "I know well how those in authority seek to make vice, virtue and virtue, vice. For that reason, we moved from Sepphoris palace to Jerusalem, braving the dangers of Herod's anger." His eyes met Joanna's. "The peace we have had since my resignation has made our loss gain."

Nicodemus said impatiently: "No doubt. No doubt. But you are still in favor with Pilate, are you not? You can intercede for Jesus?"

Chuza rubbed his chin thoughtfully, then nodded. "Yea, I can. But there is still a better way. Pilate listens to anything his wife says and, instead of going directly to him myself, I think success would be more certain if my wife Joanna speaks with Claudia."

Joseph said promptly: "A wise thought. Let us have Joanna go."

Mary looked at Joanna whose lips were parted, and whose dark eyes were luminous with determination. Joanna would do her best for the Master, there was no doubt of that. When Chuza's wife rose, Mary rose, too— suddenly conscious of her drab attire and disheveled hair. Wearily, she swept a lock back from her forehead.

Because it was dark, they went out to the broad street through the Joppa gate. Turning to the left in front of the west gate of the temple, they came out on the wide Damascus road which they climbed in silence for some distance before turning into the very narrow lane in which two people could not walk abreast and which led to the

Tower of Antonia. Pilate's residence was directly north-west of the tower.

Because it was the night before the eve of the Feast of the Passover, every house was lighted in celebration, and the streets were, even yet, quite lively.

When they reached Pilate's mansion, Mary bade fare-well to Joanna.

"Nay," said Joanna, clinging to her. "You must come with me, Mary."

"But I can't go before the governor's wife in these clothes," protested Mary.

She wanted to get away, to run in all haste back to Bethany. Lazarus must hear of this, and Martha, if she were returned from her journey. Her brother would have words of courage for her. In his eyes, ever since his resur-rection, there had been the calm of complete assurance.

But Joanna's hands held her. "Nay, leave me not. I need the comfort of your presence, Mary. As for raiment—here, put on my coat. I am wearing a ceremonial robe, so it matters not if I have a coat or not."

Joanna was so insistent that Mary agreed, and together they entered the courtyard. The surroundings were very strange to Mary of Bethany. Her friends were all girls from the lower ranks of society and tonight was her first glimpse of the environment of the upper classes of Rome and Jerusalem where dress and formality were strictly observed.

They were ushered into a large room on whose mosaic floor was spread a rich red carpet. Mary's sandaled feet sank into it. But she was hardly impressed, save that, for a moment or two, the awful fact of Jesus' arrest ceased to possess its full measure of reality. This was merely the pleasanter part of the night's dream. She, humble Mary of Bethany, treading the crimson rugs of the governor's palace!

Pilate's wife appeared at once. Whether for the festival or not, she was dressed like a Greek goddess in a gold-embroidered gown, her hair in Grecian style held up by gold pins.

"Joanna!" She clasped her guest's hands and spoke in Latin. "It is long since we have met. I heard but recently from Pilate that you had left the household of Herod. How was that?" She searched Joanna's face with concern.

Joanna answered hesitatingly, not as fluent in Latin as Claudia, making a brief explanation. Then she introduced Mary. "She is one of the disciples of the prophet of Galilee. It is about him we have come. Have you heard what has happened?"

Claudia shook her head.

"He has fallen into the hands of the high priest Caiaphas and his father-in-law, Annas."

"We have heard nothing of it," said Claudia, concerned. "When was he taken?"

It took so long, Mary thought. All the questions, all the answers. While they talked, sand was running out of the glass. Time was sliding like water between the fingers, and none could stay it.

"I think it was early this evening," Joanna was saying.

"That Annas!" said Claudia explosively. "He's a great trial to my husband. The man is really responsible for the aqueduct revolt of last spring. At first, he promised a share of the temple revenue for the project, and a start was made, but before long he made the excuse that it was costing too much, and made my husband the culprit!" She gestured expressively. "And he himself started the revolt! And now what is he up to?"

Jesus was bound in the house of the high priest. Jesus

was in the hands of his implacable enemies. Pilate's wife ranted about aqueducts, temple revenue, and revolts—and the Master was captive. Mary tried not to think what might be happening to him. That he would be treated with the respect due him was too much to hope. She had seen too clearly the envy and hatred in their eyes as they baited him in the temple. She had seen them daily growing more desperate for words to catch him with. She had heard, too, their mumblings and threats at Jesus' denunciations of their hypocrisy and greed. Well, they could not trap him with phrases, however, skillfully knit, nor, with staves, had they dared take him bodily in the city. But, in a lonely place, surrounded by but few followers, they had captured him. And now—now that they had him—what?

"That man!" said Joanna. "That man, Annas! You know, he says that as long as the prophet of Galilee is alive, the coffers of the temple will never be full, and tonight he has seized him." She wrung her hands. "I know he plans to crucify him. Doubtless tomorrow he will be brought before your husband, and we beg you to intercede on his behalf. Ask your husband, I pray you, to discharge him as guiltless."

Claudia, her face grown serious, left her guests and went into the next room. The sound of an octachord, which had been playing throughout their conversation, was immediately stilled. Then, after a little, Pilate entered the room with Claudia.

The governor carried his octachord with him, and looked annoyed at being disturbed. He sat down on a chair nearest the door, and waited impatiently for Joanna to speak.

Mary had often heard that the frequent uprisings of the Jews had affected Pilate's health, but she was unprepared for the nervousness of the Roman. He moved continually, head, hands and feet. Muscles jerked in his cheeks. He bit his full under lip. His thin hands plucked at the strings of the octachord, filling the room with weird inharmony.

Claudia, apparently resigned to her husband's difficult temperament, spoke soothingly: "Won't you listen to Joanna's request? You remember, she once talked to us of that famous prophet of Galilee. Now she is much disturbed about his arrest by Annas."

Pilate straightened. He put his harp down on the chair beside him. "What's that? Annas has seized the Galilean prophet? Annas hasn't any such authority. Haven't you confused him with Caiaphas?" His mouth twisted. "That Annas is a sly fox. Just the sort to try something like this." He looked around at them petulantly. "He broke his promise to me and then linked himself with the Zealots and stirred up trouble in the city. A wily fellow. You can't tell what he may do. Evidently that good prophet, Jesus, was interfering with him in some way." He smiled mirthlessly, as if liking the thought of interference with Annas, from whatever source.

Mary was tempted to speak out, to bring him back to the important matter under consideration. In her mind now, there kept flashing sharp and dreadful pictures. Scenes in Caiaphas' house, in which Jesus played the victim's role. Scoffing. Insults. Perhaps, she shuddered, even physical abuse. Ah, lord of Rome, cease your petty, selfish reminiscing, forget your own troubles for a moment, and think on the enormity of this crime against God. His Son in the hands of evil men!

Claudia said: "Joanna has come to ask me to intercede for him. They think his captors will send the Galilean to you tomorrow to ask formal judgment, hoping you will sentence him to death."

Pilate started. "Death!" he snorted. "Nonsense. What evil has he done? The fellow may have been unwise—yea—but from what I hear it was courageous foolishness. He walked openly in the temple and denounced the thieving Sadducees and the sanctimonious Pharisees." He slapped his knee. "By the gods, I would that I had seen it!"

Claudia said: "These followers of his know that you are an upright judge, and they beg you to pronounce him innocent of the charges against him. That's your request, is it not, Joanna?"

Joanna bowed. "That is our great desire. I believe it probable that Annas will accuse the prophet of something like stirring up a revolution, but as Claudia well knows, he is far from being an insurrectionist. As a matter of fact, last spring, when about five thousand Zealots were gathered together and wanted him to be their leader in revolt, he hurried away to Tyre and Sidon instead, and would not allow himself to be involved." Joanna's voice trembled in her earnestness. "He is a strong and peaceful man, and that is why Annas and Caiaphas, chafing under their loss of temple profits, will doubtless demand some unreasonable punishment. Please do not listen to anything they may say but judge him fairly and uprightly."

Pilate looked convinced. "I'll do my best for you. As you say, Annas is a wicked fellow, and there is no prophesying what he may try to do." He sighed gustily. "He gives us a lot of trouble." He got up, nodded briefly, and, with his octachord, disappeared into the adjoining room.

Mary of Bethany was weak with relief. He had promised. Pilate had promised. He would take the Master's part against the chief priests. And without Pilate's consent, as representative of Rome, there could be no death verdict against the Nazarene. No death verdict!

She hardly heard Joanna thanking Claudia, barely remembered her own manners. Claudia was escorting them to the door. Stopping, she took Joanna's hands in her own.

"Joanna, do come again when you have not such business as this. When Cypros was in Jerusalem, she came often, and I was not lonely, but since Agrippa quarreled again with King Antipas and has had to go to Egypt, there has been no one. I have been so lonely of late! Won't you come tomorrow?" She turned courteously to Mary. "And bring your friend."

Mary heard Joanna promise, and she herself murmured something—she was not sure what. As they went out through the courtyard, she thought that once such an invitation from the governor's lady would have meant a great deal to her. Now it was subordinate to the thought that perhaps the Master might be freed tomorrow. That perhaps he would share with them the Passover. Her anxiety that he was still in the hands of the priests remained, but the great terror for his ultimate safety had lifted.

She murmured: "Master . . . Master."

CHAPTER XXX

Now, thought Mary, she ought to start back to Bethany, to the quiet streets and restful gardens, to the little stone house asleep under the stars. But her anxiety for Jesus would not let her go. It was a web which bound her to Jerusalem, which drew her, inexorably, to the residence of Annas and Caiaphas.

She and Joanna talked of the Master as they walked. Venus, which had shone brightly in the early evening, was now hid, and the moon was white above the remnant of the south wall of Jerusalem. That was the wall, Mary remembered bitterly, said to have been built by David. And now he whom men hailed as the Son of David had been taken prisoner by jealous and spiteful men.

Reaching Caiaphas' house, they saw a young man running through the gate. It was John Mark.

Mary caught him by the sleeve. "Mark!"

He stopped trying to pull away, and looked into her face with relief. "I didn't recognize you," he panted. His eyes were restless and apprehensive.

"What of the Master?" asked Mary. "Is he all right?"

Instead of answering, he whispered: "Come back, come back! If you are found here, you will also be arrested."

They followed Mark back to his house. No one was there. Inexplicably, Mary shivered.

Joanna said in a strained voice: "I must pray." She

climbed the stairs to the upper room where, but a few hours before, Jesus had eaten with his disciples.

Young Mark was full of the night's events, and the story poured from him.

"Jesus had scarcely gone from the house before strange things began to happen," said Mark. "First the men led by Judas Iscariot came to the house in search of him."

Mary gasped: "Judas Iscariot!" Words, expressions of the Master came back to her with sharp clarity. She remembered too, the look of Judas when, leaving the supper, he had gone past her. Oh, had she known—had she known—she would have done anything to stop him. Yet, she thought in bewilderment, Jesus had known. Jesus had known!

"You were in the basement kitchen," Mark was saying, "so perhaps you did not hear. Mother and I were alone and when I saw Judas, who had left the house earlier, come back with the soldiers and lead them upstairs, I was amazed. I knew how mother would worry if I said anything to her, so I hurried out without telling her. I remembered that Jesus went often to the garden of Gethsemane to pray, so I took a short cut there, hoping to warn him before the soldiers arrived."

She was right, then. The Master had been seized in the garden he loved so well. But why had he gone there, knowing Judas' familiarity with his habits? Why? It would have been a simple thing to elude his enemies. He had done so often.

"Just as I arrived," said Mark, "a great band of men with staves and swords also appeared. It was very dark, but I managed to find Peter. 'The soldiers are coming to seize the Master. They have just been to the house. Behold, there they are. Warn Jesus to flee!'" Mark put his head in his hands and said chokingly: "But it was already too late!"

Mary twisted her hands together. She could visualize the scene. Men with torches, lanterns and weapons invading the prayerful privacy of the garden Jesus loved. What was he doing when they came? Kneeling beneath some whispering olive tree, communing with his Father, or talking quietly to his disciples?

"Rabbi was perfectly calm, however," said Mark, lifting his head wonderingly. "He met the soldiers and asked: 'Whom seek you?' " Excitedly, Mark swept back a lock of dark hair which had fallen over his forehead. "And they said they sought Jesus of Nazareth. He said at once: 'I am he.' The men were so astounded and frightened, too, I think, that those in front stumbled backward against those behind, and some fell upon the ground."

To meet the fearless purity of Jesus had been too much for such worldly men, Mary thought. They had, no doubt, expected him to attempt flight, or some sort of resistance. They might well fall back from the courageous impact in those eyes!

"Then," Mark continued, and his voice trembled with anger, "Judas Iscariot stepped from among them and— and put his arms about Jesus and kissed him! I'm sure it was a signal, for at once a soldier stepped behind Jesus, trying to bind his hands. And Jesus said: 'Judas, do you betray the Son of Man with a kiss?' "

It was as incredible, Mary thought, as a dream of insanity in the night. How often she had heard from Judas' own lips the account of his conversion to the Master's teachings! How often had she given to Judas the reverence due Jesus' chosen disciples! How often he had dined with them—yea, dwelt with them. Judas, quick-tongued and likeable, canny in business and agreeable in society.

She had often thought that Judas, had he cared to do so, might rise to worldly heights. And now—and now, might he not? He had exchanged his loyalty to Jesus for the favor of Annas and Caiaphas. Surely his reward would be ample.

"When Peter saw Malchus from Caiaphas' house also trying to molest Jesus, he struck out wildly with his sword and cut off the servant's right ear. But when Jesus saw it, he—he reached out and touched the wound and—healed him!" Mark's voice was awed.

There was a tightness in Mary's throat and yet, deep, a singing in her heart. Even in the midst of hate and injustice, Jesus still possessed that unselfishness and love which made him, without doubt, the Son of God. What chance had revenge against the greatness of that spirit? Surely, he would be delivered out of their hands!

"Then he offered himself for their binding. But when I saw the soldiers bring out the rope, I snatched it from them. One of them turned and laid hold of me. Jesus said to them: 'Are you come out, as against a thief, with swords and staves? I was in the temple with you every day, yet you made no attempt to take me: but this is your hour, and the power of darkness.' Then they bound him. But I loosened my girdle and slipped out of my robe. Thus I escaped."

As he finished speaking, Peter entered the house, his face hidden by his turban. He walked as if in his sleep, going past the two without a word.

Mary cried: "Peter, what of the Teacher? How does he fare?" She dipped him a drink of cool water and brought it to him. The cup fell from Peter's shaking fingers. He bowed his head and wept unrestrainedly. His great convulsive sobs brought Mary's first terrible fear alive in her.

She stood there, her frightened eyes upon him, and could not speak.

In the distance, a cock crowed. Peter roused himself. "There, the cock crows! The Master said, 'Before the cock crows once, you will deny me three times' and lo, his words are true! Alas I have failed him! I have failed him!" Bowing his head again, he gave himself up to uncontrolled weeping.

At the outer court before the house of Caiaphas, Mary found no porter nor any other person. Fearlessly, she went on to the second gateway and entered the great courtyard. At the four corners of the yard, great torches burned red. On the western porch below a window, Mary saw Caiaphas leaning against a Roman chair. With half-closed eyes, he watched a servant blindfold Jesus with a towel and then force one of the bystanders to strike him on the cheek.

"Prophesy!" bawled the servant. "Who is it that struck you?"

The crowd gathered in the courtyard shouted derisively. Mary cried out, and pushed desperately against the bodies blocking her way.

But Jesus remained silent.

The brother-in-law of Malchus came up behind him and with doubled fists smote him over the head again and again. Mary of Bethany's moan was drowned in the raucous laughter of the crowd.

"There, prophet!" cried the Nazarene's persecutor. "Who is beating you now? Guess if you can!"

Jesus said nothing.

A short, dark-faced man darted forward. "You're the impertinent fellow who upset the temple stalls and drove honest merchants from their business. Do you remember the lash that struck me? It is my turn now!" He hit Jesus across the mouth.

An elder shouted from where he stood, a little apart among the priests and wealthy Pharisees. "Who are you but a carpenter trying to make yourself great? What blasphemy! Calling yourself a prophet of Israel!"

Dull-witted Jehoiada suddenly appeared at the rear gate and called out loudly as he hurried forward: "He is a disturber of the peace! He is a ruffian who upsets money tables and destroys the livelihood of dove sellers!" His voice was high-pitched, and to Mary of Bethany it sounded like the screaming of a desert wind. "Yea, he is the one who dared come and free the sacred sheep and cattle reserved for the Lord's sacrifice! Punish him! Punish him!"

It seemed to Mary that her jostling progress through the packed watchers was a long and bitter journey. She tasted salt all the way.

"Let me through! Let me through!" she begged. But for every five steps she took, she was thrust back three. Men jeered at her, catching her arm as she passed. Someone recognized her and called out: "This woman is one of his followers. Let her pass! Let her see how her beloved looks now!" Eyes half-blinded, throat aching, Mary pushed on until, at last, she could see him plainly.

"Master!"

Jesus, blindfolded, was sitting on the ground in the center of the middle courtyard. His hands were tied behind his back. Jehoiada, standing over him spraddle-legged, struck Jesus on the cheeks with both hands.

The multitude roared, but Mary could bear it no longer.

"Jehoiada, stop!" she cried out with all her strength. "Let him go! Let him go!"

The crowd hushed in amazement as she ran forward and pushed the priest aside. "Stop," she sobbed. "Let him alone, I tell you! How dare you treat him thus—how dare you!"

Malchus seized her by the collar of her robe and threw her to the ground.

"Here's another trouble-maker," he shouted. "We'll attend to her, too!"

There was a roar, quickly stilled. In the silence, Mary felt the toe of a servant's heavy boot and heard, inexplicably, the voice of Joanna, Chuza's wife. She struggled to sitting position, her head throbbing. Joanna was standing in front of Caiaphas.

"That girl is a friend of mine. With your permission I'll take her with me."

Caiaphas frowned, hesitated, then inclined his head with a jerk. Joanna went swiftly to Mary's side. "Mary, I have something for you to do. Please come away with me."

Mary of Bethany looked at Jesus. He still sat in the same place with his eyes blindfolded, but he looked—almost calm. Certainly he was, she thought with astonishment, more self-controlled than any of those about him. His head was erect and turned in her direction. He appeared unconscious of bruises and scarlet finger marks upon his skin. In his face was, it was true, struggle and sadness—but no uncertainty. No uncertainty!

"Come away!" whispered Joanna. "Your arrest, Mary, would but give him more pain."

Mary, hesitating and reluctant, saw Jesus' lips move. They were forming a word.

"Go."

Turning, Mary was aware that Caiaphas' brother-in-law, Jonathan, had come boldly out of the house and had joined them. With Joanna, he led her outside the gate.

"Do not fret about him," said Jonathan. "Despite all this

persecution, I am convinced that with the power given to him from God, he can free himself whenever he wishes."

Joanna said excitedly: "I believe that, too! He is but waiting for the proper moment."

Mary tried to believe it, too. It was a heartening thought. By a great miracle, Jesus could gain his freedom from his tormenters whenever he wished. Whenever he wished!

CHAPTER XXXI

THE sun was yet pale upon the roofs of Jerusalem and the pillared grandeur of the temple when Mary reached the west gate. She had spent the night in prayer at the house of Joanna. This morning Chuza had brought the disquieting news that the Sanhedrin, at a special meeting before dawn, had voted the death penalty for Jesus.

Chuza's face had been grim. "It was to be expected. The verdict was virtually decided at the last meeting. This was merely a formality."

"But—but what reason do they have?" faltered Mary.

The steward laughed shortly. "They don't need any reason! They can't do their temple business as long as he lives, so they cannot rest until he is put out of the way. They are capable of inventing anything." He paced the room, steps quick, eyes narrowed with anger. "They are giving as the chief reason that he planned to start a revolution in Galilee."

"But—that's untrue!" cried Mary.

"There's another reason, too. They claim that when he said, 'Destroy this temple and in three days I will build it up again,' he was disturbing the peace and order of the city. Jehoiada was the principal witness to that."

Joanna said scornfully: "Jehoiada!"

"What really angers them most, however, is his saying, 'The God of the universe is my Father' and 'I am the Son of God.' That is enough for Caiaphas. He declares such words make Jesus a criminal." Chuza smashed a fist down upon a polished table top. "Greed thwarted knows no scruples, it seems."

"And now," said Joanna, "I suppose the next step will be to take him before Pilate."

Hearing that, Mary had come at once.

The procession, with Jesus in its midst, must surely pass this way. She had but a few moments to wait. There they came! Soldiers with glittering spears. The high priest, Caiaphas, slow-footed and self-righteous in his robes of office. Four of his servants following reverently after.

Mary uttered a little cry. Jesus was next! There was no mistaking the quiet dignity of that tread. Though his hands were still bound behind his back, though he was surrounded by guards, his blue turbaned head was high and his eyes looked straight before him. It seemed to Mary that his gaze went through and beyond his accusers, past dingy buildings and narrow streets, out of Jerusalem, on . . . on . . .

The last two men in the march were Jehoiada, chief of the temple guards, and his assistant, Pedahzur, son of Asaph. Jehoiada was wagging his head with his customary foolish solemnity as Pedahzur, gesturing toward Jesus, babbled shrill denunciations.

The procession did not go through the temple grounds, but instead passed through the gate of Damascus, turned to the right and entered the Judgment Hall which was close beside the tower of Antonia.

Entering quietly, Mary found but forty or fifty persons there. Doubtless few knew of Jesus' trial. Caiaphas came only to the entrance of the Hall, but would not come in, declining to defile himself by crossing the threshold of a Gentile on the Passover. Truly, thought Mary, this was "straining at gnats and swallowing camels." His body followed the groove of holy ritual while his mind lusted for the blood of the Son of Man.

Mary, without raising her veil, found an inconspicuous place in the far corner of the room. A guard carrying a long spear entered, followed almost immediately by Pilate wearing the full wide toga symbolizing his position. Two more guards preceded their captain who wore a silver helmet, shield and carried a long sword in his left hand. From the right hurried a scribe, carrying a roll of parchment and a pen holder. He took his place importantly in front of Pilate's desk.

A guard's loud voice called: "The court convenes. The accused is the carpenter Jesus."

Jesus, his hands still bound, stood up before Pilate. At the same time Benezra, representing the Sanhedrin, and Jehoiada, chief of the temple guards, took their places on the plaintiff's stand. The law of Rome, thought Mary, was indeed advanced in matters pertaining to trials, for though the Jewish law permitted trials in secret and settled them without ceremony, the Roman law would not tolerate such disorder. She was grateful for this now. It might be the saving of the Master, for certainly no honest judge could condemn him.

Pilate turned to Benezra. "What complaint do you bring against this man?"

Benezra smiled obsequiously. "Your Honor! We pray for the everlasting blessing of heaven upon the great Emperor of Rome and we proffer our gratitude for the untiring efforts of your honor, our governor."

Mary, glancing toward the entrance where the priests stood, saw Caiaphas wink slyly at Annas and the latter smile derisively. It occurred to her that the faces of both men were those of children grown old. Their countenances showed the wearing away of years, but none of the wisdom which should come with maturity.

Benezra was continuing. "Your Honor, this man called Jesus opposed the gathering of the taxes from the people. Moreover he dares to defy Rome by calling himself the King of Judea, and he is active in revolutionary agitations."

Lies—all lies! Accusations subtly molded to fit the garment of Roman law and the ear of the hearer. Mary twisted her hands together. Her lips parted indignantly. Pilate, however, seemed neither surprised nor impressed by these indictments, having been prepared by Joanna for such details. He looked curiously at Jesus.

"Do you call yourself the King of the Jews as the plaintiff says?"

Jesus' eyes, which had been closed in silent prayer, Mary knew, opened.

"Do you ask this of yourself or have others told it to you?"

A murmur of amusement went through the room. Pilate flushed, and said testily: "Am I a Jew? Your own nation and the chief priests have delivered you to me: what have you done?"

Jesus' clear steadfast gaze was upon the governor's face. Mary saw Pilate grow first annoyed, then bewildered under it. His own eyes, shadowed and bloodshot, dropped. Then, after a moment, he seemed to remember his authority. Squaring his weary shoulders, he sent Jesus an impatient glance.

"Well?"

"My kingdom is not of this world: if my kingdom were of this world, then my servants would fight that I should not be delivered to the Jews: but now is my kingdom not from hence."

In Jesus' voice was the same quiet assurance with which he was wont to address those gathered in the temple to hear him, or upon the hillsides, or on the banks of the Jordan. He spoke to Pilate as he would to one of his followers, gently as to a child.

Uncomfortably, Pilate began to question Benezra. "Since this is clearly a matter of religion, should not your Sanhedrin take it under consideration?"

It was Jehoiada who answered, drawing himself up to his full height. "Your Honor, if this matter had been one which could have been settled by our religious council, we should not have bothered you at this early morning hour, I assure you. Has not your Honor heard that this criminal has sown the seeds of revolt from Galilee in the north to the remotest corner of Judea? If we had the authority to decree the death penalty for this—this revolutionist, we should have done it long before this, but since we have no such power, we have brought him here for your verdict."

Mary's fingernails bit hurtfully into her palms. She had never liked the wily Jehoiada, although Martha had often declared him a harmless fellow, the tool of Annas and Caiaphas. Tool or not, he was an implement being used to torture the Master, and she hated him. Hated the wagging head, the watery eye, the veined, reddened nose. Hated most of all the thinking—or the lack of it—which based his brazen words.

Pilate seized upon one name. "Galilee? Galilee, you said?" He turned to the court scribe. "Is this man a citizen of Galilee?"

The short-haired scribe replied in terse Latin. "He is a native of Nazareth in Galilee."

Relief smoothed the strain from Pilate's face. For a

moment his eyes rested upon Jesus, then moved to the Nazarene's two accusers.

"According to the law of the Roman empire, a governor is not permitted to try a prisoner who belongs outside his jurisdiction. Since the accused is a Galilean, he should therefore be taken before Herod for judgment." He looked toward the entrance where Caiaphas and Annas stood. "If you wish, I can send a messenger to the king, asking his convenience." He sat back in his chair, awaiting an answer.

Jehoiada looked confused, and conferred with Benezra in a low tone. Finally, he called out in a high voice to Caiaphas.

"Your worship, the high priest! Have we your permission to take this case before Herod?"

Caiaphas' fingers stroked his long beard. Mary saw that he was muttering something to Annas. When he spoke at last, his voice was loudly impatient.

"Very well—very well! There is nothing else we can do, apparently."

One of the guards disappeared from the stand, taking the message from Pilate to the king whose palace was a few blocks away. The public trial was adjourned for the time being, and the disappointed onlookers filed slowly out into the narrow street. Jesus, however, remained where he was, and Mary could not bring herself to leave him. She moved nearer to him, hoping that she might have an opportunity to let him know that she was there, watching and praying for him.

But Pilate also wanted to speak with Jesus. He asked him again whether or not he was King of the Jews.

"My kingdom is not of this world," said Jesus again.

"But you admit then, you have a kingdom. Therefore you must be a king."

Jesus smiled. Mary was filled with wonder. In the midst of persecution, while trouble seethed about him, and no one could foresee the end, whether it be good or evil, Jesus could smile!

"You say that I am a king. For this purpose was I born, for this cause came I into the world, that I should bear witness to the truth. Everyone that is of the truth hears my voice."

His head on one side as he listened, Pilate frowned. His interest in the man who stood so calmly before him was deep. Mary could see that he was pondering the master's words. Her heart beat fast. Ah, if Pilate might only believe! Surely the manner of Jesus' speaking, the courage of his words, the wondrous expression of his face must convince the Roman governor! How was it possible for one speaking with Jesus of Nazareth not to be persuaded?

Pilate leaned forward, his mouth curved cynically. "Truth? Truth? What is truth?" He did not wait for Jesus' answer, but rose at once and walked nervously from the Judgment Hall.

CHAPTER XXXII

Mary leaned against a pomegranate tree in the south courtyard of Herod Antipas. The priests, the scribes, the money changers, merchants and Pharisees crowding around her seemed figures in a distorted dream. Weariness weighted her eyelids, made her hands limp and her body heavy. Only her mind was clear and sharp, strangely detached from flesh and bone. It was as if she thought outside her mortal boundaries and, for that reason, more distinctly. She was certain of but one thing. Jesus of Nazareth possessed or was possessed by reality. His life was potent as sunshine piercing mist—as solid as rock in water. He stood now, lean and straight, and somehow regal, in the midst of his brawny Roman guards.

A little while ago, she had stationed herself by one of the great pillars in front of the palace. She had called out to him loudly, hoping he might hear as he passed.

"Master, I am praying for you!"

He had heard! His head lifted, turned toward her. For the breath of a moment, his eyes rested upon her in tender acknowledgment. The words he answered were not for those others, the unknowing deaf, but Mary of Bethany had ears to hear. "Thank you, Mary."

She wound one arm about the tree trunk and felt the pattern of the bark in her palm. Overhead the pomegranate leaves stirred against the cloudless sky. "Thank you, Mary." Yea, there was a language of the soul which, sitting at the feet of the master of it, she had begun to learn. To learn at least to recognize the tongue and a few of the simplest phrases, though indeed the speaking came hard to an unpracticed scholar.

Joshua, Herod's captain of the guards, was talking with Caiaphas, Benezra and Jehoiada. Now and again, he glanced toward Jesus, and there was uncertainty in his keen glance. His swarthy, lean-jawed face was not unkind, Mary thought, and remembered hearing that, after the death of John the Baptist, he had treated the prophet's desolate disciples with consideration. She imagined that she could detect in his expression now a certain distaste for this business.

With pomp and music, Herod Antipas, tetrarch of Galilee and Perea, entered. Over the scarlet robe which his father had worn, he was wearing the cream-colored toga sent to him by the Emperor Tiberius. When he reached the throne, ten tall guards wearing Roman helmets and carrying long spears took their places on either side. The court scribe, Florus, sat below him to the right. As in the Roman court, parchment, ink and pens were in readiness for the trial.

This time, however, Caiaphas himself stepped forward. His eyes were veined and puffy-lidded. The dark skin under them sagged. Long lines pulled at his mouth corners. His breathing was harsh. Mary could not but contrast his appearance with that of Jesus who, despite the hours of abuse and persecution, the present strain, showed but slight fatigue.

"Your majesty!" Caiaphas rubbed his hands together as if they needed support to keep from trembling. One eye and the corner of his mouth jerked spasmodically as he talked. "We felicitate your majesty on your august virtues.

We appear thus unceremoniously before you because it is absolutely necessary that we receive your wise judgment on this case. The accused, whom we hereby bring before you, is Jesus, a carpenter of Nazareth in Galilee." Caiaphas turned to Jesus, then looked quickly away. He coughed nervously, cleared his throat. "I am sure that your majesty has heard of the accused, but with your permission I shall recount the accusations briefly. He opposes the Roman collection of taxes and has a scheme of revolt against the Roman Empire."

Herod Antipas sat staring at Jesus, making no attempt to hide his curiosity. Obviously he had heard much of this Nazarene teacher and was glad of the opportunity to see him. Indeed, Mary thought, he looked as if he half-hoped for a miracle. To Caiaphas he gave little heed, save for flicking him occasionally with a watery eye as one slaps at an insect. The high priest was an old and tiresome familiarity. Jesus of Nazareth was an intriguing novelty.

When Caiaphas ceased, the king merely sat gazing at the master. The high priest somewhat impatiently repeated his accusations. Herod started, rubbed his chin uneasily. He peered down his nose at Jesus.

"Have you ever planned a revolt against the Roman government?"

Jesus was motionless. His eyes were upon the palace window and they did not leave it.

One minute.

Two minutes.

Why doesn't he speak? Mary gripped the tree in an agony of suspense. Why doesn't he say that never—never—did he plot against Roman rule? Why doesn't he say that he fights only Satan and the powers of darkness?

Three minutes.

Four minutes. . . .

The quivering of Caiaphas' lips became a smile, cautious at first, then triumphant. The carpenter-prophet did not deny it! He stands brazenly before the king and will not answer! Surely such conduct amounts to a confession!

Herod moved restlessly upon his throne, as though, quite suddenly, he found it uncomfortable and ill-suited to his form.

Across the courtyard, there was a twittering of sparrows building a nest in the eaves of the palace. Busily the little birds were flying to and fro with mud. Mary saw Jesus' eyes leave the window and go to them. "Is not one sparrow sold for a farthing? Yet not one of these shall fall to the ground without the knowledge of God." She remembered that Jesus once said these words in the meadows of Galilee. Perhaps he was thinking them now. He surpassed life and death, she thought, and began to understand now that he was, as he had said, a Limb of God, dumb before those who would deliver him to death. Humility swept over her. She bowed her head in contrition.

The scribe, Florus, spoke arrogantly. "Carpenter, did you hear his majesty's question? Why do you not answer?"

Still Jesus uttered not a single word. Caiaphas' eyes gleamed. His body shook like an individual earth convulsion. "Your majesty! This fellow is impertinence itself. He dared to say, 'Destroy this temple and in three days, I will build it up again!' The temple, mind you, that took forty-six years in building!"

Caiaphas shook his fist. The spectators burst into laughter. Herod, relieved from the uncomfortable silence, also guffawed. The high priest began to laugh, too, then looked about suspiciously. Were they laughing at the ridiculous statement of the carpenter—or at him? He frowned. Incredible.

But Jesus remained motionless, his eyes upon the light banding the window sill.

Caiaphas glanced at him sharply then grunted. "And that is not all. After we seized him last night we examined him and what do you think? He claims that God, the creator of the universe, is his Father—and he calls himself the Son of God!"

Herod pursed his lips and looked at Jesus to see if he would not say something to this. When there was no response, he turned a large jade ring round and round upon his fat finger, frowning at it.

He, too, Mary saw, was confounded in the presence of the Master, just as Pilate had been and, like Pilate, was loath to pronounce sentence. Hope stirred in her. Perhaps —perhaps Jesus would go free then!

Herod made another attempt. "Did You really try to instigate the destruction of the temple?" he asked in a low rasping voice.

But Jesus answered not a word.

At a loss, Herod turned to Caiaphas. "Your worship, the high priest, as far as I can learn from the testimony given here today, I think this case comes under the jurisdiction of the Roman governor. If this man had committed murder or robbery, then certainly he should come before me, but such a thing as a plot against the Roman Empire must certainly come before His Honor, the Roman governor." He sat back in his chair, looking well satisfied with his decision.

Disgruntled, Caiaphas rubbed his head. "Since you put it that way," he muttered, "it seems reasonable enough."

Jehoiada laughed vacantly. "Whoever heard of such a complicated case? When we take it before the governor, he says it is outside his jurisdiction, take it to Herod. But when we take it to Herod, he says it has to do with the peace and order of the Roman Empire, therefore it must be returned to the governor." He wagged his head loosely and waved his hand before his face. "Now who can tell us what to do?"

The crowd roared, but Herod's mouth grew grim. Caiaphas, quick to catch the king's annoyance, barked sharply to Jehoiada: "Quiet!" The king beckoned the high priest and they whispered together.

Jesus alone seemed untouched by all the confusion and turmoil. He remained motionless but, lifting his eyes to heaven, appeared to be engaged in prayer. Mary of Bethany also lifted her eyes and tried to pray. "Father in heaven, save Your Son from the malice and ignorance of these men."

She was distracted, however, by the appearance of Herodias, who came out from the back courtyard. Herod's second wife was wearing a scarlet robe and a Roman toga. Joanna was with her and they were followed by Philip, the son of Herod's concubine and a half-brother of Antipas. He had but recently married Salome who soon hurried after wearing a dress of Damascus cloth. She looked about her brightly at the crowd, posturing and widening her eyes childishly. She was seeking admiration, Mary knew—and cared little where she found it. It was wine to her.

The crowd had broken into groups now. Herodias and Salome, careless of hearers, began to speak together.

"He doesn't look a bit like John the Baptist, does he?" asked Herodias. There was relief in her tone. "You can see what nonsense it was—the story that this Jesus was John come to life!"

Salome, cocking her head, was eyeing Jesus critically. She shrugged. "He certainly doesn't look like anyone who'd have so many women disciples. I'd have supposed him to be much more—more dashing." She turned to Joanna. "Whatever do you seen in him, Joanna?" She laughed. "Really!"

Joanna did not answer, but moved to Mary's side. Their hands met and clung. Tightly. Tightly.

A group of money-changers in the center of the yard began to shout at Jesus. One of them filled an old shoe with horse dung and threw it at him, jeering: "Here, Christ! Here's our offering for you!"

Missing Jesus, it struck instead a dove vendor standing nearby. The crowd became hilarious. Money-changers and temple merchants followed one another in attempts to torment and abuse Jesus. Some took off their sandals and threw them at him. Since many of the missiles fell dangerously close to Herod's throne, one of the soldiers of the Imperial guard led Jesus away to where Herodias was standing.

Benezra, standing by, began to ridicule Jesus. "How now, prophet! Working miracles is a little difficult under such—unfriendly conditions, isn't it?"

Jesus made no answer. A tall nervous money-changer joined Benezra. "Greetings, Messiah!" He hit him a stinging blow upon the cheek.

Mary cried out and started forward, but Joanna's hand held her.

"But that man is Shallum, well known for his evil ways. How dare he strike the Master!"

Joanna said gently: "We can help the Master more by prayer."

But now the money-changers and temple vendors were crowding around Jesus, closer and closer, arguing with one another who should smite him first. Mary could endure it no longer. She wrenched her hand from Joanna's, and ran forward, crying out in a sharp voice: "Stop it!

Stop it at once, I tell you! That man is my Teacher. If you must hit someone with your foul hands, hit me, cowards!"

Herod looked up from his conference with Caiaphas. He ordered the guards to bring Jesus back to his former position and to stand with spears outstretched to prevent the crowd closing in upon him.

Mary fell back, then, and soon found the comforting arm of Joanna about her. She was trembling and tears were running, hot and salty, from her lashes.

"Joanna—Joanna!" she moaned. "I cannot bear it."

There was suffering in Joanna's dark eyes, too, but she said quietly: "He can bear it. See how patient he is, Mary."

Dashing the tears away with one hand, Mary saw. Yea, in the face of Jesus of Nazareth was the same gentle strength as of old. She gazed at him in wonderment. No anger. No resentment. Not a vestige of fear. Instead, in that countenance, an endurance that was almost peace. Surely, she thought reverently, the will which sustained him was not human, but divine.

"If they'd only tease him a bit more," said Salome, her lips full and petulant, "I'm sure he'd work a miracle. Wouldn't that be amusing?" She giggled. "I'd like to see the face of that old fellow there, if this Jesus should set his beard afire!"

Her mother smiled. "You mean Caiaphas, the high priest, child? For shame, Salome!" But her glance at her daughter was both tolerant and admiring. She looked at Philip. "What do you think might make the man do a marvel, Philip?"

Philip looked dubious. "I have no idea. Indeed, this is the first prophet I remember seeing—if he is one."

Herodias stared thoughtfully at Jesus, then struck her hands together. "I have it! The garment he wears is not suitable for miracles. Salome, fetch a better robe for the

Messiah!" She laughed. "Imagine if he should be gathered up in a cloud to heaven as was the prophet Elijah!"

Mary leaned back against the pomegranate tree, love for Jesus and hate for his tormenters mingling, so that her mind was in a turmoil. She watched Salome dance away into the palace, and return presently with a handsome crimson robe over her arm.

"You don't mind his having this, do you, Philip?" she asked carelessly. Without waiting for his answer, she summoned a soldier. "Put this on the—the Messiah. Perhaps it will encourage him to do a miracle. If he would I'd ask the king to pardon him."

Benezra and Jehoiada scowled at her, watching apprehensively as soldiers put the king's red toga over Jesus' goat's hair robe of brown. Once more, the crowd laughed derisively.

Mary knew what Salome's motives must be. She knew that Joanna's only son had been cured by Jesus, and was therefore a little in awe. She was also aware of the widespread adverse criticism of her conduct regarding John the Baptist. She hoped by her speech to curry the favor of the crowd. Thus, with the mixed emotions of sympathy and amusement, she proffered her husband's robe to the Master.

Herod's messenger returned at this moment, and immediately ten soldiers fell into place about Jesus and led by the captain of the guard, they went out again through the palace gate. The high priest, Benezra, Jehoiada, Shallum, the money-changers, the vendors and the rest of the throng followed. Outside, pilgrims, seeing the procession, also joined the crowd in expectation of excitement. Mary went by herself through the Joppa gate, turned north toward Herod's gate, and reached the Praetorium before the

Roman soldiers. There she stationed herself by the great limestone steps leading to the Judgment Hall.

It was some time before Jesus came. At last she went to the gate to see if she could catch sight of the approaching procession. Finally it came into view, turning into the tower of Antonia. Jesus, Mary saw, was not wearing the red robe now, but entered the hall in His robe of brown.

Two hours had elapsed since the early morning six o'clock trial. The appearance of the court was entirely changed, for this time the huge stone plaza before the Judgement Hall was filled with people. Jehoiada and his scheming friends came at once to the front, completely surrounding Mary. As before, Caiaphas stood at the entrance, not deigning to enter the house of a Gentile. Shallum, too, did not enter. As in the previous hearing, the accusers took their places on the right of the platform, and the accused on the left.

Pilate addressed Jehoiada immediately. "What is your wish? Herod did not release the prisoner, but has sent him back to this court."

Jehoiada bowed, rubbing his hands ingratiatingly.

"That is so, your Honor."

Pilate moved uneasily in his chair, looked at Jesus questioningly and then back at Jehoiada. "If you insist on our handing down judgment on this man we prefer to judge him, not as instigator of a rebellion but as one who disturbs the peace. We would judge his offense as one against the police regulations."

How far these civil courts, even the fairest of them, strayed from the simplicity of truth, Mary thought. Fear and dishonesty warped words and twisted the law into an ill-fitting robe. Formality here, as in the strict rites of Pharisaical creed, blotted out the shining of the spirit. Man's courage faltered under the heavy chains. Man's vision dimmed. Expediency blurred inner knowledge as now it did Pilate's. What he wanted to do was obvious. That he dared not was also clear.

The pilgrims brought a new element into the gathering. Seeing that the governor's sympathy was with Jesus, they shouted from one corner of the room where they had assembled: "Free the prophet! By what right do the vendors of Jerusalem accuse a man from Galilee?"

The merchants of Jerusalem quieted, Mary noticed. She guessed why. The pilgrims of Galilee had the reputation of being the best money spenders in the city during celebrations, and the vendors knew that if they incurred their enmity, losses would be great. They were more subdued here, therefore, than in the palace grounds.

Pilate was quick to sense the temper of the crowd. His tired eyes went from Jesus to the pilgrims. Then, finally and with distaste, to the priests and Pharisees of Jerusalem.

He called for silence.

"We have found the carpenter Jesus guilty of disturbing the peace and order and do hereby sentence him to flogging."

He arose at once and left the hall.

Jehoiada broke the stunned silence. "What kind of a sentence is that?" he roared. "Ridiculous!"

"If this is all it amounts to," shouted the disappointed temple vendors, "we would have done better not to bring him before Pilate."

"If it is only flogging," shrilled Benezra, "the high priest can administer that sort of punishment!"

Mary of Bethany felt faint. The Master's life was safe. No death sentence. True, it was unjust that he was to be punished at all, but still . . . still . . .

She groped toward the door.

CHAPTER XXXIII

Twenty-six."

There were still thirteen strokes before they reached the
end. Father in heaven, thirteen more—and at every cut of
the barbed leather lash in the hands of the burly Roman
soldier, the flesh was torn and blood gushed forth. Mary's
fingers were pressed hard over her mouth. She must not
cry out. She must not. Jesus, her Master, made not the
smallest sound as the blows fell.

She tried not to see, not to hear, to think instead how
dazzling the sun was upon the tower and upon the golden
walls of the temple directly across from it. She told herself that most of the punishment was over, and when it
was, Jesus of Nazareth would go free. She would take
him back over the brook Cedron, through the garden of
Gethsemane which had known his lonely agony, along
the mountain path to Bethany, to the quiet garden and
the little stone house where peace was waiting. How
tenderly she would anoint those ghastly wounds—how
gently would her fingers move upon that furrowed back!

"Twenty-seven." A harsh, blaring voice.

Mary closed her eyes, but she could not close her ears.
Each time the lash fell, it was as if it sunk into her own
quivering flesh. Enough—surely it was enough! Since last
night the Master had been tormented by Annas, mocked
in the house of Caiaphas, beaten at the palace of Herod.

An ordinary man would have been crushed by the continuance of such shame and abuse. But Jesus of Nazareth, she whispered to herself over and over, was no ordinary man. He was the Messiah—the Lamb of God. As such he suffered and endured.

Several of the Pharisees standing near began to count strokes with the soldier.

"Twenty-eight."

Once again, Mary looked at him. Such patient forebearance! He did not raise his head nor take any notice of the blood streaming down his back. He was bowed, she knew, in silent weeping, and she, too, wept.

"Twenty-nine." The cruel drone of voices. The whine of the whip as the wielder cracked it in the air before the stinging blow. Mary wanted to break through the rope which held off the bystanders, and take his place. She closed her eyes and tried to pray. God of Israel! Why should the sinless Son of Man have to suffer thus? Was it because he healed the sick and comforted the sorrowing? Was it because he drove evil spirits from harassed minds? Was it—was it because he raised the dead?

"Thirty." She could not open her eyes. She was remembering what Jesus had said, that his blood must be shed for mankind. He was prepared for this, then. Prepared in all humility for the results of his blessed ministry. He had known that hate and envy would not rest until the lash curled about his shoulders. Yea, she remembered, but still rebelled. Was there no other way? Father, help him—help your Son. Heal his wounds, even as he healed those of others. Comfort him. Still his anguish!

"Thirty-one." Mary forced herself to look. Jesus' back was lined with long swollen welts between deep gashes cut by the whip. The flesh was torn like earth freshly hoed after summer rain.

"Thirty-two." Father in Heaven, we are not worth such sacrifice! Surely, we are not worth it. . . .

A man behind her spoke. "He's a stubborn one! Almost anyone else would have collapsed ere now. I know. I've watched many a scourging." He spoke with admiring condescension, and as casually as one might mention the gladiatorial games.

One of the onlooking soldiers said suddenly to his comrades: "Wasn't it this fellow who cured the Capernaum centurion's servant?"

"Thirty-three."

A lean dark soldier scratched his head, then nodded. "Yea, even so."

Another said: "But I think he had some connection with the viaduct rioters. That man Jehu, imprisoned here in the dungeon, just asked about him."

The first soldier said dubiously: "He appears meek and gentle ——"

"But the truth is he has been planning a revolt against Rome!"

"Thirty-four!"

Mary went forward to the rope and, holding to it, fell upon her knees. O God! Forbid that Jesus' blood should flow in vain!

Sebastian, the centurion, appeared and called out ringingly: "What of this criminal? Is he to be returned to court?"

The man with the scourge stopped swinging it and moved his shoulders wearily: "Nay, this is all."

The short man behind Mary called out to the centurion: "This fellow must have a charmed body. He doesn't appear to be weakening in the least." He laughed. "Perhaps he cannot be wounded!"

The centurion nodded briefly, but said nothing.

"Thirty-five."

"Thirty-six."

The lashes fell to the side, on Jesus' ribs. "He'll go out with this!" exclaimed the flogger. "If he doesn't, it's because he uses magic."

Blood spurted from the Nazarene's sides. Mary of Bethany closed her eyes. Her hands squeezed the rough rope, skin taut over knuckles. "Master! Master!" Her lips moved numbly.

"There! I tell you, He uses enchantment!" shouted the flogger in exasperation. "A few strokes should have finished him." He swung the lash until it made fearful music in the air.

"Thirty-seven!"

"Thirty-eight!"

At every blow, Mary's hands gripped the rope convulsively. But Jesus sat as if his flesh were as insensible as earth. He did not even wince. How long-suffering he was! She prayed that she might not forget his wondrous courage through all eternity.

"Thirty-nine!" The lash was laid across his hips.

"Well, 'tis over at last! Thrashing this charmed creature made my own arm pain." Carrying his thongs, the flogger walked off scowling.

Jesus bowed his head in his bound hands. Mary clutched the rope, her eyes smarting and her throat aching. It was over at last. The lash would fall no more. They could go home to Bethany.

"Free him!" ordered the centurion gruffly. "Punishing this man was a disgrace. He is a victim of the high priest's jealousy. Caiaphas despised his good reputation."

But someone called out from among the bystanders: "Sir! You are misinformed. He is one of Barabbas' crowd. He is one of the aqueduct rioters."

Mary turned. The man who had spoken was Shallum. His eyes gleamed with satisfaction as they fell upon the bent form of Jesus.

A guard threw to Jesus the red toga he had received at Herod's palace.

"Put this on him!"

A soldier picked the garment up. "How did this get here?" His hands caressed the material and his eyes were greedy.

"It belongs to the prisoner," said the guard. "It is for the king of Judea."

"Who? This fellow?"

"Yea," shouted Shallum, "that's what the vendors of Jerusalem say. He claims it is all right not to pay taxes to Rome, and moreover he has tried to spread the seeds of revolution so that he may be king himself!"

"I understand," said the soldier. "The gown is but part of the jest. Very well, we will carry it through. We will treat him as befits a king." He strode to Jesus and roused him with a kick. "Arise, King of the Jews! Now begins your coronation ceremony!"

Jesus permitted the soldiers to have their way. They draped the toga from his left shoulder around his hips and caught it up again on the left shoulder.

"But this isn't good enough. He needs a crown as well. Now what shall we do for a crown?"

A short stocky man snatched up a scythe and ran off to make a search. One of the soldiers pulled a reed out of the woven sun screen.

He held it up triumphantly. "Behold his scepter!"

His fellows cheered and clapped him on the shoulder.

The short man came back with some thorny branches, and proceeded to weave the pronged strands into a crown.

The bystanders applauded hilariously. He handed it to the guard who, taking it, cried out in pain.

"By the gods, I'm stabbed!" He dropped it to the ground.

The man who had woven the crown laughed. "Here, take my gloves."

Pulling on the gloves, the guard picked up the thorny circle and pushed it down hard on Jesus' head. Blood sprang from the cruel points, but Jesus neither moved nor spoke.

Mary sobbed aloud, but no one paid any attention to her. Why did they not release him? Why? Then she remembered with sharp emotion how often Jesus had repeated a favorite passage from the prophet Isaiah.

"He was despised and rejected of men; a man of sorrows and acquainted with grief: and as one from whom men hide their face, he was despised: and we esteemed him not. Surely he has borne our grief and carried our sorrows; yet we did esteem him stricken, smitten of God and afflicted. But he was wounded for our transgressions, he was bruised for our iniquities; the chastisement of our peace was upon him; and with his stripes we are healed."

Looking up, Mary saw Jesus open his eyes and gaze across at the golden wall of the temple. Was he too remembering those words of Isaiah? Now, for the first time, she began to understand the Nazarene's constant awareness of his divine mission.

Jesus' quietness angered the guard. He struck him on the cheek, then spat upon him.

"Hail, King of the Jews!"

A great crowd of soldiers, just released from morning inspection, came from behind the tower at the shout. One of them, seeing Jesus, stopped in horrified amazement, then ran forward.

"What goes on here? What are you doing to this good man? He is no criminal. He healed my brother of a broken wrist."

The guard turned upon him sharply. "Would you worship the King of the Jews then? Very well, to your knees, traitor to Rome!"

The newcomer fell back, discomfited.

Mary of Bethany was in distress, fearing they might torment Jesus to death. She turned to search for aid in securing his release, but at that moment a messenger appeared.

"Centurion! Is the prisoner whom you have flogged still there? Do not free him, but return him at once to the Governor's residence."

Mary stood motionless while the crowd surged around her. Voices beat against her ears. "Do not free him . . . do not free him . . . do not free him. . . ." Over and over again. It could not be. There was some terrible mistake. Even Jesus could bear no more. She must get him away—away to Bethany! But the words repeated themselves mockingly in her mind. "Do not free him . . . do not free him. . . ."

She turned and ran to the Judgment Hall, arriving just as the guards brought Jesus in, half staggering and still wearing the crown of thorns.

Pilate's face grew a sickly yellow. His hands shook. He stood up and called for silence, his lips compressed and his eyes bleak.

He said: "Behold the man!"

The crowd burst into shouts and cheers. The room was a great caldron of noise, in which hoarse voices mingled with the shrill and all, it seemed to Mary, were heated by the fire of human passions. Her own cries would not come. Here and there in that Roman courtroom, there were others standing silent. Others, too, who bowed their heads and wept. But only a few. Only a few.

The tumult began to form a pattern. Sound which had been but a tangle became a word, a phrase, a terrible sentence.

Pilate demanded order.

"Citizens! Citizens! Hasn't the prisoner been punished enough?" There was desperation in his manner. "You have a custom that I release unto you one at the Passover. Will you therefore that I release unto you the King of the Jews?"

"Nay, not this man! Release Barabbas! Barabbas!"

In amazed fright, Mary looked about her. Where were the followers of the Master? Then she caught sight of Annas, and understood. Surreptitiously, he was sending his servants into the crowd with sacks of coins which they distributed, whispering to each bystander as they did so. The pilgrims who had defended Jesus previously had apparently gone on, believing that the trial was over. But Annas and Caiaphas, it was clear, had demanded a new hearing, and Pilate had given in.

"Give the amnesty to Barabbas. Crucify Jesus!"

Mary felt like a leaf caught in a tempest. Powerless. Weak. She looked at Pilate and saw fear in his face. He could not make himself heard. He was the representative of the mighty Roman empire, yea—but at this moment he was only a man in an alien, hostile country. His own life, his own career were in the balance. The long series of insurrections, cut down only to sprout again, the ceaseless incidents of nagging insubordination, the strain of keeping a decent garment of apparent peace over the naked body of animosity, all these had been costly. Pilate's once iron nerves were that no longer. His agitation as he stood before the clamorous citizenry of Jerusalem was almost womanly. He was, quite obviously, desirous of saving Jesus of Nazareth, but he was also afraid of offending powerful Jews. If he could please the Jews by releasing the Nazarene, all the better. If not . . . Mary tried not to think about it.

A slave entered with a message for Pilate and he left the room. Had Claudia summoned him, Mary wondered hopefully. If so, she would surely remind him of his promise made to Joanna. She prayed that Pilate's wife would bolster his determination to let Jesus go free.

With Pilate gone, no one checked the crowd. The uproar increased.

"Pilate! We want Pilate!" Angry. Insistent.

"Release Barabbas!"

"Kill Jesus! Crucify the temple thief!"

Presently Pilate returned. He ordered a marble basin brought into the Judgment Hall.

Standing up before the people, he cried in a clear voice: "Having once sentenced the prisoner to flogging, we cannot pronounce another sentence."

Mary felt swift relief, but in the entrance Caiaphas pulled at his beard in sharp annoyance. He motioned to Benezra who at once cried out: "We have a law, and by our law he ought to die, because he made himself the Son of God!"

Pilate said: "I find no fault in him." Standing there, in the sight of all the Jews, he began to tremble. He motioned to Jesus. "Whence are you?"

Jesus said nothing.

"Do you not speak to me?" burst out the governor. "Do you not realize that I have the power to crucify you?"

Jesus lifted his head. His eyes under the crown of thorns were far calmer than Pilate's. "You could have no power at all against me, except it were given you from above."

Mary gave thanks to God. The same clear voice, a little weary now, but still assured. The Son of God knew whereof he spoke.

Pilate started, and now he sought again to persuade the Jews to release Jesus upon the Passover. But Caiaphas whispered furiously to Annas, and Annas sent his servants into the crowd again to spread the skein of whispers.

Jehoiada cried out: "If you let this man go, you are not Caesar's friend: Whoever makes himself king speaks against the Roman Empire. Your Honor, are you an accomplice of these plotters?"

Benezra rubbed his hands. "If so, report of this matter must surely come to the Emperor's ears."

"Pilate is a traitor to the Roman Empire!" shrieked the crowd.

Mary saw Pilate's color fade. Her own hopes thinned. Surely in this Roman Judgment Hall this day all the powers of Satan had gathered. Jesus' persecutors had found the way to influence Pilate.

Pilate made a last attempt. "Behold your King! Shall I crucify your King?"

Caiaphas called out: "We have no king but Caesar!"

"Pilate, Empire traitor!" howled the throng.

The governor stepped nervously to the marble basin. His eyes avoided the face of Jesus of Nazareth. In full view of them all, he washed his hands. To Mary, it seemed as if he were wringing them together in helplessness. Drying his hands, he jerked and the basin tipped, spilling water down upon the vendors who sat at the front.

A tall merchant bellowed: "Our governor seems distraught!" Derisive laughter echoed through the hall.

Pilate resumed his dignity, readjusting the folds of his toga, and took his place again upon the judge's bench.

"Be you witnesses, men of Jerusalem, that I am innocent of the blood of this just man."

Surely, the uproar which greeted this announcement was more animal than human, Mary thought.

The chief captain of the guard, striking his spear against the scribe's desk, called the court to order.

"Silence! Silence!"

A hush fell.

Pilate tried twice to speak, and could not. Then he lifted his hands and let them fall heavily.

"Do with him what you will."

The voice of Mary of Bethany was the first to pierce the quiet. She heard the jagged scream, and thought it came from another's throat. Then, immediate and merciful, darkness closed in upon her.

BOOK SIX

AND YE SHALL KNOW
THE TRUTH . . .

CHAPTER XXXIV

Mary MAGDALENE and the mother of Jesus waited before the gate. Both were standing very still and tense. They had stood there for hours in the quiet of the prison yard, shoulders almost touching, hands folded into their dress fronts where rigid fingers clutched the cloth as though fearful it might be torn away. What they were thinking, if they were thinking at all, could not be learned by looking at them, for the faces of both were masked with the dead, dry mask women often wear who have endured great suffering or come through travail that has touched them to the depths. They had the appearance of being attached to the ground, so rigid they were and silent, like women of stone with stone hearts and cold unseeing eyes; and yet, that they were not all stone—all unfeeling rigidity and insensitivity was shown by the occasional quivering of their lips and their strange spasmodic breathing.

Mary Magdalene wanted to speak but she could not. There were no appropriate words of comfort any more within the range of her experience. There were no words that had sufficient expressiveness and feeling. What was there in any language, spoken or unspoken, that could say to a mother: "Be of good cheer, though your son is persecuted and reviled. Take heart, dear mother, your first born is being done to his death; his wounds bleed, his flesh is tortured."

Mary Magdalene could feel the presence of the woman next to her. It was a strong presence that could not be confined to position or space, or be restricted by physical bounds of any kind. At times the whole weight of her was upon Mary's bosom and again upon her mind or, strangely, at another time, pulsing in the blood that ran into her cold fingers. She remembered now how this mother's son had affected her also; at first when she was near him and later whether she was near him or not. All that was necessary to have his presence or his influence—whatever it was—was to think deeply and reverently, not of him, but of his doctrine of the eternity and oneness of love. That he was not here with them this very minute waiting for himself to emerge bearing his cross, and being flogged by his guards, was due, Mary realized, to her own harassed state of mind. In such a state she could not think deeply or reverently of anything. In such a state, she was controlled almost wholly by grief, resentment and hatred—not to mention a fear that grew hourly that not anything within human means could prevent his crucifixion.

She believed that Jesus' mother, this sweet, very womanly woman at her side, also realized it. And this was true. Mary, the widow of Joseph the carpenter, had what Mary Magdalene could not have—and it was almost destroying her reason—the certain intuitive knowledge mothers have of disaster to their own, the sense of an impending catastrophe. She had had it, not for a day, or a week, or a year even. She had always had it. She had had it before his birth—yea, before his conception. It had been to her flawless motherhood the one irreconcilable and unendurable thing—the black stitch in her secretmost heart.

She thought: "Now they are to take him from me."

Her lips were tightening. Her eyes were much too dry

for tears. She was remembering what they had said when they had brought her the news of his arrest. "They will release him almost at once." Though she had pretended to believe, prayed, hoped—she knew better. They would never release him. That knowledge had always been with her, though never had she accepted it with a calm mind. She would say, "It is not true" and strive desperately to believe it was not true. Sometimes she nearly succeeded. It was pleasanter to think of Jesus as living a long and fruitful life of accomplishment, divinely exalted and beneficently protected from all worldly harms.

Poor Mary Magdalene, waiting with her before the gate, had not, thank God, to endure a mother's intuitive knowledge. In one way it was to be regretted, for her hopes would be blasted the more. As for herself, she was already resigned to it, or hoped she was. Resignation made it easier. Or did it? Would it ever be easy to see one's son die such a death? Could she hold it as one holds a full and streaming cup steadily to her lips without spilling a drop—and drink it all down and never choke? Drink it as her own son would have said, to the bitter dregs?

Mary, the mother of Jesus, kept her eyes upon the prison gate, expecting it to open any moment now. She both dreaded and wanted it to open. It would open and release her son. But she couldn't bear to look—her beloved son—to look and see his torment. Her precious one—to feel his pain. Her child, grown to man but still living,—clarified in her memory—an infant at her breast, his baby lips feeling for nourishment, his tiny fingers gently, gently. . . .

"Nay!" Her thoughts screamed. "Nay, it must not be!"

But she had not spoken. She had not moved. The gate was shut. The light was bright in the prison yard. There were sounds coming to her from the street. She could hear them and know them for what they were, all the sounds of a city merged into a not unharmonious drone, flowing from this street into another and another, rising and falling not unlike the sea. All the sounds of this wicked city were the sounds of an army on the march, near, then far, undulating and rolling along. There was the clang of spears now and again striking upon her ears. There were voices—voices of command and voices of assent. "Take ye her precious son and deliver him to the high hill of Golgotha."

Mary, mother of Jesus, kept her eyes upon the prison gate. And now it seemed to her, because her eyes were so dry and burning—it seemed to her there was no gate, only a wall. It was high, this wall, with no opening in its hard bricks and cold immutable stones. Neither an entrance nor an exit. No way over or under. Just a thick impenetrable wall that encompassed him around and about forever and forever.

"Nay!" said Mary. "Nay!"

But she was not saying it. She was only thinking it. Yet she knew that her thinking was a wail and cry louder than human voice.

Suddenly she could hear the other Mary sobbing beside her. And like a flashing light there came the realization that the gate was open. It was open!

Two soldiers came out. Then two more. Mary, the mother, put out her hand and let it fall gently upon the arm of her companion.

Mary Magdalene caught in her breath, quick and sharp. Little by little she mastered her grief. But, when she saw Jesus, the sorrow of his mother broke out again like a wound pressed together but unhealed. Like the streaming wounds upon the back of this thorn-crowned staggering man who came through the gate toward her, bent under the heavy weight of wood.

"Master!" Mary Magdalene's voice was a whisper.

Master? Nay, here was no teacher, no Rabbi. Here was, and Mary felt the full impact of it on her heart, her son. Her first-born. The babe whose first cry had startled gentle-eyed oxen bedded in the same manger. The child, at whose birth events transpired which, to this day, his mother kept and pondered in her heart. The star, hanging luminous and breathtakingly near above the streets of Bethlehem. The simple shepherds gasping out a tale of wondrous angel voices from the sky. The wisemen who, they said, had traveled far and with heavenly guidance, to kneel before her infant son and present costly gifts of gold, frankincense and myrrh. Yea, this was her son, the kind, soft-spoken elder brother of James and Joses, Juda and Simon and the little girls. This was the lad who at twelve confounded wise men in the temple of Jerusalem, who laid claim to no father save the one Father. This was the young conscientious carpenter, the man who called her not "mother" but quite as reverently "woman."

Nay, now as she beheld him, she saw him with the eyes of Mary Magdalene. Not entirely, but partially. He was her son, but was he not also her Master, too? Was he not, even now, and perhaps more than ever before, a teacher? She gazed at him wonderingly, full of the new widened knowledge. Yea, was he not even at this moment teaching his followers the hardest lesson of all? Was he not demonstrating the humble triumph of love perfected? In his eyes was a patience which suffered all, feared nought, condemned none. Marveling, his mother was swept for an instant clean of personal anguish. She took no step toward that beloved figure, made no physical move to touch him. She had already reached him. She had touched the shining reality of his life.

She became aware that Mary Magdalene's hand was urging her onward.

"We must follow him," the other Mary was saying. "Come. We must follow him."

Yea, they must follow . . . through crooked dark streets . . . along a road where the feet slipped on small pebbles and bruising stones . . . through throngs of raucous bystanders who jostled and mocked because they were not given yet to understand . . . up, up the rugged path where each must walk alone, one after the other . . . to that high windy hill called Golgotha.

There were those who wept for him along the way. Women who had served him, those who had been healed and comforted, those who had looked to her son to overthrow the Roman rule and establish his peaceful kingdom here upon earth. There was a man, too, from Cyrene—a man who said his name was Simon—whom the guards compelled to bear the cross for the fainting Jesus. Mary, his mother, was grateful to see the burden lifted—yet she knew that, in actuality, he bore it still, that the mark of the wood was grooved deep.

Step by step . . . one foot before the other . . . walking blind sometimes except for the arm of Mary Magdalene, blind because one could not look so steadfastly inward and retain an outward vision . . . climbing now . . . nearer . . . nearer.

A voice reached her ears, high and agonized. Mary turned. A young girl, thin and ragged, had darted through the guard and flung herself at the second of the two malefactors who followed Jesus in the procession.

"Father! Father!" she sobbed. "Don't let them! Don't let them!"

Mary Magdalene said, her voice husky with compassion: "It is Drusilla, daughter of Jehu the Zealot."

Drusilla clung to her father, convulsed in body and in mind. He was going to his death, and she was not able to save him. A week, a few more days perhaps, and there would have been enough to buy his freedom. But Rome would not wait. The imperial law was a boulder which crashed down a mountainside and no young tree, nor bush, nor flowered branch, could stop the brutal onrush. There was no pause, no hesitancy. She had come early this morning to the house of John Mark. She had found it empty. While the sun climbed inexorably, she had waited. Then desperate anxiety had hurried her all the way to Bethany. No one at the house of Martha, either. Back again, gasping and near to exhaustion, to the tower of Antonia. Jehu? He was gone . . . on his way to execution. She was too late.

"Here, none of this!" the guard called out angrily. "Away with you, girl. You can't touch the prisoner here." An iron hand descended painfully upon her shoulder, fingers clamping into her flesh.

"Drusilla, child." Jehu spoke quietly. "Behold, the prophet Jesus is to be crucified, too. Shall I complain?"

"Jesus? The Nazarene?" Amazement stemmed her sobs. As the soldier dragged her away from her father and flung her beside the path, she thought only of the strange thing Jehu had said. Jesus of Nazareth was to die upon the cross? She lay for a stunned moment in the dust, then struggled to her feet. For the first time, she took notice of the other two who bore crosses. She ran beside the procession peering first at the great burly man behind Jehu, and then at the man ahead, Simon of Cyrene, who bore the cross. This was not he, surely. Fear must have unbalanced her father's mind. But—what of this man who wore the wreath of thorns and the blood-stained robe? She caught her breath. It was—it was Jesus the Teacher. But how changed—how changed! She wailed aloud, and it seemed to her, listening in fright to the sound of it, that her voice was not hers alone, but the voice of many. The noise of a world convulsed beat upon her eardrums, and she was powerless to stop either utterance or hearing.

"Daughters of Jerusalem, why do you weep for me?"

Whose words? Drusilla lifted her head. The procession had paused for a moment as it neared the summit of the hill. Jesus was speaking. "Weep for yourselves, rather, and for your children. For the day comes in which the childless shall be accounted fortunate, and men shall begin to cry to the mountains and to the hills for help. For if they do these things in a green tree, what shall be done in the dry?"

They climbed again. Drusilla, seeing that Jehu sweated and groaned under the weight of his cross, went to him and took part of the weight of it upon herself. This time none of the soldiers interfered. Drusilla knew why. The time was short. They were almost there. Almost there. Her thoughts were no longer rational. They no longer existed. In their place was an aching knowledge, an inconsolable despair. "Jehu—my father," she whispered. And then: "Jesus—Master!"

Even her grief could not flow into one channel, but was tortured by division. In her agony, she would cry: "Father, let me die for you!" Then, the next moment: "Master, let me perish in your stead!" But no one heard. There was no strength in her voice.

She strove to take more of the burden of her father's cross upon herself, but Jehu, even in suffering, would not. Suddenly the weight was gone from her shoulders. Drusilla straightened, drawing air into her lungs in great gasping breaths. Blessed respite!

On the slope above, the Nazarene was standing, as if in prayer. Below was Jerusalem. The roof of the temple shone like a jewel in the grasp of the sky, and, to the west, near the Joppa gate, the tower of David reached upward. Jesus' eyes were inexplicable as they gazed down upon the holy city, then lifted above and away. Unmindful of his shackled wrists and the shouts of the soldiers, he was praying.

Realization came to Drusilla like a dagger to the heart. They had reached the top of Golgotha.

CHAPTER XXXV

JOANNA stood apart among the reeds. The air was still and sultry. Underfoot were wild daisies and dandelions, but their beauty was nothing to her. They flowered upon a hill of blood. They covered a skull. She put her hands over her eyes, felt slow tears trickle through her fingers, and wondered that there were tears left. She had wept so many. Perhaps it was cowardly of her to leave that place, to leave those three holes which the slaves were digging, to flee from the sight of Jesus lying upon the cross. He had lain there calmly, Jesus, as one might lie upon a bed. His eyes had been open to the blue sky. Neither anguish nor pain were upon his countenance. Nay, not even when the long spikes were driven through his palms and the red blood had spurted up. It was then that he had said the words which repeated themselves over and over in Joanna's wondering heart. "Father, forgive them. They know not what they do."

"Father, forgive them!" Strange words from a man who was dying for the good he had done, rather than the evil. An astounding attitude for one facing the most cruel of deaths, for one whose healing and saving footsteps had been dogged by the jealous, the greedy, the vindictive and, finally, the murderous.

Joanna dropped her hands and looked down at Jerusalem. Pilgrims were still thick upon the Damascus road, two hundred feet west of Golgotha. Some of the more curious were even now climbing the steep path to watch a Roman execution. They were in good spirits, gaily attired for the festival, and eager to witness a spectacle. Joanna shivered. Tomorrow was the Feast of the Passover, and tonight the Lamb was being sacrificed.

The sharp metallic sound of nails came to her clearly, mingling with the groans of the two malefactors and the bitter wailing of Drusilla who had begged the soldiers on her knees to stay her father's sentence for just one day. She needed but fifty shekels more to buy his freedom, she had sobbed, and these had been promised her. But Sebastian, the centurion, had had no authority to stay the execution. "It is the sentence of the Roman governor," he had said. "You are too late, no matter what you do."

Pilate will not easily forget what he has done today, Joanna thought. He will dream at night of a thorn-crowned, bleeding Jesus. In the daytime, he will find accusation in the eyes of those he meets. He will feel condemnation growing, growing. . . .

There were shouts from the direction of the execution ground. Joanna looked. Jesus and Jehu lay quietly upon their crosses, but the third malefactor was struggling with half a dozen men. He was a strong, great-framed fellow whom even long months in the dungeon of Antonia had not been able to weaken or to tame. For the moment his name escaped her, but he had been one of those at Capernaum with Barabbas. Finally, a soldier brought a rope and bound him, still writhing and protesting, to the cross. The clanging blows of the hammer driving the spikes were punctuated by his curses. Joanna turned her head away.

She started. Something dark was sliding along the ground to her left. Wild dogs, perhaps, which frequented this place? Nay, three shadows, swaying, taking shape

before her eyes. One after the other. She saw then what
was making them. The crosses were being erected. She
heard the thuds as slaves, handling them as if they were
large trees, dropped them into the holes. The two malefactors screamed as the full weight of their bodies tore
at the flesh of hands and feet.

Joanna ran toward the crosses. She could stay apart no
longer. She must join those others, the sorrow-wracked
mother, tight-lipped Mary Magdalene, Salome the mother
of James and John, Mary the wife of Cleophas and the
other loyal women. They were kneeling in prayer at the
foot of his cross. She, too, must be with him now.

The centurion in charge of the execution was talking
to a soldier. He, Sebastian, had been reminded of the in-
scription Pilate had ordered placed at the top of Jesus'
cross.

"It explains the crime," he said to the guard, "and must
be put up."

He wiped sweat from his forehead and licked his lips.
He was hot. He was tired. The whole business nauseated
him. He had believed himself hardened to floggings, tor-
tures and crucifixions. He had seen enough of them, by
Jupiter, in his thirty-eight years. He was acquainted with
blood and terror. Who in the Roman army was not? Sebastian prided himself on hardihood and soldierly indifference to all pain, another's or one's own. Carrying out his
orders unflinchingly, unthinkingly, he looked forward to
a raise in rank and additional power in a conquered world.
But now, quite unexpectedly and certainly against his
volition, he was sickened. Not the screams of the malefactors, nor the wailing of the women was responsible. It
was the sight of forbearance which had changed him,
which had brought this inward trembling, this despised

weakness. His throat ached, his head throbbed. Sebastian was possessed of a great hatred of his life.

The soldier was staring stupidly at the writing on the board.

"Well, why do you hesitate?" asked Sebastian. He was annoyed. The guard was no better than a beast. Had he no humanity? Did he not see that the prisoner upon the center cross was no ordinary person?

"There is no crime printed here," said the soldier dully. "It but reads: 'Jesus of Nazareth, King of the Jews.'"

"Do you presume to criticize Pilate?" roared Sebastian. "This was inscribed at his behest. Carry out your orders!"

Through a haze he watched slaves bring a ladder. The soldier clambered up to nail the sign to the Nazarene's cross. At every hammer blow, the wood shivered. Jesus did not flinch. Nay, even now he did not utter a sound. What sort of man was he who could thus endure the cruelest death Rome could devise? Sebastian closed his eyes. The look of this Galilean was unendurable. The centurion felt as if he, with his own hands, were slaying this man. Yet he was not responsible. Surely not. Or was he? Was, perhaps, the whole world oddly to blame? Nay, this man was a condemned seditionist. He had plotted to overthrow the empire. He was deserving of death, of every moment's exquisite torture, of every agony of body and mind. He, Sebastian, would not pity. To pity a revolutionist was disloyalty to Rome. He would look at this Jesus coldly, as he had looked so many times before at men dying upon crosses. He walked forward defiantly a few paces and stared upward at the Galilean. Watching, his mood changed again. He melted as a candle melts under flame. He was confused and disturbed. It was unaccountable.

Sebastian backed away. It was said that this man was a worker of miracles. He could well believe it. But from whence had he this power? From what mysterious source? From the Jewish God he professed? Sebastian refused belief. He had long been skeptical of the supernatural influence of any deities, Roman or otherwise. He had seen too much of priesthood with its hypocrisy and greed, to say nothing of rampant immorality, to credit divine ordination. He had seen too much of men, he considered, to think them sprung of ought but passion. Secretly, Sebastian believed in nothing but ambition and physical force. But now . . . he did not know . . . this man had a strange doctrine, it was said. His fellow soldiers had often laughed about it among themselves, recounting, to them, fantastic sayings of the Jewish prophet. He had said that God was his Father. He had said, too, that God was a Spirit. Did he then believe himself bodiless, incorporeal? Did he still believe it, bleeding upon the cross?

Sebastian could look no more at Jesus of Nazareth. His eyes traveled instead, in a kind of relief, to the little group huddled at the foot of the center cross. Usually, he remembered, those condemned to death by crucifixion were unattended in their last agony. Occasionally one or two relatives were present, but not often. Today, however, there were half a dozen women about the Nazarene and, of course, that poor girl Drusilla, daughter of the insurrectionist, Jehu. Drusilla, he noted, was being comforted by none other than Joanna, the wife of Herod's former steward. He had not been able to restrain surprise that a woman of her rank should be here. She had made no disturbance, however, and the others, too, were well behaved and orderly. Not the sort one would expect to find at an execution. Even Jesus' mother, Mary, had caused no trouble. He examined her expression curiously and then turned from it as he had turned from her son's.

Another woman was hurrying up the incline from the

Damascus road. The young woman called Mary Magdalene, beholding the newcomer, said: "It is Martha."

Martha was panting. Her legs ached and her throat was dry. Her eyes were wet, and the three crosses which rose before them blurred continually. This, she told herself with what firmness was left within her, was not happening. She would awake presently and her heart would flood with relief that it was not so. She would tell Jesus about the dream, if it remained in memory to oppress her, and he would calm her as he always did when she brought him her trouble. He would say: "I am Life eternal." He would say: "Fear not. Believe only."

But now, while the dream was upon her, she could not stay her sobs, nor stop her hands from tearing at her dress, nor stop the groans come unbidden.

Mary Magdalene was beside her. Warm arms were about her, and Martha was weeping as she had not wept since Lazarus' burial in the tomb from which Jesus had called him. Her graying head was pressed against Mary Magdalene's bosom, pressed tightly. Odd that she, the elder, should seek solace with one younger. She had always been the one who wielded authority in their family, who had advised, made decisions, borne responsibility. And now, she had become as a child weeping upon a mother's breast. She had wept so in the arms of Mary her sister when she brought the news. She had clung to Lazarus, wailing and incoherent. She had come ahead of them now, running nearly all the way, gasping over and over again: "Nay, it is not so. It is not so."

Mary Magdalene was speaking to her. She was saying: "Drusilla waited and waited. She begged the centurion to spare Jehu's life a little longer but he would not."

Jehu? Drusilla? What names were these? There was only one name. Jesus. Jesus of Nazareth. A voice, thin and hopeless, murmured in her ear. "Did you get the money?" Martha looked up. Drusilla was standing beside her, hair wild and face haggard, repeating over and over, not as if she cared, but as if it had been in her mind and must come out now: "Did you get the money? Did you get the money?"

Martha remembered then. Mary had told her briefly of Drusilla's need, had begged her to take the purse containing fifty shekels to Jehu's daughter. "I promised," Mary had said wearily. "It may be too late, but go nevertheless." That was why she had come ahead of her brother and sister. Mary had needed rest before she could walk again, and take the long road to Golgotha. Lazarus had stayed with her.

"Yea, I have the money here," said Martha. She fumbled at her girdle, then thrust the purse into Drusilla's limp fingers. It dropped to the ground. Then, as if come to full realization, the girl picked it up and ran forward to the foot of Jehu's cross.

"Father! Father! Here at last is the money. Come down, father. Come down!"

But Jehu could not answer for his suffering. Salome went forward and drew his daughter away. Martha fixed her eyes upon Jesus. How still he was. The others were groaning, but the Master uttered no sound. She would remember this, that even in her dream, he had shown forth spiritual courage. She heard the centurion, who was standing by, exclaim: "There is not a Stoic who could bear suffering like this!" Jehu's burly guard laughed. "How now! Our great centurion has turned philosopher!" The other soldiers laughed. How could they laugh, Martha wondered. Jesus was dying. Jesus was dying but he made no disturbance. His face was calm. A ray of light broke through the clouds which were gathering in the sky, and shone down on Jesus' face.

A falcon flew across the mount from west to east. In Martha's ears the faraway clamor of Jerusalem echoed as shadows reflected on the waters of a pond. She groped for coherent thought. Cattle were feeding on the hillside. A flock of doves flew from the temple to Golgotha and presently returned. What was it Jesus had said? "A grain of wheat must die that much fruit may be brought forth."

The earth shook. The clouds shut off the rays of the sun. Martha was unafraid. It was part of the dream, part of the dark wild beauty of the illusion.

Caiaphas climbed the path to Golgotha with Benezra and Jehoiada. He was consumed with the desire to see the fanatical prophet die. All had gone well, as he had planned it. There had been no tricks, no sudden and impressive works of magic. Perhaps the carpenter's son could work miracles only among the credulous, those who "believed" as he called it. For it was obvious, was it not, that had he possessed any mysterious power, he would have used it to save himself? Only a fool would have been so passive, so annoyingly submissive in defeat. Well, Israel would be well rid of Jesus of Nazareth. Seeing what befell a man who criticized priesthood, set himself up as the Son of God, overthrew the tables of the holy temple, others would be slow to interfere with established practices. A year from now Jerusalem would have forgotten that a man named Jesus, an upstart carpenter from the hills of Galilee, had ever existed. Death, a death of shame and ignominy, would blot his name and spurious deeds from mind and tongue.

Reaching the top of the hill, Caiaphas stopped for breath. Ah! There they were, the three crosses! He rubbed his hands together.

He smiled. "Behold," he said to Benezra and Jehoiada as they came abreast, "the miracle-working carpenter!" Jehoiada ran forward, wagging his head and grinning. "You there," he called out, "you, who destroy the temple and build it again in three days, save yourself now if you can!"

Caiaphas nodded, pleased. Jehoiada, he considered, was basically unintelligent, but he had a wily way with him, and a faculty of happening on to apt phrases. He repeated softly: "Yea, save yourself if you can."

Benezra picked up a stone and flung it toward the center cross.

"If you be the Son of God, come down from the cross!" he bawled.

Caiaphas walked forward, not in haste, but with dignified and pompous step, as befitting his position. He peered up at Jesus' face. How placid it was—how undisturbed. Did he not feel the spikes? Did he not hear the reviling of his triumphant enemies? Rage swept through the high priest. He would make him hear! He would bring some expression of pain or other emotion to that still face whose eyes did not lower to his, but stared off to the horizon. Yea, he would make Jesus of Nazareth, even on the cross steadfast in his self-designated superiority, look down.

"He saved others," he called out mockingly to Jehoiada and Benezra. "Himself he cannot save!"

No movement of that pinioned body or thorn-crowned head. No glance from Jesus.

"If you be the King of Israel," shrilled Caiaphas, "come down from the cross and we will believe you." He approached the cross, shaking his fist. "Do you hear? You trusted in God; let Him deliver you now, if He will have you: for you claim you are the Son of God!"

Behind him, Caiaphas could hear the throng of money-changers and scribes who had followed him. They took up his words and the sultry air was filled with their abuse. Stones rained about the crosses, but none touched the Nazarene. Jesus made no reply, but gazed off to the pyramid-like mountain in the north where, of old, the prophet Samuel had lived. The sky darkened. Caiaphas glanced about him apprehensively. By the looks of the heavens, a great storm was gathering. A little while ago as he came from the temple, there had been a slight shaking of the earth. Best go back now. There were many things to be done. All the preparations for the festival tomorrow. He regretted now that he had condescended to climb Golgotha. He, the high priest of the temple, had no time for such trivial expeditions. What happened on Golgotha was of no real importance. What had he expected to see? A miracle? Nay, no matter what a man had done or what he claimed to have done, he died. When disease ravaged him, when old age came, when his flesh was pierced and blood flowed from his body, he perished. Caiaphas' lips twisted. Life eternal! The only eternalness belonged to death. That was certain, irrevocable, permanent. Those who belonged, as he did, to the exalted sect of the Sadducees, knew that there was no resurrection, now or anytime, of the earth-born. Let the Pharisees and Essenes dabble with the childish notion, if they wished. They would learn. They would learn by never knowing!

Caiaphas beckoned Jehoiada and Benezra and, with a last scornful but somewhat puzzled look at Jesus, went down the hill.

The two thieves were talking now. Jehu had answered some of the taunts the money-changers hurled at Jesus. Now that he had started to speak, he could not stop. Somehow, the movement and sound of his lips lessened the pain, or seemed to.

On the other side of Jesus, his fellow malefactor, Onesimas, was also crying out, but his were words of condemnation. He, too, was reviling Jesus.

"If you are the Christ, save yourself and us!"

But Jehu, shocked at Onesimas' mockery, answered and rebuked him. "Do you not fear God, Onesimas? In our suffering, we receive the due reward of our deeds: but Jesus has done nothing amiss."

As he spoke the pain lessened, but Jehu felt very weak. He licked his lips, rolled his head toward Jesus. "Lord, remember me when you come into your kingdom."

Jesus turned his head. For an instant, their eyes met. Jehu's, pleading and agonized. Jesus', forgiving and calm. Jehu was comforted. Let the night come now. Let the darkness close about him. There would be light again. For him. For the world.

Jesus said: "Verily I say unto you, today you shall be with me in paradise."

It was enough, Jehu thought. It was enough—and more.

CHAPTER XXXVI

$\mathbb{A}$ MAN with a black beard and dusty, torn garments ascended the steep slope of Golgotha, praying. No one who chanced to look his way would have been aware that he prayed, for his black, brooding eyes were full open and his parched lips were stretched tight over broken teeth. In the deep hollows of his cheeks there might have been the faint, ever so slight, quivering of live tissue under the dead, dark skin. Yet one could not be sure of this. The shadow of his beard encroached there, and the glare of the sun but made its mark higher on the rounded knobs of his cheekbones.

Yet he was praying as might have prayed his master once as he strode along through the blotted, sandy reaches of the wilderness. Or as he went, shaking his shaggy mane, to the muddy slopes of the Jordan and plunged in to raise the baptismal waters in strong brown hands.

"God," prayed Akkub, "deliver from me the sins of this earth plight, and the struggles of my conscience. Permit me here not to look upon death, but life everlasting."

And presently he was standing below the three crosses, just a few paces behind the Roman guard, and quite close to a little group of men and women who were either weeping or too choked with suffering to weep. He was raising his chin to look up.

When someone near him said: "If I mistake not, you are Akkub, once a disciple of John the Baptist."

Akkub did not at first remember the voice, but the sound of it presently awoke a memory and the memory, in turn, expanded into definite form. . . .

Night in Capernaum, starless and very black, and very hot, with the odors of an unnumbered multitude pressing to his senses. Here to his right was the low, clinging shape of a house—Peter's house, and beyond that a garden. In the garden a torch threw down the only light there was, making a walled-in circle. To the left, nothing was to be seen. Behind him was nothing. Ahead there was nothing. Yet, in that nothingness, one saw clearly all one imagined. One made shapes of all the sounds coming forth—for it was easy to put flesh around a groan, the thin body of a child around a whimper, exposed bones as covering for a cavernous cough. Yea, sounds made sights in that darkness. It was from the darkness itself, not what it hid, that the sounds seemed to be borne. It was as though all these were the night itself, constituting the night and the night was eternal.

The feeling that the night could not end he remembered as he now did the voice of a woman, repeating: "You are Akkub, disciple of John."

And Akkub answered: "Yea. We met in the darkness at Capernaum."

The woman moved closer. "I am Mary Magdalene," she said.

Akkub looked down at her. On her quiet face were the marks of tears and long suffering. She seemed much older than at Capernaum, except for her eyes which were like a child's but recently awakened in a strange room.

"You left us," she said reprovingly, "to go with Barabbas."

Akkub could not deny this. Nor was there any reason

to. He answered simply: "Yea, I went with Barabbas for a short time. Then I returned to John."

"But John is dead."

He ignored her statement. "Now I have returned to Jesus."

Mary glanced up at him questioningly. But he did not see her, for he had become lost in another memory. He stood alone before the strewn ashes of a cave in a mountain retreat beyond the Jordan. He had come back. He was biting his nails and recalling that here one time his master sat glooming over a fire whose dying sparks in the twilight were as the evening's first pale stars. Soon the sparks were gone, but the stars lingered. Then the stars were gone, and he went in spirit with John to the top of a hill to watch the sun rolling like a great wheel along the rim of the horizon.

The unspoken, but clearly heard words of John, who stood with him in spirit, declared: "In like manner so has arisen the Son of Man. And you have left him to go with thieves."

Akkub had sat down and wept. And his days in the wilderness were days of communion with John. There he had lived the past and had prayed for his soul and, presently, after hunger and hardship and distress, he had set out, as many another pilgrim, for Jerusalem.

There they had told him of the crucifixion. Three crosses on a hill. Three lives shedding the red blood of agony. The center cross, they had said, supported the frame of the peasant preacher. He had not complained. He had gone willingly. He had been tortured as few men had ever been tortured before, yet he had withstood it and forebore to cry out or squirm or plead mercy. A brave one, indeed, that Galilean teacher now nailed to the cross. "Heed what we say, stranger, and stay away, for there is no telling what may be the next whim of the governor, spurred on by the ranting temple priests. Room for more crosses on that hill, and yours may be one of them."

Akkub had said: "I shall go nevertheless."

Muttering, they left him, made signs on their foreheads, and leered back at him. He would go, but where was the road? A beggar directed him to a wrong place because he had no coin to pay for proper information. Presently, he was beating a path through a thicket of brambles in a close, hot gully. A small clearing showed ahead. Perspiring, he came out upon it and there, to his horror, saw a man hanging by his neck, quite dead. The rope had strangled him. His red hair hung loosely over his face, but when, with trembling fingers, Akkub brushed it back over his temples, his horror was the more because he knew who it was almost immediately. Jesus' disciple, Judas Iscariot.

The certain knowledge moved Akkub to step back, quite without reason, and wipe his hands upon the grass. Then, once more, he stared at the dead man in the hope that he might be mistaken. He marked his height and said: "He is of that height." He computed his weight, of which he could not be sure. Finally, he sat down.

"It is he, Judas," he said.

Akkub rose again, for plainly it was his duty to lower the body and remove the rope. With this thought, he advanced until he was once more almost within reach of him. But he could go no farther. Fear, more terrible than anything he had ever known, pressed his feet solidly upon the ground and held him there. Though he might step back, he could not step forward. All he could do was to look, with growing intensity, into a dead face whose expression was alive.

So Akkub went on, and presently found his way to Golgotha. He was standing beside Mary Magdalene when a soldier of high rank passed in front of him, then stopped. They exchanged looks.

It was Joshua, Herod's Captain of the Guards, who had delivered to him the mutilated body of John the Baptist.

"My greetings," Joshua said. "For a moment, I did not recognize you."

"I will never forget you," Akkub said, "nor the debt I owe you."

An embarrassment came over them. Akkub could find no words to say, though thoughts were burning in him, and he was recalling this man to the past . . . walking again at his side over a mountain road. The clank of Joshua's sword, the faltering beat of steps behind them, and the steady creaking of a long wooden box were thrown like futile pebbles upon a silence graven in stone.

And he could feel between him and the stalwart soldier the same embarrassment he now felt, yet realized that from him came a humanity and understanding quite irreconcilable to his position and calling. In Akkub's ears were still the words he had once spoken: "Gather up your packs. Find your staffs. We will proceed at once on our way to this strange man whom you call Jesus."

Now they were together again. Somehow, Akkub knew that Joshua's embarrassment was due to what had happened here on this high hill. His manner was one of apology. It was as though he were actually saying: "I had no hand in this. You must not think ill of me. Secretly, I grieve with you."

To break the wall between them, Akkub reported the finding of Judas Iscariot's body. Mary Magdalene overheard him, and closed her eyes to regain her composure and beat down the hatred rising in her heart.

"He betrayed our master," she whispered, "but may God rest his soul."

Akkub said: "His sin is less than mine, for I betrayed two masters."

Joshua remained silent. Little drops of perspiration were forming upon his cheeks, where they glistened like crystal sand. He looked up at the center cross, sorrowing and tight-lipped, then drew a breath which he expelled, sighing.

All this while Akkub had not dared to look. For it was true. He had betrayed the Master. Now that he had come too late, how could he justify himself or beg forgiveness, or be in the consciousness of the Lord as a true man whose erring ways were no more? And how, by coming so late, could he relieve by one jot the distress Jesus now endured? How at this time could he offer to ascend the cross in his place, that Jesus might be spared? Yea, how could he? He was too late. The crushing wheel of events had made its turn. No human power could set back what, in the order of things, had come to pass.

And he, like Joshua, felt beads of water come to his paling face, when he would that they might be drops of blood. Yet Joshua had more strength of purpose. More courage had he. Though he made no pretense of being one of them, though he never openly acknowledged his belief in divinity and his certitude of the Son of God—he was a better man.

So Akkub sweated, standing before the cross. The prayer he had said coming up the hill mocked him. The spirit of John had risen like a ghost at his side, declaring: "The Son of God has arisen and yet you chose to go among thieves."

Blindly, with tears streaming, Akkub looked up. At first he could not see. There was a mist between. It was too late—too late. In his shame, he had not the strength to hold up his head. He could not see. He was too late. He had chosen to go among thieves. He had betrayed two masters—who strangely now were one. One master—one life—one shame—one retribution that would endure forever. . . .

The mist cleared. Jesus' eyes were open—and in a moment of supreme and utter happiness, Akkub saw them smile with a certain undoubted meaning, and knew he need grieve no more. . . .

CHAPTER XXXVII

Ben ISHAM walked back and forth, back and forth. An endless vigil in which seconds were long as minutes, and minutes, curiously swollen, were hours. Hours were years, and the night—the night was eternity. It wasn't so, of course. Ben Isham was a man whom years of soldiering had made realistic. Actually, by reasonable measurement, it was but nearing the fourth watch. Not too long before dawn pearled the far hilltops. He would think of that.

Thick clouds rolling overhead made a barrage which neither moon nor stars could penetrate. The garden was so black he could not see a stone's throw away. Posted at intervals, he reminded himself, were nearly a hundred men, yet he could not shake off the feeling of solitariness. Perhaps it was the beat of his own footsteps, the loudest sound in the night. Hollow. Lonely. Perhaps it was that, from the first, this assignment had been distasteful to him. He was accustomed to long watches, to eerie, often dangerous, surroundings, but always before his duty had been to guard the living. Now he guarded the dead. At the behest of Pilate, petitioned by anxious priests and Pharisees, he had marched a hundred Jewish soldiers to this remote garden belonging to Joseph of Arimathea. They had rolled a great stone to seal the sepulcher of the crucified Nazarene, had made it secure against intrusion. The high priest feared, it was said, that the disciples of Jesus

336

of Nazareth might steal hither and bear the body away. This was highly improbable, Ben Isham held, since all had fled at their teacher's arrest in Gethsemane. None had been seen since save one, a certain mild-mannered fisherman called John who had been present at the cross. Was it likely that men, so easily scattered in time of stress, would now have the temerity to approach a tomb in the dark of the stormy night? Nay, thought Ben Isham contemptuously, they were in hiding in some dingy corner of Jerusalem, quaking at every knock or strange step, or— more likely—they had escaped to the hills, fleeing to the wild crags of Hebron or to the desert of Arabia. He had seen it happen again and again. When leaders were seized, their followers tarried not but were sped as leaves by the winds of terror. These disciples of the carpenter-prophet were no exception. Their little revolution was over. Their ambitious dreams sagged to nought. There was that in every man, reflected Ben Isham, which led him to defend his own flesh above all, protect his bones, hoard every drop of his own blood.

Ben Isham stopped. A twig snapped under his feet. Except the Nazarene . . . yea, he had heard, though he had not been present, that the man had made no resistance to capture nor to persecution, that he had seemed almost indifferent to the torturing of his body. Indeed, it had been noised about that he was always declaring that the flesh profited nothing, that it was the spirit which bestowed and maintained life. Strange philosophy. Strange person. . . .

Ben Isham leaned against an olive tree, suddenly weary. Well, Jesus of Nazareth was dead now. He was crucified, and the gullible might mourn him as the Son of God, but they could not bring him back. There was no returning from the grave.

It was the fourth watch finally. Sleepers wakened grum-
blingly and stumbled to their posts. Those relieved settled
down with yawns and grunts. Only Ben Isham could not
rest. He was in charge. Death was the penalty for him to
sleep on duty. Oddly enough, tonight he did not mind.
Ordinarily about this time, his lids dragged against burning eyeballs but now, although he was somewhat tired, he
did not feel like slumber. Something kept him awake. A
feeling that something was about to occur. A foreboding
or, possibly, an expectation. He knew not which.

He began to walk again, striding monotonously. Time,
broken by the changing of the watch, healed and became
once more a long cobweb stretching to nowhere. . . .

Reaching the far western limits of the garden, he
turned. Light seeped through the garden. Relief swept
Ben Isham. Dawn. He strode forward eagerly. Before
long, others would come to take their places and he and
his men could return to their quarters. Dawn—but was
it dawn? The light came not from the east, nor did the
rays fall impartially upon the hillside. Rather, it was a soft
illumination concentrated in one spot. The soldier stopped,
wondering. The glow came from the direction of the
sepulcher. Had women disciples come at such an early
hour to embalm the body of Jesus, as was the custom?
How had they passed the guards? Orders were strict. No
one was to be allowed to approach the sealed cave. Ben
Isham started forward angrily. But, as he ran, the light
grew and spread. It was as if the petals of a great shining
flower, star-hearted, unfurled, and the whole garden was
filled with its strange blooming. Simultaneously, Ben
Isham seemed to see great crowds about him shouting and
singing. They were dressed—terror struck at him—they
were dressed in grave clothes! It could not be! Voices all
around about him and from above, as if from heaven itself,

blended in a great symphony, music such as he had never heard before. One theme there was, repeated and repeated in varying tone and volume, rolling from horizon to horizon. Praise to God in the highest.

Ben Isham shouted hoarsely. He called out orders, but his own voice was swallowed, lost. He could see his men running from the sepulcher, and could hear a great rolling as of thunder. Under his feet the ground began to reel and swim, and a faintness came upon him so that he fell, weak as an infant . . . and under his clutching fingers the earth had no substance any more, nor any form. . . .

As they climbed the slope to the sepulcher, the four women went, in unspoken accord, more slowly. The journey through Jerusalem's narrow and deserted streets had been black and desolate beyond the telling. They had reached the outskirts of the city when a sharp earthquake occurred and the sky overhead took on a queer unfamiliar color. They had huddled together for long frightened moments, rolling eyes upward at the great heaped clouds and feeling the road tremble as if with palsy. Salome had suggested turning back, but Mary Magdalene would have none of it. With resolution now she led the way up the twisting path to the garden of Joseph of Arimathea, a dark silent figure in the gloom. Salome and Mary, the mother of James, wept and moaned a little as they mounted the incline, their grief steady and resigned. All rebellion had gone out of them when they had watched with Jesus' mother at the foot of the cross. Only the sorrow, deep and beyond human stemming, remained.

Joanna, like Mary Magdalene, could not weep. A great heaviness was upon her, the weight of spirit and of body and of the night. Her thoughts were slow as words thickly spoken in alien tongue. Her feet dragged as if shackled.

The jars of spices which she bore were an almost intolerable burden. She could go no farther. She could not. Yet—she must. She, with those faithful others, must minister to the broken body of her Master.

"But who will roll us away the stone from before the sepulcher?" wailed Salome in sudden anxiety.

"Perhaps the guards will help us when they see we mean no trouble," said Mary, the mother of James.

Joanna thought of the size of the boulder. "It will take at least three score."

Only Mary Magdalene said nothing. Rounding a group of thick-leaved trees, they stopped. There were lights in the garden ahead, and much confusion. Nay, there was one light, a strange radiance from the sepulcher. Soldiers were running toward them, away from the tomb. Others stood huddled together in groups. Some knelt with faces covered, sobbing like children.

Joanna was stricken with consternation. The stone was rolled away from the cave's mouth! Father in heaven, what had happened? She started forward with her companions. No voice challenged them. None of the guards made any attempt to halt them.

Mary Magdalene was first at the sepulcher. Joanna followed her, stooping down to look into the cavern. She heard Mary Magdalene's quick intake of breath, and then she herself felt the quickening of her startled heart. The body of Jesus was not there!

The jar of sweet ointment fell from Joanna's nerveless hands with a crash. She looked down blindly at the shattered pieces on the cave's floor, and fragrance drifted up to her slowly. Her throat was painfully tight. Her two fists ached. Was it not enough that they had crucified him? Could they not let the dead rest in peace?

Beside her, she heard Salome breathe: "Behold!"

She lifted her head and through eyes blurred with moisture saw, in the dimness of the tomb, two white figures, one at the head and one at the foot, where the body of Jesus had lain.

For the shaking of her lips, Joanna could utter no sound. Nor could she look longer upon the figures, for the strange glistening of their raiment.

There came a voice from the sepulcher, and it was like no voice which Joanna had ever heard.

"Fear not: for I know you seek Jesus which was crucified. He is not here, for he is risen, as he said. Go quickly and tell his disciples that he goes before you into Galilee. There shall you see him. Lo, I have told you."

When Joanna came to herself she was with Salome and Mary the mother of James hastening along the road back to Jerusalem. How or when she had left the sepulcher, she knew not. Only one thing she knew. They must find Peter and John and the others. They must tell them of the astounding events.

Salome said suddenly: "But—but where is Mary Magdalene?"

"Is she not with us?" asked Joanna. She turned her head, half expecting to see a figure hurrying to overtake them. But there was nought upon that road but the pale dawn.

Mary Magdalene could not leave. She stood without at the sepulcher and the tears she could not shed before, fell now. She was frightened, bewildered and, above everything, desolate. In her agony, she knew not what to think. Were those gleaming figures in the sepulcher part of a dream or vision, or were they representatives of evil men who had robbed the tomb of the body of her beloved master? She walked blindly in the garden, not able to see her way because of tears. She stumbled into bushes. Branches caught at her garments, and she bruised her sandaled feet on sharp, upthrusting stones. Dimly, she was aware of a man approaching and turned a little away from him, bowing her face in her hands.

"Woman," said the stranger, "why do you weep?"

She did not answer. Why did she weep? There was reason in plenty. None, she moaned inwardly, had ever known such cause for grief. She had been thrust from a height into a pit where no light came and out of which she could never climb.

"Whom do you seek?"

The man's voice seemed to her far away, and she wished that he would go away and leave her with her sorrow. Yet, he might know something of what had occurred here. Perhaps he was the gardener.

"Sir," she said pleadingly, "if you have borne him hence, tell me where you have laid him, and I will take him away."

"Mary!"

That voice! That voice of infinite compassion. That tone of tender rebuke. Father in heaven, who was it spoke thus to her—who? She turned, shaking from head to foot, and blinked the tears from her eyes.

"Rabboni!"

It was he! It was her Master! It was Jesus of Nazareth. Joy crowded into her heart. There was room for nought else. She flung herself forward to touch him, to hold him. . . .

Jesus said to her: "Touch me not, for I am not yet ascended to my Father: but go to my brethren, and say to them that I ascend to my Father and your Father; and to my God, and your God."

Mary Magdalene sank to her knees in the dew-wet

grass, and her prayer had no words, for it needed none.
. . . When she lifted her head, Jesus had disappeared.
Nevertheless, she doubted not that she had indeed seen
him, and returned to Jerusalem with rejoicing to seek out
the disciples.

The doors of the room where the disciples had gathered
were shut, for fear of the Jews. Wild rumors streamed
through Jerusalem and crowds in the streets had strange
tales to tell of dead men risen and walking, of astounding
sights and bewildering sounds. Hot words flew in the
temple where priests and Pharisees gathered. Caiaphas bellowed and shook his fist at Ben Isham. Annas brought a
great pile of silver to bribe him and his Jewish soldiers.
"This is yours if you will say nought but what we tell you
to say. Your story is fantastic. No one would believe it, no
one of intelligence. Still, there are fools abroad who might
repeat it. That would be dangerous—for Israel and for the
Romans. Say, therefore, that his disciples came and stole
him away."

All this was known to the followers of the Nazarene.
What had actually occurred at the sepulcher they dared
not guess. John and Peter, hearing the report of the
women, had hastened to the sepulcher, greatly wondering
when they saw not the body. But Jesus did not appear to
them in the garden, and they returned, bewildered and
still sorrowful, scarce crediting the story of Mary Magdalene. What she had seen, they said, was a spirit. A beautiful vision had been hers, nothing more.

"But how think you the stone was rolled away?" asked
James. His dark eyes were thoughtful, and he looked
around the circle with a wistful eagerness. Would none of
them open their hearts to the hope that filled his? Did
none of them believe that Jesus had risen? He wanted to

believe. He was filled with ineffable longing. If only someone would share his credulity, then—then he might attain
complete faith.

James heard Philip say: "It was a trick, I think, to trap
us. The Romans or Pharisees stole him away, so that we
might believe him risen. Afterwards, they mean to produce his body and mock us."

James would not accept this explanation. He heard the
others gloomily admit its logic, but something within him
cried "Nay!" He went to the small window and looked
up at the evening sky. All was calm. Stars frosted the sky
and the moon rose over the housetops like a great glowing
pearl. It was as if the world had found peace and reas-
surance after turmoil.

Behind him he heard Simon Peter cry out sharply—and
then silence. He turned. Jesus of Nazareth stood in front
of the barred door. Jesus—or his spirit, for how could
corporeality come through heavy wood?

Sound clogged in James' throat. He heard his own
breathing, harsh and loud.

"Peace be unto you."

Yea, it was his. It was the voice of the Nazarene. The
familiar gentle tones filled the room, soothed the swiftly
beating heart, cooled the hot terror of the mind.

Again he spoke. "Why are you troubled? And why do
thoughts arise in your hearts?" He came forward a few
steps, but some of the disciples drew back in alarm.

Patiently he stretched out his arms. "Behold my hands
and my feet, that it is I myself. Handle me and see; for
a spirit has not flesh and bones as you see me have."

James started. He could see clearly the cruel print of
the nails in the palms and feet. Yet, so great was his joy
that even yet, he could not rationally believe. He could not
say to himself with quiet assurance: "This is indeed our

Master, risen from the dead and now triumphantly alive." He dared not be convinced. He could only delight in the vision, if such it were—and thank God for it.

The eyes of Jesus of Nazareth searched each upturned face. No one spoke. In every gaze was a mute longing to believe, but no conviction.

"Have you any meat here?" asked Jesus quietly.

No one stirred. Then John rose and brought a piece of broiled fish and a bit of honeycomb. Without a word, and with shaking hands, he handed it to Jesus. And before them all, the Master received it and ate.

Peter ran forward and fell down before Jesus, clasping his feet and weeping bitterly. "Master! Master!" With one accord, they came together in a circle about the Nazarene.

Thomas looked at the other disciples pityingly. Grief had unbalanced them. What had they said—"We have seen the Lord!" Why could they not face their terrible loss reasonably as he did? Men should be brave enough to look at the bowels of the dark, and not falter—not turn to wishful fancy to allay their grief. Jesus was dead. Dead. Yet here was Peter babbling like a child who had had a pretty dream. Here was John, ordinarily so reliable, with a face all alight and lips curved with happiness. Here were Andrew, and Philip and—and all of them. Laughing, crying, pouring words of idiocy upon him, trying to persuade him that not only was the improbable true, but also the impossible. He looked at them, his face drawn and bitter.

"I have told you, and I tell you again: unless I see in his hands the print of the nails, and put my finger into the print of the nails, and thrust my hand into his side, I will not believe."

Peter said: "But we have seen!"

Thomas did not answer. He sat down sullenly and looked at the floor. Chill silence fell upon the others, and he felt a little guilty, for he knew that his stubborn incredulity had caused it. Yet, could a man lie and say he believed, when he did not? Surely, honesty demanded . . .

He was conscious of a presence. In an instant, the atmosphere, the mood of the room was changed, transformed. Thomas swallowed. It had always been thus, when, after an absence, Jesus of Nazareth had returned to them.

He raised his head. Jesus stood before him.

Thomas shut his eyes. He would not be fooled. He would not be deluded. If it were a vision, one could deny its reality and it would vanish. If not . . . if not . . . he opened them. Jesus was still there, his gaze upon him, Thomas called Didymus—and such reproof was there that tears filled the disciple's eyes.

Jesus said to him: "Reach hither your finger, Thomas, and behold my hands; and reach hither your hand and thrust it into my side: and be not faithless, but believing."

Trembling, Thomas summoned the courage to approach and to do what he was bidden. His finger touched the Master's hands, felt the warm flesh.

He bowed his head in contrition. "My Lord and my God!" Awe swept over him. The impossible was possible. He who had been dead was alive. God, the Father of all, ruled heaven and earth.

Jesus was speaking again. "Thomas, because you have seen me, you have believed: blessed are they who have not seen and yet have believed."